THE COURT
OF MIRACLES

THE
COURT
OF
MIRACLES

Kester Grant

HARPER
Voyager

Harper*Voyager*
An imprint of HarperCollins*Publishers* Ltd
1 London Bridge Street
London SE1 9GF

www.harpercollins.co.uk

First published by HarperCollins*Publishers* Ltd 2020
1

A catalogue record for this book is
available from the British Library

ISBN: 978-0-00-825477-3 (HB)
ISBN: 978-0-00-825478-0 (TPB)

Printed and bound in the UK by
CPI Group (UK) Ltd, Croydon CR0 4YY

MIX
Paper from
responsible sources
FSC www.fsc.org **FSC™ C007454**

To Mum, who filled my world with stories,

and Babu, who gave me the words to tell them

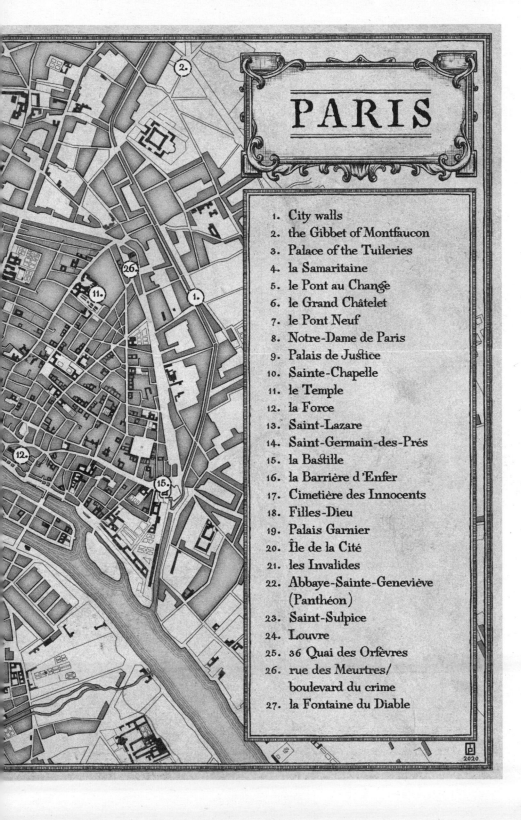

PARIS

1. City walls
2. the Gibbet of Montfaucon
3. Palace of the Tuileries
4. la Samaritaine
5. le Pont au Change
6. le Grand Châtelet
7. le Pont Neuf
8. Notre-Dame de Paris
9. Palais de Justice
10. Sainte-Chapelle
11. le Temple
12. la Force
13. Saint-Lazare
14. Saint-Germain-des-Prés
15. la Bastille
16. la Barrière d'Enfer
17. Cimetière des Innocents
18. Filles-Dieu
19. Palais Garnier
20. Île de la Cité
21. les Invalides
22. Abbaye-Sainte-Geneviève (Panthéon)
23. Saint-Sulpice
24. Louvre
25. 36 Quai des Orfèvres
26. rue des Meurtres/ boulevard du crime
27. la Fontaine du Diable

The Miracle Court

LEGION OF GHOSTS

THE GUILD OF BEGGARS

Lord Orso
Loup, Master of Ghosts

FORTUNE FAVORS THE ROGUE

THE GUILD OF CHANCE

Lord Ocan Maloni
Maoko Fujiwara, Master of Dice

SLEEP ETERNAL

THE GUILD OF ASSASSINS

Lady Charlotte Corday
Col-Blanch, Master of Poisons
Montparnasse, Master of Knives

DOES THE MAD DOG BITE?

THE GUILD OF MERCENARIES

Lord Rime Temam
Kais Sansal, Master of Brawn
Gan Khenbish, Master of Arms

MOTHER SEINE, BROTHER RAT

THE GUILD OF
SMUGGLERS

Lady Nihuang
Tamar l'Aure, Master of Tides

IN INK IS TRUTH

THE GUILD OF
LETTERS

Lady Gayatri Komayd
Artemon Bansele, Master of Paper

TAKE WHAT YOU WILL

THE GUILD OF
THIEVES

Lord Tomasis Vano
Thénardier, Master of Beasts

FLESH IN CHAINS

THE GUILD OF
FLESH

Lord Kaplan
Lenoir, Master of Flesh

DREAMERS OF THE DREAM

THE GUILD OF
DREAMERS

Lord Adlen Yelles
Kitoko Eyenga, Master of Visions

CONTENTS

PART FOUR: The Black Cat's Hunting

THE LAW OF THE MIRACLE COURT

Now these are the laws of the Miracle Court,
as old and as true as the sky;
the Wretched that keep them may prosper,
but the Wretched that break them must die.

All the Wretched are equal before the Miracle Court;
neither blood nor race, religion, rank, or name is
recognized.

All the Wretched are free; slavery is forbidden in the
Miracle Court.

The Lord or Lady of a Guild is its Father/Mother.
Their word is law to the Guild.

Keep to your Guild for protection and strength.

Let Guild leaders parley before risking the welfare of
their Guild or the Miracle Court.

Physical attack on a member of another Guild is
considered an act of war.

If your activities put the livelihood of the Miracle Court at risk, your Guild Lord will deal with you appropriately for the protection of the Court.

Children of the Miracle Court are protected by their Guild Lords first, and the Court second.

Daytime is the time of the Court's enemies: Those Who Walk by Day, police, and nobility. Children of the Miracle Court work best at night.

You must have permission to enter other Guild Houses.

Commit crime for survival and prosperity and the benefit of the Guilds, but never for pleasure.

Each person may divide their spoils only after first sharing with their Guild Lord.

Don't forget the weakest among you. The Guild must provide for all its children.

Keep the laws, or punishment will be swift and certain.

PART ONE

How Fear Came

1823

He heard a cry that had never been heard since
the bad days. . . . A hideous kind of shriek . . .
A mixture of hate, triumph, fear, and despair . . .
that rose and sank and wavered and quavered
far away.

—*The Jungle Book*

THE FOUNDING
OF THE MIRACLE COURT

FROM L'HISTOIRE DE PARIS, BY THE DEAD LORD

In 1160, Ysengrim the Boar was appointed grand prévôt. *His commission was to keep order in the streets of Paris, which was a dark and lawless place. He led violent assaults on the city's poorest spaces and its hives of beggars, thieves, and outcasts, killing or imprisoning all in his path. Those who survived the purges knew of no one who could be trusted, as Ysengrim's men had a legion of spies alongside their corrupt officers.*

To protect themselves, the city's Wretched formed nine guilds: Thieves, Beggars, Assassins, Gamblers, Mercenaries, Smugglers, Prostitutes, Opium Eaters, and Men of Letters. The Lords of each guild sat together to form the Miracle Court, bound as brethren by laws that they had written.

Among the outcasts of the city were Lombards, Corsicans, Moors, Africans, Maghrebi, Mughal, Romani, Qing, Jews, Ottomans, Edo, alongside the leprous, the maimed, the sick, the elderly, and those accused of witchcraft. They were despised and rejected by prévôt, *king, and country. But all were welcomed into the shelter of the Miracle Court, beneath whose roof all are equal and free.*

1

※※

Le Début de l'Histoire

It is a time of famine, a time of hungering want that threatens to eat you from the inside out, leaving you good only to wait for the coming of death. And Death the Endless always comes.

It is before dawn, dark and silent. The corpses of the starved have been laid out on the cobblestones overnight, waiting for the carts to bear them away. The dead are wide-eyed, unhearing, uncaring, unafraid. They remind me of my sister, Azelma.

Azelma, who never cries, cried for two whole days. She wouldn't eat or sleep. I tried everything, even saying that Father was coming with two bottles of whiskey in his belly and rage in his eyes. But she didn't move, unhearing, uncaring, unafraid.

She's finally stopped crying. For the last few hours she's been lying on her bed, staring into the distance. She won't answer me, won't even look at me. I think I prefer the crying.

Azelma used to wake me with a murmur of *"Viens, ma petite chatonne,"* and I'd lean into her warmth while she brushed my hair and helped me draw on my clothes.

Now I slip from the bed without her and change in the cold, putting on a dress that's getting too short. Giving my hair a few tugs with a hairbrush and teasing it into a lopsided braid. I splash my face with icy water poured from a heavy porcelain jug and sneak a look back at her. She's on her side, eyes open but seeing nothing.

The inn is quiet at this hour. I hesitate a moment longer, but she doesn't move, so I go downstairs and grab a pail, take a faded scarf from a peg by the door. The scarf is Azelma's and is too big for me, but the well is many streets away from the inn and the walk will be cold. I hate making the trip alone, in the darkness, but I must.

Outside, the freezing air burns my throat. I hasten to the well, trying not to look at the bodies I pass on the street. At the well I lower the pail and heave it back, full, my numb fingers straining with the weight of it.

The road back is treacherous, and with every cautious step my breath rises in clouds. With every breath I think of my sister, and the fear eats at my insides.

When I reach the inn, my shaking arms are relieved to put the bucket down. I pour some of the water into a pan and set it to boil, then look around. The floor needs mopping, even though that never keeps out the smell of spilled wine, and in the dim light, the main hall is a disarray of plates, empty tankards, and jugs; all need scrubbing.

I have dried hundreds of plates while Azelma flicked soapy bubbles at me. I duck and complain. She wrinkles her nose and tells me, "Kittens hate water."

I sigh and decide to start on the floor. The mop is heavy, and it makes my tired arms ache dreadfully, but I push it back and forth with vigor. Maybe if I can scrub away the stains, I can also scrub away the sick feeling growing in the pit of my stomach.

My sister, my sister.

Last night Father said nothing when Azelma didn't emerge from her room for the third night in a row. It was as if he'd forgotten she existed. He hummed, drumming his fingers on the table cheerily. He even threw me a hunk of warm brioche, which was so unlike him that I couldn't bring myself to eat it. There's barely flour in the city for bread, let alone for brioche, so I don't know where he got it. My father is a thief; he's stolen many a shinier jewel or weightier gold purse than this scrap of dough. But what use are jewels or gold in a time of famine?

My stomach growled low and heavy at the scent of the pastry. But fear was gnawing at my bones worse than hunger, so I brought the bread to Azelma, and now it sits, growing stale on a chipped plate beside her bed.

My hands are red with cleaning, and there's a sheen of sweat on my brow, but still I shiver. If Azelma doesn't eat, she'll soon be lying with the corpses outside in the cold, waiting for the carter to pick her up. But she's not feverish, I checked; there's something else wrong with her, something dreadful. What's worse, I can't do anything to heal it. I feel like the kitten Azelma likens me to—tiny, fragile, batting my paws against the wind.

There's a sound at the top of the stair, and when I turn, Azelma is there: clothed, hair plaited, looking straight at me. I should be relieved, but her expression is unnerving.

"I'll finish up here," she says in a flat voice. "You need to find Femi."

I should be happy to drop the cleaning, but my fingers tighten around the mop handle, and I frown. Why should I get Femi Vano, the one they call the Messenger? He comes and goes as he pleases, whispering things in my father's ear. He speaks to Azelma in murmurs and makes her laugh. But it's not even dawn and the inn stands empty; Father is snoring in his bed. Why must I get Femi now? Can we not clean as we always do, side by side?

Azelma comes down the stairs and takes the mop from me. My sister has a way with words; her voice is soothing, like honey, and the customers like her for that, and because she's pretty, soft. But now, even hushed, her voice is dagger-sharp.

"Bring him around to the back, and tell no one. Do you hear me?"

I nod, reluctantly heading for the door.

Azelma always asks me if I have a scarf or reminds me I

need a coat. She tells me to be careful and not to dawdle. But now she turns away, saying nothing. I don't know this hard girl. She's not my sister. She's something else, a hollow thing wearing my sister's face.

I call Femi by whistling the way he taught me, and suddenly he appears, swooping down from nowhere.

"Kitten," he says with a low bow, but I've no time for his gallantries and drag him by the arm to the inn. Azelma looks at us dead-eyed and tells me to scrape the wax from the tables into the pot so we can melt it down for new candles. When she slips out the back door to speak to Femi, I tiptoe to the kitchen and climb onto the tall red stool I sit on to wash the dishes. I can just make out the tops of their heads through the window. They're standing pressed against the wall.

"He is coming for you," I hear Femi say.

A long silence follows. When Azelma speaks, her tone is bitter. "Father will bargain. He always does. While they are occupied, you must take her. They will not notice that she is gone."

"We can run." Femi's voice rises in desperation. "We can hide."

"Who has ever escaped him? How far do you think we'd get before he found us? Even if by some miracle we could escape now, we'd damn her if we brought her, for he will surely find us. And if we leave her behind, then who do you think will taste my father's rage? Have you thought who he might throw at Kaplan to appease him? Or to punish me?"

Azelma shakes her head, then turns to the window, as if she senses me watching. I duck so she won't see me.

"Whispers and sweet stories you have given me, Femi Vano," she says, and I lift my head in time to see her gently touch his cheek. "But words will fade where I am going. If I am lucky, I will not remember anything. Give me your oath in bone and iron that you will find a protector for her."

Femi raises his hand, and with a single gleaming movement of his knife, his opposite palm is marked by a long, dark line as drops of blood begin to bead like black diamonds.

"My word, my blood," he says. "I give you my promise in bone and iron."

She rests her head on his chest, and her voice softens.

"Do you care for me?"

"You know that I do."

"Then do not cry for me," she says. "I am already dead."

"No, not dead. The dead, at least, are free. . . ."

When Azelma comes back inside, her face is a mask. Femi trails behind her. Like his Maghrebi ancestors, who hailed from northern Africa, he wears his thick hair in coiled braids. No matter the weather, he is always swathed in a heavy brown cloak streaked with rain marks and frayed at the edges, giving him the impression of having large folded wings. His dark skin is like burnished copper, his nose is slightly hooked, and his eyes burn fierce and golden—and right now, they are rimmed in red.

Azelma beckons to me. I take her hand; mine is small and hers is cold as she leads me back up the stairs to our room.

There are some old clothes laid out on the bed: boys' things, oversized and fifteenth-hand.

Her eyes travel over my thin frame unforgivingly. They pause at my face, studying me, as if looking for something. "*Dieu soit loué,* at least you're not pretty." Her voice catches.

She's right. Where Azelma is softness and curves, I'm bones and angles. The only thing we have in common is our olive skin, the legacy of the *pied-noir* woman who birthed us. When I was small and winter winds rattled the panes like vengeful spirits trying to get in, Azelma would put her soft arms around me and tell me stories. "What do you want to hear, little cat?" she would ask.

"Tell me about our mother."

Father says she was nothing but a rat for leaving us with him.

"The woman who birthed us is not our true mother," Azelma would say. "Our mother is the City."

But even I knew it was not the City that had gifted us our olive skin and raven hair.

Now Azelma's gaze falls to the thick braid that I struggle to plait by myself. She reaches out and I go to her. She unties the braid with deft, gentle fingers and begins to brush.

"Our mother the City is not a merciful mother," she says as she gathers my hair in one hand. "To be a girl in this city is to be weak. It is to call evil things down upon you. And the City is not kind to weak things. She sends Death the Endless to winnow the frail from the strong. You know this."

I hear the sound before I realize what is happening: a sharp, shearing scrape. Then I feel a sudden lightness at the back of my neck. My eyes widen, but before I can say a word, a tail of dark hair lands softly at my feet. Azelma takes the shears to the rest of my hair, cropping it close to my scalp.

"Keep it short," she says, and when she is done: "Take off that dress."

I wonderingly obey, my hands trembling to undo the buttons she sewed on. She used to force me to stand like a statue, arms outstretched, while she fit one of her old dresses to my frame, her mouth full of bent, rusted pins. I always squeezed my eyes shut, afraid she would draw blood. She would laugh at me through pinched lips. "I've not pricked you yet, little kitten."

I peel off the dress and hand it to her. I stand before her in a much-patched linen shift.

"That too."

Fear and cold prick my skin.

"Hear my words, for they are all I have left to give. Wrap them around your flesh like armor. You may forget my face and my voice, but never forget the things I am telling you."

"I won't," I say, trying not to tremble.

"Eat only enough to stay alive. You must get used to hunger so that it won't break you. Stay small so you will fit into tight spaces and they will always have need of you."

I want to ask her who "they" are and why they might need me, but her tone is solemn and my tongue is stuck to the roof of my mouth.

"No dresses anymore. Do not let men look at you with desire." She wraps a length of gauzy cloth around my chest, binding it tightly.

I can barely breathe.

"Wind bandages around any parts of you that are soft."

She hands me an oversized pair of trousers so faded that no particular color could be ascribed to them. I pull them on quickly, and follow them with a large shirt.

"Wear clothes like a mask so no one will see you, do you understand? Wear them to hide your true face. You are not Nina the kitten, you are the Black Cat. Show your teeth and claws at every opportunity so they remember that you're dangerous. Only then will you have won a small portion of safety. One shut eye's worth of sleep."

I tie up a pair of thick boots that have seen several owners and don a large cap that engulfs my small head.

"Father might have given me his silver tongue, but he gave you his sharp brain. You're clever, Nina. That is a weapon. You're small and you're quick, and those, too, are weapons."

She grips my wrists and peers into my face.

"Be useful, be smart, and stay one step ahead of everyone. Be brave even when you're afraid. Remember that everyone is afraid."

I'm afraid now, of her. Of the two days of awful crying and the blank stares and the fire that burns in her usually gentle eyes. What has happened to my sister?

"When you think the darkness is coming for you, when you are small and frail and fear that our mother the City is trying to destroy you, you *must* not let her. Do you hear me? You must survive."

"I w–will, I swear it," I say, my voice trembling.

We go downstairs to where Femi Vano waits in a shadow.

"You're to go with Femi and you'll do what he tells you," Azelma instructs me.

My heart races with fresh panic. "B–but I want to stay with you!"

This carved-out form of my sister bends and looks me in the eye. Her voice is hollow.

"Sometimes we must pay a terrible price to protect the things we love."

I don't understand what she means. There are a hundred questions I want to ask her, but I can't find the words; they choke my throat as tears roll down my face. She ignores them.

"You must look after yourself now."

She glances at Femi, her eyes like chips of ice.

"Take her, then."

There's no goodbye, no hug, no proclamation of her love

for me. Instead, she pushes me away as if she doesn't want me anymore.

"Zelle?"

She begins moving through the tables, cleaning.

"Zelle—" I start toward her, but Femi holds me back.

"Hush." Worry laces his voice. He's scared, and I don't know why.

Then I hear it. Over the drumming of my own heart, I hear the crunch of boots on gravel, voices outside.

"Go now!" Azelma hisses.

Femi picks me up, pressing me to him, and I feel the fear thrumming through his bones and into mine.

He drags me to the kitchen, away from Azelma, who for the barest second throws an anguished look at us over her shoulder. Then she turns away and straightens her spine. Her head is held high; her hands make fists at her sides.

I start to call her name, but Femi's hand clamps hard across my mouth.

"Thénardier!" A roar from the front of the inn splits the silence, a growling, penetrating command.

Femi freezes. I hear clumping and thumping overhead; the shout seems to have to stirred Father from his slumber. I marvel that whoever has come has been able to wake him from the stupor of a drunken sleep with one word.

Femi dares a glance out the window, his eyes darting back and forth as he checks the yard for anyone standing there.

The front door opens.

I hear the honeyed but unsteady tones of my very hung-over father from the top of the stairs, the uncertainty in his voice. "Lord Kaplan?"

The visitor has entered, while in the darkness of the kitchen, Femi inches us toward the back door as quietly as possible.

"Forgive me," my father continues. "I did not think you would see to this trifling matter yourself."

"A trifling matter, Master of Beasts?" the voice growls back, seeming to rattle the very roof of the inn. "Do you forget who I am? Do you forget how I came to be? I wanted to see if you would actually do it—if even a man like you would truly sell his own kin."

Sell his own kin? Understanding strikes me like a fist, leaving me winded.

Azelma . . . *Father is going to sell Azelma?*

"I've twelve gold coins here, Thénardier."

"Twelve . . . ," Father echoes, but his voice is considering, wheedling. A rage wells in me because I know that tone: he's doing what he always does. He's actually *bargaining,* this time for a better price for his own daughter.

I bite down on Femi's hand, but he doesn't loosen his grip, and with a last fumble at the door, he drags me out into the night.

2

The Keepers of the Gates

I can't remember how long it took Femi to tear me away, only that I scratched at him like a wild thing, howling till I lost my voice, hoarsely begging him to bring me back to Azelma, but he never once loosened his grip.

His voice was unsteady as he murmured to me, "I am taking you to a place that you must get into. In the west wing you will find a room. Inside that room is a boy, and around his neck is something you must take or all will be lost."

These were his instructions as emotion churned within me. Perhaps if I did as he said, I could go home.

I look up at giant iron gates, where six heads have been impaled on spikes. They are the Keepers of the Gates, ever staring. The heads have been preserved in oil so they will not rot, but the wind and rain have nevertheless turned them sour and hideous. It is a gruesome warning to all the land of what happens to those who cross the nobility.

This is the place I must get into.

A gold-wrought cage, the Palace of the Tuileries.

I feel a knot of fear in my chest.

Remember that everyone is afraid.

I close my eyes and think of Azelma's words, the stories she wove around me.

Il était une fois . . . there were six mice that lived in a city of cats. They dwelt in a time of great suffering and terror. One day the mice started to speak and ask questions that no mice before them had ever dared whisper.

I open my eyes and count the heads on the spikes again, mouthing the names as I go.

And these were the names given to the mice: Robespierre the Incorruptible, Marat the Hideous, Danton of the Golden Tongue, Mirabeau the Wise, Desmoulins the Brave, and St. Juste the Beautiful, the Angel of Death.

Father has been taking me out on his burglaries for over a year, so I know well how to silently clamber and slip into small spaces. After all, I am a mere whisper of a girl, more shadow than flesh.

I am afraid to break into the palace. But I am more afraid of what will happen if I don't. All I know is that I must get back to my sister, so the quicker I do what I'm told, the quicker I can return. Which is why I throw myself between

18

the wheels of a moving carriage and grab the underside, letting it carry me into the grounds, past the guards. I hang there until feet in jeweled slippers step from the carriage onto bone-white gravel and the servants in leather slippers and hard boots close the doors with a resounding thud. The carriage starts to move toward the hulking building, and at last I release my grip.

I somehow manage to slip past blurs of noise—for even at this hour, there's the clamoring of guards, carriages, and servants—and scale the wall that will lead me to the west wing.

My fingers are bleeding by the time I get to the right balcony and drag my body over the rail, collapsing in a heap.

It takes me a few minutes to look around. There's a large shuttered door. But Father showed me how to pick a lock before I could even walk. I reach into my trouser pockets and find the pins that Azelma placed there for me. Thanking her silently, I pull them out and get to work. Father taught me well. The door opens in seconds, gliding outward, leaving me staring into a massive room cloaked in darkness. Roaring fear pulses at my throat, driving me ever forward. I take a step and let my eyes adjust.

Inside that room is a boy . . .

He is at the far end of the room, asleep in a mountain of a bed.

I ignore all the ornaments, the fine furniture, the baubles shining eerily in the moonlight that gently filters into the room. The curtains around the bed are not drawn. I wonder

19

why a boy like this would want to look out into the darkness at all.

Breath catching in my throat, I pad toward him, move-
ments fluid, forcing the panic down. I wonder who he is.
Surely he's a noble of importance, his room being the size of
Father's whole inn.

Around his neck is something you must take . . .

A collared nightshirt betrays an inch of pale skin. But I
see nothing around his neck.

Although Father sends me up walls and down chimneys
to grab whatever he instructs, I have never stolen anything
from someone who was actually present for the theft. The
rule is always to hide until they are gone. But that is not the
rule tonight.

I rub my hands together to warm them and lean over
the boy. He has long eyelashes and dark wavy hair. He
looks peaceful, and by the sliver of moonlight I imagine
that he is quite handsome, like a boy from one of Azelma's
stories.

I lower gentle fingers to his shirt—it's best to move neither too slowly nor too quickly. I keep to the shirt fabric,
trying to avoid his skin. There it is! A chain, long and heavy,
which is why it wasn't high about his neck. The length and
weight also mean it's loose, easy to tease out. The end of
the necklace slips from under the covers, and I pause for a
mere second as it glimmers in the moonlight. It's the largest
stone I've ever seen, a sapphire set in a gold casing thick with
smaller pearls and jewels. It sits heavily against his chest. He

will surely wake if I lift it, or if not then, when I try to get it over his head.

You're small and you're quick, and those, too, are weapons.

I count to three and then I move. As smooth as water, the necklace is whipped off, and there's only a whisper of a second when the metal chain brushes his skin. When he opens his eyes, he's looking right into mine.

You're clever, Nina, and that is a weapon.

If he shouts for help, he will rob me of important seconds I need to escape. I might make it to the balcony, but not beyond.

This is the art of thieving. . . . Femi's words echo in my ears. *Deaf are the distracted, and blind are the surprised. Those mesmerized by a face do not notice where the hands may creep.*

I need to distract him, keep him surprised—or at least, more surprised than he currently is. His mouth opens, so I do the first thing that comes into my head: I kiss him, pressing my lips to his in a style that I've seen played out too many times in dark corners of Father's inn. He tastes like chocolate. And that's the last thought in my mind as I push away from him and start to run, leaping for the balcony.

I'm over the edge, into the freezing night, my lips still burning. I hear a strangled sound as I drop and roll onto the balcony, then start to scale the wall down to the ground.

"Wait! Please!"

I should not look up, but I do, fingers raw and wind at my back. He's staring down at me from two floors above. He's going to call the guards; he's going to demand I give the necklace back; he's going to have me arrested, and I will have failed Femi and Azelma.

"Who are you?" he asks.

I pause for only a second before I smile at him. "The Black Cat," I say. Then I let go and drop like a shadow into the night.

Femi and I travel over rooftops in the dark, high above the noise of heaving, sleepless streets, far from the city center, over warrenous rookeries and pitch-black alleys. Femi nearly flies, moving with fearlessness and grace. Every now and again he whistles, each time a different sound, as clear as the bells of Notre-Dame. I think I hear the echo of an answer on the wind, but I can't be sure it's not my tumultuous mind playing tricks on me.

"Keep up, little cat!" Femi calls, his voice soft, eyes gleaming in the moonlight. "Don't think, don't hesitate, just leap when I leap."

Every step I take is filled with terror: I never know if my foot will land solidly or if I'll fall behind. Father taught me how to scale buildings but never how to soar, leaping like a bird from rooftop to rooftop. With every leap, I think of my sister and my stomach turns inside out.

When we pause so I can catch my breath, Femi whispers to me in urgent tones the reason for our mission, words I am to repeat, gestures I am to make. The jumble of things I must remember is terrifying. Panic rises, choking me, but I think of Azelma and bite my lip, forcing myself to concentrate. Then we are off again. And in the darkness, I repeat Femi's words to myself over and over till I know them by heart. I will do whatever I must to get back to Azelma.

Finally, he stops, and I nearly whimper in relief, overcome by the journey, my ears ringing with the instructions he has given me. In the silvery dawn, I see that we are on the outskirts of an abandoned neighborhood, its buildings ravaged by time. We scramble down the side of a crumbling edifice, push past a half-open gate, dwarfed by the shadow of a ruined church. A pair of heavy doors awaits, our arrival upsetting a murder of crows nesting in the roof. Inside, what hasn't decayed has long since been scavenged: the benches, altars, and stained-glass windows are dark open wounds along the crumbling walls.

"L'église de l'évêque Myriel," Femi says, his low voice echoing into the ruin. "They say it's haunted by the ghost of its founder, a man violently converted from a life of nefarious crime." He reaches out to me, drawing me into the darkness after him.

"And there are others who say that l'évêque Myriel never gave up his criminal ways. Becoming a 'man of God' was the perfect cover for his illustrious career."

Femi gently pulls me toward a small side door that must once have led to a vestry. We enter and step through another decomposing room and down a dark staircase. He slows a little for me, pointing out which stones are likely to shift beneath our feet. At the bottom of the staircase in the meager half-light is a monster of a door, darker even than the darkness of this lightless place. Femi places a hand on it, and I follow. It is cold beneath my touch. Iron, which does not rot, or burn, or fade . . .

The giant door swings open before us. A blaze of light blinds me.

"Welcome to the Guild of Thieves," Femi murmurs.

3

The Lord of Thieves

"Fret not, little one. Thénardier is not here tonight."

I shiver at the sound of my father's name, but Femi nudges me gently on the shoulder.

"Look up."

He points overhead, and I crane my neck to see. The vaulted ceiling glimmers like a net of pure shimmering light.

"The true beauty of the Thieves Guild lies there," Femi says. "Once a year, during the feast of l'évêque Myriel, patron saint of Thieves, each member of the Guild offers a stone, a crystal, or a shining gold coin. Each Cat of the Guild is given a share, and they race up the walls and climb ropes thrown from high windows. The Cat that reaches the top first has the honor of embedding the gift in the ceiling."

Our mother the City is draped in a coat of fog and smoke

so thick that I have never seen the stars in the night sky—but I imagine that this is what they look like. Something inside my chest thrills to the beauty of it. But there's not much time to admire before Femi is steering me away. I blink and take in the noisy chaos of the hall.

It's like a palace, if a palace had no organization and great treasures were left all over the place. It's a chaos of graceful statues of white marble and ancient blackened gargoyles that must have come from Notre-Dame herself. The floors are covered with overlapping carpets of thick colored silks no doubt taken from the best houses in the city. Every inch of wall is hung with gilt-framed paintings large and small, depicting battles, ships at sea, landscapes, romantic images of myths, religious icons, and portraits.

The hall shimmers and buzzes with wine, heat, and ribald conversation. Beneath it all, a strange current of danger pulses. The place is alive—teeming with people of all ages, shapes, and sizes, of all skin colors and dress. I see sharp-eyed faces, old women swathed in layers, and merchant-class men in stiff cloaks, as well as the odd priest.

"There are no family names in the Miracle Court. There is no race or religion," Femi says to me. "Faith, caste, blood— these are not bonds that tie the Wretched together, for that is how the world sees us, as *wretched*. And thus, Wretched is the name given to all children of the Miracle Court. What binds us is our Guild. It is a bond stronger than family, thicker than blood. All you see here are brothers and sisters of the Thieves Guild."

Femi indicates a horde of ragged, barefoot boys and girls only a few years older than me.

"Those are the Dogs: Thieves who conduct their business at street level. There are also Horses—highwaymen—though there are only two left in the entire Guild, since the Gentleman no longer rides."

For any of the Wretched who appear to be everyday persons from the city streets, there are ten others wearing impossibly bright clothing, jewels that glimmer and shine. Men and women with diamonds and rubies dripping from their necks, noses, wrists, ears, fingers, and toes, every knuckle coated in shining stones.

"Those are the Cats," Femi mutters, indicating the brightly clad figures. "Burglars that prefer to sneak along rooftops and slip through windows and chimneys."

His eyes narrow at a particularly rotund gentleman garbed in purple, gold, and pink. Every part of him is shining with jewels so weighty it must be impossible for him to lift his hands.

"Cats are always showing off."

Along one side of the hall is a long, crooked line of people. Femi gestures toward them.

"All Thieves hand their take to the People of the Pen—clerks, on rent from the Guild of Letters. They serve as accountants, lawyers, and auditors to all nine Guilds of the Miracle Court."

I squint at the row of pale, expressionless men and women seated behind a long table, wearing robes of indistinct color.

Their heads are bent; they are all taking copious notes, barely saying a word.

"The People of the Pen are obsessive with information," Femi whispers. "Their devotion to order and detail is stronger than their will to be corrupted. They're both feared and respected by all the Wretched, for there's nothing about us they don't know. The location of each Guild House is a strictly kept secret, except to myself, as Messenger to all the Guilds, and to the Guild of Letters. When the People of the Pen come knocking at the door for an audit, even the most fearsome of Guild Lords lets them enter."

Once the takes are noted and signed for, they are handed to clerks with magnifying glasses and monocles that give them the strange appearance of owls. They inspect each item, testing silver and gold, setting things alight, striking them with hammers, even biting them before announcing their findings, which are sometimes met with laughter at the Thieves' expense, or murmurs of jealousy at some of their better takes.

In the center of the room is an intricately carved black chair. Hanging from its high, pointed back are piles of sparkling necklaces, a glittering diadem or two, and several fine embroidered tapestries. Sitting in the thronelike chair is a man a little older than my father. He has the same copper-brown skin and cunning golden eyes as Femi.

They must be kin, I think.

He is dressed more modestly than many of the Thieves around him, in a well-cut coat and shirt of unexceptional color. In fact, nothing about him is exceptional except for two chains of varying lengths that encircle his neck: one a shimmering rope of pure diamonds, another a collar of rubies gleaming in the light of a hundred burning candelabras.

"Tomasis, the Lord of Thieves," Femi says, nodding toward the man.

Standing beside the Lord's chair is an older gentleman. His face is a map of heavily powdered wrinkles, his hair is hidden under a wig, and he is shod in the worn, gilt-edged finery of a noble gone to seed.

Femi inclines his head toward the powdered man. "There are only three Merveilles—Wonders—still living in the Court. They are criminals of such fame and notoriety they've become living legends. The most any child of the Court can hope for after their death is that their songs will be sung, their stories told over and over again. But the Merveilles—their exploits are recounted to every child of the Court while they still draw breath. The three remaining Merveilles are le Maire, the Fisherman, and the Gentleman. Le Maire is a member of the Guild of Letters, and he's been missing for more than a decade. The Fisherman is Nihuang, the Lady of the Smugglers Guild. The last Merveille is the man standing beside the Lord of Thieves. 'Gentleman' George, infamous highwayman. And if you earn his favor, there is much that he can teach you."

The Gentleman spots us and inclines his head to whisper something in the ear of Tomasis, the Lord of Thieves, who turns to glance lazily in our direction. Femi squeezes my arm.

"It is time, Nina. Remember all I have told you. There is no going back."

Femi marches me toward the men. People move away to let us pass, looking at me with a hungry interest that I can't quite like.

We reach the throne and Femi drops to one knee, pulling me with him. "Monseigneur. Vano, Lord of the stolen, Father of thievery and plunder . . ."

"I'm listening, *mon frère*," Tomasis says.

I find myself pulled back to my feet as Femi rises.

Tomasis glances at the powdered gentleman, who nods at Femi.

"Messenger," the man says in a honeyed voice.

"Gentleman," Femi replies with a slight incline of his head; then he turns back to Tomasis.

"I have a new child for you, Monseigneur."

I immediately lower my eyes to the intricate silken rugs that cover the floor. Femi has told me that I must be prepared to watch much of the proceedings from beneath lowered lashes, but I risk a glance up.

Tomasis smiles a leathery smile, taking a sip of wine from a jewel-studded goblet.

"A child?" he asks, placing the goblet on a delicate mother-of-pearl table beside him before pinioning me with his eyes.

Had I thought his eyes lazy before? They positively eat me whole now. Beside him, the Gentleman tilts his head at me like a bird, considering my potential.

"She is a Cat, Monseigneur," Femi says.

30

Tomasis considers Femi, and I can't help but see the clear resemblance between them: they must be brothers.

"Isn't recruiting kittens the role of the Master of Beasts? Last I checked, you were still Aves, the Elanion—Messenger to the Miracle Court. Strange, then, that one who carries messages should suddenly take on this new responsibility, especially when you have never shown particular interest in the Cats of this Guild."

Tomasis is famously suspicious, Femi told me as we crept along the rooftops. *You have to be suspicious to become a Guild Lord, and you have to continue to be suspicious if you want to remain one.*

Tomasis focuses on me, and when he speaks, his words are deceptively gentle.

"And who are you, little one, that the Messenger of the Miracle Court himself pleads for you?"

I swallow, my throat suddenly dry. Despite the swarming buzz of conversation around me, I feel the burning of hundreds of eyes on my back.

"My name is Eponine Thénardier," I say.

Around us, surprise makes the volume of conversation raise.

Tomasis narrows his eyes at this, taking in the lines of my face, reading me as if to see a resemblance.

"Thénardier is the Master of Beasts of this Guild. He rules beneath me and manages all my children, Dogs, Cats, and Horses. He knows all my business and holds tremendous power within the Shining Hall."

31

Power he won after several other Masters died in frequent and mysterious succession, Femi told me. *Thénardier has never been shy of slitting a throat or two when needs must.*

"Explain what reason I might have to take his own kin from him behind his back?" Tomasis turns to Femi, his gaze burning bright.

Femi doesn't flinch. "Thénardier has been using his own flesh and blood to perform his best takes—perhaps all of his takes—for the last two years now. The offerings he presented to you were not his to give."

"A *thief,* then? Is that what you accuse him of? Thievery is quite a common practice between these walls."

The hall comes alive with laughter at that. Tomasis smiles pleasantly, but there's no denying the hardness to his eye and the grim line of his lips.

"And if the offerings he gives me are ample tithe," Tomasis continues, "what is it to me how he came by them?"

"She is not of the Wretched. She is no child of the Miracle Court, bound by no Guild, bearing no mark—"

"You avoid the question. Why would I insult the Master of Beasts before the whole Guild by taking a Cat, his own flesh and blood, behind his back?"

"Ask her what she has for you." Femi's voice is barely a whisper, yet it resounds in the hall.

I reach into my coat and pull out the chain with trembling fingers; the heavy stone follows.

"*Rennart's balls!* Is that the Talisman of Charlemagne?" The Gentleman steps forward and lifts the stone delicately from my palm. He fishes a monocle from his waistcoat pocket and inspects it, turning it over before setting it once again in my hand.

"This stone is one of the crown jewels," he says.

"Yes," I say, even though I had no idea.

"They are kept at the Palace of the Tuileries."

I nod.

"Where was the stone?"

"Around the neck of a boy." I try hard not to let my voice waver.

The Gentleman starts at that. "A *boy*? The Talisman is currently worn by the dauphin of France."

So that's who the boy was: prince of the realm. Future king, heir to the throne of France. I let out my breath heavily. I kissed the future king, and he tasted of chocolate. . . .

Tomasis laughs, a tremendous sound bursting with warmth and humor that fills the hall and bounces off the walls and ceiling. "The Talisman of Charlemagne, stolen from the neck of the dauphin. It is worth a sight more to me than Thénardier's pride," he says, wiping his glittering eyes.

Femi raises his eyebrows subtly at me.

"This is the offering I bring before you," I say quickly, reciting the words he taught me on the rooftops. "A gift from the"—I pause to recall the name—"*caliph* to the king of Those Who Walk by Day, containing the hair of one of their most holy saints." I drop to one knee, head bowed. "Take this gift, Lord of Thieves. May it please you and grant me favor. And take me with it, as daughter to you. Let me

33

dwell in your presence as one of the Wretched, a true child of the Miracle Court, and I will serve you for all my days."

The Gentleman glances to Tomasis, who nods. The powdered man steps forward, clearing his throat.

"What is your name?" he intones.

"I have none until my Father has spoken it."

"Who is your mother?"

"I have no mother but the City."

"And who is your Father?"

"I have no Father but the Lord of Thieves."

The Gentleman lifts his head and looks out at the Thieves in the hall before continuing. "Today you shed your earthen skin and are reborn in the darkness to your Guild and the Wretched—your brothers and sisters.

"Hereafter you will be called by your true name. . . ."

He pauses, glancing at Femi, who, tilting his chin up, says, "Black Cat of the Thieves Guild, daughter of Tomasis, child of the Miracle Court. May they sing your songs forever."

May they sing your songs forever. The words ring in my ears as a hundred voices repeat them around me.

Tomasis gestures for me to approach. I rise and bring the necklace to him. He leans forward, lowering his head, and I put the heavy chain around his neck. The stone nestles against his chest, glimmering defiantly against the rubies and diamonds beneath it.

"From this day forth I will be your Father," Tomasis says.

"You are bound to me by bone and iron. I lay my mark upon your skin, and you will recognize none but me above you."

"Thank you, Father," I say. From the corner of my eye, I see a thin woman dressed in silks approaching, a bottle of dark liquid and a metal quill in her hands.

"From this day forth I will protect you from all things, and you will serve me in all things and abide by the laws of the Miracle Court."

"I will, my Lord," I say, trying not to stiffen as the woman reaches me. She tilts my head to the side, exposing my neck, and with a swiftness that is astounding, and a biting, burning pain, she tattoos a shape into the soft skin behind my ear.

"From this day forth, the Guild of Thieves will be your family, and you will serve them, and never shall you betray them."

I feel blood beading under the sting of the woman's quill; smell its metallic tang as she finishes. My neck is aflame with the pain of it.

I know the mark is a diamond, because I have seen Thénardier's mark when he was passed out on the floor after a drunken rage.

"It is not often, little Cat, that I am honored with so worthy an offering." Tomasis holds the Talisman in his palm and tilts it so it catches the light. "I will give you a gift, if you desire it. Ask anything of me and it shall be yours."

Beside me, Femi twitches. I sense his warning and ignore him.

"I wish for you to save my sister," I say hurriedly. "For you to give her your protection as you have done for me."

I hold my breath and try not to hope.

"Save her?" Tomasis asks. "From what does she need saving?"

"She has been taken, sold . . . ," I say, the words heavy in my mouth.

"Sold? That is indeed lamentable. And Thénardier allowed this to happen?"

I bite my lip. My father is Master of Beasts of this Guild; I dare not speak ill of him, not here.

"I see," Tomasis says, frowning, my silence clearly explaining it all. "Thénardier always has been unnaturally fond of the coin." He touches his necklace, considering. "Buying her back can be done. But consider this, little Cat: What if the one who bought her does not wish to sell?"

I raise my eyes fiercely to his.

"Then there is someone I wish to see dead," I say.

Tomasis laughs, and the hall laughs with him. Only Femi shakes his head frantically, trying to get my attention.

"How very bloodthirsty of you."

The laughter scratches at my skin. I have said the wrong thing, and it amuses them.

"You do not kill people?"

Tomasis smiles widely at me. "Not usually," he says. "But I know others who are quite good at dealing in death. So tell me: Who is it that has taken her? Say his name and it shall be done."

Femi makes a strangled noise.

"I heard him called Kaplan."

The hall itself immediately goes silent. Beside me, Femi is frozen.

Tomasis rises with the dangerous grace of a jungle beast and in two strides is standing before me. The blow comes out of nowhere, sends me crashing to the ground. I try to ignore the sting of my cheek, the cold stone beneath my fingers as I struggle to my knees.

"Please!" Femi is saying, his voice urgent and shrill. "She does not know what Kaplan is."

The whole hall stays silent.

"You would bring the Tiger's enemies to my house?" Tomasis asks Femi, his eyes glittering darkly. "You would trick me into taking them as my own?"

"Forgive me, my Lord. She does not know what she is asking!" Femi says again sharply, his words like a blade parrying Tomasis's rage, holding it back.

"Then why do you bring her to me?" Tomasis roars. "Why would she ask me to kill *him*?"

The question echoes off the walls. Everyone is listening.

I will myself not to tremble, sucking in the air around me to steady myself.

"Fath— Thénardier sold my sister to him," I say, looking at his feet, trying to keep the fear from my voice.

Tomasis sighs and bends, putting a hand beneath my chin. When I look up, his eyes are boring into mine. "Violence is rare here in the Shining Hall. Unlike the other Guilds, we rely on our speed and our wits. It is said we Thieves are good at stealing even the outrage from a brother's heart." He steps back, sitting heavily on his chair. "I'll forgive you your impudence because you're among the youngest of my children. None would bring me what you have. And none would dare ask of me what you have just asked."

He nods to Femi, who grabs me by the arm and yanks me to my feet.

"Lord Kaplan, the Tiger, rules the Guild of Flesh," says Tomasis. "He sits at the high table with the eight other Lords of the Miracle Court." He shuts his eyes and rubs a hand over his temple as if weary. "We have . . . agreements with the Guild of Flesh. They don't interfere with us, and we let them be. I would not defy Lord Kaplan even for one of my own. For to attack a Lord would plunge the Court into war. It is forbidden; thus sayeth the Law."

"Thus sayeth the Law." The murmurs echo around me.

"We the Wretched, children of the Miracle Court, are bound by the Law," Tomasis continues. "It binds us, it keeps us, protects us, constrains us. It is engraved on the scales of our eyes, it is written in ash on the blackened tablets of our hearts."

"But my sister!" I cry.

"I will give you a hundred new sisters," Tomasis says with mournful eyes. "But I cannot return to you that which has been taken. Grieve for her, but know that she is gone."

I fight down the bitter disappointment that rises in me.

I thought this man who rules so powerfully over the Guild of Thieves could help me save Azelma.

A trembling starts within me. I try to control it, making fists and holding my limbs taut, but it takes over, my body no longer able to contain everything it feels. Tomasis catches me by the arm and pulls me toward him. His voice softens and lowers so that only Femi and I can catch his words.

"Do not be afraid, little one. You are a child of this Guild; Kaplan will not touch you. And you will be safe here from Thénardier's wrath—I know his violence when the bottle has him. Look at me now: you are no longer his kin, you are *my* daughter. If he raises a hand to you, it will be as if he has struck me—and even he has never been drunk enough to try such a thing."

"I am not afraid for myself," I say, biting off each word with chattering teeth. I look Tomasis in the eye and see pity swimming in the depths.

If I can find out what the Tiger has planned, or where he has taken my sister, then surely I will be able to do something. . . .

"You said you will give me a gift, so I ask you for the truth," I say, my voice small. "Is he going to kill her?"

Tomasis shakes his head slowly and looks away. "I will not gift you this truth, for it is one known to all. Death would be a mercy to her," he says quietly. He smiles at me, a smile wreathed in sadness, and for a moment he looks just like Femi. "But the gift I have promised you will keep.

Know that one day you may ask it of me and I will bestow it on you." A stern look comes over him. "Do not go looking for her, for you will not find her. Do not try to help her, for there is nothing that can break the Tiger's hold once his claws are in. Do not make Kaplan your enemy; you will not sing the hunting song in his name. Swear to me that it will be so."

Azelma sacrificed her one chance at escape to send me here, to give me the small bit of safety that even now stings behind my ear. Femi risked the wrath of his brother to save me, and now the Lord of Thieves has pledged to protect me from the Tiger, and from Thénardier. I must heed their words; I must respect their sacrifice. I must forget my sister. I would be a fool to do otherwise.

I nod.

"I swear it, my Lord," I say.

And the lie tastes bitter on my tongue.

4

She Who Sleeps

Breaking into a place under cover of night is usually a simple matter of finding an entry point. A loose window, a door with a lock begging to be picked. Sometimes you have to toss up a rope or scale a wall to get to a building's weak spots. Other times you might creep across rooftops and let yourself down a cold chimney. But the same techniques are much more difficult by day, when you're likely to be spotted by any number of people: the merchants and workers; the laundry-women hauling their linens to the boats floating on the Seine; the musicians, the beggars, the tradesmen, all the common people of the city, who aren't children of the Miracle Court. By day the city seethes with life: it is a nest of mice scurrying to and fro, everyone hurriedly going about their business.

I shift impatiently under the lowering sun as the city

hums its frenzied song. It is not yet time for me to be about; every inch of me longs to retreat until the daylight is truly gone. Dogs of the Thieves Guild work by day, and we Cats despise them because of it. Cats glide across the rooftops in the moonlight like dancers, while Dogs roam the arrondissements and slip silky hands into rich men's pockets. Cats would never lower themselves to such petty work.

But today I'm not even a Cat. Today I'm a flower girl. I stole a dress, an apron, and neat slippers from a girl down at the floating baths. She likely walked home half-naked, poor thing. I took the basket of flowers from a distracted woman who was eating breakfast. Breakfast is a luxury for most of the Wretched, one I am rarely afforded.

A building looms before me, all yellowed stone and tiny windows. I've watched it since sunup, and it's been silent all day.

My heart is skittering in my chest; the hair at the back of my neck stands on end. I know the danger of what I am about to do, and I am afraid.

Everyone is afraid.

Azelma's words float toward me on the cold breeze. And I do what I always do when the fear threatens: I remember her whispering to me by candlelight. I wear her words like a shield as I set forth.

It's been three months since Femi first brought me to the Thieves Guild. Three months of delivering takes to Lord Tomasis while secretly scrambling up the walls of every Flesh House I can find in the city. Three months of watching and waiting and learning that the houses of flesh come alive only after the sun has set. Three months of cramped limbs from perching on window ledges in the rain, counting the heads of a hundred girls, searching for one that looks like *her*. I climbed a hundred walls, slipped into a hundred windows before I found her.

I take a deep breath and approach the building from the side, avoiding the front, with its door of flaking blue paint, and the outrageously fat man sitting on a barrel. Weeks of spying on this house have shown me that when he's sober, he's as strong as an ox and as violent as a caged bear. But right now, he's still in the depths of a daylong hangover. Last night was a wild night. He indulged in too much wine—*good* wine. I would know. I stole it from the cellars of the Marquis de Loris, an avid collector, and dosed it with poppy purchased from the Guild of Dreamers to ensure he would sleep deeply. Although the guard is snoring, I won't risk the front door and instead slip to the side entrance, where kitchen deliveries are made. I push open the door, and as I knew they would be, the kitchens are empty at this hour.

I ease into a corridor. At its end is a door to the chamber of the madam who runs this establishment. Her door is ajar, and from inside comes the sound of snoring. *Good.* Her wine, too, was laced with poppy, and I paid a sailor on his way in to make sure he delivered it to her. He was delighted to do so. A grateful madam would earn him more time with the girls.

I should leave. I always leave at this point. It's too

dangerous to stay. But today will be different. Today I am going to rescue her.

I look up the stairs.

Do not go looking for her, Tomasis said.

I should obey him, but I can't.

As if mesmerized, I'm drawn up the stairs, creeping quietly, hand on the banister. The gaudy peeling wallpaper shows exotic scenes of the Qing lands.

The top of the landing is lined with doors half-open in invitation. But only one room calls to me: the last one on the left. I walk to it with purpose and push against the door, and my breath catches in my chest.

She's lying on the bed, her body curled into a ball as if to protect itself. The room is seedy: an open cupboard with a few fading costumes, a small dressing table with a cracked mirror, a clutter of colored bottles of watered-down perfume, cheap powders and rouge, a brittle calling card from a customer, two syringes lying used and empty.

My heart contracts as I look at her. Her makeup is smeared across her face. Her hair has been curled into unnatural ringlets. In the last few months, she's grown thin and hollow-cheeked. The dress she's wearing is torn in several places, with uneven stitches along the hem. She who once sewed so quick and neat can make only uneven stitches now, her hand unsteady from the drugs, or from a beating. The syringe has tattooed her arm with black pinpricks, each one flowering into a yellow-blue bruise. Her skin is bumpy with gooseflesh, but she was too tired to pull the threadbare sheet over herself.

I reach out and gently trace the mark of her Guild. The Tiger doesn't tattoo his children with ink. He has other ways of marking them. Her mark runs across her eye like a stripe from her cheek to forehead, a scar of raised flesh against smooth skin.

At my touch her lashes flutter groggily, her gaze heavy and unfocused with the poppy they've shot into her veins. Her eyelids close again. I know that she does not recognize me. Perhaps she thinks I'm a dream, a memory of another time when she was another girl. While in other beds throughout this building, and in hundreds of houses around the city, her sisters dream uneasily as well.

It wasn't always this way. When Lady Kamelia led the Guild of Sisters, there were five thousand women of the night. But hers was a reign of seduction and luxury, and all of her daughters flourished under the protection of the Law. Since the Tiger wrested control of the Guild, it is said that twenty thousand Sisters sleep under his thrall.

"Zelle, Zelle!" I hiss softly in her ear, but she doesn't stir. I shake her, and when that fails I grab a jug at her bedside and spill icy water over her face.

She splutters awake, gasping. One eye is dark brown, the other filmy and blinded by the cat-o'-nine-tails that cut into her, marking her as a child of the Guild of Flesh.

She tries to sit up but is too weak, so I try help her. Trembling, she edges away from me, her hands raised to protect herself—she's afraid I'm here to give her a beating.

"Zelle, it's me. It's Nina. . . ."

Between her fingers her good eye finally focuses on my face and she gives a sharp intake of breath.

"No, no, no . . ."

She's shaking violently now, wet and cold, as I try to drag her to her feet.

"Zelle, please, we have to go before they wake. Come quickly."

"No!" She twists out of my grasp and tears herself away from me, backing into the wall. "I won't go, I won't, I won't. They broke his hands. They broke him. . . ." She stops, and something in her gaze hardens.

"Zelle," I say calmly. I approach her slowly, like a person trying to tame a frightened beast.

I hear the creak of a door opening downstairs, and a raised voice berating someone. I curse under my breath. The Fleshers have arrived, and they must have realized that something is wrong. Voices grow louder. I don't have much time.

"Zelle, it's me, *Nina*," I say.

"Nina? Nina, no . . . not Nina. Not Nina . . ." Her words are slurred, her voice ragged. "You must leave, before they come. . . . They broke him. They broke—"

"Shhh," I say, even as footsteps pound up the stairs. It's only moments now until they begin to check on the girls, until they find me here with her.

Azelma's eyes focus on my face, and for the first time since I have stood here before her, I think she truly sees me.

Boots thunder down the hallway. Doors slam. Voices call

out that the girls are asleep. Azelma's eyes dart to her window, terror raw on her face.

"You must go," she says urgently.

"Not without you." I reach for her. "Come with me." She looks at my hand, and she takes it. We dash to the window, which I throw open, and I clamber onto the ledge, then turn to her.

I see it then, the clarity amid her confusion, the resolve beneath her fear. My sister stares into my eyes; she is so close I feel her breath against my cheek.

"Run," she says, and she pushes me as behind her the door flies open. I watch my sister's face as I fall in slow motion, and then abruptly she is gone and a man is leaning out, yelling and pointing.

I hit the ground with a shuddering impact. Pain laces my side. The wind has been knocked out of me, and I gasp for breath, willing my limbs to move, finding that they obey far more slowly than I can afford. I barely manage to rise to my feet as several men burst out of the building. They're giants, like all of the Tiger's sons, chosen for their brawn, their complete absence of morals, and their unspeakable propensity for inflicting pain. They circle me like sharks. They ask no questions; they don't want to know who I am or why I am there. My being there is enough for them.

The sun is setting fast. I have time to call out only once, so I whistle loud and sharp, the call of the Thieves, knowing that even if anyone hears, it will probably be too late.

5

The Claws of the Hawk

A voice rings out, and the words are so ridiculous that even in the depths of my fear, I almost laugh.

"Six grown men against a child seems incredibly cowardly to me." The voice is amused, young. Its owner clearly has no idea that he is addressing some of the most dangerous men in the whole city.

"If we could return home without getting into any trouble for once, I would be most grateful," says another, wearier voice.

"They've got a *child* there, St. Juste. Take a look."

"Dear heavens, you're right." Which is followed by a barked order. "Unhand that child immediately or you will have cause to regret it!"

The voice—St. Juste's, it seems—is well modulated, educated; the voice of someone who is used to being listened to.

The Fleshers, however, listen to no one but the Tiger, so they ignore St. Juste and lunge at me. Two of them grab me from behind, and I'm thrown to the ground. They begin to kick me, and I scratch and yowl, striking out with a dagger that's been tucked into my boot.

Then someone fires a gun and the Fleshers freeze: men unaccustomed to being crossed rarely carry weapons.

"I will shoot you if you do not unhand that poor child. And what's more, Grantaire will shoot you as well, and he is far less likely to kill you."

"I object to that!" says the other man now. "I can shoot perfectly well in my cups, I can! Watch . . ."

Another shot rings out, and one of the Fleshers yelps and raises a hand to his ear.

"See, I *meant* to clip that one."

The Fleshers look at one another. As a Guild, they are not known for their brains. The Tiger adopts only the most violent children, the ones who will obey without question; figuring out a complex problem like this is beyond them.

He takes a second shot, and another Flesher swears and grabs his leg, nearly crumpling to the ground. I can hear the Fleshers scuttling heavily away, but surely only to get weapons and return. I take a second to appreciate the fact that I am still alive.

"I say, Grantaire, that was good! Did you mean to get him right above the knee?"

Someone turns me over, and I am greeted by the sight of two faces staring down at me. One has a mess of black hair, a green waistcoat, and a roguish smile.

"Oh, good, it's alive!" he says.

The other face scowls at me as if disappointed that I have survived. Even from this perspective I can make out the grim features of a young god, his face carved of marble and determination and framed with a halo of ice-blond hair tied at the nape of his neck. He is beautiful and terrible at the same time in his tailcoat of deep red, with a cravat artfully undone at his throat. In his hand is a fine pistol of gold filigree, which he tucks into his waistband so he can scoop me up and put me on my feet.

"Can you stand?" the dark one asks with concern. Then he wobbles and topples over, making the blond one roll his eyes and go to his aid. The dark one is drunk. They probably both are.

"I'm fine," I say shortly, biting down at the stinging in my side.

"You seem to have fallen into extremely bad company," the dark one says from the ground, where he sits batting away the blond one's attempts to bring him to his feet. "If you want to paw at me, St. Juste, you'll have to ask for my hand first."

"No one will ever want to paw you until you are less of a drunk, Grantaire."

"You are to blame for the depth of my drunkenness,

St. Juste. Your meetings positively bore me to tears and drive me to the bottle."

The blond one gives up and turns to look at me, and it is not a look that I will ever forget. He seems to see right through me, scanning me swiftly and taking in the lines of my clothing, the blood on my cheek, on my hands and my feet.

"We should introduce ourselves to our new friend," the dark one says. "I do believe this urchin owes us his life."

I wince at that. The idea of a child of Miracle Court owing a debt to one of Those Who Walk by Day is unthinkable.

"I am in your debt, sirs," I say, the admission sticking in my throat.

"What is your name, little boy?" the dark one asks.

The blond one's eyes narrow. "Girl," he says.

I try not to let my surprise show. Almost nobody can tell I'm a girl.

"Girl? Where?" Grantaire looks around comically, and seeing no one else, he blinks at me and points unnecessarily at my face. "*That* is a girl?"

I raise my chin defiantly. "They call me the Black Cat," I offer in response.

"Oh, that is good," says the dark one. "I want an animal name—can I have an animal name too? What about the Drunken Ferret? And you, St. Juste. You can be . . . the Oppressive Eagle of Judgment."

"You can call me Nina," I say, trying to suppress a smile.

51

"Well, m'lady Nina, I am Grantaire," the drunkard continues with a swift return of grace and manners. "And this pinnacle of humanity is Enjolras St. Juste."

Now it's my turn to stare. St. Juste, the beautiful. St. Juste, the Angel of Death, whose head is one of the six impaled atop the gates of the Tuileries. One of the *six little mice*— revolutionaries who set the city aflame and nearly toppled the king and queen only a generation ago. And for their pains the nobility fed them to the guillotine and hunted down all of their known relations, hanging them from the gibbet of Montfaucon.

"You call yourself by that name openly?" I ask.

"Oh, here we go. Don't get him started about his ancestry," Grantaire says, and takes a swig from a flask that has appeared in his hand.

"I am not ashamed of my kin," St. Juste says. "I was in the womb when my uncle tried to change the world. I was brought up under my mother's name, and so I lived, but what kind of living is it when gangs of brutes set upon children? When little girls are so scared they must hide what they are under layers of shapeless cloth?"

I stare at him. "You're mad," I say.

"Perhaps, for only the mad would see the endless darkness, the great evil that reigns around us, and stand against it."

"They're going to kill you."

"Probably," St. Juste says with a grim smile. "But by all hells, I'll set this city on fire and take as many of them down with me as I can." His eyes gleam with a passion I've never seen before. It's both frightening and mesmerizing. Here is a boy who is marching toward his death, and he is delighting in it.

"They'll hang him from Montfaucon for sure, and us alongside him," Grantaire says so mournfully that I am released from the spell St. Juste's words have cast over me. "But we are all his lackeys, for there is a truth in what he says. This city is a broken thing, and the world itself is wrong, and we cannot sit by and do nothing about it."

"Falling over in taverns is not doing something about it," St. Juste retorts sharply.

Grantaire smiles at that. "I drink to you, Son of Rebellion, Oppressive Eagle of Judgment." He raises his flask and salutes his friend before downing its contents.

As he swallows with a heavy hiccup, a sharp cry rends the night. It is the call of Aves, the Elanion; Femi.

"What on earth is that?" Grantaire asks.

"It sounds like some sort of hawk," offers St. Juste.

"What kind of devil bird preys at this hour?"

Suddenly there is a tinkle of breaking glass, and the solitary streetlamp goes out. I cannot help but grin in the darkness.

"Sirs, I will take my leave of you, and am mindful of the debt I owe you. It would be wise to leave before the Fleshers return. They will no doubt be armed this time."

In the sudden darkness they are half-blind, so they barely see me slide past them and clamber up the wall of a nearby building.

"Wait!" Grantaire shouts, but I ignore them. I'm not

afraid they'll shoot me, because, unlike me, they are not ac-customed to darkness. Well, that and I've stolen their pistols.

"Well, that was fairly rude. We did save her life," comes Grantaire's voice as I climb higher and higher, ignoring the pain in my side. "Then again," he continues, "I can't blame her for fleeing. You probably drove her away with your weary justice speech."

"I am going to let you find your own way home if you don't shut up, Grantaire," St. Juste's voice says clearly.

"Hold on a minute. . . . Where's my gun?"

My laughter carries on the wind, curling around them, caressing their skin like a kiss, before I am completely gone.

⤛⤜

The Messenger is waiting for me, perched on the edge of an old gabled roof, so still he might be one of the city's weath-ered gargoyles.

"Femi—"

"What did you think you were doing?" His voice is a snarl.

His barely controlled anger hits me like a wave, and I take a step back. "You took your sweet time," I retort sharply.

"Aye, and if those two fools had not intervened, I'd have arrived only to sing a death song over your corpse."

Femi turns, and it strikes me that there is something odd in the way he is standing.

"You took an oath that you would not seek her out, that

you would not attempt to rescue her. Beating you to death was the most merciful thing the Fleshers might have done if they had discovered you were a girl. But the Tiger is afraid of nothing and no one. Law or no Law, he'd probably take you, just to see what the other Lords would do. He'd feed you the poppy, and turn you into . . ."

I blanche at his words.

"You *swore* you would not do this, Nina," Femi says again. "You cannot help her. Not this way."

Though I know his words are true, a storm of rage rises within me. "How can you speak of oaths while she is in there—you who swore you cared for her!"

It is as if I have slapped him across the face. He stops, trembling and towering over me in anger, his face turning hard and cold.

"It is because I care for her that I promised to protect you. It was the last thing she asked of me, Nina—the *only* thing she asked of me. If she'd asked me to flee with her, I'd have gone. If she had asked me for Death the Endless, I'd have given her a blade." He swallows and looks down, cradling his hands. "And even though she did not ask it of me, did you really think I wouldn't try to find her? I who hear all and see all that happens in the Guilds. Did you think I wouldn't have called in every debt, paid every coin and jewel in my possession, to try to save her? Did you think I would not come for her myself?"

They broke his hands. Azelma's terrified voice lances my brain.

I look in fear to his hands. He stills as I reach out and push back the long sleeves of his cloak to find a tangle of misshapen fingers, little more than gnarled claws, bruised, twisted, and broken.

"I am Aves, the Elanion, Messenger to the nine Guilds of the Miracle Court," Femi says in a trembling voice. "But seeking to steal from a Guild Lord could not go unpunished. It is the Law. And only because I am trusted, only because I am Tomasis's blood-born brother and he pleaded for me— for this alone I was spared."

Horror seeps into every pore of my being. Horror, and fear and sickness at the sight of what they have done to him.

"I swore to protect you," Femi says, his voice still quiet. "I promised her. What will I have left if I fail her in this as well?"

I turn from him, light-headed. I close my eyes and try clear my thoughts. "I cannot just forget her, Femi."

"And you cannot rescue her. It cannot be done, not *this* way."

I turn his words over in my mind, until I finally see the meaning behind them. My eyes snap open. "You believe there is another way?"

Femi straightens, tucking his ruined hands back under his cloak. I wonder how he managed to climb with his fingers so broken.

"She cannot be stolen, but perhaps she can be bought," he says. His words are careful, deliberate.

Hope swells in my breast. "For how much? More than

56

twelve coins of gold?" I can raise an impossible sum if needed. Stealing precious things is what I am good at.

Femi shakes his head. "The Tiger is rich beyond measure," he says. "Gold means little to him. But he is a man who is never thwarted in any of his wishes. What you must find is something that he wants but cannot have. Make him desperate for it until he is ready to pay any price to attain it. If you are lucky, you might have power to dictate a price: the freedom of your sister."

His words are genius. But I frown as a new thought blossoms.

"What is it that the Tiger wants?" I look up and find Femi staring at me, his face a grimace.

"What does he always want?" he asks.

The question hangs between us, unanswered. But even now I am aware; I have seen my sister, and the truth of what she has become is so terrible I dare not speak it aloud.

Sometimes we must pay a terrible price to protect the things we love.

Is there any price I will not pay to save my sister?

No. There is not.

PART TWO

The Dead Wolf

⟫— 1829 —⟪

When a leader of the Pack has missed his kill,
he is called the Dead Wolf as long as he lives,
which is not long.

—The Jungle Book

THE FOX RENNART'S REVENGE

FROM STORIES OF THE MIRACLE COURT, BY THE DEAD LORD

Il était une fois . . . Rennart the Fox came to the house of Ysengrim the Boar, stealing into his lair in the darkness. The Fox's blade was sharp, and his teeth hungered for the taste of blood. He stood before the crib where the daughter of Ysengrim lay sleeping, and he gazed upon her beautiful face.

It was for revenge that the Fox had come. Ysengrim and Rennart had once been like brothers. And yet Ysengrim had given to Rennart the gift of the seven hells. First he had betrayed his friendship. Then he had taken the Fox's house and his name. He had killed the Fox's loyal men. He had murdered his wife and his daughter. Lastly, he had cast the Fox into the darkest dungeon, les Oubliettes du Châtelet, the place of forgetting. And in the last of these seven hells, Rennart sat in the darkness and waited.

With time and patience, the Fox escaped. And under the cloak of darkness he came to stand before the crib of Ysengrim's daughter.

"Slay her, I must slay her," Rennart cried to himself. "Does the blood of my men, my wife, my child not cry out for vengeance? All has been taken from me. I have earned the right to do this midnight deed."

And though Ysengrim had wounded him beyond healing, despite all that he had lost and suffered, Rennart knew that if he slew the child he would be no better than his enemy. He knew that he could not kill her.

And so instead the Fox took her. He stole her from her crib, and carried her away to his den, and in doing so inflicted a thousand hurts on Ysengrim, worse than burying a wife and child, worse than seeing men fall, worse than losing all that you have built. The Fox gave Ysengrim the Boar a terrible gift: the gift of never knowing what had become of his daughter, the guilt of wondering endlessly whether she had lived or died.

6

The Tiger

I watch Ettie from the corner of my eye. I have to; Thénardier will beat her if she doesn't learn fast. And I cannot afford for her perfect face to be marred. Not today of all days.

The inn is crowded early this evening, voices merging into a dull roar. They'll get louder as the night goes on and people get drunker. The air is thick with the scent of beer and wine long soaked into the floor and the sweet smoke of poppy from the pipes of the Dreamers in one corner. It's roasting in here, too many bodies in too small a space. Carrying drinks to any table means walking through a maze of wandering hands and lecherous grins. I avoid the men with tattoos behind their ears: those are the ones you don't want to trip over.

I glance back at Ettie, who's struggling beneath the weight of a jug. Her skinny arms aren't used to lifting such things.

I take a deep breath.

I can do this. I've rehearsed it in my head a thousand times.

I weave through the customers and bump my hip into a table just hard enough that the man at the far end is jostled into Ettie.

She is fighting to keep her hold on the jug when a large hand darts out and grips her shoulder, steadying her.

"Not used to waiting on tables, are we, little one?"

The voice is a rough, warm growl. My heart sinks into my boots, when it should be soaring.

The world seems to slow. I drop whatever I was carrying onto the nearest table, ignore the protests of the customers, and push through the crowded floor to her.

The man has stood to help her with the jug, and, relieved, she lets him take it.

Don't look at him, Ettie, I think, despite myself.

But she does, a single golden curl escaping from her white cap as she tilts her head up to see who has saved her from a fall. She's small and he's a giant of a man, exuding strength and warmth. He has yellow eyes, a face tanned dark from years spent at sea, hair bleached orange-blond by the sun. The long, corded scars that cross from his forehead to his cheek don't take away from his magnetic charm. He smiles at Ettie, a smile that is all teeth, and God forgive her, she smiles back.

"What is your name?" the smiling Lord asks.

"Ettie," I blurt out before she can answer.

She turns to me, her eyebrows raised in question.

"I'm sorry she disturbed you, Monseigneur," I say, not looking at his face. Definitely not looking at the scars. "Come with me, Ettie. You're needed in the kitchen."

I reach out to her, but his hand clamps down tight on her shoulder again.

"Lord Kaplan! Are my daughters bothering you?"

I've never been so delighted to hear Thénardier's voice. The customers watch with interest as he moves through the crowd toward us. It's a promising spectacle so early in the evening. After all, someone might be about to die—and that someone isn't them.

Kaplan, the Tiger, is a Guild Lord, and he dresses his huge frame in rough sailor's garb: loose shirt, trousers, boots, and an old naval jacket he legendarily took from the back of an admiral at sea. He carries no weapons; he doesn't have to.

Thénardier, in contrast, is only a Guild Master. He is a small man, thin and wiry. He can be recognized from afar by the purple-and-yellow-striped waistcoat he favors. He's a distraction, like a peacock fanning its brilliant tail. Like many members of the Thieves Guild, he's given to wearing fine jewelry. His right hand is heavy with rings of gold. I've felt the mark of them on my skin too many times to count.

"Eponine, take little Cosette outside." Thénardier rubs his hands together, as he's wont to do when bargaining, for he sees Kaplan's interest; he knows there's something to be gained here.

My stomach churns. I remember the night the Tiger came for Azelma.

Stay calm. It's all going according to plan.

I step forward and take Ettie's hand. Everyone is staring at her and she doesn't know why.

She tries to pull away from Lord Kaplan. But he doesn't let go.

"Your daughter too?" Kaplan's yellow eyes flick to my face.

"Nina is my little Cat," Thénardier says.

Like everyone we know, he says one thing and means another. He says I'm a Cat, but he means I'm a full member of the Thieves Guild, so touching me is making argument with the Thief Lord. Thénardier is saying *back off* in such a way it comes out dripping in sweetness. He smiles, his mouth full of gold teeth. He cut them from the gums of soldiers dying on the battlefield and paid a butcher to put them in for him when his own rotted away.

"Your Cat has claws."

Kaplan releases his hold on Ettie. She sways into my arms.

I grab her and begin moving us toward the door, hoping the Tiger's eyes will follow us. Hating that they do.

"And the blond one?"

"My ward."

"I didn't know you were in the habit of dispensing charity, Thénardier."

"Her mother pays me for her keep."

We're almost at the door, and Ettie is protesting because

I'm pulling her arm too hard, but I must, to get her out. Out of the room, out of sight, out of *his* presence.

I yank the rough door open. The wind comes racing in, biting at my cheeks. Ettie is saying something about the cold, but I ignore her. I drag her out and tug the heavy door closed behind us. The last thing I hear is Lord Kaplan's voice, as clear as the bells of Matins: "How much can I pay you to take her off your hands?"

I suck in deep breaths of the cold air. My mind is racing. I've just heard the words I needed to hear. He's taken the bait.

So why, then, do I feel so miserable? I look Ettie over. She's a little thing. Twelve years old and unable to fend for herself. At her age, I had been a member of the Thieves Guild for three whole years. She hasn't the cunning to survive the Miracle Court. And yet I find myself trying to hide her, winding baggy boys' clothes around her like armor to protect her from hungry eyes. I tuck her rebellious golden curls into an old cap so she'll look like me.

You hide her like Azelma hid you. The thought comes unbidden.

An act, I tell myself, *so as not to be too obvious until the time is right.*

"Is Thénardier sending me away with that man?" she asks curiously, digging the toe of one oversized boot into the watery muck on the ground, as if perhaps it mightn't be so bad if Kaplan took her. She thinks anything would be better than living with Thénardier and his drunken rages.

She has no idea.

"That man is the Tiger," I say.

Ettie takes a step back. Young though she is, she recognizes the common name whispered for the Lord of the Guild of Flesh.

I shake my head roughly; I can't afford to think about it now.

"Will he harm me?" Ettie's little body shakes. "Nina . . . ?"

It's the same reaction I had only a few years ago, when I stood shaking before the truth of what the Tiger was.

Ettie always looks to me for answers. I'm the one who tells her how to keep out of trouble. I shouldn't have bothered to disguise her; it was a silly, disjointed attempt to protect the lamb I was planning to offer up. To keep people from seeing what she is. For Ettie is beautiful, the kind of beautiful that would draw attention even clothed in rags. The kind you spend years hoping to find, the kind you convince Thénardier he must take in, the kind you know the Tiger will want.

"Will he kill me?"

Ettie's words shake me from my reverie. I need to get her away now, to hide her so that neither Thénardier nor the Tiger can find her; thwart them, make them mad with the wanting of her. Only then can I demand my price.

I catch my breath.

"Yes, he'll kill you," I lie. He won't kill her. What he'll do is much worse. She will look for death and it will not come.

Ettie's face crumples. She breaks into little sobs.

The first night I brought her back to the inn, she looked around and promptly burst into tears until Thénardier's reprimand left her cheek a mass of blue-black bruises. When the last customer was gone and dawn was peeping through the wooden shutters, I crawled up to my bed and found her curled in a ball, shivering under the bedsheets. She was half frozen with fear and sorrow. I should have given in to my exhaustion, ignored her, and fallen asleep. But she stared at me entreatingly with those enormous blue eyes. So I lay down beside her, put my arm around her for warmth, and told her a story.

"Stop crying," I say shortly, and grab Ettie's hand. "Come on."

"Where are we going?" She sniffles.

I smile. A smile that she should never trust.

"Somewhere he will not be able to find you," I say, which is only partly a lie.

We rush down a tangle of back streets, keeping to the shadows.

She's breathless and struggling along behind me, but at least she's stopped crying.

She thinks I'm going to save her. When I'm sending her to a fate far worse than the seven hells.

But sometimes we must pay a terrible price to protect the things we love.

7

The Black Cat's Choice

After the revolution failed, the city was carved into two parts. Half of Paris is rigid, boxtree-lined avenues haunted by the aristocracy. The other half is a murky jungle of crime and misery.

I wear this city like skin wrapped around my bones. I know each street by the feel of the stone beneath my feet. It speaks to me; it shows me where to go. It would have been safer to go the long way, cutting through the manicured streets of the sheltered nobles, but we don't have time. And it would have been faster to go over rooftops, but Ettie doesn't know a Cat's way of racing along tiles and leaping sure-footed from one house to the next.

So instead, we run down the villainous-smelling streets, weaving between wagons and Those Who Walk by Day.

Dodging an old lady sitting on a crate with a sign that says she'll mend clothes for a few sous; darting down an alley, throwing out a prayer that we'll find it empty. We skitter along the alley's length before ducking into another one.

Ettie's boots are too big, and she can't run fast. But I bring her along at breakneck speed. We have to keep moving. The city assumes that anyone hesitating too long in one place is issuing a challenge.

Ettie pulls on my arm to slow me down.

"Nina, if we could find a carriage, I could go to my *maman*."

I shake my head. Her *maman* stopped sending letters months ago; we both know what that probably means.

So we hurry along till we get to a ramshackle factory in the Gobelins, shut down by the banks for debt.

"Where are we?" Ettie asks.

I ignore the question.

It takes a ridiculous amount of time to clamber through a window and hoist Ettie up, since she's awful at climbing. She's awful at a lot of things. . . .

Ettie wrinkles her nose at the stench; a toxic smell from the arsenic used to dye the wall coverings, hats, and dresses of the nobility hangs in the air.

"How long will we stay here?"

I'm in no mood for Ettie's questions. "I'm not sure—a day or two, maybe."

She looks around, not liking what she sees. "Will you tell me a story?"

"This is hardly the time for a story!" I snap, making my voice as hard and ugly as I can, for it is an ugly thing that I am doing.

She shrinks from me, eyes wide.

I try to calm myself, but my thoughts aren't so easily cowed; they whir and screech in my head, accusing and shouting, clawing at me with a thousand knives of guilt. What kind of person sells another?

The kind of person who would do anything to get her sister back, I remind myself grimly.

I've no choice; it's the only way. *Azelma safe.* Isn't that worth the cost?

And yet I know I'm not just condemning Ettie to the Guild of Flesh. Whispers speak of Sisters smuggled in boxes, of living cargo traded to the Tiger's allies overseas.

The horror rises and threatens to overwhelm me. What he does, what he is, is an abomination, forbidden by the Law. The Law that is meant to protect us, to keep us safe.

And yet I cannot help the Sisters hidden in the shadows. I cannot save all the women in the Fleshers' houses. But I might free one of them. I can make Azelma safe.

For a terrible price.

I eye Ettie shivering in the corner.

"I'm sorry," I say, for snapping at her. And for what is about to happen, and for my part in it. I am so filled with regret that it threatens to burst out of me.

As if she can sense the turmoil I'm in, she gives me a small, forgiving smile, which is so typical of Ettie. It is not enough that she is beautiful; she is also kind. She rises and comes nearer to me and sits down on the floor.

"Tell me what happened to Ysengrim's daughter when Rennart found her."

I swallow. Ettie is obsessed with stories. And yet . . . what harm is there in finishing the tale? In giving her one last good thing before the end? And so I begin.

"Rennart the Fox went to the house of Ysengrim the Boar," I say. "He stole into his lair in the darkness. There he found the daughter of Ysengrim, and he gazed upon her beautiful face as she lay sleeping."

Ettie inches toward me and leans into me, like she did on the nights when she couldn't sleep; like I did when Azelma relayed stories to me.

"It was for revenge that the Fox had come," I continue, relaying the betrayal of Rennart by Ysengrim, the murder of his wife, the casting out of the Fox to a dark hell until he could escape and have justice.

But my voice grows unsteady. I try not to remember Azelma wrapping her arms about me like this, the warmth of her. Azelma, who protected me, who would never have done to me what I am contemplating doing to Ettie.

When a warm tear rolls down my cheek, she reaches up to wipe it from my chin.

"Don't cry, Nina," she says in her small voice.

And I know then that even for Azelma, my sister, even for her, I cannot go through with this. And the knowledge defeats me. For if I can't exchange Ettie for Azelma, then I cannot save my sister at all. I've lost her again, lost her forever.

The pain of it slices at me, but I cannot let it drown me, not now. I did a terrible thing setting this plan in motion. Ettie's life hangs in the great and terrible balance, and if I fall apart now, there will be no one else to help her. I must concentrate on the only thing I have any chance of changing now. . . . I must think of Ettie.

I glance sideways at her. She is so vulnerable, in her oversized shirt and boots. Like the beast he is, the Tiger has gotten the scent of her. I made sure of that. He'll come for her, and it will be my fault.

What am I going to do?

When we don't return, they'll look for me; they'll know I had a hand in it. She can't hide in this building forever. Nor can I.

Be useful, Azelma said the day she was taken, *be smart, and stay one step ahead of everyone.*

And then it comes to me. Breathtaking in its simplicity, really: the only way to protect someone is to give them to the protection of another Guild.

I remember Tomasis's reaction when I was given to him, and I frown. No Guild will want the Tiger's prey, for all the Lords fear the Tiger.

Except, perhaps, the Dead Lord.

I sit upright so suddenly that Ettie looks at me, blinking. "What is it, Nina?"

My mind is racing as I begin to make a new plan, and

I am faced with an inconvenient fact: no one has seen the Dead Lord or his Ghosts in weeks. His absence is strange enough to be whispered about in the Court. There is only one person who might know what has become of him.

The thought is so insane it is laughable.

What choice do I have?

"Where are we going?" Ettie asks.

"To find Lady Corday."

"Who is Lady Corday?"

You don't want to know.

"The Lady of the Assassins Guild."

Ettie catches her breath. "Where will we find her?"

Somewhere no one goes—at least, not if they want to walk out alive.

8

❧〜〜❧

The Dealers of Death

In times past, terrible wars threatened to tear the Miracle Court apart, which is why the Law was created to govern all the Guilds. But even with the Law, the Guilds can't quite give up the moldering suspicions that make them so distrustful of one another. The location of almost every Guild House is a closely guarded secret, known only to Femi and the People of the Pen. One of the exceptions is this house.

The building is impressive: tall, ancient, built of white marble. Its architecture is spare compared with the extravagant Gothic style of its decaying neighbors.

My mouth goes dry looking at it. They say it used to house the finest undertakers in all of France; some say it still does. We walk up a manicured path of smooth white stone leading to a large terrace. The front door is tall and black; its knocker is a heavy brass skull.

The Assassins don't need to hide their Guild, because members of the Miracle Court usually aren't foolish enough to seek them out.

I take a deep breath, wrap my fingers around the cold brass, and rap on the door. The noise thunders through the house, and an eerie, unnatural silence answers us. I pray that no one opens the door.

No one does.

"Are you sure this is the right place?" Ettie whispers.

It's the right place.

No one may enter a Guild if they are not a child of that Guild. It is a Law of the Miracle Court. The punishment for entering a Guild House uninvited varies by Guild. Thieves like to hang people from the Pont Neuf by their nether regions, which could be why no one ever tries to visit them. There are stories that say entering the front door of the Assassins Guild without an invitation leads to instant decapitation via hidden guillotine. Invitations are scarce. We'll have to do without one today.

Every nerve in my body is alive with dread as I push the heavy door open. That it's not locked frightens me more than I can say. I pause for a moment. No guillotine falls.

We stare down a long corridor lit by dim sconces; the floor is a chessboard of black and white marble. There's a small fountain gurgling delicately at its far end.

Beside me, Ettie is rigid and quiet. My fear is contagious.

"Good hunting," I call as loudly as I dare, making Ettie jump. My greeting goes unanswered.

"Maybe they're not home," Ettie offers. I shake my head.

The Bats are always home.

We walk down the corridor; my heart beats a wild staccato.

This Guild House, like its children, is stark, elegant, and devoid of feeling.

Ettie approaches the fountain. I grab her by the collar to stop her.

"Half the members of this Guild have devoted their lives to concocting deadly poisons. Don't drink *anything*." She nods, and we proceed with small, cautious steps. Ettie runs her fingertips along white markings on the dark walls as we go. I glance at them and my blood runs cold. The marks are carved into the wall. Each group of four is crossed with a fifth line. It's a running tally.

Ettie is wide-eyed as she inspects the paintings hung on the walls. On the left is a smudged mural of a skeleton dancing with a beautiful young woman: the oldest existing depiction of the danse macabre. On the right is a cluster of portraits: gentlemen and women of varying ethnicities, all dressed in fine black velvet, each holding a goblet filled with what looks like red wine but is actually blood. Rumor has it the portraits are painted in blood too. Each figure either holds a dagger or has a snake wound around their free arm to show which of the two houses of the Guild they belong to: Poisons or Knives.

"Who are they?" Ettie whispers.

"The Lords of this Guild."

The last portrait depicts a slight woman holding a dagger to show she's of the House of Knives.

There's a breeze.

The hair on the back of my neck rises, and every nerve in me screams *danger.*

"Can I help you?" asks a voice like a dagger point.

Ettie leaps in surprise. Out of nowhere a tall, thin young man has appeared beside us. His hair is black and barely curls. His skin is tanned, showing his Maghreb heritage. He's dressed from head to toe in varying shades of almost–black. He looks at us with dark, expressionless eyes.

He is Montparnasse of the House of Knives, Master of the Assassins Guild. Children of the Miracle Court are respected for the threat their Guild poses. Montparnasse is one of the highest-ranked Masters of the most dangerous Guild of all.

"Bonjour," Ettie says politely.

Horrifyingly, slowly, I become aware that the space around us is full of people. An ebony-skinned young man and a Corsican with an eye patch stand on either side of us, watching.

"Master of Knives." I try to keep the tremor out of my voice. *"Nous sommes d'un sang."* We are of one blood. I give the slightest of bows while keeping my eyes firmly on him.

He tilts his head and looks me over, and in a blur, he is inches from me. He raises a hand and I incline my head, a sign of submission, offering my neck for slitting if he sees fit.

Something cold and sharp touches my skin like a whisper, brushing my hair behind my ear, to reveal my diamond tattoo, the mark of my Guild.

Montparnasse is so close I am sure he can taste my fear. I try hard not to shake as he looks at me, close as a lover. I try very hard not to think about the fact that he smells of steel, salt, bone, and blood.

"Thieves Guild," he whispers, like a caress on my skin.

Do I imagine the tiniest glimmer of surprise in his voice?

Then we're grabbed from behind, dark sacks thrown over our heads. Ettie cries out through the rough cloth. This is bad. I was mad to have come. No one walks into the Assassins Guild and leaves alive.

I make a noise for Ettie to keep quiet as I feel the point of a blade at my back.

We're marched through countless corridors, twisting and turning. I won't remember how to get out of here. There are sounds—doors opening and closing, footsteps echoing on marble. Splinters of light dance through the weave of the sack.

A fire roars somewhere; its crackle and warmth sneak through the cloth. There's a murmuring of voices.

"Madame," Montparnasse says.

"Master of Knives," a woman's voice answers.

"I've brought you a gift."

"I'm no gift, not even to the Dealers of Death." My voice is muffled through the sack and doesn't sound as dangerous as I would like.

I'm pushed to my knees, the hood is removed from my head, and I stare blinking into the sudden candlelight. Ettie is next to me, looking terrified and perplexed.

Seated in front of us is a petite woman in a dark velvet dress. Her thick brown hair is pinned back tight, and she gives an impression of meticulous neatness. My heart drops at the sight of her so close. Charlotte Corday, Lady of the Assassins Guild. The only Assassin ever to come to her office by murdering the previous Lord in a crowded room, without going anywhere near him. Stories are whispered about her: that she came into the world dead, a corpse with skin like marble and cold, hard eyes; that those who have seen her smile rarely live long enough to talk about it; that she has sworn an alliance to the Dead Lord.

At her right stands a pale bald man wearing small spectacles and a waistcoat of dark gray satin. His white shirt collar is starched so stiff at the neck, it looks like it's trying to stab him. He's still except for his hands, which are wrapped in kid gloves; I have heard the acid-stained fingers constantly wring themselves together. He is Col-Blanche, Master of Poisons. At Corday's left stands Montparnasse, who is playing with a long, thin dagger and watching us.

"People don't usually come to us seeking their own deaths," Corday says, her voice like ice. "However, I'm sure we can make an exception if you've brought appropriate payment. Alternatively, the fee could be waived if you volunteer yourselves to the House of Poisons. Our newest recruits are always in need of fresh subjects on whom to test their concoctions." She pauses significantly. "Although that option is usually quite painful."

I blink several times before I realize what she's saying. "What? No, we're not here for that. . . . We're here for your help." I stumble over my words.

Lady Corday tilts her head. "You wish our aid in matters unrelated to death?"

"Yes."

Corday's eyes widen the tiniest fraction and her hands rise from her lap, fingers pressing together as she stares at me with an intensity that makes me feel like she's looking through me.

"You must forgive my presumption. I assumed you wanted help dispatching yourself from this life, since that is our trade. But then, we Death Dealers are not used to *un-invited* guests." And there it is, the threat lacing her measured words. She leans back in her chair, making herself comfortable. "In what way may we be of . . . *help* to you?"

We're probably dead already, so it makes no difference if I tell her the truth.

"My Lady, I'm the Black Cat of the Thieves Guild."

She watches me.

"I'm looking for a Guild to take Ettie." Nervousness makes me ineloquent.

"Who is Ettie?" Corday asks.

"I am!" Ettie lifts her head and shakes her golden curls out of her face.

Corday transfers her gaze to Ettie and pauses.

"Very beautiful."

Ettie colors beside me. "Thank you."

Corday raises an eyebrow before returning her attention to me.

"The Thief Lord won't give her his mark," I say.

"And I thought Tomasis was always eager for new pets." Corday runs her fingertips over one another as if she's testing them for sharpness.

I shake my head. "He won't, because the Tiger wants her."

Silence fills the room. The Death Dealers are good at silence. They wield it like a weapon.

"The Thieves won't take her, but you think I will?" Corday says in a tone of mild amazement.

"N–no," I stutter. "I would never . . . That is to say, I am looking for the Dead Lord. He is the only one who might take her despite the Tiger's interest. But I have heard that his seat at the high table has been empty, and the Ghosts have not been seen in the shadows." Even I know how stupid that sounds, but I've started and I must finish before I am condemned. "I know that you and the Dead Lord are allies of old. I have heard the stories."

"What stories?"

"That the Dead Lord saved you as a child and brought you to the Dealers of Death."

"Come here, child."

Montparnasse is at my side in a second, his fingers burning into my arm as he guides me to my feet. I walk toward Corday, leaving Ettie behind me.

"You would ask the Dead Lord, a Lord of the Miracle Court, to defy the Tiger by giving this child a mark?" she asks.

"Do you know what happened to the last Guild Lord who defied the Tiger?" a voice interjects.

I turn to a fireplace tucked into the farthest corner of the room, before which is seated a plump little brown-skinned woman draped in colorless robes, a sturdy scarf wound around her head, her thick graying hair tied back.

Hers is a face I know well, for she is usually seated at the Lords' high table when the Miracle Court meets. She peers at me now like an owl through large spectacles that dwarf her face. In the flesh she is not particularly intimidating, but appearances are deceiving, for this is Gayatri Komayd, Lady of the Guild of Letters, Mother of Ink, Keeper of Secrets, Head Auditor of the Miracle Court.

I do my best not to frown, confused by her presence here at the Assassins Guild. I'm so distracted, I almost miss Corday nodding to Montparnasse.

I swing around in horror to find that he has Ettie on her feet, his blade at her cheek. Ettie's eyes are wide with terror, the razor-sharp dagger pressed into her skin.

"Please!" I cry.

"You're daring, Black Cat of the Thieves Guild." Corday's face is a picture of calm. "And for that I'll give you some free counsel." Her eyes flicker back to Ettie. "Slice up her pretty face, and perhaps the Tiger won't want her anymore."

"Please. Don't!" I plead.

"I doubt Kaplan would be put off by a disfigurement at this stage. You know what he's like when he wants something," says Col-Blanche.

"It's true he doesn't like being defied," Corday agrees.

She glances again at Montparnasse, and at the merest blink of her eyes he lets go of Ettie and puts his blade away. Ettie breathes out in a long, loud sound.

I dare not even go to her. I try to still my trembling hands and keep my eyes on Corday, who seems to be measuring me up for something. I hope it's not a coffin.

"You're very small."

I nod.

"And you're a Cat."

"Yes, my Lady."

"You must be very good at getting into hard-to-reach places." Her eyes flicker toward the fireplace at Komayd.

"Nina can break into anywhere," Ettie pipes up from behind me. "She once broke into the Tuileries!"

I could kick myself for having told her about my burglaries, but Ettie so loves stories.

Corday looks at Ettie in amusement. "Did she? Well, that's very good, because everyone else has failed."

I frown. *Failed at what?*

Corday's and Komayd's eyes meet; they're having some sort of silent conversation.

"The Cat speaks truth: there's only one Lord mad enough to openly defy the Tiger," Komayd responds. "Only Orso."

The Dead Lord.

Corday agrees with a tilt of her head. "So you are right, little Cat, to seek an audience with him."

She motions to Montparnasse, and the bonds at our wrists are sliced with the whistle of a sharp blade.

"You must find the Ghosts," Corday says. "They are incomprehensible at the best of times, and I hear the absence of their Father makes them . . . even worse. I wish you both the best of luck. Shall we drink to your endeavor?"

I'm left with the feeling I've missed a fundamental part of the conversation. Did we just walk into the Assassins Guild looking for clues about the Dead Lord, only to be sent to find the Ghosts? Nobody has seen them in weeks. Was this some sort of test?

Col-Blanche moves to a small side table and pours sparkling white wine into two cut-crystal glasses. He carries them over on a tray and offers them to us.

I hesitate. The Master of Poisons is offering me a drink. A drink no one else in the room is drinking. *This* is definitely a test.

"I thank you, sir, but I'm afraid we can't accept your generosity," I say.

Corday smiles, showing her even white teeth. The sight fills me with dread.

"Wise, little kitten." She pulls a gold pocket watch out of a fold in her dress. It's a small, intricate thing hanging on a long chain, with a brass serpent twisted around its face.

"Now, if you could both look closely at this." Corday's tone indicates we have little choice.

I squint at the tiny gilt thing; it has Roman numerals of black, and hands like knives behind its glass face.

As the watch moves back and forth, the numbers blur together. I try to focus on them, but my thoughts seem to slow and the room grows wider, stranger; the crackling of the fire is loud in my ears.

Behind me, Ettie gives an odd sigh.

I try to turn to her, but my feet won't obey. My fingers scrabble uselessly at my coat, trying to grab for my dagger, but I can't seem to lift them. A wave of dizziness overcomes me. Have the Death Dealers given me some drug after all?

With a thud, Ettie crumples to the floor.

"You're a fighter, aren't you?" Corday says to me, her voice seeming to come from far away. "That's good."

"We came for your help." My words catch on my tongue and trip at my teeth.

I slump to my knees.

"It doesn't work on everyone. Some can fight it. Few are immune. The trick, little Cat, is not to look."

The last thing I see are Corday's eyes, wide and bright, drowning me inside them.

I hear a sound like someone clapping their hands together.

"*Nous sommes d'un sang,* little Cat. I hope we meet again soon."

9

The Dead

The first thing I do when I open my eyes is to make sure I'm not floating on the festering waters of the Great Serpent—the Seine—with my throat slit. My head aches, my mouth is dry, and my stomach churns. I narrow my eyes and peer away from the streetlight into the darkness, smelling the rain as it falls, trying to make out where we are.

Ettie wakes, too, and leans her head on my shoulder as we try to clear our minds from the heavy fog that shrouds them.

"How did they drug me if I drank nothing?" she mutters.

I ignore her, because my head is ringing. I should be relieved. We survived a direct encounter with the Lady of Assassins, even if it feels like someone has stabbed at my brain.

"Maybe it was a mist in the air," Ettie muses. "I always feel strange after the Dreamers have been smoking their pipes in the inn."

"There was something about the watch." I hesitate. "It did something to us."

Ettie rubs her eyes and shakes herself. We get to our feet, and she looks around at the dark street.

"Do you think the Dead Lord will want to take me?" she asks doubtfully.

I smile. "I think so. We have to find him first."

Each Guild of the Miracle Court has hundreds of its own calls, to speak over long distances, to give warning, to summon, or simply to announce their presence. The Thieves even have a complicated language of day and night calls. Then there are the Master Calls, calls that are universal in their meaning and that every child of the Miracle Court is taught to recognize.

I raise my chin and sound a Master Call, a short, sharp whistle. Ettie turns upon hearing the noise on my lips.

"What are you doing?" she asks.

"Calling the Dead."

A shadow moves in the fog. I slip my dagger into my hand as I wait for the person to materialize; I find comfort in the weight of it in my palm.

The shadow has a name: it is Montparnasse, Master of

Knives. I wonder what he is doing here. Is he here to protect us, or to do us harm?

More shadows shift. I blink several times. I see them before Ettie does: broken mountains of gray, hollow-eyed specters in ashen robes, their faces pale as death. Some are missing limbs or eyes; others have faces that are labyrinths of ancient wrinkles. These are the Dead Lord's children. The Ghosts.

Montparnasse looks at me. "You found your Ghosts, so I suggest you run along unless you want the Hyènes to find you."

I've no desire to encounter the Hyènes, the children of the Guild of Mercenaries, men and women paid to do violence.

I turn to say something, a small word of thanks, perhaps, for his not having murdered us. But there's only an empty space where he was standing.

With Ettie holding tight to me, we move toward the ghostly figures.

"We're looking for your Father," I say.

"Father?" The whisper comes back to us as a question.

An ashen boy who can't be older than five opens his mouth. "Do you know where he is?" he asks in the high, lost voice shared by all the Ghosts. I pause, surprised. The Dead Lord is Father of their Guild. Surely *they* know where he is.

"I think I might," I say noncommittally. I don't know, of course, but I'm not about to betray that fact, or they might lose interest in me . . . or worse.

A murmur goes through their ranks.

"Take them to Loup."

"Yes, come," says the boy. And where they were as still as statues, they're suddenly in motion, pulling us along with them. The small one leads the way, without hesitation, with surprising speed.

As we go, more shadows join the troupe, till we're walking surrounded by a gray wall of Ghosts.

Ettie looks at me, worried, as she should be. The Ghosts are among the most dangerous children of the Miracle Court, second only to the Assassins. Because there are so many of them.

"It's all right," I mouth at her.

But that's also a lie.

<hr />

The train of gray Ghosts walks together, pressing in from all sides in an odd, jostling wave. Ettie's tense beside me. Her arm is linked with mine; we'd get carried away from one another otherwise.

"I thought you meant real ghosts," she mutters, her tone deeply reproachful.

"People mostly ignore or look through them," I explain, "so they call themselves Ghosts because they think they're already dead."

Ettie is staring at a girl with milky eyes and long gray hair hanging down her back. She's blind. Beside her an older Ghost walks with a crutch; he's missing a leg.

"What happened to them?"

"Their Father."

There's a long and horrified silence as Ettie takes this in. But it's the truth of it. The city weeps tears of silver coins to the unfortunate. So the Dead Lord occasionally takes a hand, or a pair of eyes to encourage the silver. That's how he loves his children.

I lean over to whisper in Ettie's ear, trying to distract her from the horrors.

"Do you know why they're gray? They sit so long in one place begging that the dust from the carriages and street becomes part of them."

Like the smell. It wasn't so noticeable when there were only a handful of them, but now, as the bodies press into us, it's overwhelming. Sweet, sour, stale.

"What's that?"

I narrow my eyes to make out what she's seeing. The gray road ends, but the Ghosts still move forward.

Overhead is a large barrier. One of the Portes de Paris, the sixty-two gates in the wall that imprisons the city. Its name carved into the ancient stone.

La Barrière d'Enfer. The Hell Gate.

And beyond it, only darkness. The Ghosts are disappearing into it. The closer we get to the gaping hole, the more it grows. Holding hands, we let the darkness swallow us.

We're in a tunnel of some sort. In the distance, a single flaming sconce burns over an archway. The light illuminates the walls, which appear to be decorated with odd, detailed patterns carved in white stone.

"Nina!" Ettie gasps, her hands flying to her mouth.

I look closely. The delicate patterns of animals and flowers framing the archway are not carvings; instead, they're made of hundreds of human bones intricately fitted together, and rows of skulls above them.

Carved into the bones, an inscription over the archway reads: *L'empire de la mort*—the empire of the dead.

Ettie shakes beside me.

The small boy looks at her. He points beyond the archway into the darkness.

"It's all right," I whisper as we get dragged with the Ghosts deep into the catacombs.

The tunnel finally widens into a giant cave, ten times the size of the Shining Hall. The walls are lined from floor to ceiling with bones. The cave is lit by sconces made from the bones of human hands, the flame emerging from wicks fitted into palms, making the light jump and casting shadows everywhere.

The Ghosts settle down, sitting on the floor or perching in the many other tunnel entrances riddling the cavern. Their numbers must be in the hundreds. Their whispery, childlike voices echo around the cave.

Ettie and I stand together. The boy still holds on to her hand and looks around.

"Who are you?" comes a voice, loud and clear.

The Ghosts begin to murmur again, taking up the question.

Who are they? Who are you—

"And what are you doing among the dead?"

—Among the dead. What are they doing?

"We're looking for the Dead Lord." I try to sound brave. Their whispers echo my words.

The Ghosts are like a swarm: you can't make out where they start or end. The gray shapes morph and move in the dim light until through them a figure seems to rise from the ground itself. A thin boy, he is all pale skin and gray rags, his hair white, and in the middle of his face, where his nose should be, is a hole. I grip Ettie so she doesn't say anything. She remains admirably silent.

The thin boy bows low. I follow suit, dragging Ettie down with me.

"And what do you want with our Father, Thiefling?" The noseless Ghost's eyes are sharp with accusation.

"*Bonne chasse,* Master Loup. We've come to beg your mercy."

Loup looks at us, frowning. "*Bonne chasse* . . . Speak then, quickly, or we'll add you to the pot with the others."

The pot! The pot! comes the whispering cry.

I take only the briefest moment to wonder what others have been added to the pot; Ghosts are mysterious at the best of times, and their words are as garbled as a sphinx's riddle.

"I've business with the Dead Lord."

"You may speak your business."

"No," I say firmly. "I was sent by Lady Corday. I have matters to discuss with Lord Orso alone," I add, twisting the truth.

Loup crosses his arms. "Then we must await his return." The conversation is over. He turns his back on us, his torn cloak swishing as he goes.

"And when will he return?"

Loup pauses but doesn't answer. I have the unsettling feeling that I'm seeing only part of a puzzle. First with the Assassins, and now here among the Ghosts.

The pot! The pot! Feed them to the pot! his brethren begin to chant again.

Loup sighs, and nods, and a hundred gray hands rise to grab us. We are pushed and pulled by the living wall of hands and feet and gray faces, all snapping teeth and voices whispering over and over.

"Wait! Wait! Master of Ghosts! What is this?"

"Nina, they're not actually going to eat us, are they?" Ettie shrieks beside me.

I decide that avoiding the question is the best course of action at the moment.

We are brought to another large cavern, so hot the thick air hits us in waves. At the room's center is a giant cauldron, big enough to hold a man. At its base roars a giant fire, stoked by Ghosts on every side.

"The pot is unusually full. I am not sure I can fit you

in at the moment," Loup says mournfully. He points a finger toward someone in a corner of the cavern. "He will be going first. You will be after him."

I blink. The heat is making the world shimmer and move. I see a tousle-haired blond boy in a dark red coat, trussed like a chicken. He sees me, and though it's been several years, I know who he is: the beautiful son of the rebellion who saved me from the Guild of Flesh. St. Juste. He must recognize me, too, because the look he gives me is clear enough. For someone so used to giving orders, St. Juste doesn't need words to make his meaning clear.

You owe me!

"Master Loup! Not that I would ever question the wisdom of a Master of the Beggars Guild, but is there a particular reason you are going to cook this Day Walker?"

Loup looks at me and sighs. "He followed us into the Guild." He sounds offended at the effrontery of St. Juste's behavior. "He entered without an invitation."

We both look at St. Juste squirming in his bonds.

"Well . . . ," I say. "Before you cook him, have you asked why he dared to follow the Ghosts?"

Loup shakes his head, looking sullen. He gestures to another Ghost to remove the gag from St. Juste's mouth.

He gasps, dragging in long breaths of air.

"You—" St. Juste starts.

"You have very little time, and even fewer words to use, so I suggest you put them to good use," I advise him. "Why did you follow the Ghosts and enter their Guild?"

"I was looking for Lord Orso. I had a rendezvous with him, and he never appeared."

"Why would the Dead Lord have rendezvous with a Day Walker?"

"He said he that knew my uncle, that he would tell me stories about how it was when they were young men together, before the revolution failed, before my father was fed to the guillotine, before every man, woman, and child in my family was hunted down and hanged at Montfaucon simply for bearing the name of St. Juste.

"I have never met anybody alive who could tell of them. So when he did not come, I was worried, and followed the beggars to this place."

A lie! A lie! Feed him to the pot!

The cloth is stuffed back into St. Juste's mouth, and he scowls, trying to talk, but nobody can decipher what he is saying.

I look around at the Ghosts, crammed into every space in the cavern, their eyes glimmering with a strange madness.

"Before you suck the marrow from his bones," I say, "is there anyone who can verify his tale? Is there any among you that saw the Dead Lord with this Day Walker?"

A silence greets my question, and then a movement, a pushing and shoving, and the smallest Ghost, the ashen little boy who led us here, appears at the front.

"Did you witness this, Gray Brother?" Loup demands.

The boy solemnly nods.

"Was it before Father went away?"

He nods again.

"And were you ever going to speak up, Gavroche?" Loup says in a tone that is both exasperated and threatening.

Gavroche looks slightly put out, and I step hurriedly between them.

"Master Loup, what is happening? Where is the Dead Lord? What has become of him?"

"He cannot return," Loup says. "They took him, and they put him in the place where we cannot reach him."

All around us, the Ghosts wail their strange screeching cries.

I frown. "*Who* did this? Who took him, Master Loup?"

As I ask the question, I realize I already know the answer; it hums in my bones, with a certainty.

"That *fiend*," he spits.

And there it is. The tone of Loup's voice, that bitter loathing, could only be used to talk about the Tiger.

Of all the children of the Miracle Court, the Ghosts prize the Law above the rest. Many years ago, Kaplan broke the Law; he twisted it to his needs and never paid the consequences. His existence is a blasphemous outrage to all, but especially to the Ghosts.

"If you bring me to where the Dead Lord is," I say, "I'll give you revenge. You see, I have something the Tiger wants, and your Father can take this prize from him."

Loup hesitates, and I can see I've piqued his interest. The Ghosts are many things, and one of them is curious. Their

Father is famous for his stories and legends. I must make this engaging.

"Master, this is my tale." I raise my voice, spreading my arms out dramatically in my best impression of a storyteller. "My sister is desired by the Tiger."

"And what have the children of the Dead to do with the Lord of Flesh?" Loup asks.

"She has no Guild, no family to protect her. The Thief Lord won't cross the Tiger. We asked Lady Corday and Lady Komayd, and they told us only Orso is unafraid of the Tiger. And rightly so, for with such numerous children as he has, whom should he fear?"

The Ghosts are beside themselves, echoing my words until the cavern is loud with their whispers.

"I will give my sister to the Dead Lord as a gift."

Beside me, Ettie gasps. "Nina! Please!"

I ignore her.

Loup comes toward Ettie, inspecting her. She shudders and steps away from him.

"Where is he?" I ask. "Where is the Dead Lord?"

"In a place we cannot remember," Loup says. The Ghosts always speak in riddles.

I try again. "What place, Master Loup?"

Loup looks at me. "A place you cannot enter. We have lost many to trying already," he says, his voice a low warning.

That's what Corday said too. *Because everyone else has failed.*

I'm confused, but I won't let them know it. I need them

to take Ettie—it's her only chance. I shake my head confidently.

"I'm the Black Cat of the Thieves Guild; there's no place I can't enter."

Loup turns to survey the Ghosts. His eyes wander over them. Then he raises a hand and points. Four of the Ghosts rise and glide toward us noiselessly.

"Thank you."

"Thank you, Master."

"We are grateful."

"We are grateful."

Ettie edges near. "What are they doing?"

"I think they're coming with us."

"Gavroche knows the way." Loup indicates the small boy.

"Gavroche." Ettie looks down at him. "Is that your name?"

He nods and pulls at Ettie to start off.

I hear a muffled yell from St. Juste.

"I will also need the boy—the Day Walker," I say hurriedly. "He is known to me, and I need his skills." I have no idea whether this is true, but I owe him for the night he saved me from the Fleshers.

Loup hesitates. "If Orso summoned him as a guest, then what will he say when he returns to find his children picking the boy's bones clean?" I ask.

Loup sighs dramatically and makes a motion. St. Juste is untrussed, but when they go to remove his gag, I stop them.

"Leave it in—I've need of silence while I make my plans.

And keep his hands bound, too." That way he can't betray us by shouting or throttle me for stealing his pistol years ago. "Just untie his feet so he can run."

St. Juste gives a noise of deep discontent. It makes me smile.

"Keep close. The tunnels are treacherous," Loup warns me as the four ghosts, dragging St. Juste along with them, set off into the dark tunnels.

"Thank you, Master of Ghosts." I bow. *"Nous sommes d'un sang."*

"D'un sang," Loup answers. "If you survive, and if you find him, tell our Father we wait for him."

10

La Vallée de Misère

Loup is right: the bone-encrusted tunnels, elaborate as a spider's web, crisscross in a huge network beneath the city. Gavroche and the others move with ease, taking sharp, sudden turns, bumping St. Juste along behind them while I follow closely, realizing that without them we will be lost in the darkness.

Eventually, the Ghosts slow, and the tunnel narrows as we start our ascent. Winding stairs, slick and damp, lead to the surface, until patterns of light illuminate a grate above us. The largest of the Ghosts reaches up and, with only a faint noise of metal scraping, moves the grate aside. Gavroche scrambles up the larger Ghost's shoulders. And out we go.

I emerge, blinking, beneath the blinding streetlamps. Then there's the smell. Salt and rot. Old blood.

I know where we are.

We have come out under a bridge, the Pont au Change. It's low tide, and the waters of the fetid Serpent, the Seine, have rolled back, leaving a thick, rank sludge, the sewage and waste of the whole city. Beside me, Ettie points, and I turn my head. On the banks of the river, the dark mud appears to move, heaving and slithering like a great monster with a thousand glittering eyes. I smile.

"Mudlarks."

The city has a way of breeding a certain desperation. So it is for the mudlarks, the urchins and the ragged elderly who brave the river's poisonous banks, hunting among decaying animal flesh, burning chemicals, and human waste for any-thing they might salvage: bits of metal, leather, an ancient coin from the time of the Parisii, a ring from one of the river's many suicides.

We clamber up the slippery steps to street level. The bridge continues into a road that turns into a courtyard. To the left of it is a gendarmerie. I frown. Children of the Miracle Court tend to keep away from the police. They're corrupt, inept servants of Those Who Walk by Day.

The lights of the gendarmerie blaze. A large building with towers looms beyond it, its shadow casting a deep dread over me.

My own words come back to mock me.

I'm the Black Cat of the Thieves Guild. There's nowhere I can't enter.

Stupid.

103

"Where are we?" Ettie asks at my shoulder.

"Le Grand Châtelet."

She tenses, looking up at me with incredulous eyes.

This is what the Ghosts meant.

They knew. They *all* knew. Corday, Lady Komayd. Even Loup, though he tried to warn me.

You must be very good at getting into hard-to-reach places, Corday said.

They don't care about Ettie.

They want to free the Dead Lord from the Châtelet, the most feared prison in city.

No one has ever broken in to the Châtelet. No one has ever broken out.

I glance around to get my bearings. A street sign reads *la Vallée de Misère.* The Valley of Misery. An apt street name. In the darkness, I hear the clear chimes of la Samaritaine, the giant clock tower, which sings out every hour.

Think, Nina.

There are two guards at the entrance to the Châtelet, and two more on the top of its tower. Their rotations will be timed so there's always someone on watch. There's no way of getting in. In fact, you can't get anywhere near the tower, because it backs onto the gendarmerie, and there will be police patrolling the streets at regular intervals. How do you get into an impenetrable prison? How do you slip past so many guards unseen? And for that matter, once you're in, how do you get out with a whole other person? It is impossible.

"How often do the guards on street level make rounds?" I ask the Ghosts.

"They dance continuously through darkness and daylight."

I shake my head at the typical Ghost answer. One has to know how to talk to the Ghosts.

"How many dances between the chimes?"

"Four sets," they reply.

"Every fifteen minutes," I translate for Ettie.

Not enough time to slip past them from the street. Or to scale the Châtelet tower without being spotted.

I close my eyes and listen to the voice of the city. I hear its pulse; years of death, war, and suffering. The worst of all humanity lies here. These are streets washed in blood, filth, and pain.

I raise my head and sniff the air again: rot, death, and waste. I grin.

"I think I have a plan."

I signal to the Ghosts, and keeping to the shadows, we move together, avoiding the glow cast by the streetlamps.

"One stays here to watch," I order when we come to a stop.

Gavroche looks surprised. He points at the dark tower insistently. I know Orso is in there, but we're not marching straight into a lit courtyard full of patrolling police. We're going the long way around.

First I order the Ghosts to leave St. Juste in a dark alley

and rebind his feet. He growls at me through his gag, and I reward him with a quick smile.

"It's only for a little while. I'll be back, I promise," I call over my shoulder as we shamelessly abandon him. He will only get in the way, and we can't afford to have him slowing us down.

We stick to the houses and dart down the rue de la Joaillerie, circling the Châtelet on the right, heading toward the source of the smell: the numerous slaughterhouses that give the city's butchers their meat and the Châtelet its sour perfume of rot and old blood.

"Another watches here," I command. The Ghosts nod in perfect submission. They're good at taking orders, and I watch them melt into the darkness with satisfaction. I'm light-headed and dizzy with anticipation. Can I do this? I glance at Ettie. She's curled herself into a dark corner. If I don't try, he'll take her.

I disappear into the shadows with Ettie and the two remaining Ghosts.

Somewhere in the distance there's the low hoot of an owl—a Master Call. I plaster myself to a nearby wall, flattening Ettie next to me, my hand over her mouth.

Two police officers appear. One holds a lantern and is walking a little ahead of the other. From the cut of his uniform and the absence of badges, it's clear he's accompanying a senior officer, whose dazzling array of badges and trim betrays his inspector's rank. They must be heading to the gendarmerie.

I squint. The inspector cuts a slim figure. Most officers on a dark street would march quickly, not wanting to look into the darkness for fear of what might be looking back. But this officer walks with a measured step, his eyes taking in every shadow. He comes right alongside us, and in the halo of the lantern, I see that "he" is in fact a woman. Her face is white in the lamplight, her red hair tied behind her neck into a long tail. Policewomen are rare. Only the Sûreté have them. And the Sûreté are never good news.

She moves on. I watch in silence till she has disappeared from view.

I count to ten, then call the nearest Ghosts with a low whistle. I cross the street. Around the back of the Châtelet is a smaller edifice. There are no lights or guards, yet it is one of the most popular sights in Paris. By day, rich and poor alike line up for hours to press greasy faces against the glass of its window in the hopes of a better look. At night, nobody keeps watch over the contents because no one would steal from this place.

"I need two of you to carry," I say.

Their eyes travel from me to the dark entrance.

"For your Father," I add, and make short work of the two meager locks on the door.

Another time I'd have let Ettie practice her lock-picking. But the sight of the inspector spooked me. I want to be done with this. We push the door open and face the stench of decaying flesh. I breathe through my mouth. Beside me,

Ettie hastily lifts her scarf over her nose and tries not to gag. I should have warned her.

The building is one giant room with a grimy storefront window. The whole space is filled with long wooden tables arranged with as little room between them as possible. They have raised edges so that their contents don't slip off, and they are tilted so the Lookers can get a better look. Laid out on each table is a body.

Men, women, and children of differing ethnicities and backgrounds lie equal on the tables of the city morgue. Some bodies are whole: pale, terrible, eyes wide and staring. Others come up swollen from the Seine, with cut throats or missing limbs. The ones I hate seeing the most are the infants, little shrunken figures of skin and bone. The Lookers buy packets of peanuts and stand at the window asking *What could have happened to that pour soul?* in horrified delight. The people of Paris come to look at their dead for the price of a few sous.

"I want the freshest one," I say into the darkness, and around me the Ghosts whirl into action.

11

⤜⤝

The Dead Lord

The tower of the Châtelet looms above me, reminding me there's no way to breach it. I flex my fingers, which I've wrapped in rags, and steady myself. I'm the Black Cat of the Thieves Guild, and I will do what I always do: I'm going to steal something. Fearful excitement ripples up my spine as I move between the shadows, noting the guards at the tower's summit. There's a building constructed of wood; it looks like it was added as an afterthought. It's tall, rising to the platform where the guards patrol every quarter of an hour.

It has a crude door, rough-hewn and without a lock. It's not guarded, and for good reason: only a madman would try entering the Châtelet this way. Most madmen wouldn't fit. I lift the metal latch and pull Ettie's scarf over my nose, tightening it behind my head as if it'll make a difference. I don't think she'd have lent it to me if she had known where I was going. My insides are churning, as they do each time, no matter how many jobs I do. It's always the same.

Everyone is afraid, Azelma used to say.

I pull open the door, and the smells assail me. My eyes burn with tears. The entire room is covered with mountainous piles of human excrement. Even in the cold, a storm of flies is swarming overhead with frenzied buzzing. Welcome to the cesspit of le Grand Châtelet.

I take a breath and go in, closing the door behind me and giving my eyes time to adjust to the darkness. The only light shines from a small, round opening high above my head. I reach into my coat and take out my claws—hooks I've spent hours honing. Sharp ends and blunt grips. I attach one to the cap of each boot and wind the others around my gloves, fastening them tight. Then I turn to the wooden wall, and lifting my leg high, I kick with all my strength. The hook catches fast in the wood; I step up, testing to see if it will carry my full weight. It holds. I drive the other hook in, then each of my clawed hands, one at a time, and so I rise. I climb to the top of the building slowly, in half an hour, to avoid any noise. At the top I embed my hooks in the ceiling and hang there. The hole in front of me is too small for any grown man to fit through. Thanks to a lifetime of malnourishment, I'm just the right size. I hook my gloved hands around the rim and climb through into the garderobe. It's a small room containing only a bench to relieve oneself through. I head to the door and open it an inch. My observations were correct: the guards are at the far end of the tower, with their backs to me. I look around. A metal door leads into the tower. I rush to it, pull it open, and slip into the prison.

I try to recall every tale I have ever heard about the Châtelet. It has three levels. The upper floor, which I tiptoe through, is large and well aired. The cells here are rooms, with doors and tiny grated windows. Inside are the rich prisoners, those who can pay for the meager comfort the upper levels afford them.

There's a clattering of boots on stone from the end of the corridor. My heart leaps into my throat. I've mistimed my entry, or the guard is early. The twinkling of a distant lantern grows stronger in the dark stairwell before me. I have only seconds and so I climb, scaling the wall, till I'm at the ceiling. I dig my claws in above, and my toes into the corner. Here I hang, suspended. Patience is ninety percent of being a Cat: sitting, waiting in the shadows till the right moment. I relax my muscles to avoid cramping and try to calm my breathing, to ignore the sweat gathering on my forehead as, below me, the guard arrives. Most people who walk into a room never look up. Neither should he. Bored, he strolls through the corridor, lantern in hand. Then he pauses, and sniffs.

Ysengrim be damned! The smell of excrement coming off my boots is strong. I hold my breath. He looks around for the source of the odor but sees nothing. He rubs his nose, sighs, and walks through the door beneath me, just seconds before a soft lump of something foul dislodges itself from my boot and falls to the floor.

Once I'm convinced that the guard is safely gone, I head down the winding stone stairs, counting the floors as I go. Le Fosse, la Gourdaine, le Puits. The staircase gets damper and steeper, and each corridor I pass has more cells squeezed into the same amount of space. I speed up, not knowing when the guard will return. Finally, the staircase ends, in a corridor of complete and utter darkness.

A place we cannot remember, Loup whispers in my mind.

My fingers brush the plaque on the wall, which bears the dungeon's name: *les Oubliettes.* The place of forgetting.

The air down here is stale. The floor is covered in rough straw. Something scrambles near my foot, and I keep myself from flinching. It's only a rat.

There are ten cagelike cells with iron bars. I reach into my jacket and pull out my tin box of matches. I light one and hold it up to the first set of bars. An emaciated man, more skeleton than human, barely moves. He might be dead. In the next cell is an old man with long hair and a beard. His cheeks are hollow, his fingernails long claws, and though his eyes are open, he doesn't seem to notice the light. I move on to the third cell, casting my light before me. A pile of rags in the shape of a person faces the wall. I go nearer to the bars and, in a low voice, whisper, "Good hunting."

The pile of rags moves, stiffly at first, and the figure turns as if its untethered limbs are gathering themselves together. Hands take hold of the bars: the fingers ravaged, scaly. As it gets closer, his terrible features are illuminated in the match-light: his face looks like it's melting, the skin peeling and flaking in layers.

Orso, the Dead Lord, Father of the Ghosts of the Beggars Guild, keeper of histories, teller of tales.

"Monseigneur." I half bow in the darkness in the way of the Wretched, my head tilted to expose the mark at my neck. "I'm the Black Cat of the Thieves Guild."

"I remember." His voice is hoarse, as if he hasn't used it in a while. "The youngest Cat in the history of the Court. You knew the Law by heart."

I also remember. It's hard to forget the first time you look upon the ruined face of the Dead Lord. It takes everything in you not to shudder. But I knew the words by heart, and he could find no fault in my knowledge of the Law.

He pauses; then, in a measured voice, offers: "You've gone to a good deal of trouble to speak with me, child. As you can see, I'm at your leisure."

I take a deep breath. "I have a friend," I say. "I ask you to give her the mark of the Ghosts."

He looks at me, considering. "And what is so wrong with your friend that you would break into this godforsaken place to ask me to take her?"

"The Tiger wants her."

He seems to think about it. Then he laughs, which makes his face even more horrible to behold.

"And you alone are not afraid of the Tiger," I continue.

"The Tiger doesn't like to be crossed," he says.

"Perhaps it's time for a change?"

His withered fingers strangle the metal bars. "If you could get me out of this prison, I'd give you everything you ask, but you must know, little Cat: there's no way for me to escape."

"Escape, my Lord? I'm the Black Cat of the Thieves Guild." I smile in the darkness. "I'm here to steal you."

———

We move like the darkness itself, in the complete silence that only children of the Miracle Court have mastered. The prisoners on each floor hear nothing and see nothing, deep in their nightmare-laden sleep. When we make it to la Gourdaine, I hear a sound: the tiny squeak of a mouse. But it is the rhythm that makes me stop. The squeak comes once, twice, and a third time, in a pattern I know well. It is one of the hundreds of Master Calls. In the darkness, Orso stills, and just when I have convinced myself that I was mistaken, a whisper floats toward us on the darkness.

"Nous sommes d'un sang."

We can't afford delays, but Orso makes a gesture with his hand that I should investigate. I glide silently away from the stairs and into la Gourdaine. Cells line my path, and everyone sleeps. Except for a huge shadowy figure whose eyes glint at me through the bars. The man's bearded face tells me he must have been imprisoned for at least a year. He holds his hands out to me, palms up, so that I see he bears no weapons, but the size of those hands makes me pause—they look strong enough to crush me, should I be so foolish as to go too close.

"Sister," he says, in a whisper so light it's as if he did not speak. He tilts his head, exposing his neck. In the darkness, I cannot make out a tattoo, and I dare not light a match here, but if this is indeed a child of the Miracle Court rotting away in these cells, at least I can inform his Guild that he is alive. I reach out, my pulse racing, and gently touch my fingertips to the skin behind his ear, where I feel it.

It is the shape of an X, the mark of the Guild of Letters—the guild of auditors, lawyers, extortionists, forgers, and moneylenders. The guardians of secrets and information, whose spies are said to have infiltrated every position of power in France and abroad.

"Sister, thou art a Cat?" the man whispers.

I nod, swallowing.

"I don't know how you are aiming to escape, but I can tell you that whatever you have planned won't work." He wrinkles his nose. "Although apparently you got in through the privy? Clever. He won't fit out that way, though." He motions at Orso, who has silently joined me. "And even if you got out, there are the gendarmes, and among them the Sûreté—"

"I have procured a gendarme's uniform for Lord Orso," I interrupt. I grabbed it from the cloakroom of the gendarmerie before I broke in to the Châtelet.

The prisoner pauses, bows his head at Orso in respect. Orso, for his part, eyes the prisoner with curiosity.

"They know the names and faces of every guard," the prisoner continues. "The number of them and the number of prisoners. The roaches can't sneeze here without someone noticing." He rubs a large hand down the side of his face. His eyes narrow cunningly. "But if you get me out of this cell, I'll show you how all three of us can walk out of here."

I don't have time for this. Another rescue, another body, another opportunity for things to go wrong. But then again, he is a son of the Guild of Letters, trained in the art of espionage and subterfuge. If anyone knows how to escape a prison such as the Châtelet, he probably does. Of course, trusting him could be unwise. He is a criminal, after all, locked up for some reason I can only guess. But I have to save the Dead Lord, and we must choose our allies wisely in times of great trial. That, and I'd be a fool to miss the opportunity for the Guild of Letters to owe me a debt for freeing one of their sons.

I sigh and take out my lock-picks.

On the prisoner's instruction, I open the locks of every cell in la Gourdaine, moving like a whisper between the iron cages; the inmates don't even wake as I do my work. The Dead Lord, dressed in the garb of a guard, silently watches me. If something goes wrong, it was my decision to set this son of the Guild of Letters free. The giant, on his release, towered over me like a threat, murmured his quick instructions, told me he would return, and then disappeared, moving surprisingly quietly for a man of his size. A few thumps later he is back, carrying the body of a dead—no, just unconscious—guard. He strips him of his uniform, throws him into the cell, and swaps clothes with him. Some of the prisoners start to awaken. It is a testament to how long they have been there that they simply stare at me without making a sound. They are dumbfounded at my presence.

"*Liberté*," I say to them; their eyes travel to the open doors of their cells. Pandemonium ensues.

12

Les Oubliettes

I make it back to the top floor of the tower at a run. Behind the door, I peer into the courtyard as a cry pierces the night. The Ghosts are wailing. The guards on the tower are confused; half of them rush toward the balcony's edge to stare down at the commotion, giving me time to dart behind their backs across the courtyard into the garderobe. I unwind a rope I found in one of the guard rooms and attach it to a vicious-looking hook, which I fasten to the stone ledge of the privy. Then I grab the rope and in one fluid movement I dive through the hole, dropping headfirst into the cesspit. The rope stops my fall, tearing at my muscles. The stench chokes me, burning my nose and eyes. I climb down the last few inches and lower my feet into a squelching pile. I tug at the rope until the hook comes free and follows down after me. Then I take a deep breath and lie down in the vile muck, allowing it to cover me completely. I do my best not to gag, or move, or let myself think about what's happening. I'm already covered in the stuff; a little more can't hurt. Outside, men yell, doors slam, the Ghosts wail louder, and voices shout at them. I close my eyes in my soft, putrid resting place and wait.

Moments later the clatter commences: the door of the cesspit opens. The night-soil men have arrived right on time to empty the cesspit. They appear unconcerned by the running gendarmes and the wailing Ghosts causing chaos around them. They have one job to do, which hasn't changed for over a hundred years, and they're going to do it no matter what. They wedge the door open, allowing glorious night air to rush in, and they return to their wagon to get their shovels. I rise, camouflaged by my coating of muck, and dart out the door. Armed with their shovels, they return to the cesspit, and while their backs are turned, I clamber onto their large wagon and hunker down between the foul heaps of excrement.

I lean over and squint between the wagon's wooden slats toward the light of the gendarmerie, where Ettie and the Ghosts are gathered around a body. Ettie is wailing loudly. The policemen are standing nearby, trying to calm the Ghosts' hysterical cries of *"Murder! Murder!"* The slim inspector is there in their midst, barking orders and taking control, her red hair gleaming in the light.

She bends over to study the corpse.

"This victim has been dead for hours," she says, straightening. She frowns as her eyes wander over the Ghosts. Then she looks up at the tower.

"Something is not right. Check on the inmates," she says.

My stomach tightens.

"But, Inspector Javert—" a gendarme starts to argue.

"Now!" she barks, and the men hurry away, disappearing inside the Châtelet.

"PRISONERS ESCAPING! PRISONERS ESCAPING!" screams a guard rushing toward them moments later as a frantic bell cleaves the night.

Javert swings sharply around. "Report!"

"Inspector Javert, the prisoners are loose inside the prison! We have been overwhelmed. It is only a matter of time—"

"Gendarmes! Prepare the horses. Not a single inmate is to make it past these gates."

The gendarmes have barely had time to assemble, when a handful of blue-coated guards come running, fleeing from a swell of prisoners in rags, their eyes mad with hope.

The Châtelet spews forth so many prisoners that even the gendarmes on horseback have to hold tight, rocked by the wave of men flooding the courtyard, scaring the horses.

There's the sound of gunshot and the acrid smell of grapeshot. The gendarmes have to choose whom to stop, and for each prisoner they manage to restrain, ten more go rushing past, threatening to trample them. Two of the horses buck and lash out, throwing their riders, then rush about in panicked circles. In the total chaos, the Ghosts and their corpse are forgotten. As instructed, they slink away into the night, taking Ettie with them. In the middle of the fray, I see two guards in blue uniforms halt the riderless horses and mount them. I know they are not the same guards who were thrown.

The prisoners have passed the gates, battering them down and flowing into the streets and alleyways. Javert screams at the top of her lungs for the gendarmes on horseback to go after them. They carefully back out of the swell and lead their horses after the prisoners. . . . She has ordered them to go, and so they do—though two of them won't stop riding till they're far beyond her reach. And they're not out of danger yet: there's time enough for the gendarmes to realize that neither of those riders is one of their own. I fear for the Dead Lord and his new ally. I need to increase their chances of a smooth escape. I need to cause a distraction.

The night-soil cart, now loaded, starts to move toward the river. The workers will carry their fragrant cargo to a soil yard in the south, where they spread it out to dry with used hops from breweries before selling it as fertilizer to the farmers outside the city walls. I wait till the cart is on the bridge before I leap off, rolling as I hit the street. I duck down the alleyway where we left St. Juste and appear out of the darkness before him. Dagger out, arm raised, I register the widening of his eyes as, with a single arc of my blade, I sever the bonds at his hands and feet.

"I don't have time for explanations. Just do what I say and we'll all get out of this in one piece," I order as I remove the gag from his mouth.

He gives a loud sigh, relieved to be free.

"Quick, put this on!" I thrust a garment at him.

He hesitates, considering whether to trust me, as behind us the cacophony of chaos plays like an orchestra. I smile sweetly at him. He frowns and grabs the garment, then throws it over his head, his hands getting caught in the sleeves, which I tied in knots so he wouldn't have time to lash out at me.

Then I scream, a shrill scream that echoes in the night.

"Escaped prisoner! Escaped prisoner!" I screech, backing away from him.

He has just pulled the garment over his head and stands, chest exposed, fighting to make sense of his sleeves, preparing to defend me from an escaped prisoner. But his cramping muscles betray him and he falls over.

I bend toward him. "Forgive me, St. Juste, but I daresay they won't hold you for long."

The look of sheer confusion on his face is a beautiful thing. Raised voices and the thunder of boots on cobblestone ring through the darkness. I turn and flee, running into ten guards. I point at him over my shoulder and put on my best sobbing voice.

"There! One of the prisoners! *Mon Dieu,* he must have gotten out through the privy, for he reeks! He grabbed me and tried to slit my throat!"

The privy smell thus explained, the guards hurtle toward St. Juste, who has struggled to his feet and is still trying to shrug on the prisoner's robe that I gave him—making it look as if he might just be an escaped prisoner trying to free himself from the incriminating uniform.

"We have you cornered," the guard nearest St. Juste crows as I disappear into a shadowy side street and start to scale the wall. I reach the roof in seconds and shelter in the shadow of a gable.

The scene below me would not work in daylight, where the guards might see St. Juste's clean-shaven skin and the clean but rumpled clothes he wears. But in the darkness, even by torchlight, all these things are made invisible by the guards' desire to have captured a prisoner.

"Put your hands up and get down on your knees!" they roar at him.

St. Juste's face is a portrait: comprehension sweeps over him, as well as clarity, anger, and something else. He looks past the guards and searches for me at the roofline, his eyes blazing.

"You are making a mistake," he says in a voice weak from so many hours of disuse.

"Not another word from you!"

"I am not a prisoner. My name is Enjolras St. Juste."

"St. Juste?" The guards pause. "We've got a stupid one here. Don't you know all the St. Justes are dead?"

The guard speaks the terrible truth. All the Marats, the Dantons, the Robespierres, the Mirabeaus, the Desmoulins:

every man, woman, and child bearing those family names was set dancing by the noose of Montfaucon, where what's left of their bodies still hangs today.

There's a strange steely light to St. Juste's eyes as he answers, his jaw set in a rigid line.

"I know," he says.

The guard sniffs, unsure how to interpret this but knowing they have a job to do.

"I think I'd rather be a prisoner of the Châtelet than be called by the name St. Juste in this city," the guard says, shaking his head as his colleagues drag St. Juste away.

As he passes, St. Juste raises his head to the darkness where I have disappeared. He can't see me, I'm sure of it, and yet I feel the burning of his eyes upon my skin. I swallow down guilt. They won't keep him, not once they realize he's not actually an escaped prisoner. At worst, they will rough him up to get out their frustrations, which is better than ending up in the Ghosts' pot. He should really be thanking me.

I keep moving and pretend it doesn't bother me at all, that I can't feel the heat of his glare on me as I let myself down under the shadows of the bridge. The Ghosts and Ettie are waiting for me. We climb into the entrance to the catacombs, drag the metal grate behind us, and flee down the tunnels, hoping desperately that everything has gone according to plan.

When I hobble into the Halls of the Dead, Loup's first words are a gracious suggestion that I clean myself. When a Ghost tells you to bathe, you know you must smell bad. Gavroche leads me to a sulfurous pool of steaming water. Ettie sits by my side and informs me that this is Orso's favorite pool, a fact I wish I didn't know.

I'm freshly dry, with tight, clean skin, and I'm wearing the dusty gray cloak of a Ghost, when the Ghosts erupt in loud cries. I run to the Halls of the Dead, knife in hand and Ettie trailing behind me, in time to witness Orso's entrance on horseback, like a great hero of legend, amid hysterical cheers from the Ghosts, who weep and wail with delight, throwing themselves at him and greatly frightening his stolen mount.

Orso is enveloped in the guard uniform, a scarf at his neck swallowing his face and his hat pulled down low over his brow. He leaps from his horse and is immediately engulfed by a wave of gray figures, some at his feet, others pulling at his arm or face. He laughs and looks around; spotting me, he gives a roar.

"My children, behold: my savior." He inclines his head at me. I frown and back away as the Ghosts swarm me, batting them away ineffectually. They touch my face with dusty fingertips, whispering and moaning their thanks. It takes another roared order from Orso for them to unhand me, and Ettie stifles a giggle at my expense.

I straighten my robe and turn to Orso. "Monseigneur." I

bow. Beside me, Ettie does the same. She's getting the hang of this.

Orso has seen Ettie. His eyes narrow, and he crosses the room to inspect her. He tilts her face up to examine it.

"It's no wonder he wants you." He releases her. "You're so very lovely."

He catches my glare.

"Don't look so ferocious, little Cat." His eyes are bright with laughter. "I won't scar this one. Her face is far more useful to us intact. She'll be the jewel in our crown. The little Lady of Ghosts. I will give your friend the Ghost's mark, and that will resolve our debt."

The feeling of St. Juste's reproachful eyes still scorches my skin.

"My Lord, there is a boy who calls himself St. Juste."

The Dead Lord stills at the name; he watches me intently.

"He said you summoned him to our Guild House, Father," Loup tells him in a voice that demonstrates just how unlikely he finds the story. "That you sent Gray Brother to him with an invitation."

"They were going to eat him!" Ettie squeaks.

"And where is this boy?" Orso asks. "Or has he already been consumed by my children?"

I clear my throat. "In the Châtelet. He, er, volunteered to aid in your escape by creating a distraction. They won't hold him long. They'll realize he isn't a prisoner, since he insists on proclaiming his birth name to everyone he meets."

The Dead Lord scratches the scaly skin on his cheek. I

try not to stare. "Well, he won't live much longer if he continues doing that," he says.

Orso turns to Loup. "They will release him at some point. Send some of your brothers to meet him when they do."

My heart lurches, but there is nothing I can do. St. Juste knows the location of the Beggars Guild; his days are numbered. And yet he did save me from the Fleshers. True, I saved him in return from the pot, but that was little more than a temporary reprieve from a now-inevitable fate.

"My Lord, I ask you to spare him," I say impulsively. "Then your debt will be paid."

Orso's heavy gaze seems to see through me.

"You have developed feelings for this boy? Even though he is not of our kind?"

"What? No!"

"He is very handsome," Ettie interjects unhelpfully.

Orso stares at me, and I feel myself start to blush.

"Is he?" Orso asks with great interest.

"He is handsome, but—"

"Is that why you saved him from the pot, Nina? Are you in love with him?" Ettie's voice is breathy and hopeful.

I silently curse myself for giving in to her constant begging for stories, especially the romantic ones. I clear my throat. "I— He saved my life. I owe him a bone debt."

I could be mistaken, but there is a flash of something that looks like humor in the Dead Lord's eyes, and his voice is not scolding when he replies.

"Fear not, little kitten. Your paramour is safe. It was

indeed at my invitation that he sought me out. Sadly, I was otherwise occupied and unable to receive him. But we will scoop him up now, and I promise you sincerely that we will not eat him."

I raise my eyebrows at Orso.

"Or maim him," I add.

"Or that."

"Or pay the Hyènes to beat him, or the Assassins to kill him, or submit him to a Dead Trial."

"Indeed!" says Orso. "You have my word that no harm shall come to him under my care. I have plans for him. We will have much use for him in the days to come."

Under Orso's lordship, the Ghosts have flourished and grown to the size of a small army. They say the Great Bear's mind is always turning. Whatever plans he has for St. Juste, it is probably best that I keep well out of them. I have my own battles to fight.

"And our other *new friend* sent a message," Orso adds under his breath.

I look up at him; he must mean the son of the Guild of Letters.

"He bade me carry it to you, as if I were the Messenger."

I give a wry smile at the thought of Orso scrambling over the rooftops like Femi.

"He, too, took a bone oath, pierced his flesh before me, proclaiming that he is in your debt." He looks at me un-blinking, calculating. "It would seem we all are."

I nod shortly, as if having Guild Lords and People of the

Pen in my debt is an everyday occurrence and I expect no less. Orso seems to find this funny and laughs as he gathers his children around him like a king in his court. They flock to his side, pressing into him.

The Ghosts cry out enthusiastically to hear the tale of how he escaped. And Orso's laughter rumbles through the caverns and echoes off the walls over his excitable children's cries.

Every story I've ever heard was lifted from Orso's mouth. It was from his lips that Femi heard the tales, and from the Messenger that they were whispered in Azelma's ear so that she could weave them, a net in the darkness, around me, to keep me safe and warm on cold nights.

Orso's ruined face splits into a wry smile.

"*Il était une fois . . .*"

When the last tale fades away, I see that Ettie looks stiff and pale. Loup notices and leads us to a side cavern, a small room with delicate frescoes of bone animals.

We collapse in a heap on the floor.

"Nina, what's wrong with the Dead Lord?"

"A disease of the skin. It's not contagious."

She shivers violently, winding her fingers around the edge of her cloak; her eyes flit nervously to the ivory-encrusted walls. The bones were taken from the dead of the Cimetière des Innocents, where the ground swelled so full with bodies that they broke through into the cellars of houses, poisoning the air with fumes potent enough to kill.

"It's been a long night," I say wearily. "You need to sleep."

"Yes," she murmurs, curling against my back. Little Gavroche appears silently, as is his way, and sets himself down beside her, leans his head on her, knots his tiny hands in her cloak.

I turn over, close my eyes, and try to think of all that has happened.

I visited the Assassins and survived. I visited the Ghosts and rescued St. Juste. I broke into the Châtelet and stole the Dead Lord. I freed a member of the Guild of Letters. I kept Ettie safe. I'm the Black Cat of the Thieves Guild, and these are the things I have done. I won't think about anything else. I won't.

13

The Miracle Court

"Nina!"

Ettie's voice wakes me from a deep sleep. Like a good Cat, I leap instinctively to my feet, dagger in hand before my eyes are fully open.

Ettie is sitting up, staring at me. She giggles.

I blink, taking in our surroundings. Sulfur and bone, we're still in the Halls of the Dead. I lower my dagger.

"How long have I been sleeping?" I ask.

"I don't know. I just woke up myself."

There's a smell of food in the air. I can't remember the last time I ate.

My things have been cleaned and left in a small pile beside me. I grab for them as I sit down. My lock-picks, climbing claws, tin of matches, rope, and hooks. I'm naked without them. I tuck them into various pockets of the gray robe. Ettie's scarf is still slightly damp. I also pocket a tin cup I stole from the prison, with the emblem of the Châtelet stamped into it. A gift for Tomasis.

"They left these." Ettie points to two bowls of brown stew. My stomach growls. I grab a bowl, tip it to my lips, sip, and swallow.

Ettie is pulling bits of brown meat out of hers and inspecting them.

"Do you remember them threatening to feed us to the pot?" she asks worriedly.

I laugh. "Do you remember the horse Orso rode in on last night?" I ask.

Ettie goes slightly green.

"Better eat fast," says a voice. Loup is at the entrance of our cavern holding a candle; its wavering light casts horrifying shadows on his face and the hole where his nose should be.

I finish a last gulp of stew, put down my bowl, and wipe my mouth with my sleeve.

At the entrance of the cavern a parade of lights dances past us. The Ghosts are on the move.

"Eat up," I tell Ettie. "It's time to go."

Ettie finishes her bowl, and I pull her to her feet. We grab candle stubs and slip into the sea of moving Ghosts. The sea parts and there's Orso, freshly clad in a massive gray robe, his scarred face alight with a crooked smile. He's carrying Gavroche on his shoulders. A chain of silver is draped around his neck with six dusty signet rings hanging from it. Ghosts are not given to wearing jewelry or anything distinguishable, so I've always wondered what the rings signify. In all the years I've known of him, he's never added to their number. Perhaps they belonged to the previous Lords of the Dead.

Around us the Ghosts are buzzing and bouncing with excitement, pulling at one another and cavorting like puppies.

"It is time we were off," the Dead Lord says. "Are you ready, little ones?"

His children's agreement echoes off the walls.

"Where are we going?" Ettie asks.

"To Court," Orso says, and motions for us to walk beside him.

The Miracle Court gathers at unpredictable intervals. Summonses to the Court are whispered from the Messenger to the ear of each Guild Lord. They pass the call through the Masters to their children, and so the Wretched come.

The Dead look like a gray worm winding through the catacombs and up dark stairways to the street. Through the city we go, until we come to the ruins of a neighborhood so broken that even the poorest have long since fled. When the Ghosts go marching, the people of Paris know to close their windows and doors and not look out for fear of what might look back.

There are entrances all over the neighborhood. Through a hole in the wall, a broken doorway, the Wretched squeeze, climb, and clamber. The Cats dance on rooftops and swing from chimney to chimney on long ropes. The Assassins prefer to use windows, and therefore no one else does. Inside, the buildings are falling apart. Ettie watches her feet; the floorboards are rotten, and one false step could send her crashing to the story below. Orso, in front of us, moves like a spirit, gliding through the broken corridors of peeling paint.

"Welcome," Orso whispers to Ettie at the threshold of a great room, "to the Court of Miracles."

Tonight's Court is held in an ancient theater long abandoned by Those Who Walk by Day. Its ruined elegance is lit by candlelight reflecting off a crystal chandelier. The Wretched pour in from every door, holding their candles aloft. The shining light is meant to remind the Court of the long darkness in which it was born.

The Court is a great rookery of crime, the haunt of Death Dealers, Thieves, Mercenaries, and Beggars, as well as a nest of immigrants: Lombard, Jew, Romani, Maghreb, Corsican, African, Qing, Edo, Mughal. We all come to the Miracle Court as equals. The Court recognizes no race, no religion, no marriage or tie of blood. The Wretched have only one Father, their Guild Lord; one family, their Guild; and one Law.

Tonight, the Wretched spill in, filling the hundreds of dusty seats that line the mezzanine and the galleries above. Music comes from the pit, where an out-of-tune piano is being played. There's laughter, talking, murmuring, whispering.

The Ghosts enter last, slowly flooding the auditorium. The other Wretched pay them no heed as they begin their silent vigil. Orso grasps Ettie by the hand, and I watch her face as she takes in the stage, the backdrop a giant oil painting of wolves roaming an ancient forest, the set framed by dark velvet curtains.

On the stage, candelabras brighten a long table. Around it are nine seats, one for each of the Lords of the Court; eight are occupied. Standing at the edge of the stage are the Masters of the Guilds.

Orso steps with us out of the darkness and starts the long procession to the stage. I swallow hard. It's against the Law to address a Lord at the high table without invitation. Following Orso like his shadow, I feel the weight of what we're doing.

Conversations come to a stop. Orso's name is spoken and then hushed. People crane their necks to see my face or Ettie's, but we keep going, our heads held high, a sea of Ghosts behind us.

The Lords at the table are talking to each other. Lady Corday looks up first. Somewhere behind her is the shadow of Montparnasse.

Tomasis's sharp eyes spot me, and he raises his eyebrows. Doubtless Thénardier is lurking nearby.

And seated right in the middle of the table is the Tiger. All the hairs on the back of my neck go up, and my fingers curl into fists.

Orso has reached the stage and climbs the steps with us trailing behind him. Gavroche has appeared beside Ettie and is clinging to her gray robes, half hiding her.

"Nous sommes d'un sang," Orso says with a reverential bow of his head. Then he raises his hands in greeting. "Good hunting, my Lords." Orso is the keeper of knowledge for the Miracle Court, the teacher of the Law. When he speaks, everyone listens.

The Lords bow their heads in recognition, murmuring their answered greeting. All save the Tiger. His mouth is closed in a tight line, and his yellow eyes don't leave Orso's face.

"I see you've started without me," Orso says as he takes his seat. "What a pity. It's almost as if you thought I wouldn't be present."

Ocan Maloni, Lord of the Guild of Chance, speaks up. "My Lord Orso, we heard you had disappeared and no one knew where you were."

"We heard you were never coming back," says Rime Temam, Lord of the Guild of Mercenaries, glancing sidelong at the Tiger.

"I wonder where you heard such vicious rumors." Orso's chin dips.

"How did you get out?" the Tiger asks bluntly, betraying that he knows where the Dead Lord was.

Orso smiles. "My dear Kaplan, I'm the Father of Ghosts. I'm not like the mortals of flesh and blood. There's nowhere that can hold me."

"You lie like Ysengrim." The Tiger spits on the floor.

"And yet here I stand." Though Orso is smiling, his eyes are as hard as nails. "And while we're on the subject of my absence: Do you know, Kaplan, that my last memory before I was, er, misplaced is of five men ambushing me, two of whom bore marks of the Guild of Flesh?"

"You accuse me of having a hand in your imprisonment?"

"I tell you only what I saw. Do you doubt the word of a Lord?" Orso's voice is like steel.

The Tiger grimaces. He crosses his arms and gives a short whistle. His Master appears at his shoulder. Lenoir sees out of only one eye: when he took the mark of his Guild, a single blow from the tail of the Tiger's cat-o'-nine-tails struck his face. The Tiger murmurs something in Lenoir's ear, and he nods, rushes off. Seconds later, two burly Fleshers are brought forward.

"On your knees," the Tiger says.

The men's faces darken, but they obey. No one defies Lord Kaplan. Lenoir hands him a pistol. He takes it and, without ceremony, points it at the first kneeling man. The Flesher barely has time to raise his hands before the pistol cracks: Kaplan shoots him straight through the heart. I flinch. His body falls slowly, in a cloud of gunpowder. I look away as the second man lowers his head. He knows there's no getting out of it. I've never liked watching deaths. I hear the thump as he hits the floor a heartbeat later.

"Two men bearing the mark of my Guild," the Tiger says to Orso. "Consider the accusation met."

"You are all goodness and deference, my dear Kaplan."
Orso bows as Lenoir drags the bodies away. Then he smiles.
"But enough death and retribution. Let us celebrate our
reunion. I want to share with you a moment of great joy."
He draws Ettie out of his shadow and gently moves her
forward.

Seeing her, the Tiger half rises from his seat and turns to
Thénardier, who has materialized beside Tomasis. Thénardier is staring at me, his lip curled in anger.

"A new mortal is passing through the gates of the living
and into the kingdom of the dead," Orso says.

The Tiger gives Thénardier a glance laced with signifi-
cance.

Thénardier steps forward, red-faced and flustered. "Monseigneur Orso." His voice is like treacle. "You seem to have
both my ward and my daughter in your care."

Orso looks at him as if he's a worm.

"Do you address me without invitation, Thénardier?"
Orso asks in an icy tone. "You are only a Master and have
no voice at the high table."

Thénardier hesitates, glancing at Lord Kaplan. "But
they're my children. . . ."

Orso's hand comes down on my shoulder. "This one is a
child of the Thieves. Tomasis is her Father. Is that not what
the Law says?"

What does the Law say? the Ghosts echo behind us, hundreds of voices raised, till the question bounces off the walls
and thrums through my entire body.

Tomasis's eyes burn into me. I meet his gaze squarely. I'm probably in a world of trouble.

"And this one has asked for the mark of the Ghosts." He puts a hand on Ettie's shoulder. "It will be given to her, in your illustrious presences."

Lord Kaplan makes a sound of fury and stands, a finger pointed at Orso. "You wouldn't dare, you old bear! She's mine!"

I see Ettie shiver in Orso's grasp.

"Yours? I see no stripe upon her, my brother."

I look at Thénardier. His face is contorted and pale.

"Thus, she's free, and has a voice to ask to join the Dead. Is that not the Law?" Orso continues.

It's the Law! It's the Law! the Ghosts whisper in a frenzy.

The Tiger looks around the table, and the other Lords remain silent. Grim. Voiceless.

"Do you defy the Law, my Lord?" Orso asks coolly. "Or do you think to twist it to suit you, as you once did before?" Orso tilts his head, addressing the table of the Lords. "How far can the Law be bent before it breaks upon our backs, destroying us all?"

The Lords look uncomfortable, except Corday. She seems amused, though only slightly.

The Tiger sits back down at Orso's words, trembling with ire.

The Dead Lord stands and pointedly turns his back on the table of his peers. He looks out over the spectators of the Miracle Court, who are watching with hushed attention.

Then he turns his gaze to Ettie. "This night, the Girl Who Walks by Day will die, and you will be born anew among the Dead. This night, you join the Wretched, giving yourself as a child to the Court of Miracles, as a daughter to the Ghosts." Orso turns Ettie to face him and asks, "Are you ready, my child?"

Ettie looks at me in confusion. She doesn't know what's coming. I should have warned her, but I didn't want to scare her. Fear so often makes the pain worse.

I nod for her to agree.

"Y-yes."

"Good girl." He pushes her gray cloak from her shoulder and tilts her head, baring the tender flesh below her ear. Loup steps forward; he's carrying a long metal rod that is glowing red with heat.

"It will hurt," Orso warns.

Ettie looks at me, eyes wide with fear. I take her hand.

The burning rod comes down on her skin. She screams and sways, and I feel a bitter tug of guilt as I catch her. I want to whisper, *I'm sorry.* But the Court is no place for sympathy. Loup takes the metal from her skin, and she collapses onto me. I hold her tight as her body shakes with dry retches. I pin her arms to her sides as the tears pour down her face and she tries to claw at her neck, which must feel like it's on fire. She sobs in my arms.

The song starts, in whispers at first, till it grows and swells, soaring about us.

"We were born in the darkness, thou and I, my brother,
All forgotten, all in the grave,
All tooth, and club, and steel, and claw,
Side by side and unafraid."

As voices join the chorus, they echo and ring around the hall, a thousand voices melding into one.

"We are of one blood, thou and I, my sister,
Bound by pack and Law the same.
When hunger or sickness or war shall take you,
I will sing the death song in your name."

Ettie's sobs have quieted. From time to time she trembles with pain.

"Cry no more, my sweet," Orso says. "I know it hurts, but this is not a time for tears. There's great joy after the pain." He nods at me.

I lead Ettie off the stage, refusing to meet Thénardier's eye. Orso perches on the steps of the stage. The Ghosts crowd around him like shadows. They make space for me, and I settle in among them as they coo over Ettie's mark. Ettie lays her head in my lap and I stroke her blond curls. She's shaking. Or maybe it's me. I can't tell anymore.

14

The Master's Hand

The Tiger's face is pale and taut. After the song fades, there's only silence in the Court. Every eye is on Orso. He smiles widely and raises his hands. "Well now, this is a somber affair. I thought we were celebrating my return."

The music starts up. A crowd of singing Ghosts, Gamblers, and Thieves is accompanied by a piano.

Loup appears at Orso's side with a goblet of wine. Everyone starts to laugh and chatter. The Hyènes come down from their perches and grab reluctant partners, swinging them around in their violent dances.

Ettie looks at up me. She's stopped trembling. "I'm safe now, aren't I?"

"Yes," I say. "They can't hurt you now."

Which technically is true—the Law protects her. But the

Tiger is watching Ettie with hungry, determined eyes. He has never been one for obeying the Law.

Tomasis catches my eye. I know from the slight raise of his head that he wants to speak. I slip away from Ettie and sidle up to him, my head bowed reverentially. He cocks his head to one side, studying my face with searching eyes. His necklaces sparkle, catching the dancing light of the candles.

When he speaks, his voice is low enough for my ears alone to hear what he has to say.

"Justice is a fire that rages through your bones. The Law hangs upon your heart like a burden." He reaches out with a leathery hand and runs a finger down the side of my face, tracing the line of my cheek and neck, pausing at the Guild tattoo behind my ear. "You'll make a good Thief Lord in your time."

I flinch, recoiling at his words.

I don't want to be a Lord. Tomasis is my Guild Lord, my Father in the Miracle Court. To consider anything else would be blasphemy.

"I won't always be around, little kitten," he says, as if reading my mind. His eyes dance with amusement as he watches my expression.

I can't bear to think about what his words mean. A world without Tomasis would be unthinkable. How could I ever watch him be cut down by age or infirmity? How could I watch other hands lift the jewels from around his neck and wear them against their own skin as Lord of the Guild of Thieves? I myself could never do it.

"A Guild Lord does whatever he must to protect his children," Tomasis says gently. "But a Guild Lord also chooses his enemies wisely." He glances over at the Tiger, who's still sitting rigid at the Lords' table, watching Orso and Ettie. "There are things even I can't protect you from."

He holds out his hand, and I take it in my own and kiss his large knuckles. I whip out the tin cup I "rescued" from the Châtelet and offer it to him. He frowns, taking the battered piece of tin and raising an eyebrow at me as he turns the cup over, inspecting it. Then he sees the words stamped into its underside—

LE GRAND CHÂTELET

—and he laughs.

We watch the dancing late into the night. The musicians play our best-loved songs, and all the Guilds join in singing while I staunchly refuse to explain the lyrics to Ettie. I try to still the nervous thrum inside me. Try not to think about what will happen tomorrow. Here I am surrounded by my brethren. Let tomorrow take care of itself.

Throughout the night, various acquaintances nod at me in acknowledgment of what I've accomplished. Gentleman George doffs his hat and offers to teach me some of dances of the noblesse. I try to control the fluttering of my heart: one of the Merveilles of the Miracle Court has just condescended to talk to me. Femi demands to know how I did it, while all around us the hall buzzes that the youngest Cat of the Thieves Guild broke the Dead Lord out of the Châtelet.

I pretend I can't hear them and attempt not to preen too much. But I'm tipsy with pride. Renown is meat and honey to the Wretched. I squash a desire to glance into the long shadows, where a certain Master of Knives might be lurking. I try my best not to care about what he might be thinking.

Wine is passed around; a goblet reaches us from Loup. We raise it, toasting with the drinking words of the Court: "Come, brothers and sisters, let us forget." The wine is so strong it hits me like a wave, dizziness and warmth going from my head to my toes. Ettie has a sip and coughs.

"You'll get used to it," I chuckle.

Ettie is safe now. As safe as she can be. But Thénardier's face was a promise of rage. And when he drinks, his temper is ugly and unreasonable; his fists itch to batter something. I drink deeply to give myself courage, to steel myself.

A few hours before dawn, the music winds down and the singers turn to ballads and tragic love songs. The hall is drunk with the laughing and cavorting of the Wretched. Orso rises from his perch, and the Ghosts rise with him. I get up and help Ettie to her feet.

"Time to go, little one," Orso says.

We leave the theater together, passing back through the old houses. I stop, and Ettie continues ahead of me before she notices I'm no longer next to her. She turns, confused.

"Let's go," Ettie says.

"I can't," I say as gently as I can.

"What do you mean?" She sees the determined expression on my face and her lips tremble. "You can't leave me,

Nina." Ettie's voice is small and terrified. She glances at the Ghosts. "You can't leave me with *them*."

I've no choice; she's safer with them.

"Nina."

I take her hand. "It's only for a while."

"Nina, don't go. . . . Stay with me, stay with us."

"I'm a Thief," I say. "Not a Ghost."

"You said w-we look after each other now." Her words are sharp, like a slap across my face.

"Ettie—" I try, but she shakes my hand off and steps away from me.

"You're a liar." The tears run down her face. "You're like *Maman*. She said she would come back, and she didn't. She left me here, with you." All of Ettie's fear and anger spills from her. "And now you're leaving me."

"I'll be back, I swear." It's a promise I can't keep.

Ettie won't take my hand. She won't even look at me. She steps back among the gray shadows of the Ghosts, but I can see her expression. Right now, she hates me.

Hatred is all right. It means she's still alive.

I walk alone down the cold street, away from the Ghosts, who watch me go; away from Ettie, who doesn't.

I go to face what's waiting for me.

You have to be brave, Azelma said.

I square my shoulders and pretend I'm not afraid.

✂∾✄

Minutes later, shadows blur before me.

"What do you want?" I ask, trying to calm my voice.

Montparnasse cocks his head, and I suppress the desire to shiver.

It's strange to think that a few days ago I'd have been afraid of him. I now feel nothing but a dull-edged anticipation. It's easier to face what's coming if you don't think about it. I've had a lifetime of not thinking about it.

"You've done a service to the Dealers of Death tonight. Lady Corday is"—he fishes for the right word—"happy."

It sounds foreign on his tongue. I have problems imagining Corday expressing any emotion, especially happiness.

"I thought you might need this." He offers me the handle of a dagger—his dagger. The one he's always playing with in a suggestively threatening manner. One of the ivory-handled daggers that Assassins carry with them until their deaths. I've never heard of an Assassin offering his dagger to another.

I'm amazed, recognizing the honor of this gift.

"I have several more, and you, it seems, have enemies."

I take the dagger. It's light. The blade is keen and wicked-looking. The ivory handle is wrought with skulls and filigree.

But it won't protect me, not from this.

He looks at me; his eyes search my face for some sign. For a wild moment I consider asking him to stay with me. Does he know what's about to happen?

He knows, or he'd not have given me the dagger.

But he can't get involved; he's an Assassin and I'm a

Thief, and he's not allowed to interfere. So he's giving me a weapon to defend myself.

"Thank you," I say.

Because I don't know what else to do, I keep walking. Leaving him behind.

I think of the dagger inlaid in ivory. I think of Ettie.

The sun is rising ahead of me. The first light is breaking. We the Wretched are creatures of the night. And this night is ending. I raise my head and whistle the Morning Song.

Another voice joins mine.

"Making new friends?" Femi appears beside me. "As if your current ones weren't problematic enough."

I smile. "You don't have to go with me," I say.

Femi nods but keeps ambling along by my side. He's remembering a promise he made to someone long ago. A promise to look after me. I'm glad he's here.

They're waiting for us down a side street. Thénardier's face is an ugly mask of violence. He's drunk and accompanied by four of the Flesh Guild.

"Nina," Femi says, "we can run."

I remember him saying those same words a long time ago, when I was a child. It didn't work then either.

"He's my blood kin. He's the Master of my Guild. How long can I hide from him?"

Femi looks at me as if he's looking at Azelma. He knows all the words I'm not saying. If Thénardier takes his anger out on me, he might not hurt Ettie. Hurting Ettie is forbidden, but from the way Thénardier is swaying, I'd say he's in no state to care about rules.

"Well, well. If isn't my little *chienne* of a daughter."

Thénardier reaches out and grabs me, slamming me back against a wall. I feel my ribs crack as the breath gets sucked out of me, leaving me reeling.

"Do you know how much money you lost me?" he asks.

I smell his sour, wine-soaked breath, and a thousand memories tear through my mind. Blurred words, burning rage, a hundred bruises, a dozen broken bones. Azelma begging him to stop.

"Beating me won't get her back. She's under Orso's protection now," I say through gritted teeth.

"You're right. It won't get her back, but it will give me great satisfaction."

He throws me and I fall, hitting my head on the cold stone.

"Thénardier!" Femi yells. "Tomasis won't be happy if you hurt his best Cat." He leaps in front of Thénardier, who drunkenly bats him away.

"Tomasis can go to Ysengrim," he slurs.

Insulting Tomasis in front of Femi is a mistake, but Thénardier seems too drunk to care.

"She brings in ten times more than you ever have, Thénardier. Think about it. If you injure her legs or her hands and she can't bring Tomasis her cut, what do you think he'll say?"

Thénardier smiles. "Ah, but *I* won't be the one injuring her," he says.

He snaps his fingers and the Fleshers close in.

If someone is going to kill me, I'd like to get a few blows in first. I'd like to go down fighting. But if I fight here, if I land one punch, Thénardier will take his temper out on Ettie. He'll wait patiently till he can waylay her and give her a taste of his rage. That's the kind of man he is.

"Thénardier!" Femi says, his voice raised in warning.

"It's not me who sent them." Thénardier steps back to observe with a gleam in his eye. "Think of me as the messenger," he says, laughing at Femi's barely concealed rage.

"Are you the Tiger's jackal now, Thénardier? This will end badly for you."

Thénardier looks long and hard at me through the hulking forms of the Fleshers. "Ah, Elanion, I would love to intervene, but you know me." His face splits in a vicious gold-toothed grin. "I always back the winning side."

I hold on to the wall and haul myself to my feet as the Fleshers circle me like jackals.

When the first blow comes, I fall without even raising my hands to defend myself.

I taste metal. My fingers scratch at the cold, wet ground as the pain sings in my ears. It's easiest not to think. It's easiest to close down.

I feel the heartbeat of my mother the City beneath my palms, and I murmur the words of my childhood, words I used to say like a prayer into sticky, wine-stained floors.

It's all right; it's only pain. It'll be over soon.

"For *Rennart's sake,* she's your daughter!" Femi pleads.

Rage screams through me, fueled by my pain. I might as well get it over with quickly. I raise my head.

I shouldn't say it, but I do.

"I will never be his daughter. I'm a child of the Thieves Guild. Tomasis is my Father."

Thénardier laughs.

A boot comes down on my face, and the world turns to darkness.

I fall into muddled dreams of Ettie shrieking in some distant place and Femi arguing with someone. Then the sensation of being lifted into the air, a voice like a whisper of cold wind against my ear.

"Don't die, little Cat."

～⌒～⌒～

Time is a blur, long stretches of silence and darkness. Days, hours, or weeks, I can no longer tell its passing.

Sometimes Ettie is beside me, her voice coming out in little choked sobs. Other times I have the impression that Gavroche is watching me carefully with his expressionless dark eyes.

Sometimes there are moments of startling clarity, pain lacing my body as every detail comes sharply into brilliant focus.

Sometimes there's movement as the Ghosts whirl into

action, fetching foul-smelling ointments, burning things, boiling water in large steaming vats, changing bandages, offering blankets.

Sometimes there's a whisper of almost-black linen, the glint of a silver blade, the suggestion of coldness and death.

Much later, when I'm awake, a box is delivered. It's black, with a ribbon tied around it. It has written on it *Pour la Chatte Noire.*

"Tomasis sent it," the Master of Knives tells me in an icy voice. "With his regards."

It'll be better than the vile medicine Montparnasse usually brings. Brewed by the Poison People, a gift from Col-Blanche that is meant to heal but burns my throat. I assume since I'm not yet dead that the Master of Poisons isn't trying to kill me.

Ettie undoes the ribbon, lifts the lid of the box, and almost drops it.

Inside is a hand. Bones protrude from the wrist, blood is coagulated at the stump. The knuckles are hairy, decorated with rings I recognize instantly because they've marked my face many times.

Thénardier.

It is a statement from Tomasis to the Miracle Court. He has proclaimed with flesh, blood, and bone that I am a child of the Thieves Guild. That he is my Father now, and that I am under his protection; that anyone who harms me is striking at him and will be punished. Even if that person is his Master of Beasts.

Deep within the thick waves of my pain-fogged stupor, I smile.

⋙⟨⟩⋘

Sometimes Orso's rumbling voice echoes through the giant cavern and into my small cave as he tells his children stories of mice in a kingdom of cats, enchanted birds, and violent snakes. If I open my eyes, I can just make out a sliver of the main cavern, the Halls of the Dead. Gray mountains of sleeping Ghosts lie piled on top of one another: the Dead, sleeping in their bone-laced tomb deep beneath the city streets. The caverns hum with a low medley of snores and whispers, a broken lullaby that settles over my heavy heart.

Ettie is one of them now.

She is safe.

Still, the Tiger's face flashes through my mind, his ceaseless, roaming gaze determined and hungry.

Within the Halls of the Dead he cannot touch her.

She is safe.

For now.

I close my eyes. I don't open them for days.

PART THREE

The Bread Price

O blind and foolish! Thou hast untied the feet of
Death, and he will follow thy trail till thou diest.
—*The Jungle Book*

THE TALE OF THE SIX LITTLE MICE

FROM STORIES OF THE MIRACLE COURT,
BY THE DEAD LORD

*Il était une fois . . . There was once a land so full to the brim
with mice that they overflowed into every city and town.*

*They were busy little mice, growing crops and building all
the fine things in the city, from the shining roads to the great
houses.*

*At the heart of their country was a court of cats. Now, the
cats were few in number, but they had the silkiest fur, and they
walked with the most graceful step, and of course they knew
they should be in charge of the whole land.*

*So the cats took everything, leaving the mice with little,
and sometimes nothing at all. For the land belonged to the
cats. And the houses and roads that the mice built belonged
to the cats. The cats even sent the mice into battle for them.*

*The mice were hungry and poor. Their children died for
want of bread, and although there was bread to be had, the
cats had it all; they held great feasts at which they drank and
ate until they could consume no more. They kept anything left
over just in case they needed it later, and because they didn't
like to share.*

*Now, there were six brave little mice that thought, Why
do our children starve when there's food we've grown with our*

own hands? They spoke to one another first, and then to other mice. They spoke the truth about what is good, what is right, and what is just. And far and wide across the land, the mice listened. And those that listened asked them to go reason with the cats for their children's sake.

The six little mice asked the cats if they could have a small amount of bread. The cats said there was no money for bread because of the war. But the mice knew that was a lie, because they had grown the grain themselves, and they had fought in battles and knew how much bread there should be. A great anger grew within them.

One night, the six quietly led every mouse in the land to the cats' palace. And while the cats slept, the six little mice bade their companions tie the cats' paws together, front and back. And they carried off every last cat to a place where they would have to answer truthfully for the terrible troubles they had brought on the mice.

The cats, once awake, were angry. And when the six brave mice demanded answers, they refused. They had no fear of the mice, nor tears for their suffering.

The mice decided they did not need the cats in the land anymore. They would make a new land, and their children would no longer hunger, thirst, and die. And so they built a scaffold and made nooses for the cats' necks.

When the cats saw the scaffolds, they caterwauled so loudly that their brethren in other lands heard them. There came a fierce army of felines, who snuck up on the mice and took over the city. They burned everything in their path, rescued the cats from their nooses, and killed one-third of the mice for reason and one-third for sport.

In the end, they took the six brave little mice whose questions had inflamed the whole land, and they called all the remaining mice to bear witness. Then the cats hanged the six before all of their brethren to teach the mice fear.

Legend says that one of the six survived, a mouse born without a tail. For in the confusion, when the mice knew the cats were coming, one bold young mouse said, "If all of the six die, we'll forget the truth they have spoken. We'll forget we were brave once. Let me take your place, brother. I'll hang from the noose for you, and you will live with my name."

"How can you take the noose for me?" asked the sixth mouse. "I'm known to all, for I've no tail."

But the bold little mouse cut off his own tail and took the place of the sixth mouse.

And the cats, who could not tell one mouse from another, caught the bold young mouse, saying, "Here's the one!" They hanged him with his brothers, and all the mice that witnessed it were afraid, and from that day there was a great silence in all the land.

But they say that sometimes on the wind you can still hear a voice whispering about what is good, what is right, and what is just. And that somewhere out in the wilds, a mouse without a tail still lives.

15

The Fountain

It has been two months since I received Thénardier's hand. And a month since I could walk normally again after the beating.

In that time, Death the Endless has begun to haunt the city, taking the weakest: the old, the frail, the young. The bodies are piled high in the streets. It's best not to look too hard at them. Especially the ones that are still moving; desperate families have put their sick out on the street to die, no longer able to bear the sight of their suffering.

It is an evil time; either we live or we die.

The dead are laid out in the place de Fouche, waiting for the corpse carriers to cart them away and leaving the square mostly deserted of Those Who Walk by Day. That's where I find Ettie, sitting cross-legged on the ground, dressed in her dust-gray robes. Loup is going through the pockets of a body nearby.

"That's a dog's trick," I say to Loup. Ghosts aren't known for stealing anything, let alone from corpses; the dead are their kin, after all.

"Looking for food." He turns to glance at Ettie.

She's sitting with her back to us. Loup goes everywhere with her now; he's Orso's eyes, ever watchful for the Tiger.

"We have one here that can't endure long."

There is never enough food, but it has been weeks since there was any bread or grain to be had—unless you are among the nobility. Police are stationed outside the city's bakeries to prevent riots. Starving urchins turn themselves in to the poorhouse of the Hôtel-Dieu, ready to risk death within its infested walls, in exchange for a mouthful of gruel. Those Who Walk by Day have declared days of fasting and humiliation. They bring out the reliquaries of Sainte-Geneviève and parade them around the city. From Notre-Dame to the Tuileries the procession walks daily, led by barefoot penitents dripping blood from the wounds of their flagellations.

The Guilds have no time for such archaic superstitions. But we, too, are powerless to feed our numbers. All the amassed wealth of the Court means nothing if there's no grain to be purchased. My insides are scraped out and hollow, aching with constant hunger.

Ettie is not as strong as Loup and I, not as used to feeling her insides shrink in preparation for the long famine. I've tried my best to steal what food I can, but since the beating, I'm not as strong as I was, and hunger makes me even weaker. Plus, anything I forage for Ettie gets shared with at least ten other Ghosts. She can't bear to see them hungry.

Loup glances over to make sure Ettie is not listening and says sotto voce, "She has a shadow."

I give a start, look around at the dark corners of the buildings. There's a Ghost on every street between here and the city gates. The Ghosts are everywhere, and they see everything. If Loup says there's someone following Ettie, I believe him.

"A child of the Court?" I ask, fearing Thénardier or the Tiger.

"No," Loup answers.

I try to rid myself of the fear gnawing at my insides. I give a low whistle and Ettie turns to me; I'm pleased that she has started to learn some of the Master Calls.

"Nina!" She greets me, but she's slow and unsteady on her feet, her eyes sunken. I take her arm and feel little more than bone between my fingers.

"Have you brought anything to eat?" she asks hopefully.

I shake my head.

Her face falls. "The pot has been empty for days. Gavroche doesn't get up anymore. He barely takes any water." Typical Ettie. She's dying of hunger and all she can think about is Gavroche.

I glance at Loup. He nods solemnly; the little ones are always the first to go.

"How many have you lost?" I ask him quietly.

"Ten so far."

Ten Ghosts dead of hunger. Perhaps I'll sing the death song after all.

"It will pass." It *will* pass. But whether we survive it or not is another story.

"Does it hurt?" Ettie asks. "To die of hunger?"

"If it is merely hunger," Loup says, rifling through the pockets of a dead man, "then why do the plague doctors come?"

The plague pits have been reopened, and carts trundle through the streets, pushed by men wearing masks with beaks like birds, calling as they go for people to bring out their dead. There are so many ill that even the plague doctors, those birds of death, are overwhelmed.

"I tell you, it's hunger and sickness," Loup says. His hands come up empty and he pushes the corpse over, rolling it away so he can get to the next one.

Ettie shivers, though there's no breeze.

"Let's go get water," I tell her. "The fountain isn't far." I slip my arm through hers and bear the weight of her.

She leans into me and smiles at Loup. "I'll bring you water, my Loup."

He nods, unhooks a water pouch from his cloak, and throws it at her. I catch it, since she doesn't even lift her arms.

My heart wrenches. She's too weak; she won't survive. And there's nothing I can do.

The Fontaine du Diable is a disorder of town criers, brandy vendors, shoeblacks, and barefoot match sellers with hollow eyes. A bony-limbed boy dances for pennies while his blue-capped monkey plays a tiny hand organ beside him. Ettie claps in delight and begs to watch. She can hardly see the dancer since the crowd is so thick. But I let her have a minute or two of fun as I scan the area.

I'm not a Dog, used to daylight activity. The throng unnerves me; the sunlight blinds my eyes. Perhaps it's the mere idea of the shadow that Loup spoke about, but I'm jumpy, twitchy with nerves.

When he comes, he appears out of nowhere. First he was not there and suddenly he's beside her: a black gentleman, excessively broad of shoulder, wearing a brown velvet top hat. He watches her stretch on tiptoe trying to see past the crowds, an indulgent smile on his face. I see a million details in one second: the smile lines at the corner of his eyes, his shiny boots, his country coat of olive green, and the end of a silver-and-ruby rosary peeking out of his pocket. How he fidgets with his sleeve, an unconscious nervous tic.

Could this be the shadow? There's an intensity to his dark eyes I dislike, as if he's planning something. Every muscle in my body tenses, my dagger ready in my hand. The gentleman moves suddenly, strong arms whisking Ettie up as if she were a leaf of paper. He lifts her higher just as

I stick the sharp edge of my dagger against his gut, and he freezes.

He's deposited Ettie on his shoulders so that she can get a better view of the scene, and she, oblivious to what's unfolding below, is laughing in delight.

Our gazes are locked, and to the gentleman's credit, he doesn't even raise an eyebrow.

I bare my teeth. "Put her down," I command.

His voice is calm and deep as he begs my pardon. "Forgive me, little Cat," he says.

How does he know I'm a Cat? I am not familiar with this man's face, and yet he knows my Guild. He gently lowers Ettie to the ground.

"Oh, Nina! The little monkey is adorable!"

I take her firmly by the arm and draw her away from the man before lowering my dagger. My eyes remain fixed on his, and he slowly raises a hand, palm up, to show he bears no weapon. And on his palm is a scar, as if someone stabbed his flesh with intent. The mark of a bone oath.

"We are of one blood, thou and I," he murmurs.

My eyes widen. He cocks his head slightly in a motion that means he wants to speak. I glance at Ettie, and when I look up again, I see nothing but a mass of people. Then I spot him, on the move, swallowed by the crowd.

The crowd is like an ocean, thick and heaving. With a careful eye on the gentleman, I jostle past a knife grinder sharpening a cleaver on his treadle and a stick seller waving whips, crops, and walking sticks at anyone who will listen. Ahead of us, the brown velvet top hat bobs.

We plunge into a crowd lining up around the fountain. If people can't eat, at least they can fill their bellies with water. There's no semblance of order, and we pass some poor maids and kitchen boys. I stop behind a servant wearing a fine velvet coat; his clothing tells me he is employed by an important house. I wink at Ettie and she nods in understanding. I push her gently and she falls into the servant.

The man curses. Ettie is all apologies and pleas for forgiveness. Meanwhile, I slip a hand into his coat and relieve him of a coin for water, and another for luck. I whistle low, and Ettie disentangles herself and meets me a little away in the crowd. I pull out the coins and show them to her. She laughs the silvery laugh that I love.

I give Ettie the coins. "Ask for half a bucket and drink your fill. We've got nothing else to put in our stomachs."

I push past some fine-liveried footmen but do not see the gentleman. I look around. There's a stand of trees nearby, and I head toward them. If he's anywhere, he'll be there, where it would be harder to see us between the trunks.

Indeed, he is waiting for me, arms crossed, leaning against a tree.

"Good hunting, sister." He greets me with a bob of his head.

I am nervous, and try to hide it. But I keep turning back to the fountain, Ettie always in my sight.

"Who are you?" I ask sharply.

"A son of the Guild of Letters, one of the People of the Pen. And a brother who owes you a debt of blood. You set me free from the Châtelet."

I blink in surprise, studying his features. The beard is gone, but yes, it is him.

He smiles. "I have come by some information that I thought might be of use to you." He moves to glance over my shoulder to where Ettie is. "The Tiger is going to take the girl," he says.

My heart drops, Ettie: she's there, handing the water man her coin.

"He can't. Orso will go to war with the Flesh Guild."

"He will use your father, Thénardier—"

"*Thénardier* is not my father," I say, baring my teeth.

He raises his eyebrows.

I shake my head. "How do you know that he will take her?" I ask, even though Loup's warning of a shadow pounds in my head.

"Is there anything the Guild of Letters does not know? All things come to our ears eventually. My brethren learned that Thénardier plans to kidnap her and give her to the Tiger."

"I'll tell Tomasis." I frown as I watch Ettie. She's got her bucket and is carrying it slowly away from the crowd, where no one will jostle her. She's so weak her progress is unsteady.

The man gives a small, grim smile. "The Thief Lord will

not involve himself in such a matter. There is an . . . understanding between the Guilds. He won't defy the Tiger."

My mind is racing. I look at the crowd, suspicious of everyone, as Ettie unhooks the water pouch and dips it into the bucket.

"When?" I ask, turning back to the man.

"There was no time or day specified," he begins; then his eyes go wide. "Sister—"

I whip around. One glance shows me that the water pouch lies on the ground and a desperate-looking stranger in a loose shirt and ragged boots is pulling Ettie away from the fountain and toward the streets.

Part of me is amazed that anyone would dare take a child of the Guilds in broad daylight. But the part of me that is the Black Cat of the Thieves Guild is already moving, racing after them, dagger in hand. I sing a call so sharp that people turn to look, and every Ghost within a mile must be able to hear it.

Ettie is kicking and flailing, but the man's arm is tight around her neck. She sees me loping after her and reaches for me, tries to call out but can only choke.

I repeat my call again and again, and as I run, an echo begins to hang in the air. The Ghosts have heard me. They're answering.

The man reaches the street and drags Ettie around a corner just as I spot the first Ghost. Like a shadow, she seems to melt from a wall, her voice picking up the call.

By the time I reach the corner, my breath is spent, but that's not why I stop.

I stop because my ears are ringing with the sound of a hundred calls as Ghosts fill the street, pouring from corners and doorways like gray rats.

The man has loosened his grip on Ettie, who is taking great drags of air and clutching at his arm to keep herself upright. He looks around wildly, not sure whether to push forward or turn another way, but the Ghosts are everywhere now.

They walk with the deliberate shuffle of those who never have to run anywhere. They're not afraid for Ettie. They don't have to be. There's no way the man can escape them. They're too many, and they know it.

The man's eyes are bulging like those of a maddened animal. He turns this way and that, finding himself surrounded. Leading the Ghosts is Loup, like a terrible vengeance, fearlessly staring down this man three times his size, because he knows what happens next.

"Au secours!" the man yells in a panic. *"Au secours!"*

Anyone near enough to hear, and who is not a child of the Miracle Court, turns away. Young boys carrying giant buckets of wash disappear down alleys. Windows that open onto the street close. The City knows when to shut its eyes.

"Quelqu'un! Aidez-moi!" the man cries piteously.

"Let her go," I say, lunging toward him.

He drops Ettie. She lands in a heap and I rush to her, taking her by the arm and pulling her away; she doesn't need to see what will happen. The Ghosts part for me, flowing back into place like water once we've passed.

"Please!" The man's eyes are white and wild with fear, his hands raised to fend them off. "Please, don't hurt me."

There was once a war between the Guilds. And among those who wrought death and destruction, it was the Ghosts that were the most feared. For theirs is the most populous of all the Guilds, and carries with it a burning belief in the Law. Once roused, their wrath is more terrible than that of all of the other Guilds put together. The stories of how they claimed their victims forever haunt the minds of every child of the Miracle Court.

Loup smiles a wicked smile, and a shiver runs down my spine. "Take him."

16

❧

The Dead Trial

The Ghosts tumble over themselves to lift the nearest grate in the street, and they descend into the darkness and stink of the city's sewers. With reluctant hearts, Ettie and I follow.

The city's great stone-walled sewers are darkness and rot, stained with layers of waste. I breathe in deeply. Most Thieves have had to hide in these slime-covered corridors on bad nights when a burglary went wrong. I've learned it's easier to let the smell burn your throat and bring tears to your eyes than to try to shut it out.

My eyes adjust quickly to the darkness. Eventually we come to a platform of sorts, and spilling off every part of it are the Ghosts. They're packed into the tunnel, some knee-deep in the stinking waters, waiting.

With a hiss, a lantern is lit, revealing Orso, Loup, and a

hundred glittering black eyes staring at a broken thing that looks like a naked man tied to a wooden post. He's already a mass of bruises crisscrossed with streaks of blood. His right hand is a bleeding stub of raw flesh. I wince. They've taken his fingers for daring to touch Ettie. The Ghosts carry no weapons, nor are they schooled in combat. Any wound inflicted on this man was done with bare hands and teeth and slow, careful purpose. I almost feel sorry for him.

"Does he live?" Orso asks.

Loup nods.

"A Trial, then." Orso smiles grimly. "You are invited to attend, little Cat." He bends his head in mock respect.

I shudder. I've never seen a Dead Trial before. The stories are the stuff of nightmares, but I dare not refuse so direct an invitation; it would be an insult to the Ghosts.

I glance at Ettie, who was so overwrought she has fallen sound asleep in a nook, away from all of this. Good.

"He has no mark on him," Loup whispers to Orso.

No mark or tattoo means he's one of Those Who Walk by Day.

"My children," Orso says. "We have been wronged. There must be justice."

The Ghosts break into terrible, deafening cries as Orso approaches the man and looks him over.

"Why would you lay a hand on my child?" Orso asks.

The Ghosts repeat the accusation, echoing it again and again, till Loup barks at them to be silent. "Let him speak!"

"I w–was f–forced," the man tries to say through swollen lips.

His answer is received by a hiss from the Ghosts.

"Forced?" Orso's voice is laced with disbelief. "How were you forced? Speak the truth here and perhaps you'll be shown mercy."

The man looks at Orso through the slit of a ruined eye. "I—I had a debt," he moans piteously. "He said he'd call it off. . . ."

"Who is 'he'?"

It's a needless question. We all know who wants Ettie.

"I can't tell you. They said he would kill me."

"Do not fear, my friend." Orso traces a finger along the man's broken face. He smiles a devilish smile. "*He* will not kill you."

And all around him the Ghosts cackle and whoop.

Orso looks at the Ghosts and spreads his hands wide. "What do you say, my children?"

Guilty! Guilty! Guilty! Their voices roll and echo off the walls, a tangled mess of whispers.

Loup raises a hand, and the Ghosts move to engulf the man like a swarm of rats. His cries are muffled, there are so many upon him. I turn my head away.

Orso lumbers toward me.

"You know who did this," I say, my voice hard.

Orso surveys me and murmurs under his breath. "The Tiger is no fool; if he were named, this act would force us

174

to go to war. You heard the Day Walker; he would not give a name."

Orso's gaze wanders over his children as they taunt what's left of the broken man.

"We can ill afford such a confrontation." His voice is low and soft. "Not when we're so weak from hunger and sickness." He shakes his head.

The Dead Lord is silent for a moment, his eyebrows knotted.

"It has become much bigger now than just her," he says, looking at Ettie. "You've publicly thwarted the Tiger, and he can't allow that. If a mere kitten can stand up to him before the Court, anyone might follow. He will have his vengeance or lose the power he holds over us. She has become a symbol he must destroy. Nothing will stop him."

"But you can protect her!" I insist.

"Can I? He had me thrown into the Châtelet, attempted to kidnap her in broad daylight. If he's bold enough to try take to her once, he'll do it again."

My heart sinks. If Orso can't protect Ettie, then who can?

"There are at least four Guild Lords who would aid the Tiger if he asked them, because they fear him too much to refuse," Orso says.

"But the Law!" I cry. "Does it count for nothing? He's not allowed to touch her. She's one of your children!"

"He's weakened the Law. He's tested it and made it his plaything."

He puts the tips of his fingers together thoughtfully and looks at me. "Do you know how the Assassins take names?"

I shake my head.

"If someone wants to end a life, he gives the Keeper of Records the victim's name and pays for the death. Most of the time the Assassins carry out the task, especially if they've anything to gain from it. But every now and again, they go to the one marked for death, the dead wolf, and they tell him the price that's been offered, letting him counter. If he can pay the price they ask, the Assassins will cancel the contract forever because they will be richer if he lives."

I listen, confused.

Orso sees this and elaborates. "You must pay a price higher than any the Tiger can offer to any child of the Guild. And you must pay it to all the Lords. Or she'll never be safe."

My mind reels.

"How much gold do you think it would take?"

"Gold?" Orso throws back his head, laughing heartily. The sound booms across the sewer.

Ettie is startled and wakes. She looks around, bleary-eyed.

"Would you pay the Lord of Smugglers in gold? Would you pay Tomasis in gold? What is gold to them?" Orso's eyes challenge me. "Come now, little kitten, where's that sharp brain of yours?"

I don't understand.

"What weight has gold to the dying? Of what worth is gold in a time of famine?" Orso says.

Then it comes to me: Gold has no value to the dying. It

can't stop the hands of death. What the dying want is to live. And to live they need to eat.

"Bread . . . ," I say as it dawns on me what the Dead Lord is saying. I must find a way to feed the entire Miracle Court. Dread fills the pit of my stomach.

There's only one place in the city where there's always bread, even during a famine. Bread enough to save Ettie, to save us all, though no Thief of the Miracle Court would dare steal from there: the Palace of the Tuileries, nest of viperous, lawless nobility, and home to the king and queen of France.

17

~~~

The Pont Neuf

There are several ways to get into the Tuileries, the most heavily guarded building in the city. The last time I slipped into the palace, I was smaller and more desperate—and un-encumbered by Ettie, who is useless at most things that require any sort of stealth. But I can't risk leaving her behind. It has been two days, and the Tiger will surely have heard that his plan to kidnap her failed. Ysengrim knows what he might do next.

Ettie and I make our way to the Faubourg Saint-Germain. *He* is there, as I knew he would be, sitting among the bodies of the dead, for the dying are everywhere.

"Nina!" Ettie says in a weary voice. "Isn't that St. Juste? He is so beautiful." Her deliriousness is clearly unhinging her brain.

St. Juste looks up at me and frowns.

I've often watched him from the shadows. Not—despite what Ettie thinks—because he's handsome, nor because he's good at giving rousing speeches, which he is. But because my debt to him weighs heavily on my shoulders. I owe him a blood debt, which I've yet to repay.

Trying hard not to blush, I sit Ettie down in a spot where I can watch her. She winks at me and shoos me toward him.

Several of St. Juste's student cronies are milling around. A lot of them are crying.

Beside him, a young man with sandy hair and large round spectacles is drawing blood from a corpse with a wicked-looking needle.

"Stealing from the dead?" I ask.

The young man with the needle looks up at me, his face lined with tiredness.

"Taking samples," he says.

"Feuilly is studying medicine. He will analyze the blood and look for any abnormalities," St. Juste explains in a flat voice.

"What kind of abnormalities?"

"The kind caused by a water supply contaminated with waterborne disease," says Feuilly, carefully wrapping the chamber of the syringe in cloth and leather.

"Death in the water," slurs Grantaire, the drunkard who was with St. Juste the night they chased off the Fleshers. He is propped up against a wall nearby, watching the proceedings with an air of gravity. "I told you this when the bodies starting piling up," he adds, "and you called me a drunk, St. Juste. Well, now you know. The only reason I drink spirits is to avoid poisoning." He winks at me, taking a swig from his ever-present hip flask.

"Grantaire, it is not yet midday; can you not remain sober for even one morning?" St. Juste snaps.

"I don't like corpses," says Grantaire with a hiccup.

"It is certain that the water is contaminated," Feuilly cautions. "We are now trying to isolate the sickness, discover its origin, so that we can work toward a cure. One need only look where the death toll is the highest to know that the contaminants are isolated to the water systems in the poorest parts of the city."

"While the fountains of the nobility run pure," St. Juste says in a flinty voice.

My insides freeze. I think of what Loup said about the plague doctors, and of the piles of bodies near the Fontaine du Diable; of the poor and the servants alike, lining up to draw water from the well.

I look at Ettie, who was snatched by the shadow before she was able to take a sip from the water pouch. But how many others have drunk of this water? How many of the ten dead Ghosts?

St. Juste leans over one of the smallest corpses. He gently takes the mottled blue hand and places it on the boy's chest, closes his staring eyes. Then he turns.

"This is the world we live in, my friends," he says, his voice hard. "How much longer shall we sit by and let this continue? How many more citizens shall we watch them cut down?"

His hands ball into fists at his side, and his words are greeted with subdued nods from his friends. As if noticing my complete lack of response to his speech, he turns blazing eyes toward me.

"The last time I saw you, you had me arrested by the gendarmes."

"It is good to see you too, St. Juste."

He frowns darkly at me, and taking my arm, he drags me down the street by my elbow. Ettie watches me from a distance with a look that says, *Are you in danger, or is he getting romantic?* The glint in her eye shows that she thinks it's the latter. I sigh. Ettie is hopeless.

"Now, now, St. Juste," I say, "there's no need to get intimate—or do me grievous bodily harm."

He ignores my quips and holds me pinned tight by both arms.

"And after they arrested me, I was questioned for *hours*. It was three days before they finally released me."

I wince. I'd hoped they wouldn't keep him quite so long.

"You said you were in my debt, but you stole my pistol the first time I met you and had me arrested the second."

I loosen one of my arms from his grip and reach into my skirts. Reluctantly I pull out his pistol; it's one of my favorite things, covered in intricate gold scrollwork. "I'm sorry?" I offer as I hand it to him.

His eyes burn into me as he takes it. "The only reason I'm speaking to you now is that I recognize that you are a young woman of considerable enterprise and skill."

I frown, unused to his flattery.

"Do you know what I thought about for those three interminable days when I was stuck in the Châtelet? Aside from wondering if they were going to execute me for my name?"

He draws me to him until my face is inches from his. He licks his lips, which I find quite distracting, and I do my very best to focus on his words. Behind me, I sense Ettie positively squealing with delight.

"I thought that we could use someone like you in the Société des Droits de l'Homme."

I blink at him.

"You have all the necessary links to, er, people who can provide us with arms, and information. And you have experience in evading the inquiries of the law. You and your Guild are our natural allies—you hate the nobility as much as we do. You can recruit those who will be willing to fight alongside us. We need people of skill and cunning if we are to succeed. What do you say? Will you join in our crusade? The cause needs you."

"The cause needs me?"

"I need you," he says, as tender as a lover. Then he smiles, a ferocious, terrifying smile. "Don't you see, Black Cat? Together, we're going to change the world."

A thousand thoughts race through my mind, one of

which is wondering why my heart is racing. Another is that I owe this young man a great deal. I would be dead had he not rescued me from the Tiger's men. My answer is almost a foregone conclusion.

As if he can read my mind, he releases me.

"If you join us, Black Cat, my incarceration in the Châtelet will be forgiven."

The idea of being in any way affiliated with one of Those Who Walk by Day is deeply unsettling. But by joining his cause, I will pay back my ever-deepening well of debt. I do not really have much choice.

I sigh. "All right, I'll join you, St. Juste, but you must do something for me. I know you speak to Orso. You must tell him about the death in the water. Already ten of his children have died. He will be able to protect the rest, and can warn the others."

St. Juste studies me intently. "It shall be done. But why are you not able to carry this message to him yourself?"

Because in a world of untrustworthy criminals, I don't know whom to trust with this message, and because you are just so damned noble that I know I can trust you. . . . But I'm not about to tell him that.

"Because we need to get into the Tuileries, my friend and I." I wave vaguely toward Ettie, who waves back enthusiastically.

"The Tuileries? Why?"

I sigh again and try to rearrange the truth in the manner most likely to please him.

"I'm going to steal something from the king," I say.

If St. Juste is shocked, he doesn't show it. His eyes bore into me. "Treasure? Jewels?" he asks, something like judgment in his eyes.

"Bread," I say.

It was the right thing to do, sharing this truth with him.

He stops, his eyebrows knotted in a frown of deep thought. "I heard what you said that day in the Halls of the Dead, Black Cat. We are not so very different, you and I. We are both fighting monsters a hundred times more powerful than ourselves. We are both tiny and insignificant, and we both know that the odds say we cannot win."

St. Juste reaches out his hand to me.

"But we also both know we'll go down fighting," he says.

I reluctantly take his hand, and behind me—far enough away that she is not able to make out our conversation— Ettie makes a noise of smothered delight.

It occurs to me that perhaps St. Juste can be of help getting us into the Tuileries if he is willing to do me just one more favor. . . .

We arrive at the Pont Neuf, where, according to the tongues of Notre-Dame, the procession should be at this hour. The bridge was the first of its kind to be built: there are no houses on it, meaning that it has ample space for the cacophony of actors, vendors, quack doctors, and tooth-pullers who crowd it.

Today the traffic of coaches, wagons, omnibuses, cabs, and animals has slowed to a crawl. We have threaded our way through the clogged arteries of the city, avoiding seedy *bouquinistes* handing out illegal pamphlets denouncing the king, and colporteurs selling bawdy books from blue-papered trays. Around us, every inch of every wall is pasted over with bills bearing incendiary political gossip, historical essays, and an overflow of exclamation marks. *Here,* they cry, *royal advisor Concini was roasted and eaten! Here,* they claim, *the king's son was unhorsed by a runaway pig and died!* And over and over, posters scream:

WANTED: ESCAPED CONVICT JEAN VALJEAN
NO. 24601

We weave through the ruck till we're buried in the crowds jostling for a clear view of the procession. Every day since the start of the famine, the remains of Sainte-Geneviève have been paraded through the streets in an attempt to blackmail God into mercy.

It's great sport for the poor, who love watching hungry priests and wild-eyed penitents in their bloodstained shifts whip themselves to a frenzy. At the head of the procession is General Jean Maximilien Lamarque, one of the country's most beloved military men, who looks dismayed at having to take part in this farce when he could be abroad fighting the Austrians. He's supported by a handful of soldiers and several members of the Sûreté, riding on horseback in their bright blue uniforms, their eyes constantly sweeping the crowd.

Behind the wailing penitents, bored nobles, forced by the powerful Church to participate in the charade, are taking the agonizingly slow carriage ride from Notre-Dame to the Tuileries. Their plumed carriages of gold and glass wait in an exhausted line to cross the bridge.

The palace has decreed that each day, two poor children should be brought to be blessed and fed at the royal table. It's an old tradition called l'Enlèvement—the Kidnapping—by the city's children, started by la Reine des Gâteaux, Marie-Antoinette.

I spot a carriage that must be carrying the children; it's the least adorned, a third-class carriage fit for transporting the very poor—after all, they might sully anything else.

I motion to Ettie and she follows me till we're directly opposite the carriage. All we need to do is dart forward and slip under it. Everyone is watching the penitents, and between the noise and chaos we should be safe enough. I take a wary step forward and pull Ettie after me; we're inches away from the carriage and are about to duck under it when a Sûreté officer approaches from the side of the procession on horseback. Her eyes meet mine and I take in the long ponytail of bright red hair.

The inspector.

I don't know if she recognizes Ettie from the night at the Châtelet, but she sees that we're too close to the carriage. Frowning, she nudges her horse toward us.

Rennart's balls!

Grabbing Ettie, I pull her back into the crowd, but the inspector keeps coming, eyes narrowing as she keeps us determinedly in her sights.

"Nina, what do we do?"

Then an explosion rocks the ground and everyone turns toward the back of the bridge in time to see a cloud of smoke rise. The crowd gives a gasp of delight. Someone is blowing something up! What grand entertainment! General Lamarque yells an order, and his men go careening, guns raised, toward the explosion. Over the sound of the crowd the shouting begins. It's a blur of noise to start, but the tone is all that matters: voices raised in pure and utter outrage.

I grin. St. Juste decided to grant me this additional favor after all.

The soldiers can barely push through the trapped crowds as the invaders appear. A swarm of young men, wearing shining boots and tailored coats, carrying signs—and, to my horror, entirely unarmed—march red-faced and chanting toward the soldiers. At their head is St. Juste.

Lamarque notes their lack of arms and the seething crowd, and he shouts for his men to lower their weapons.

"We don't need your penance!" St. Juste shouts at the procession. "Take the bread from the tables of the nobility and feed the people!"

The crowd cheers in response, though it's not clear whom they're cheering for.

Inspector Javert leaps off her horse and advances on us. I dare not back too much farther into the crowd; with the agitated soldiers, horses, students, and onlookers, there's the very real threat of being trampled. Then, like a puppet on a string, the inspector jerks to a stop. The blood drains from her face; her mouth opens in surprise. I follow her gaze. There's a man in the crowd staring at her, a broad-shouldered man with a brown velvet hat and a country coat of olive green. The son of the Guild of Letters whom I freed from the Châtelet and who warned me that Ettie was in danger.

"Valjean!" the inspector shouts as the man turns and flees. She springs into action, leaping into the crowd after him like a suicide into the Seine.

A Cat knows how to taste the air and feel the perfect moment to act. In a rush of movement, I grab Ettie, push back through the crowd, and launch myself at the carriage door. Flinging it open, I leap inside, a dagger in my hand, prepared to go face to face with the poor children chosen for l'Enlèvement. I land perfectly, and in a heartbeat I'm inches from the occupant's face, the point of my dagger sticking into his throat.

Except that *he* is not a poor child. *He* is quite handsome, and drowning under such a vast amount of lace, silk, frills, and velvet that my horrified mind starts ringing every alarm bell it knows. This is not a commoner selected to take tea with the royals. Time slows down as I gaze into the exqui-sitely long-lashed eyes of a handsome brown-haired young man on whose lap I am almost sitting. I hear Ettie scramble into the carriage behind me. I hear her gasp. I catch the faintest whiff of chocolate and spice.

"Black Cat?" he says.

Oh no.

"Your *Highness*?" I say.

Perhaps it's the invasion of his personal space, perhaps I'm the only one who ever treats him like this, but instead of the fury that should overcome him, and despite the dagger pressed against his neck, his eyes brighten and his face splits into a joyous smile.

"You know each other?" Ettie asks behind me in a voice so laced with delight that between this and St. Juste I just *know* that she believes my life is far more romantic than it actually is.

Before either of us can say or do anything more, the air shudders with the sound of gunfire. The dauphin, Ettie, and I are thrown around as the horses rear, and we land in a tangled heap on the floor, with him apologizing profusely and me elbowing him out of the way. Outside, there's shout-ing, horses galloping, and the screams of a crowd now afraid for their survival. The air begins to taste of smoke and gun-powder. Lamarque's voice carries as he orders everyone to stand aside so the procession can exit the bridge quickly.

The carriage rocks and we're on the move. Ettie wobbles

and climbs onto the seat, holding out her hand to help the dauphin up. The dauphin rises, reaching trembling fingers toward the carriage window. I bat his hand away.

"Don't be a fool! Do you want to get shot?"

He opens his mouth to say something, when the carriage gives a sudden jolt, and he falls backward, slamming his head against the seat. He slumps over. Ettie gives a small screech and dives toward him, checking to see if he's alive.

I'm not sure whether she cares because he's the dauphin of France or because she hopes he's the love of my life. Either way, I feel no small sense of relief when she nods to me to tell me he's alive. I'd rather not be arrested for murdering the heir to the throne just at the moment.

"Are you going to tell me how you know him?"

I sigh. "I might have visited his bedchamber once."

Ettie gasps, happily scandalized.

"To *rob* him, Ettie. Don't look at me like that. It was several years ago."

There's a long silence before Ettie adds, "And yet he still remembers you." She lets that hang in the air between us, heavy as guilt.

I try to weigh up the chances that the dauphin is not bearing a grudge after all these years—I did steal one of the crown jewels from him, after all.

"He's also very handsome," Ettie adds, as if there is some sort of attractiveness competition going on that I am unaware of.

"Is he?" I say, as if I haven't noticed.

18

Of Drownings

Ettie is in charge of everything that happens when we arrive at the palace. Not because she knows the ways of nobility better—she doesn't—but because she is perfect combination of charming and pathetic. When the carriage door swings open, a servant with a round moon of a face and flushed cheeks pokes herself through the doorway. Ettie promptly bursts into tears, pointing at the dauphin and gasping an incoherent explanation between breaths. Havoc ensues. People run hither and thither; there are orders, there is shrieking, and the dauphin is borne away by five people, as if one person isn't enough for a royal of his *handsomeness*.

We should really flee. After all, the dauphin will probably have us arrested once he comes to—I daresay robbing the heir to the French throne is a hanging offense? But if I run,

I'll fail in my mission and have no way to protect Ettie from the Tiger. The dauphin didn't seem very angry to see me, and if I stay, then somewhere in the Tuileries there is a store-room full of grain that I desperately need.

In the chaos, nobody questions us. We are here for tea with the queen, or so Ettie keeps loudly crying, until the moon-faced servant returns and, sniffing, takes in our stink, a mixture of smoke and gunpowder.

"Not the usual standard," she says, her voice laden with disappointment.

Ettie sways beside me, and her tears become more pitiable. Moon-Face chides her and snaps her fingers, and two footmen appear at her side.

"This one's half dead, from the looks of things. Best carry her in," she says.

So even Ettie gets carried. I, however, prefer to walk.

First there's a visit to the *salle de bains,* a large room empty save for a giant mother-of-pearl bathtub set on gold clawed feet. Steam rises from the tub, which is full of peaks of something thick and white. It looks like a huge bowl of well-beaten egg whites, and it smells violently of lavender.

"What's that?" asks Ettie.

"A tub, to wash yourself in. You can't meet the queen smelling ripe as a wheel of Camembert!"

We give up our clothes, which Moon-Face threatens to

burn, but I refuse to relinquish my satchel of lock-picks, claws, and daggers, which the servants have been eyeing with growing levels of alarm. I only have to bite one person before they let me keep my weapons, and then Ellie and I are unceremoniously herded into the giant tub, which is large enough to drown five people. I am heaved in, weapons and all.

First they soak us in boiling water, to "dislodge the grime." Then they attack. Four maids dressed in cornflower-blue skirts and armed with brushes haul us up and squirt strange-scented liquids at us. I yelp and shriek, while Ettie for some reason can't stop giggling. They scrub every inch of me with a brush, until my skin feels raw. Then they get to work on my hair, roughly lathering it with some rose-scented salve that makes me wonder if it's possible to die of overperfuming. I am just growing used to their fingers rubbing my scalp in a way that's not entirely unpleasant when they dump a jug of water over my head, leaving me spluttering.

I curse them in back-alley argot.

"I've never seen such an ungrateful savage. And you having the honor to be chosen!" scolds Moon-Face.

Next we're pulled from the water and dried down with soft white linens. The maids yank at my hair with brushes as if they're trying to pull it all out.

Once considered adequately dried, Ettie's hair is braided, while mine gets fastened in a coil with my own lock-picks, which they have assumed are hairpins. We're wrapped in thick quilted robes and given slippers of the softest white leather lined with lamb's wool—I make a mental note to take them with me when I leave. Then we're led up a back staircase. Moon-Face unlocks a door and pushes us forward, then closes the door behind us.

The room is the size of Thénardier's entire inn, and of all the rooms in all the fine homes I've broken into, this one seems the most weighed down with an oppression of gilt. It frames every door and window, every corner, and marks the decor throughout, from an ornate clock to the chandelier to the candlesticks. Everything is gold. And what's not gold is silk: patterned curtains; hand-painted wallpaper, cushion covers, and bed linens. Even the draperies that fall from the gaping mouth of the bed canopy are silks, heavy with tassels, and topped with gilt carvings of frolicking animals.

What's not silk is covered in flowers. It looks as if a flower girl has gone mad and strewn her posies over every available surface. There are roses painted on the ceiling, delicate Qing gardens trailing along the walls, lilies and carnations woven into the impressive pastel Ottoman rug.

There is a click behind us: they've locked us in, which doesn't faze me at all, since I've never met a lock I couldn't pick.

Next to the obscenely large bed, almost made minute by a mountain of fluffy pillows, is a table bearing a platter of cold meats, sliced fruit, and cheeses. My stomach growls, and I go to inspect the offerings: thick slabs of pressed beef tongue, honeyed ham, and wafer-thin cured meats; a hard yellow Comté, a soft, peach-rinded Reblochon, a white-dusted Tomme de Savoie; thin slices of golden pears.

I pick up a piece of Comté and sniff it.

"It's fine," Ettie says, and I can hear her stomach growling.

I look at her reproachfully. I've told her many times not to eat or drink things offered unless you trust the giver. And sometimes not even then.

"Oh, just eat something, Nina." She passes me a plate.

Giving her a look of condescension, I choose a single slice of pear and take a tiny bite. It melts in my mouth, all sweetness and juice. I swallow carefully and wait to see if I feel any side effects.

Ettie laughs. "Not everyone is trying to poison us."

"That's what you think," I say darkly, deciding it's probably safe to wolf down another piece of the pear.

"Isn't it delightful to be so clean?"

I frown. Since I smell like I've been attacked by a lavender rosebush, I refuse to agree.

When my stomach is full, I pick through the leftovers and secrete some in the drawer of the bedside table.

"Why are you doing that?" Ettie asks.

"So we have more for later. Nobles always throw away leftovers."

"They throw away *food*?" She looks affronted.

"Yes." I stretch my body out on the bed beside her. I lay my head on the mountain of pillows and tell her every tale I know about the nobility: of la Reine des Gâteaux, who told her people to eat cake in the middle of a famine;

of leprous King Louis XV, who thought his sickness could be cured by bathing in the blood of innocents and had his men steal children from the city streets until riots broke out in protest.

When the key turns in the lock and the door opens, Ettie is suitably frightened.

Moon-Face comes in all smiles. "Well, look at the two of you, so clean and neat."

I glare at her, but she ignores me. Two new maids, armed to the teeth with torturous-looking devices, follow her in. Ettie's eyes sparkle with excitement as they go at our heads again with brushes, combs, and a variety of oils. Ettie seems to enjoy her styling, whereas I feel like they're torturing my head. She ends up with her golden curls tamed into something called *à la grecque.* I am given a more demure style of loose waves piled at the back of my head. Then we're both liberally sprayed with yet more scent, which sends us into cascading sneezes. A lady in a gigantic dress of bright yellow enters the room; her face is painted white, and she wears a white curled wig almost double the size of her head, upon which are perched several mustard-colored butterflies and a parrot.

"Madame Gelada," says Moon-Face, "royal dresser from the Grand Mogol."

The Mogol is the fanciest dress shop in the whole city; I know, since I've had to . . . *borrow* some of her creations before as disguises. The yellow lady surveys us calculatingly.

She is followed into the room by an entire retinue of men and women wearing different shades of yellow and carrying brightly colored boxes of varying sizes.

Madame Gelada delicately seats herself on a small pouf and claps her hands. Her servants get to work opening boxes of underclothing, and Madame selects the garments.

We're draped in chemises and culottes, silk stockings embroidered with tiny flowers, followed by corsets with velvet stays tied so tightly I can hardly breathe. The skirt hoops are so large, three people could hide under them.

Next come dresses of every shape and color. From pale ivories to bright scarlets, some embroidered with silk thread, others festooned with beads and sequins that catch the light and shine. Ettie gasps as she surveys the wondrous creations. But Madame has little time for our opinions. One look at us and she's already chosen: Ettie gets a dress of pale blue, and I one of dusty rose. They're dropped over our heads, fastened, straightened, and smoothed. The servants pull out ornate brass needles and thread of every color, instantly matching it to fabric and stitching hems, waistlines, and sleeves.

When they are at last done, Madame gives a short nod to show she's pleased with her work, and departs, leaving behind a flurry of boxes, tissue paper, and servants to pack up, all without having said a single word to us.

"We look so fine!" Ettie says once the servants have scurried out the door.

I snort. As if I care about looking fine. My gown has

only the barest strip of cloth on the upper arm—where am I meant to hide my dagger?—but Ettie is dragging me to a mirror and forcing me to look at us side by side.

"We are beautiful."

Unbelievably, the outfit has added to Ettie's beauty. The sheen of her blue dress makes her eyes look even bigger. The flowers in her curls make her look as if she's tumbled here from some otherworldly realm, like a princess from a story that Orso might have told us. There's pink in her cheeks, now that the food has filled her up.

I've always thought it isn't fair that she's so lovely. Her face draws the attention of those who should not see her. It turns her into a thing to possess. I'd cut her face with my own dagger if I thought it would save her. But to scar Ettie would change nothing. It's not just her features that are beautiful. Something inside her draws people to her. Innocence, a kindness that could swallow the city whole if she let it.

"You always look beautiful, Ettie. You don't need a dress and a thousand pins in your hair to change that," I say grumpily.

"You look lovely too," she adds loyally. I shake my head. Even with my fantastical get-up, I'm all angles, edges, and frowns. A bag of bones, Femi calls me. How he'd laugh at me now, parading around in a giant silk dress like an over-stuffed meringue.

"I don't care what I look like," I say fiercely, and I mean every word. It's not what I look like that has earned me my place, or the protection of my Guild. My size, my speed, my mind, and my daring make me who I am. I am the Black Cat of the Thieves Guild.

Moon-Face reappears to shoo us out of the room, whispering garbled instructions as she leads us swiftly through back corridors.

"Remember to curtsy before him, and her, if you should see her. Don't rise until they tell you to. You can't speak to them unless they speak to you first. Remember that. Don't eat with your hands. Don't take food from the table. Watch him and do what he does. Use your serviettes; no wiping your faces on your sleeves."

I don't have time to go wherever it is that we are being taken, I think fretfully. I need to find the kitchen larders.

Ettie casts me a glance of worry. I grin at her with far more reassurance than I feel. Meanwhile, the same thought repeats like a military tattoo in my head.

I must pay the bread price.

I must pay the bread price.

I've been in this golden cage for over two hours, and I still don't know where the kitchens are located. And even when I find them, will there truly be enough bread to pay all of the Lords? We are in a time of famine, after all; perhaps the nobility, too, are suffering from scarcity of grain.

As we're led down a maze of hallways, we pass a barred door flanked by two armed guards, with three heavy gilt locks hanging on it.

Every nerve in my body is instantly alert. I'm sure I know

199

what is so carefully locked away in a place such as this. And the temptation to get inside is acute.

But before I can make a plan, we round a corner and reach a door clearly made for giants, attended by footmen in blue livery. My feet sink into lush carpet. The blank-faced footmen, making no eye contact or sign they've seen us, open the door and allow us to enter.

19

The Dauphin of France

The room is like the inside of a confectioner's box, papered in soft, sugary pink. There are giant windows framed by velvet curtains with tassels the size of my head. Ten servants crowd toward the middle of the room, framing two sofas in perfect symmetry.

A fine smiling lady in a dress of palest blush, diamonds at her throat and ears and an elaborate wig on her head, sits in the middle of one sofa. Behind her stands a gentleman with eyes like a hawk's. He makes a low-voiced comment to the woman, while in the corner, at an ornate desk of eggshell blue, is a gentleman busy with something I cannot see.

The other sofa has its back to us, over the top of which I can see a dark head, hair tied back in a blue velvet ribbon.

A doorman takes his stick and bangs it on the floor, and in a loud voice says, *"Les invitées."*

I glance at him. Like all the other servants, he looks straight ahead, announcing our presence while ignoring our existence. At his words, the occupants of the room turn to us.

My Cat instincts tell me this is not a place to let down my guard. For a long moment I evaluate my situation: the number of people, the potential for pieces of decor to be used as weapons to defend ourselves, how quickly I could drag Ettie to the door, what expensive items I could take with me.

The smiling lady beckons to us. Moon-Face pushes us, whispering a reminder to curtsy. We stand right before the lady. She might be attractive under the layers of heavy paint, but it's hard to tell. I curtsy neatly, but Ettie bows. I kick myself for not having taught Ettie the rules of curtsying. In the Miracle Court all the children bow. But the lady bursts into peals of honeyed laughter.

"How enchanting." She puts out a hand to Ettie, inviting her to approach. I trail behind her.

"What are your names, little ones?"

"I'm Ettie, and she's Nina."

The lady's eyes linger momentarily on my face and run down my frame. She dismisses me, and I'm suddenly painfully aware that I'm the only person in the room whose skin is not milky white. In the Miracle Court, race, origin, family mean nothing. We are all one blood. But here . . . here, with one flicker of her eyelashes, the lady has told me that I'm not worth looking at. Not worth paying attention to.

As sudden as a viper, the lady's hand darts out and takes Ettie's chin in a firm grip. She tilts Ettie's head and looks at her.

"Charming, charming," she says almost to herself. "I am the queen of France. This is Monsieur Sagouin, our most trusted friend and advisor."

The standing man stares at us without smiling. The queen does not introduce the gentleman at the desk. Which speaks volumes about who *he* is.

"Madame." We bob our heads.

"In this time of suffering, it is our custom to invite young friends from the less fortunate neighborhoods of the city to take tea," the queen says. "I want my son to know that not all children are as fortunate as he." She raises a hand. We turn, and there's the dauphin, watching us, wide-eyed.

I try my best to smile in a friendly, Ettie-like way, hoping he doesn't instantly have us arrested.

He rises at the queen's lifted hand. He's pale and wears a jacket of midnight-blue velvet edged in silver frogging, with a scarlet pin at his chest.

"Mesdemoiselles, this is Louis Joseph Charles Romain, the dauphin of France."

We curtsy yet again, and the dauphin comes toward us, which causes his mother to raise a delicate eyebrow. Doubtless, the dauphin usually doesn't greet common guests. But now he takes Ettie's hand, while keeping his eyes on me, and then takes my hand, and whispers, "Nina—so that is your name," in a quiet tone of victory. He waggles his eyebrows at me as if to communicate something; I assume it is that he is not going to give us away, or to implicate me in the theft of his necklace, and I breathe a sigh of relief. He returns to his sofa, and a servant appears at his left and offers him a silver platter, on which is balanced a tiny cup. He accepts the cup and has a sip. Another servant appears at his right and offers him a folded serviette. He uses it to dab at his lips delicately before returning it to another servant to be taken away.

I decide that he is ridiculous. How many servants does one person need to drink a cup of tea?

A new servant appears and pours black tea. He adds a golden spoon of sugar and a drop of rich cream to each and, after stirring them, extends the tray toward us. Ettie and I both take a cup. The china is whisper-thin, the handle so fragile I'm afraid I'll snap it. It would fetch a tremendous price in the Thieves Guild. I take the smallest sip. The tea is piping hot and creamy. It tastes like heaven.

Yet another servant holds out a tray full of miniature cakes. I recognize them from the larders of the great houses I've robbed. You learn a lot of things when you're hiding in the kitchens of nobility, waiting for the household to fall asleep. One is that cooks are artists of a rare caliber. Another is the names of delicacies served to the wealthy. There are fat réligieuses filled with crème anglaise and topped with salted caramel. Milles-feuilles with their wafer-thin pastry between layers of cream, and dominoed icing. Puits d'amours, delicate tarts filled with almond paste. Charlottes loaded with raspberries. Miniature tarte tatins and plump profiteroles oozing melted chocolate.

I crane my neck to see if there is any bread anywhere, but there is only cake. Perhaps la Reine des Gâteaux was right, and there is nothing else here to eat. But looking on the piles of delicacies, I find my stomach turning.

"What's that one?" Ettie points to a tiny mountain of macarons sandwiched together with fondant. My breath catches; they are so small and simple, so beautifully colored: soft pink for rosewater, red for strawberry, dark brown for chocolate, sienna for *café*. The burned-gold ones are salted caramel, and the white, delicate vanilla.

"That one please." I point at a pale green one. The servant picks it up with silver tongs and places it on a saucer. I look at the macaron, the smallest smudge of green against so much pink-and-gold porcelain.

"That's all?" Ettie asks, surprised. Her plate is piled high with cakes. She's definitely making up for the weeks of hunger.

I can't explain; there's a lump in my throat. How can I be surrounded by such riches when hundreds of my brothers and sisters are dying of starvation? I signal to another servant. He brings a serviette of pink embroidered cloth. I take it and thank him. The prince looks at me, bemused.

"You don't need to thank them," he says in an undertone.

He's right. Gentleman George would smack me for an error that blatant. I turn my mind to a way of bringing the conversation around to the kitchens, and where the larders or bakery might be.

"I've waited years to see you again. I thought I never would," the prince mumbles to me, looking as if he is making bored, polite chatter. "You took the pendant of Charlemagne from me. I was in so much trouble!"

"Did . . . did they beat you?" I ask, curious as to how a dauphin qualifies "trouble."

He turns to me, astonished.

"Beat me? Of course not. Nobody would ever dare beat me."

I splutter into my teacup. "But you said you were in trouble."

"Yes, well, Mother was very disappointed in me, and she does know how to make life extremely uncomfortable when she chooses." He pauses to reflect. "I had a whipping boy when I was younger. . . . What was his name? They would beat him if ever I did anything bad."

A whipping boy. He's worse than ridiculous; he's horrible. I change the subject abruptly. "Do you want it back? The necklace?"

"What? Oh, well, it might be a tad difficult to explain how it's turned up now, after so long," he says dismissively, as if we were discussing a lost glove.

"It is one of the crown jewels of France," I say, deeply reproachful, even while envisioning it around Tomasis's neck, remembering the appreciation it earned me.

"Hmmm, yes . . . ," the dauphin says distractedly.

"Come here, child," the queen says suddenly, beckoning Ettie.

Ettie looks at me nervously.

"There's no need to fear," says the queen. "I just want to see your lovely face."

Ettie inches forward and the queen peers intently at her. Her words are soft and kind, but there's something hungry about the way her eyes bore into Ettie's that makes me think of a spider considering a fly.

"You're *so* lovely. Does she not make the room lovelier simply by being in it, Romain?"

Ettie blushes brilliantly.

"Undoubtedly, *Maman,*" the dauphin agrees.

"Perhaps we should keep her," the queen says.

My heart beats faster at the thought of Ettie remaining in the palace. Wouldn't that be an answer to our troubles? Surely even the Tiger would not be able to take Ettie from the protection of the queen of France. Yet there's a strange tightness in my throat at seeing Ettie here with them. She looks like one of them. And somehow, it hurts.

"You would make a fine companion for the dauphin," the queen continues. "He's quite a lonely boy."

The prince flushes. I'm not sure what he's embarrassed about, or how it's possible to be lonely when there are fifteen people with you at all times.

The queen settles on her perch and taps the seat beside her, inviting Ettie to join her. "Now, will you entertain us, my pet?"

Ettie looks panicked.

"Don't be shy. Perhaps you know a song you could sing us?"

I catch my breath, hoping Ettie doesn't sing any of the songs we know, since they are all quite vulgar.

Ettie thinks. "I can tell you a story."

"How delightful," the queen says.

Ettie has collected so many stories. I silently hope that she repeats none of the saltier ones she's heard.

"This is the tale my Father told, as it's told to all the children of the Dead," she begins. "There was once a country so full to the brim with mice that they overflowed into every city and town."

Rennart's balls!

Not *that* story; not now, not here!

20

Ettie's Tale

At first, Ettie sits ramrod straight, with her back to me so she can't see my expression of warning, and she doesn't turn as I cough loudly.

"Are you all right?" the prince asks, alarmed.

But Ettie doesn't notice me at all. She is concentrating, trying to recount the tale exactly as Orso has told it to her.

I unfold my napkin and tuck the macaron inside, carefully wrapping it, and put it on my lap.

"If you don't like the cakes, we can throw them away," the prince whispers, looking at me curiously.

"I'm sure they're delicious." I've just lost my appetite. Ettie is casually telling the tale of the failed revolution that almost overthrew the royal family, and short of a dramatic intervention, there's nothing I can do to stop her.

"You don't have to keep that one. We can have fresh ones sent up for you whenever you like," the prince insists.

"Leave me alone," I say under my breath.

He stops eating and sits silently while my head spins with possible outcomes. Will we be arrested for repeating the tale? How will we get a message to the Court or Femi if they take us?

"Do they not have a lot of food where you live?" The prince interrupts my plans. The pity lacing his voice is as subtle as a club, causing all my hackles to rise. We are in a time of famine, after all, and someone has failed to tell the dauphin.

"Have you looked outside the gates of the palace recently?" I hiss quietly. "Did you not see anything during your ride through the city today?" I look him straight in the eye. "The bodies are lying in piles on some street corners. People are *starving* to death. When we do have food, we don't throw it away, or have *fresh* food sent up."

He stares at me, dumbfounded.

I don't care. I don't have time to care, or to sit here eating frilly confections while Ettie is repeating seditious tales and I'm meant to be figuring out where the palace grains are stored and how exactly I'm going to get them out of the Tuileries undetected.

As Ettie continues her tale, the atmosphere in the room becomes charged. There's something worrying about the expression on the queen's face, though she continues to smile.

Beside me the prince is sipping his tea, pensive, quiet, annoying.

"The story. What's it about?" he mutters at me.

I'm so amazed he doesn't realize that I momentarily forget how annoying he is.

"It's about the failed revolution. The cats are the nobility, and the mice are the revolutionaries."

At that, the prince's eyes dart from Ettie to his mother, and then to the man in the corner, who has turned around now. He's pale and soft-looking, with a monstrosity of a powdered wig and clothing of delicate baby blue.

I try to get up, but the prince grabs my sleeve and yanks me down.

"Don't. You can't do anything, not now," he says, holding on to my arm tightly. "If *Maman* demands your head, then I'll beg for your life. Don't worry."

Well, that makes me feel so much better.

Ettie's voice grows more dramatic as she describes how the cats managed to summon their brethren, who rescued them from hanging and instead imprisoned the mice.

The room seems unbearably warm and close. I shrug away offers of more tea from the servants. I can't eat or drink; I can barely breathe. I can do nothing but listen as Ettie seals our fate.

The queen grips Ettie's hand as she finishes the tale. I fight the panic building in me.

"Thank you, my dear one," the queen says, planting a

kiss on Ettie's forehead. "Where did you hear that fascinating tale?"

"It—it is known," Ettie answers, thankfully not mentioning Orso or the Guilds.

"Out!" says the man at the desk, his voice sharp and high. "Everyone out."

The queen turns to look at him. She releases Ettie, who slips off the sofa and stumbles toward me, at last feeling the tension in the air around her.

Monsieur Sagouin and the servants move to the door.

Ettie and I rise to go after them. Perhaps if we sneak out now, we can find the kitchens and leave this place before—

"Not you, my dear," the queen says to Ettie, pinning her in place with her eyes.

"What is wrong, Father?" the prince asks the minute the door closes.

The queen opens her mouth to answer but is cut off by the man at the desk, who has risen and is coming to her side.

"What is *wrong*? You dare ask what is *wrong*? Did you think it a good story? Did you pity the mice? For they were indeed so small and so brave, at the mercy of a kingdom of cats!" He snorts.

The prince seems to shrink into himself at the bitterness of the words.

"Are you such a fool that you can't hear? Commoners come into our palace and tell of sedition whispered in the streets. *It is known*. These are the stories our people tell their children?"

"Father, it was only a story. I doubt she even knows what it means. . . ."

"Show him," says the queen. And to my horror, the man starts to unbutton his waistcoat.

"I was a child of six when they took the palace. They came screaming for la Reine des Gâteaux—they made her eat until she was sick, and they took the heads of all her ladies-in-waiting. They forced her to march half naked in the streets, and they made me watch." He loosens his cravat clumsily, as if he is not used to removing his garments himself.

"My mother married into this family at fifteen—younger even than you, Romain. She had no choice in the matter. They would have hated her no matter what she did. She tried to win the people's affection. My father tried. He longed for his people to love him."

He peels the cloth from his skin, and then we see them: deep, jagged scars that crisscross his chest, from neck to navel.

"They held me and my sister for fifteen days—*fifteen days* of relentless beatings. They forced me to tell lies at my mother's trial, to accuse her of unspeakable acts."

The queen sits straight and still, her eyes glittering dangerously.

"If our uncle had not invaded, they would have killed every last noble in the land. Every man, every woman, and every child."

He is shaking, and the queen reaches out and grabs his wrist. I see her knuckles clench white.

"These are the gallant little mice of which this story speaks," he continues. "Willing to torture children, to murder women. These are the helpless heroes of such stories. No matter how you pity them, no matter how you may think they suffer, you cannot lower yourself to their level, because they will always hate you for who you are.

"Instead, you must rule them, control them. You must do as we have always done, as we will continue to do. You must do whatever is necessary to protect the ones you love." His voice breaks a little at that, and he turns away as if he cannot bear to look at his son anymore.

"If these are the stories they are telling in the streets, then things are as we have long suspected," the queen says, looking at the dauphin, her voice as sweet as treacle. "If you think your crown, your blood, or your name will protect you, then you are mistaken, my son. We must show them the same mercy that they are prepared to show us."

She turns abruptly to us. Ettie is practically cowering behind me.

"Don't be afraid, child. We've enjoyed your most illuminating tale." She gives us a far-too-wide smile. "In fact, we are so grateful for the entertainment that we would like to extend our offer of hospitality. We're having a ball tomorrow evening, and we would be enchanted if you would both stay to enjoy the festivities."

Ettie looks delighted by the idea and comes out from behind me to smile shyly at the queen.

But I know better. The queen is clearly dangerous. We

should leave the palace immediately. Once I've found the grain stores we can slip away.

The queen glances at her husband, who is struggling to redo the buttons of his shirt. His belly hangs out, soft and sad, and he looks entirely forlorn. "Come, my dear," she says. She rises and takes him by his elbow, leading him out of the room.

With a swishing of silk on waxed wood floors, she's gone.

21

The Sisters

"I'll accompany you to your chamber," the dauphin says, rising. The doors open for him and he ushers us out.

"Oh, Nina, a ball! Can you think of anything more exciting?" Ettie claps her hands together in delight as we meander down the endless corridors. She turns and sees the look on my face and hesitates. "We can stay for the ball, can't we?"

"You have very little choice," says the dauphin.

I frown.

"It is time for us to leave here, Ettie," I say firmly.

The dauphin pauses. "It's better not to cross Mother," he says. "After all, she is your queen, and her command is law over you."

"What did you say?" I ask in a dangerous voice.

"Well, you're her subjects, so technically you belong to her, and to my father."

"I belong to no one," I say sharply as Ettie grabs my arm.

The prince frowns. "That's just not true. I am the dauphin of France. One day, I'll be king, and everything and everyone will belong to me. You'll belong to me. I can have you arrested if I choose. I can have you executed if I want. I—"

I slap him hard. The sound rings through the corridor like a shot.

"Nina!" Ettie scolds.

The servants gasp and start to come toward us, but the dauphin waves them away.

He stares at me, clutching his cheek in amazement. "You struck me."

"I'll do worse if you ever again presume to tell us we belong to you. We are the Wretched. We belong to no one but our Fathers. You and your kind may rule over most things in this land, but you do not rule over us."

The prince touches his jaw, emotions warring on his face: anger, incredulity, and something else. He straightens his jacket and runs a hand through his hair.

I turn my back on him and keep marching toward our room.

He rushes to keep up with us.

"Forgive me," he says in an uncertain voice.

I'm unimpressed. Ettie, ever kindhearted, is immediately taken in. She goes to him, arms outstretched.

"See, Nina? He's sorry." She strokes his arm soothingly. "We'll stay with you until the ball. We promised your mother we would."

The prince perks up, a smile wreathing his face.

I give a snort. "I'm not here to attend balls," I say.

He looks from me to Ettie and fidgets with the sleeve of his coat. "You told me that there is famine," he says. "If you stay here in the palace, even after the ball, you will never be hungry again. We have plenty of food." His voice is so piteously earnest.

I cross my arms skeptically. "And what of the people outside the palace? What of the Wretched? Should I live here in this gilded cage, stuffing myself with cakes, while they hunger and die? A pile of the stalest scraps from your table would keep them from starvation. Your smallest store of grain would save hundreds of them."

"I didn't know," the prince says quietly.

"You are the dauphin of France. One day, you'll be king, and everything and everyone will belong to you." I repeat his words back to him. "Will you still eat cake then, when your people are starving?"

The prince stands there awkwardly, silent. He has never known hunger, has never wanted for anything. I can't make him understand.

Somehow, we've made it to our chamber door.

"Time to go to bed," I say coldly.

Ettie gives the prince's arm a sympathetic squeeze and comes to join me.

The prince seems pensive; he barely meets our eyes as he inclines his head to us. "I bid you good night, then, mesdemoiselles." He swallows nervously. "A-and I'm sorry for having offended you."

"You are forgiven," Ettie says kindly. "And Nina is sorry for having struck you."

"I am not," I mutter darkly as Ettie shoos me into the room.

⋙⋘

Ettie climbs into the bed after the maids have come to help us out of our gowns.

She looks at me thoughtfully.

"Don't worry," I tell her. "I—"

"I think he likes you," she says.

"What?"

"The prince. I think he likes you."

"Ettie, you think everyone likes me," I say shortly.

"It's true. Montparnasse also likes you."

That takes me aback. I stare at her for a whole minute before I find my voice and choke out, "Don't be silly! Why would either one of them like me?"

"Because you're brave and clever." She grins. "And because you slapped him."

"I would *never* slap the Master of Knives," I say.

Ettie collapses into giggles at the thought.

"Montparnasse is only being good to us because of Lady

219

Corday. She wanted Orso to get out of prison. And anyway, boys don't like girls because they're brave, Ettie."

"Oh?"

"They like them because they're pretty."

"Well, I'm pretty, and Montparnasse definitely doesn't like me." She stretches out her legs and wiggles her toes, frowning. "When you were healing, I asked him to teach me how to fight so that I could protect you if Thénardier ever came for you again. He struck me in face and told me it was my fault, that I had to learn to block properly."

"That's probably Montparnasse's way of declaring true love."

And we laugh, the two of us under the covers, until our sides and our jaws hurt. Then we lie there in the darkness, side by side, until her voice comes again, quietly.

"Sometimes I close my eyes and think I should just let the Tiger take me. If he kills me, at least this will all be over, and you'll be safe." She's shaking, trying to be brave.

"It wouldn't be over." My voice comes out uneven, broken. "If you give yourself up to the Tiger, he won't kill you."

"But you said—"

"I lied. The Tiger doesn't kill people. He—he breaks them." The moonlight reflects off Ettie's eyes as she looks at me. "But they don't die. He destroys everything that's good," I say, taking a deep breath. "I know because he took my sister Azelma."

"You have a sister? Can you rescue her? You're the Black

Cat. You can get in anywhere. You freed the Dead Lord from the Châtelet!"

Ettie's unshakable faith in my abilities should warm my heart, but she's wrong.

"I tried," I say, fighting back tears. "But she wouldn't come. He fed her the poppy, and now she's a slave to him. Even if I could get her out, she'd fight to get back to *it,* to him. That's what the poppy does. She doesn't remember who she is anymore. She doesn't remember me."

I can't go on. I can't bear to put the evil into words.

I pull my dagger from under my pillow and open my hand. I put the blade to my palm and run it across in one swift movement. Droplets of blood bead across the line I've made.

"I won't let him do that to you." I hold out my hand to Ettie. "I swear it."

Ettie takes the dagger and, wincing, draws the blade across her skin. She wrinkles her nose in pain as I put my bleeding palm to hers and we clasp warm, wet fingers, our blood mingling.

"You are my sister now."

"You are my sister now," she whispers.

And I try not to think about Azelma. She was my sister too, once.

We let go and Ettie wipes the dagger blade on her satin pillowcase and hands it back to me. I shake my head.

"Keep it. Montparnasse gave me a new one."

Her eyes light up and she hugs the dagger close to her. Then she throws me a look of pure mischief. "I told you he likes you."

We laugh, talk, and sleep very little. Ettie forces me to tell her more stories.

I tell her the tale of how I stole the giant sapphire necklace that now hangs about Tomasis's neck from the prince. I tell her the stories and rumors about Orso and Corday. I tell her about the Merveilles of the Miracle Court—the Fisherman, le Maire, the Gentleman, the most audacious criminals France has ever seen. I talk until the sun comes up and my voice is hoarse, till Ettie's eyes are bleary and exhausted. Then, holding my hand, she gives in and lets sleep take her.

I should go explore the palace and find what I need, but Ettie's fingers are curled around mine and I can't bear to leave her. For once we are not in imminent danger, we're not starving or hurt; for once we lay together laughing at foolish things. This is how it was with Azelma. To think I'd forgotten what it is not to be afraid.

I lie awake listening to her breathing.

Could Ettie be safe here in the palace? Could she be happy? Surely the Tiger wouldn't dare take her if she were under the protection of the king and queen of France.

But I cannot feel easy with the idea of leaving Ettie with the royals, not after the story she told and the predatory look in the queen's eyes. And I cannot leave the palace without ensuring Ettie's safety from all the Guilds—I must find that grain. But even if such a vast quantity of grain can be taken, will it be enough to stop the Tiger?

She has become a symbol he must destroy. Nothing will stop him. . . . He will have his vengeance or lose the power he holds over us.

What can I, one small Cat, do against a Lord of the Miracle Court with a Guild of henchmen to defend him? Can I ever keep Ettie safe?

22

The Mesmerist

We're awakened by a maid carrying steaming mugs of melted chocolate and cream. I make the maid take a sip first, watch her swallow it, and then insist she stay for a few minutes. When she doesn't pass out or die, I let her go.

Ettie gleefully swallows her chocolate. I sip mine carefully. It's the most delicious thing I've ever tasted. The smell reminds me of the prince's lips, and I feel a pang of guilt mixed with resentment. It's late. We must have slept the whole day.

Ettie looks better. Her face is brighter, and the shadows are gone from beneath her eyes. She hops excitedly off the bed and reminds me that there's a soirée tonight.

I purse my lips. I don't have time for soirées; I haven't yet been able to slip away to search for the grain stores. And it's dangerous for us to stay on in the palace any longer. I have to act tonight.

There are two dresses laid out on a chaise longue. A silvery blue crêpe de chine for Ettie, a salmon gauze for me. The maids bustle in and strip us of our clothes, slip on skirt hoops, and tighten corsets with unnecessary vigor. Then our hair is done and we're adorned with finery. Ettie is given a necklace with a locket, I'm given a bracelet of gold and rubies, and we each get an ornate fan. We slide jeweled slippers over our silk stockings and make faces at one another as we're ushered out.

The ball is a snarling chaos of gold, crystal, and glass. The candlelight from a hundred chandeliers shimmers and bounces off mirrored walls. The air is thick, heaving with the heat of so many bodies made bold by drink, voices merging into a blur of shrieks and cries. Their faces are terrible painted masks of white, their lips blood-red with rouge, and they're unable to hide the fever that burns within them: a strange, violent madness laced up with linen stays and clothed in velvet and silk.

"This is horrible," Ettie says finally.

But for me it's a good chaos, the kind that will let me slip away to explore the palace.

"I don't much enjoy balls," the prince admits, appearing at our side and ruining all my plans. "But now that you're here, it will be much better," he adds, evidently cheered at the thought.

The prince points out several persons of interest, which bores me to tears, until I spot the flash of bright blue, brass, and red. The inspector is stationed at one corner of the room, looking grim. I spot three other Sûreté officers standing conspicuously in various alcoves.

"We could dance," the prince suggests, eyeing me hopefully.

There's loud music coming from one end of the ballroom. It fights against the nobles' shrill voices.

Ettie laughs. "We don't know how to dance," she says, watching the couples gliding around the floor in perfect time. "Not like that."

"No one taught you to dance?" The prince looks at me.

I lift my chin defiantly. Gentleman George hasn't yet taught me all the courtly dances.

"I had other things to learn, Your Worshipfulness," I answer.

He smiles and bows. "Mademoiselle," he says to me sotto voce. "Will you give me the honor of this waltz?"

I frown. "She just told you we don't know how."

He reaches out his hand. "Then let me teach you."

I could refuse him; I'll embarrass myself if I accept. What do I know but the wild *hyène* dances of the Miracle Court?

Ettie nudges me from behind, trying to get me to accept. She likes the prince. She likes that the prince likes me.

I sigh and take his hand. His face lights up, and I feel a

small thrill. He's standing there like an idiot, not letting go, not leading me anywhere.

"Aren't we going to dance?"

"Yes," he answers, clutching my fingers like they're jewels. "But first I must celebrate this hard-won victory."

The dauphin stops a servant. "Champagne," he tells us as the servant passes us each a glass of sparkling pink liquid.

I look at the glass, admiring the tiny bubbles in it. As I lift it to my lips, my ears suddenly prick up, making out a whistle so low it's nigh impossible to hear through the din. The hair on the back of my neck rises as I identify it; it's a rare call, one I was taught but have never heard used: the call of the Assassins Guild.

My eyes widen, and I see a dark face watching me from the other side of the hall.

Montparnasse.

I almost drop my glass, snatching my hand from the prince's. He protests, but I ignore him. My eyes sweep the room.

A servant moving through the crowd catches my eye; he's dressed as a waiter, but the points of his collar are starched exceedingly sharp and high. It is Col-Blanche, Master of the House of Poisons.

Two Assassins, here in the palace?

I swing around again. Scores of Assassins are here, carrying trays of champagne.

"Drink *nothing*!" I hiss urgently.

Ettie and the prince look at me.

"Stay with her," I order the prince. "Don't leave her alone for a second, and don't eat or drink a thing, *either* of you!"

My stomach is tying itself in knots as I make my way through the crowd toward Montparnasse, their raucous laughter ringing in my ears like the bells of Saint-Sulpice, like some terrible nightmare I can't escape.

When I get to where he was standing, no one is there. I poke my head through a frosted-glass door to the balcony and he grabs me, dragging me out into the night, crushing me against him with a finger to my lips, just as two Sûreté officers step into the exact spot I where was standing. The door is only open a crack, but we can hear their low conversation behind us.

". . . deserve a demotion for your behavior yesterday, Inspector Javert."

"Forgive me," the inspector murmurs.

"You can't lose your head each time you think you see Valjean."

"I don't *think* I saw him—he was there." Through the crack in the door I can just see her turn her head slightly toward the man beside her. "In all the years I've worked for you, when have I ever been mistaken?" Her tone is reproachful. "Valjean is the key to the whole criminal underworld."

The officer sighs. "There's no proof that this underworld exists."

She flinches. "How can you say that? You've seen the reports. They date back years—"

"Rumors and old wives' tales. We've no solid evidence.

And the fact remains that you had a duty to protect the procession, a duty you failed to attend to when you gave chase to a convict. The events on the bridge might have been disastrous. The dauphin was injured."

An uncomfortable silence follows.

"It won't happen again."

"It had better not." The man shakes his head, and they move away from the door, doing circuits of the room as they speak.

It's begun to snow. The tiny flakes land on my skin like icy pinpricks.

Montparnasse is still holding on to the gauze of my dress, and I realize I can't breathe. I'm not sure if it's because of the inspector or the Assassins—or him.

"The prince was holding my hand because he was about to teach me to dance," I say before I can stop myself.

His expression is unreadable.

"What are you doing here?" I snap, annoyed with myself for explaining the situation to him.

"Lord Orso sends his regards."

He looks into my eyes, and I wish I could tell what he is thinking.

"Don't let her drink anything," he adds. Then he releases me and is gone.

One thing has become clear: if the Assassins can sneak into the palace unnoticed, then so can the Tiger's men. Ettie is not safe, not even here.

I have to think. Something will occur tonight. Montparnasse

didn't have to warn me, but he did. Which means there's still a chance I can find what I came for and sneak away with Ettie before it happens.

I find Ettie and the prince at the back of the ballroom. The music has stopped and everyone is gathered around, talking excitedly.

I get to Ettie and whisper in her ear, *"We have to go."*

She starts to follow me, but the prince sees us leaving and grabs my arm, asking where we're going.

"I must fetch something in my room," I lie.

"I can send a servant."

"No. Please. It's important."

"But a mesmerist has come. Don't you want to see her? It was a last-minute engagement, but she's said to be remarkable."

I look up. Everyone is on their feet, facing a small stage decorated with exotic objects. A gong echoes through the ballroom, and a hushed excitement steals over the crowd.

"*Messieurs et mesdames,* please welcome la Grande Meresmo."

The crowd claps enthusiastically. An eerie high-pitched music begins to play as la Meresmo enters. She is veiled, draped in layers of silk, with a belt of coins around her waist and a turban on her head. Her eyes are blackened with kohl, her hands and wrists covered with rings and bracelets. Nonetheless, there's no mistaking those eyes. It's Lady Corday.

"Ettie, we *must* go."

"Oh, but, Nina, can't we watch?" Ettie doesn't recognize the Lady of the Assassins Guild in her costume.

"You've heard of the mystical powers of the mesmerists." Corday's voice rings out. "Men and women who studied the dark arts, learning to make others obey their commands. Perhaps we'll start with a volunteer." Corday looks around. She crooks a finger. "Madame Langur," she says.

Madame Langur looks horrified; she turns to the queen, who nods approval, and the lady reluctantly gives in. She goes to the stage and is helped up by two servants.

"Madame, have you ever been a sparrow?" Corday asks.

Madame Langur is confused.

Corday moves her fan back and forth in a slow and steady motion. "No, of course you haven't." She fixes the woman with an intense stare. "Look at me, madame. Look directly at me, and don't look away."

Madame Langur's eyes follow the fan.

"Now sleep!" Corday says.

Madame Langur freezes. She remains upright, but her head lolls forward, and in the hush that follows, she starts to snore.

The ballroom erupts in rapturous applause.

Corday waits for it to calm, then says, "When I snap my fingers, you will awake a sparrow. Now . . . *moineau!*"

As Corday snaps her fingers, Madame Langur opens her eyes and, putting her head to one side, begins to twitter like a bird. The audience cheers uproariously. The queen looks positively enthralled.

Corday claps her hands and Madame Langur ceases all movement.

"*Reveillez-vous.*" Corday snaps her fingers.

Madame Langur gives a start, as if shocked out of a deep sleep. She looks around, disoriented.

"Thank you, madame."

Corday's servants help Madame Langur back to the audience.

"It's my pleasure to amaze you. Now, for my next feat, I'll attempt something quite out of the ordinary."

A boy brings her a tray, and from it Corday picks up a long chain that ends in a censer, smoking with sweet incense.

"I'll ask you all to watch this vessel attentively." She swings the chain back and forth in a repetitive motion.

I look for Montparnasse, but I can't find him.

"Don't look away. Look only at the vessel. Keep your eyes upon it. Don't let it out of your sight."

"Ettie, we need to go."

But Ettie's eyes are glued to the censer.

Corday swings the chain back and forth in large arcs.

"Ettie!"

Corday claps twice. I shake Ettie. She won't even look at me. I turn to the dauphin, and he, too, is staring, mouth agape. In fact, as I look around, gone are the expressions of merriment and wonder: the whole audience is staring, slack-jawed, at Corday's censer. Just like when we left her Guild.

The trick, little Cat, is not to look, Corday said to me earlier, and I've been looking for Montparnasse, away from her and the swinging chain.

"You may all sit down," Corday says.

The nobles collapse like children playing a game. Everyone

in the room sits, except for the Assassins, who remain standing, eyes averted. I lower myself as well and watch from the corner of my eye, making sure not to look directly at Corday.

"Now I'll ask a question." Her voice has lost its mysterious timbre. This is the Corday I'm used to.

I see Col-Blanche.

"Who gave the order to poison the city wells?" She looks over the crowd. "Rise to your feet."

An older man rises and stands perfectly still, gazing expressionlessly at Corday.

I bite my lip. St. Juste's tests must have provided Orso proof of the poisoning.

Col-Blanche takes a bottle from one of the trays and pours it into several glasses.

Corday continues. "Who came up with the idea to put sickness in the water?"

Three more gentlemen stand.

"And who will tell me why it was done?"

The first gentleman opens his mouth and speaks in a cold, distant voice. "Grain was running short," he drones. "Famine was coming, and when there is hunger, the commoners rise up. We thought to reduce their numbers. Incapacitate them to avoid the uprisings we faced last time."

"Who else knew this was being done?"

Twenty more rise. Among them are Madame Langur, Monsieur Sagouin, the king, and the queen.

There in the background, Montparnasse is watching me, his face its usual blank mask.

233

Corday bows to the royals with delicate deference, and as she rises, she looks straight at the queen.

"Your Majesties."

For the first time in my life, I see Corday's face betray actual feeling: a brilliant, burning hatred. I shiver. I'd not for anything in the world have Corday look at me like that.

"Messieurs Mandrille, Vervet, and Tarsier, you have no children," Corday says, turning to the other Lords.

"No, madame," they drone back at the stage.

"Very well, then. I drink to your health."

The Assassins disperse and bring a glass of champagne to each of the gentlemen mentioned. Corday mimes raising a glass in the air.

"*Santé,*" she says, and they drink.

"And the rest of you all have children."

"Yes, madame," they reply.

"Then I have a gift for you."

The Assassins move through the room, handing a small glass bottle with a stopper to each standing person. The queen takes hers and clutches it tightly to her chest.

"You will give it to the child you love the most and make sure they drink the fullness of it."

I turn in horror to the prince, who is staring, dazed, at the stage. Panic races through me, along with the realization that somehow, I don't dislike him as much as I thought, since I definitely don't want him to die.

"Yes, madame," the queen says.

23

Les Diamants de la Couronne

Corday smiles.

"From this day forth, whoever even thinks of putting death in the waters of this city will cast their own hand into the flames until it is ruined."

"Yes, madame," the whole room echoes.

"And when I clap my hands, you'll awaken and forget all that has been said."

She claps her hands twice and everyone starts, as if waking from a dream. They murmur and mutter. Then they see they're all on the floor and begin to giggle like children, pointing at each other. Corday takes a deep bow before disappearing from the stage in a puff of heavily scented smoke. Thunderous applause breaks out all around us.

I shake Ettie and the dauphin. They are slow to wake.

"Get up, both of you. Now."

They frown blearily at me as I drag them to their feet.

"We have to get out of here."

Several nobles have been poisoned tonight. Who knows if it is contagious. Who knows what might happen next.

"Ah, there's my son," the queen calls over my shoulder.

Think, Nina. Think!

I grab the prince by the lapels of his velvet coat and he blinks at me.

"Don't drink it," I hiss urgently in his ear.

His eyes widen in confusion.

"My son!" The queen is before us, the king at her side.

I let go of the dauphin's jacket, and we bow to them.

"I have something for you," she says, holding out the crystal bottle to the prince. "I saved it especially for you." She smiles at him, her eyes soft and kind. "Will you drink it for me?"

The dauphin's eyes dart to me, then to his mother.

"Come," the queen presses. "We'll drink it together."

I grab the prince's sleeve and give it a tug.

A servant gives the queen an empty glass. She pours the clear liquid into it and hands it to her son.

He stares at the glass. He can't refuse. She's the queen. He's not allowed to say no.

I catch Ettie's eye. She's not a fool. She's noticed Montparnasse by now, as well as Col-Blanche. Two of the Court's most notorious Assassins are in the room, and drinks are being handed out. I wink and she nods in response.

The prince takes the glass, and with a last apologetic glance at me, he raises it slowly to his lips.

Ettie gives a giant sneeze and stumbles straight into him, knocking the glass out of his hand. I pretend to stumble too, and step on the king's foot. He yelps and hops away. I follow, clutching at his sleeve, begging his forgiveness in a manner so obsequious, it would cause anyone who knew me to stare. He shakes me off in annoyance and hobbles away. His snuff-box is now in my pocket.

"Oh, what a shame!" The queen surveys the spilled drink. "I shall find you another."

I glance around for the Assassins, but they seem to have disappeared.

Our time is running out.

"Don't drink *anything* your mother gives you. You must promise me this," I order the prince in an undertone. Then I turn to Ettie. "We have to go," I hiss.

She nods, and we wait till the queen's back is turned before we flee, leaving the prince watching his mother with fear in his eyes.

>✦✦✦✦✦✦✦✦✦✦✦✦<

A well-timed crash on a lower floor is enough to send the guards racing away from the door with many locks, the one we passed on the way to the queen's chambers yesterday. Then it takes only a moment of concentration for me to pick the locks.

We step inside and are stunned motionless by the sight of les Diamants de la Couronne: the crown jewels of France.

"We shouldn't be in here," Ettie says in awe.

I ignore her and step forward.

There are Fabergé eggs, heavy scepters of ivory, orbs of pure obsidian. The largest diamond I've ever seen adorns a hat belonging to a dead queen. A heavy, ancient crown of brutish gold embossed with a fleur-de-lys motif sits on an ermine cushion. There are rings, necklaces, and earrings of every stone and pearl imaginable.

"That's the Grand Sapphire." I point to a giant blue stone. "They say it's without flaw."

And then there's the king's crown. Its gold brocade cap, arches, and circlet are adorned with diamonds and colored gemstones set between two rows of pearls.

"Those are the Mazarin stones. That's the Sancy. And the Regent Diamond," I whisper.

There's also a large Bible covered in jewels, and several items of weaponry. I pocket a small dagger with a ruby in its hilt before moving on to the stunning collection of crowns, tiaras, and diadems. I reach for one.

"Nina, you can't steal a crown!" Ettie is aghast.

"Why not?"

"Because they'll notice."

I go to the largest tiara, with blue and white stones, and I pick it up.

"Nina, we *can't*!"

"Are you stealing from me again?" asks an amused voice.

I freeze. "These belong to your parents," I say carefully, "so technically I'm stealing from them." I turn slowly to find the prince behind us, relieved to see that he is alone.

"I can't let you take that," he says.

I feel my temper fraying; I'm running out of time. "This is just another piece of jewelry to your family, but it means everything in the whole world to me, because with it I might be able to keep Ettie alive."

He shakes his head.

"Give it to me," he says.

"Take it then, *Votre Altesse*." I thrust the tiara at him. "But know this: If anything happens to Ettie, I'll come for you. No matter where you are, I'll find you. Nothing will keep you safe from me. Not the high walls of your palace, the number of your guards, or the riches of your parents. I'm the Black Cat of the Thieves Guild. There's nowhere I can't enter. I'll come for you in the night, and I'll cut out your tongue so you can't cry for help. I'll cut you open so you bleed slowly, and I'll leave you to die just as you lived—all alone in your beautiful golden palace."

I'm trembling as I finish, the words of my oath heavy on my tongue. Ettie is behind me. I can practically feel her cowering.

The prince's eyes never leave my face. He doesn't seem frightened or upset. He looks thoughtful.

He takes the tiara gently from my hand and looks at it appraisingly. He walks past me and goes to put it back.

I close my eyes; so be it. I can knock him out and take

the tiara. I'm sure he won't fight me, not the way I fight. I ready myself, dagger in hand, just in case, but when he turns around, he's holding another tiara. An older one with even bigger stones, all pure white and glimmering.

"Take this one," he says. "It belonged to Margaret de Valois. It's worth far more than the other, and Mother hates it. She might not even miss it."

I stare. Ettie sobs and throws her arms around him. He seems bemused but lets her hug him and blushes when she kisses his cheek. Then he notices the dagger in my hand.

"Were you going to stab me?"

"Maybe," I say quietly, putting the dagger away.

I take the tiara and pry Ettie from him.

"We have to leave. We must find Corday and the others. They're our best chance of getting out of the palace."

"I've organized a carriage," the prince says awkwardly.

I nod.

"I'd have given you the tiara even if you hadn't threatened me," he says.

If I knew how to apologize, I might do so. But words of regret don't come easily to my lips. Instead, I say in a shaking voice, "Don't drink anything she gives you. Ever. Promise me."

It's the best that I can do.

"I promise," he says.

24

The Bread Price

We find Corday near the stables, where a retinue of carriages stands waiting. Corday motions to Ettie and me to join her. We slip into a carriage after her and are joined by Montparnasse. I sit poker-straight and alert as the carriage starts to move, still marveling at the implications of Corday's performance tonight. Ettie, however, is so exhausted she doesn't even seem worried about sharing a carriage with the Lady of the Assassins Guild.

She curls up and starts to fall asleep, her head resting on my shoulder.

I stay awake because no one in their right mind falls asleep in a carriage with two Assassins. For a long while we are silent. My stomach is all knots. I have failed to get the bread price.

I can feel Montparnasse's eyes on me, watching with the long silence that the Death Dealers have perfected. It sets my teeth on edge.

Corday clears her throat and I tense.

"I think you could go far, little Cat," Corday says. "I think you could in time be the Lady of Thieves."

I frown darkly. "I have no desire to be Lady of Thieves," I say, though I recall my conversation with Tomasis.

Corday's lips quirk slightly at the corners; she is amused at my reaction. "All Guild Lords in their time must also lie down to die. We're not immortal."

I turn my head away, as if that will stop me from hearing her words. To suggest I could one day be Lady of Thieves is to envision Tomasis's death. Tomasis, my Father, who took me in and protected me, whose care has been a shield around me. How could I think of a world without him in it?

"Death the Endless comes to us all," Corday says, as if reading my mind. "There's nothing to fear in the grave. But while we live, it is instability that we should fear. The Guilds need strong, ruthless Lords who are not afraid to maintain peace at any cost."

"Even at the cost of the Law?" I bite out, thinking of the Tiger.

Corday smiles, baring her teeth. "You must make your enemies your allies. And if you can't do that, then destroy them. Them, and all who follow them, so that fear doesn't come for you when you sleep."

We ride along in the darkness, Corday's words echoing

in my head. She's clearly been driven half mad by too many assassinations, to speak in such riddles.

"Who paid the blood price for the death work this evening?" I ask. It is a bold question, but Corday seems inclined to talk. "How many of the Guild's children partook of the water before it was known that it carried death? Did Orso send you to avenge what the nobility have done?"

Corday looks out the carriage window before speaking, and maddeningly, her answer is not a response to any question I have asked. "Is it known that those who join the Wretched shed their old skin, forgetting what came before. But sometimes, in the darkness, I remember.

"Once, many years ago, when I was a Child Who Walks by Day, I had kin, blood relatives, who could not bear the shape of the world in which they lived. So they decided to change it. They were very brave, and very naïve. For what person can truly ever change the fate of a nation? They were betrayed one day, surrounded by enemies. They knew they had failed and there was nothing more they could do. So they chose to stand and face Death the Endless. Their enemies set their hiding place on fire to burn them out, and they gave themselves to the flames rather than be taken.

"It was Orso who saved me. He had a different name then. He was a friend of my father's, and it was he who carried me from the flames."

So the rumors are true. Orso saved Corday's life when she was young. No wonder the Ghosts and the Bats are such firm allies.

"If I lived a thousand years, I could never repay the debt I owe. It is deeper than blood and bone, stronger than iron. For if the Dead Lord had not taken me into the sewers, if he had not brought me to the Court and sworn me to the service of the Death Dealers, I would have been hunted down and slaughtered like a dog in the streets. My body would have hung at Montfaucon, dancing on the wind, a feast for the crows."

I remember this. *All the families and allies of the revolutionaries were hunted down, and none were spared; wives, children, all blood, all kin bearing their name, all were fed to the guillotine or hung at Montfaucon as a message.*

"So I was not sent tonight," she says, turning to me, her eyes shining. "No Guild paid a blood price for tonight's work. It was done willingly, for when we learned what they had done, we could not let it go unpunished."

Her voice is ice.

"You sit here in this carriage, little one, and you think yourself safe because I am telling you stories. You think you can trust me because I am allied with the Dead Lord. But I tell you the truth, and mark it, for it will be your salvation: it is not wise to be so vulnerable." She gestures to Ettie. "She is your heart, and anyone who strikes at her wounds you. No child of the Guilds can hope to survive with a weakness so exposed.

"There are no friends in the Miracle Court, only allies. You may think you have purchased her freedom tonight, but others will come for her eventually, including those you think are your friends, those you believe you can trust."

A shiver runs through me, for I *don't* have the bread price. How am I to protect Ettie without it? And if Corday is to be believed, any safety I buy her won't last. I fight to keep my lips from trembling.

The carriage slows to a stop. Montparnasse alights. I wake Ettie and we climb out.

Some Assassins have gathered in the cold, near the carriage behind our own. Behind it are a dozen more carriages, all bearing the royal insignia.

"What's going on?" Ettie asks.

Montparnasse beckons to me. I approach him warily.

"The dauphin gave strict orders that these carriages were to accompany us," he says, pointing at an open door. The Assassins step aside for me, and I have little choice but to peer inside.

"Oh, Nina!" Ettie says breathlessly beside me.

For the carriage is full of bread, from floorboards to roof. I look at the line of carriages behind us and hurry to the second one, yanking open its door. This one is filled with dozens of bags of grain, all full to bursting, as are the next and the next and the next. . . .

<hr />

Two nights pass before the Miracle Court is convened. The air burns with the light of a thousand candles illuminating the Lords at the high table. Corday comes in, followed by her Assassins, who are bearing armfuls of bread. She takes her place among the Lords and calls me forward. My eyes are drawn to Lord Kaplan, who watches me with steely intent. I try not to shiver.

The Assassins put the bread on the table before the Lords; they pile it high until it makes a mountain and starts tumbling onto the floor. The Court has not seen so much bread in one place in years, and the sacks of grain will ensure that none of the court's children will go to bed hungry tonight, or for months to come.

"Speak then, little Cat," Corday tells me.

I step forward, shaking from head to toe, not sure whom to look at. Tomasis, Femi, Orso, and Loup are all watching me.

"I offer the bread price for Ettie, daughter of the Dead Lord," I say. "I have paid the full price, as witnessed by my brethren," I add, looking to Corday. "In a time of famine, there can be no higher price to pay."

"There is no higher price to pay," the Lords murmur as one.

"I have paid this price to buy my sister's freedom. She's a child of the Beggars Guild. By the Law, none shall touch her."

"None shall touch her," they repeat.

I risk a look at the Tiger. Before, Ettie had only the protection of the Beggars Guild. But now all the Guilds are sworn to protect her. That is what I've bought with carriages full of bread and grain.

In the shadows I see Thénardier turn to leave, his face twisted into a grimace, his ruined arm tucked into his coat.

I've stolen his hand and his pride, and I've stolen Ettie from him yet again.

Tomasis motions to me, and I approach him, bowing respectfully.

"My Lord." I present him with the small shining snuffbox. "It belongs to the dauphin of France."

Tomasis laughs and throws his arm around my shoulder, dragging me to himself and squeezing me till I can barely breathe.

There in the warmth of his embrace I feel safer than ever before. I can almost forget that Tomasis would not defy the Tiger to save Ettie—this man who has cared for me more than Thénardier ever has. He's the only true Father I've known.

"I don't know if I prefer this or the tin cup," he says, his eyes sparkling. "First the Châtelet, and now the palace? You will be surely be a Merveille of the Miracle Court. They'll sing songs about you when you're dead and gone. You'll be more famous than le Maire and the Gentleman!" He pounds my back, almost knocking the wind out of me.

I look around. Femi is hovering nearby; he winks.

Ettie is being accosted by Gavroche and is hand-feeding him bread.

When I join her, she glances pointedly at Montparnasse. He's standing alone in a shadow. She disentangles herself from Gavroche and, taking my hand, drags me over to the Assassin.

"Cat," he says to me. "Ghost," to Ettie.

Ettie nudges me.

"I got you something from the palace," I say.

"Why?" he asks.

I flush. "To thank you for warning us . . . at the ball—"

"She got you a present because you're friends." Ettie cuts off my awkward explanation.

Montparnasse watches me with fascination. I fumble in my pockets, find the jeweled dagger, and hold it out to him. He looks at my hand as if I'm offering him a snake.

"Go on. Take it."

He accepts the dagger cautiously and examines it, tilting it so it glimmers in the light.

"There are no friends to children of the Miracle Court," he says, echoing Corday's words. "There are allies, or enemies. Nothing else."

He walks away, leaving Ettie huffing at his rudeness yet whispering that she still thinks he likes me.

As he goes, he tucks the dagger inside his cloak, so perhaps there's something to what she says after all.

Then the frenzy starts. The Lords rise. Their Masters divide the bread, and it's given out to the Court. Everyone eats. Some only a mouthful, keeping the rest for children or sick ones at home.

Femi approaches and sweeps me up, dragging me into a whirl of a dance that has no steps. I hold on tight as he swings me around. The room spins, grows distant, and I'm laughing so hard I can barely breathe.

Then there's wine, which is always plentiful. Loup brings

us our cups. We all drink deeply. The Ghosts and Thieves gather around, demanding to hear the tale of how we got the bread and where we've been. There are songs and stories, and Ettie is there beside me, her voice raised in laughter. For hours we sit, leaning against the stage till rolling waves of tiredness hit us. Ettie grins sleepily at me, her eyes narrow slits. She yawns widely and I laugh at her.

She twines her fingers around mine and leans her head on my shoulder.

"You'll be safe, I promise," I whisper.

We can both rest for now. Here, in the warmth of the Miracle Court, everything will be all right.

Sometime later, I hear my name being called, but my eyes are heavy and refuse to open. My tongue feels like it's stuck to the roof of my mouth, as if I've swallowed glue. I force my eyelids apart.

Montparnasse is looking at me, an odd expression on his usually blank face. He looks . . . *concerned?*

Another person swims into view. Short, bald, with round spectacles and a long, pointed bleached collar.

Col–Blanche, Master of Poisons.

I give a start and pull myself up, moving as far from the Poison Master as I can. My clumsy body fails me, and I smash into a wall lined from floor to ceiling with shelves and stoppered glass bottles, which crash to the ground around me. I yelp and skitter away as the Poison Master, frowning his disapproval, inspects the damage.

I hunch in a corner on all fours like a cat.

"Calm down." Montparnasse's voice rings through my head.

The Poison Master potters around muttering darkly, picking up several vials I've spilled.

I taste metal.

"What happened?" I ask, panicked.

"You were drugged," Col-Blanche says matter-of-factly. I try to stand, but the room spins around me. Montparnasse is at my side, gripping me below my arm, helping me up.

"By whom?"

"By us," Col-Blanche says, busily uncorking bottles and testing them with a slim silver spoon. "We were paid for it."

"*What?*" Montparnasse snaps, glaring at Col-Blanche.

"Clearly, it was not meant to be fatal," Col-Blanche says. "Just something to make you indisposed for a few hours, per instructions."

I look desperately at Montparnasse, who shakes his head. *He didn't know.*

"How long have I been . . ." My voice trails off. There's something else. There is actual worry in the eyes of Montparnasse, he who never shows his feelings. There's something he needs to tell me. And he's worried about how I'll react.

"Where is she?"

"Gone," he says quietly. "They were dressed like Ghosts when they carried her away."

I push away from him as if he himself has betrayed me. I find the door, but it's closed.

"I've something here that might lessen the side effects." Col-Blanche pulls a bottle off a shelf.

There's no time.

I fumble at the door for a moment and then with all my strength burst through it.

Behind me I hear Col-Blanche tutting at Montparnasse. "I realize she has Corday's favor, but nonetheless, you show a remarkable attachment to the girl. It's not healthy in a Death Dealer."

But I don't care.

I'm already gone.

25

The Stripes of the Cat

I know where she is. There is only one person who would dare take Ettie from under the nose of her Guild and all the Lords of the Miracle Court.

Thénardier.

The snow and my grogginess slow me down. I run as fast as I can, ignoring the bite of the cold wind that howls at me as I go.

I round the corner near Thénardier's inn in time to see a large man climb into a carriage.

I call out, but he's closed the door; the wind swallows my words. And then the carriage is moving away.

There's a flash at the window: golden curls and large eyes.

A voice that cannot be my own screams her name.

A small hand presses against the glass. She sees me.

I run behind the carriage, slipping in the snow, my voice tearing at my throat as I call for her, over and over, even as the horses drag her farther away. My limbs are like lead, stiff and slow, but still I run. I run even when the carriage has gone so far I can no longer see it. I run as if I believe I can still catch it. I run as if to stop would be to give up on her. I run until all that is before me is covered in white. My knees buckle and I fall, my hands trembling as they hit the icy ground.

My voice is spent. The cold seeps into my skin and settles in my bones.

Someone is breathing, heavy racked breaths, but it can't be me. There's the pounding of a heartbeat in my ears, but it can't be mine.

Montparnasse finds me waiting for the snow to drown me. He takes off his cloak and wraps it around me.

"No." I fight him feebly. He's stronger than I am. He drags me to my feet and half carries me, my frozen limbs refusing to hold me up.

We stumble for what seems like hours through the snow. Everything is a blur: faces, darkness. The taste of blood on my lips. At first I don't know where he's taking me, but then I realize he's heading away from the city, toward the Halls of the Dead. Where I can be surrounded and protected.

I stop. "I'm going back there."

"No."

I turn on him, my fists pounding, legs kicking, finger-nails clawing at the edges of his cloak. He's the Master of the Assassins Guild, but he lets me attack him, his head bowed.

"I'm going back. You don't have to come with me."

He just looks at me.

The bells of Notre-Dame are ringing, the heavy peals vibrating through me.

It's time.

I hear the voice of the city around me: a beast, half mad with pain, clawing at my ears, demanding that I listen. Its pulse beats through the cobblestones, anchoring my steps as I climb up unscalable slippery walls that fall away beneath my fingers. But I'm the Black Cat of the Thieves Guild, and this is my hunting ground.

The bells ring out as I go. I hear the song they sing. The sky above me rolls and thunders. The buildings churn and shake. Around me, a screaming wind is roaring in my ears. Beneath me the streets cry out; above me the rooftops seem to shriek and wail. They say only one thing, but they say it over and over, like a soldier beating a drum.

My sister.

My sister.

My sister.

I enter through the roof. The rigging at the top of the Miracle Court is a disarray of ropes and scaffolding, a death trap for one less experienced than I. But I feel only determination. There's a blur of silence. My breath comes in shallow gasps. My eyes are needle focused.

I can see them from up here. The Nine Lords of the Miracle Court, still drinking and talking. The entire Court is present.

Good.

I take my dagger from my sleeve and put it between my teeth, biting hard on the blade.

I look down. The table is almost beneath me. It's heavy with the Lords' purses, their gilded knives; their jackets and cloaks are slung on the backs of chairs. I see the sapphire stone at Tomasis's neck, and the gray of Orso's head. I reach for the ropes, find the right one, and take hold of it.

I'm not afraid. Not anymore.

I leap into the air, as graceful as a ballerina, and land on all fours like a cat in the middle of the Lords' table.

The Lords jump back. All but the Tiger. He's afraid of nothing. He sits completely still, holding his drink, a look of faint confusion on his face. After all, no one attacks the Lords. It is forbidden. No one attacks them in front of the Court. One would have to be mad to do that.

They don't know what to do. It's their second full day of drinking. They're slow, and I have always been fast. Some of them reach for their daggers as the Masters thunder onto the stage, yelling.

The Tiger's eyes focus on me and widen in recognition, but he still doesn't rise or go for a weapon. He just looks at me as I lunge for him, howling. He doesn't raise his hands to protect himself as my dagger flies through the air. It slices his cheek, and he jerks away as I land on top of him.

I stab my dagger with all of my strength into his arm as we fall. He makes a noise like a growl, and I see blood flower at his shoulder.

A hundred hands pull me off him.

Corday takes my dagger.

Orso is holding me. His hands bind my arms painfully behind my back. I don't kick. I don't fight. I do nothing. But my eyes never leave the Tiger.

"You are no Lord." My voice is jagged. It makes him wince more than the wound. "You are not fit to be in this Court."

Orso tries to put a scaly hand to my mouth, but I bite him and he lets go.

"You bring only dishonor," I say, and the Tiger rises like a terrible vengeance before me. He ignores his bleeding arm and brings his face right before my own.

"You have no Law," I say.

He strikes me then, and the world spins. There is blood in my mouth, blood streaming down my face. I look at him and I laugh.

He calls for his Master, Lenoir, and says, "Fetch my whip."

They tie me to a chair and huddle behind me, their muffled voices pitched in confusion.

"She insults a Lord."

"Yet did she say anything that was untrue?"

"She attacked a Lord before the whole Court."

"We cannot allow it. An example must be made."

The Tiger is not with them; he stands in front of me so I can see him. He studies me, fascinated, as if he's never seen me before. He ignores the blood still dripping from his shoulder. He knows I could have stabbed him in the heart, that I could have killed him. He knows I wanted to do something much worse: Humiliate him. Speak the truth in front of the entire Court. No matter what happens to me now, they'll whisper about it forever. My words will chase him day and night, and he'll never escape from them. The Cat who looked the Tiger in the eye and called him Lawless before his brethren, something the other Lords have never dared to do.

Montparnasse murmurs something to Corday. She speaks to Orso, and fury crosses Orso's face. He steps toward the Tiger.

"Where is she?" he asks.

The Tiger looks away from me, meeting Orso's face with confusion.

"Where is the child Ettie?"

The Tiger looks from Orso back to me. "I've no idea. I don't have her." Then he shakes his head and asks, "Where's Thénardier?"

Femi is at Tomasis's side; he whispers in Tomasis's ear. Tomasis shakes his head; Thénardier isn't here.

The Tiger throws back his head and laughs. The sound of it echoes around the Court and bounces off the walls.

"Left early, did he?" he spits. "And so he got his price in the end."

"Kaplan . . . ," Orso says. His voice rumbles a low threat.

"I didn't take her," the Tiger answers.

"Liar!" I cry.

He turns back to me.

"I'm many things, little kitten, but a liar is not one of them."

The room is silent, because everyone knows he speaks the truth. The Tiger has never lied. He's never had cause to. He says whatever he wants because he's not afraid of anything or anyone.

"If Thénardier has anything to do with this," Tomasis says, swallowing his rage as he speaks, "then it was done without the knowledge of the Guild of Thieves."

Orso, tense and watchful, looks from Tomasis to the Tiger.

"The Thieves would not touch one of your children, Orso," Tomasis insists. He's worried about what might happen if his Master conspired with the Tiger to take my sister.

Orso fixes him with a hard stare and then finally nods.

The Tiger comes back to me, crouches, and smiles so wide the scars on his face are stretched taut.

"If Thénardier did this, then the jackal has played us both," he says to me.

I growl in response.

He stands, raises his good arm, and in a loud voice says, "Look well, O Wretched. Let all the Court be witness to my oath. If I had taken the girl, I'd have told you, Black Cat of the Thieves Guild. Because I would have wanted to see your face, knowing she was mine." He pauses and looks at me. "Nonetheless, you've broken the Law that you so fondly speak of. You've insulted and attacked a Guild Lord here, in the Miracle Court." His eyes flicker toward Orso and Tomasis. "It is forbidden," he says in tones of glee. "An example must be made."

The Lords say nothing. Their silence condemns me.

Lenoir, the half-blind Master of the Flesh Guild, arrives, huffing and puffing. He drops to one knee and presents the Tiger with his whip. A cruel leather cat-o'-nine-tails ending in metal hooks. It is rumored to be the whip that was used on him as a child, when his father sold him to slavers. They say he found the man who whipped him, cut out his heart, and took his weapon.

I'm not afraid.

The Fleshers untie me from the chair. They haul me up and turn me around so that I'm facing the Court and the Lords. Lenoir wants me to see them watching. Tomasis won't meet my eye. Orso looks only at the Tiger. Corday watches me as if I'm a fly caught in a web. Yet I won't look away from them. I'm fearless. Proud.

"How many times did she speak?" Corday asks.

"Five," Lord Yelles answers.

"The strike. She drew blood," Lenoir adds.

"But he struck her once," says Corday.

"Five lashes, then," Orso says. "No more."

They push me to my knees.

They say the Tiger can rend flesh from bone. They say he had years of practice when he was a slaver.

I tense every muscle, waiting for the blow.

Even so, I'm not prepared when the first lash hits me. It's like nothing I've ever felt. Like fire running through my body. My mouth inadvertently opens and a cry escapes me. Every part of me is aflame. Montparnasse is behind the Lords, his eyes fixed on mine. I see Loup, unsteady on his feet. Tears leave dark streaks along the ashen gray of his face; he weeps as he holds back Gavroche, covering the boy's eyes with his hand.

The second stroke tears through me, and I can't help but scream. Only two things exist: the pain that fills my body, and the thought that burns through my heart.

She's gone.

The world is darkness threatening to engulf me. Blood and sweat pour down my back. Every limb shakes. Femi is there beside Tomasis. His chin held high; his hands are balled into fists.

When the third stroke comes, everything starts to dim. The sounds around me thicken and fade. The world grows cold. The darkness grows bright, and stars dance about me. The ground beneath me trembles, and I hear it: the voice of the City whispering my name.

When the fourth blow lands, I see my whole life laid out before me drawn in threads of crimson, gray, and black. I see how it started, with a sister weeping in her bed; a child so terrified she gave herself to a Thief; a girl who was so lovely, the world would go to war to possess her. And through it all, he is present. He is the hunting song calling through the night.

The broken boy beneath the lash.

It ends where it begins.

It ends with him.

He is the nightmare, the monster. The thing that stalks in the dark. He is the fear ensnaring each one of us, gripping us in his claws.

And despite my weakness, as he tears the strength from my bones, I see my path. I hear the City whisper to me with silken words. I know what I will do.

With the last blow, my thoughts uncoil into endless shapes before me. I see Azelma sleeping. I see Ettie reaching out for me. My pulse hammers, drowning my ears with its beat.

My sisters.

I couldn't save the one who protected me. I couldn't save the one I was supposed to protect. I can't save the hundreds who sleep in the grasp of his claws. No one escapes him. And so there is only one thing left.

I make this oath in iron; I make it in bone.

I will destroy him, and then they will all be free.

PART FOUR

The Black Cat's Hunting

 1832

Thou hast all the long night for the hunting.
—*The Jungle Book*

HOW THE TIGER GOT HIS STRIPES

FROM STORIES OF THE MIRACLE COURT,
BY THE DEAD LORD

Il était une fois . . . there was a man among the Wretched of the Miracle Court who lived in a time of famine. He saw Death the Endless take half the city. Then hunger took his wife and daughters, leaving him with only one young son.

The man asked himself: Shall I sit here and wait for death to take us both?

For as all men, he was afraid and did not want to die. Thus, fear made him do that which the Wretched are bound by Law never to do.

He sold his son to the slavers of the sea. The Guild Lords heard of it, and on the day that the slavers sailed up the Great Serpent, they went to stop it. For it is forbidden to sell a brother into slavery. But when they saw a hundred slave ships on the banks of the Seine, they too were afraid. For how could a weakened, starving Court do battle with such an army? And for the life of one boy?

They watched his father take twelve gold coins in exchange for the life of his son. They watched him trade the coins for slaver's bread so that he might live. They saw the boy dragged away; they heard his cries as the slavers striped his back and face with their cat-o'-nine-tails, and they did nothing. They comforted themselves by saying he would probably not survive a day at sea, and they agreed to forget.

But things that are forgotten don't always themselves forget. One day, many years later, a slaver came from the sea: the boy, now a terrible man with stripes on his back and his face like a tiger. He wielded the cat-o'-nine-tails now.

He cleaved flesh from bone from the back and face of his father and sold him to his brethren, but that was not enough to satisfy him. He went to the table of the Lords of the Miracle Court and demanded a place.

Lady Kamelia Yelles of the Guild of Sisters spoke for all the Lords. She said that there was no place at the high table for one who trades in flesh, and there never would be.

Humiliated, the man left with vengeance burning in his heart, and set out to break Lady Kamelia. He purchased opiates from the Guild of Dreamers and bribed members of her own Guild to feed them to her. He made her unable to think or move without the poppy, until she was ready to say or do anything he asked. Then the Tiger took her Guild from her and fed the poppy to every Sister until he had made them slaves in a city that had not known slavery for a hundred years.

The Lords did not see what he had done until it was too late. And once they did, they looked upon him and were afraid. For he had turned the Guild of Sisters into a Guild of Flesh. And he had allies on a hundred ships at sea, allies who would come if he called them.

He took his place at the high table, and the Lords came to know that they should never have abandoned that boy so long ago. They had been fools. For is it not written that the Law is like the giant creeper? It drops across everyone's back. And none can escape it.

26

The Société des Droits de l'Homme

I crouch on the rooftop, darkness wrapped about me like a cloak. The sounds of the night float toward me: the sloshing of the river, the Great Serpent on its banks, proactive coster-mongers shouting their evening wares—oysters and coffee for those with an appetite.

A shape sits motionless beside me, like a giant bird of prey with golden eyes that see everything. The frayed edges of his cloak stir in the wind.

"Will you summon them?" I ask.

Femi looks at me, and he does not answer.

"You know that I will do this even if you will not help me," I say.

"I promised to protect you" is all he says.

My gut twists with guilt.

It is an impossible thing he has promised, especially given what I am planning to do. But he swore a bone oath to my sister, and he will never forget it.

"I will summon them," he says finally, and the silence that follows tells me he has already gone.

I stretch out my limbs, pins and needles prickling my muscles, and I stand, staring out over the city. Somewhere in those crowded streets Azelma sleeps; somewhere out there Ettie is afraid. The night wind buffets me, whispering around my ears, caressing the long scars that have healed into ropes across my back.

I hear the hunting song, and I know whose name it sings.

I climb in through the kitchen window of the house on the rue Musain with a basket in my hand and land on my feet like the cat that I am.

The house is many-storied, alive with thick cigar smoke and the loud chatter of excitable young men.

Thénardier's inn ceased to be my home the night he tried to strike a bargain for Ettie with the Tiger. I lived for a time with the Ghosts, then under the Pont Marie, with Femi Vano and a handful of other Cats of the Thieves Guild. Then Orso arranged for me to take a room at the top of a house occupied by students. Ever since thousands of the city's children died due to sickness in the water, we've been working together—the Wretched and the students. The nobility is our common enemy, after all.

So in exchange for my board, I'm a messenger between the house and the Miracle Court—and sometimes a gun-runner for the Smugglers Guild, who happily accept the students' generous overpayments for guns, ammunition, and anything else they need.

The students, devotees of Orso, are from the city's best universities. They're wide-eyed with the idealism that comes from having grown up with a silver spoon wedged firmly between their teeth. They gather in the school's courtyards to hear the Dead Lord's stories. But then, I should have known they were not just stories. Orso does nothing without reason and design. The old bear's mind is always turning.

Grantaire, who has the nose of a hunting dog, appears in the kitchen as if summoned. He could ferret out the scent of fresh-baked *pain au chocolat* from a mile away. I have an entire basketful, still warm, stolen from the racks of a nearby bakery. The smell reminds me of the pastries Ettie devoured at the Tuileries, and the dull ache of her absence twists inside me.

"You goddess, Nina." Grantaire kisses me on the cheek as he abducts a *pain au chocolat,* melted chocolate oozing from the ends of the crisp pastry. He grins in delight and wolfs it down. I swat him away as he tries to grab another.

"Nina, be kind," he pleads. "The big day is nearly upon us. We'll need all the sustenance we can get."

"'Big day'?" I dance away from him with my basket.

"Lamarque's funeral." Grantaire smiles, flaky crumbs around his lips.

Three days ago, General Lamarque was overcome with sickness.

"We've had word from the courier. They think Lamarque might not last much longer."

"The funeral will be a state event," Grantaire continues, licking chocolate from his fingers. "Lamarque may be a noble, but the people love him. The city will be in an uproar. It's the perfect time to stage our protest."

A protest with guns and barricades and a careful plan to take the streets, so the students can take the city, with Lamarque's funeral as the chosen signal. I can't help but shiver as I think of what happened the last time the city's people protested.

They killed one-third of the mice for reason and one-third for sport. Then the cats hanged the six little mice before all of their brethren to teach the mice fear. A strange coldness grips me; soon I'll get what I want.

I shake myself and march into the salon with my basket, where nineteen young men sit in overstuffed chairs, talking, smoking, and drinking by candlelight. Another handful surrounds a large table, on which are laid a map and piles of toppling papers.

These men are the members of the Société des Droits de l'Homme, the Society of the Rights of Man, a political club.

I've learned a lot from being around them. The walls are

paper-thin, and their voices are loud. The palace dictates that no association can have more than twenty members. The nobles made this law to prevent uprisings like the one that almost killed the king and the queen forty years ago. The Société is therefore made up of smaller groups, like this one. Grantaire is its vice president, and St. Juste, who turns from the table to glower at me, is its leader.

St. Juste was carved out of marble and determination. There are rumors he requires food and rest like other mere mortals, but they have never been substantiated. He seems to subsist entirely on passion and black coffee. His tailcoat is always red, because he cares nothing for fashion, and his cravat refuses to stay tied because he worries it when talking. He refuses any vice, taking neither wine nor smoke; he doesn't gamble, joke, or even flirt with ladies.

So when he glares at me, I face the full heat of his disapproval.

The boys' eyes fix on my basket of *pain au chocolat,* and they lose all interest in St. Juste's latest lecture. There's a stampede around me, leaving St. Juste to curse me and cast aspersions on baked goods, as if they somehow undermine the boys' commitment to the cause. He can be melodramatic like that.

I ignore him and give up the basket to one of the boys, then bend to study the map on the table. It's a detailed plan of the city, with twenty red marks placed at strategic locations. These are the positions the Société's cells will take. They will arm themselves and call out to the neighborhood to join them, will build a barricade and slowly push outward till the streets of Paris are theirs. Or so St. Juste has stated at least a hundred times.

"The rue Villmert group has moved," I comment, pointing to one of the red marks.

"The courier said that their position was too vulnerable from the east." St. Juste points at another street. "They've moved to the avenue Ficelle."

I frown. "But there's no easy escape from Ficelle, no alleys or empty houses."

"They won't need an escape!" St. Juste raises his voice. "The people will join them!"

I roll my eyes. St. Juste expects success in every part of the Great Plan. He can't fathom the thought that any aspect of their glorious revolution might fail, even though the city has a history of swallowing revolutions whole.

"Will you come to order?" he roars at the boys who are whooping as they try to steal the remaining pastries from one another.

I've heard them planning this for two years. I've listened to the recital of every tactic and strategy. I have even provided them with guns. And yet I have the strangest feeling as I watch them, as if they are actors at the rue des Meurtres, far away from me on a stage. Like boys playing games. They're all so cheerful and excited, but I care very little for their politics. I care more about the coins they exchange for guns, bullets, and information. I care about the promises they've made to help me when their fighting is done.

I steal Grantaire's chair. He places a steaming cup of strong coffee in front of me, winks, and, pushing me aside, sits on the chair beside me.

St. Juste frowns at us. They're so dissimilar. St. Juste the fervent nationalist and Grantaire the romantic drunk. There was a time when St. Juste seemed to despair of his friend, but when Grantaire and Feuilly turned out to be right about the poison in the water, a newfound respect was born. Now Grantaire is allowed to keep drinking and listening to gossip, and St. Juste refrains from anything but the occasional blistering scolding.

St. Juste is saying something, but I hardly hear him. Instead, I enjoy the first sip of my steaming hot coffee and read expressions of simultaneous excitement and fear on the boys' faces as they listen to their leader. I think of the many nights I've sat here with them, the only girl allowed in their midst. It's hard not to become fond of these boys with their irreverence, mischief, and honorable intensity.

"Does everybody know what they're doing?" St. Juste asks.

Grantaire says no. Everyone laughs.

Through the sound of the boys' laughter comes a squeak: the sound of a rodent. The boys don't hear it, but their ears haven't been trained from childhood to know the calls of the Wretched.

27

Gray Brother

I slip into the kitchen, grab a *pain au chocolat* that I hid earlier, and steal out the door into the night, where a pale gray boy waits, watching for me with earnest dark eyes.

"*Bonne chasse*, Gavroche."

He's not tall enough for his age. The great famine that almost took him has long since passed, but there still hasn't been enough food to go around, and so Gavroche remains small, a shadow of a boy. At least he survived.

During the famine, thousands of the city's inhabitants, mostly its old and its weak, were laid out on the streets for Death the Endless to take. He also took the firstborn of many of the great houses, thanks to retaliation of the Assassins Guild. I watched the coffins of the nobility traverse the city as they were borne to their resting place, and on those days, there was no sorrow to be found in my heart.

Gavroche inclines his head respectfully at my greeting, but his eyes are fixed on the *pain au chocolat* in my hand. I give it to him. He takes it and sniffs before glancing up at me slyly.

"No poison here, little Ghost."

He considers me for a minute and then takes a small bite.

As I watch him eat, I think of all things I must do to set my plans in motion.

I see the map on St. Juste's desk. I picture all the pieces in their place, like dominoes ready to fall. There is still one piece I need to make sure is ready for the game to begin.

"Do you know where the inspector is? The policewoman with the red hair?" I ask Gavroche. There is a Ghost on every street corner of the city; they know where everyone is.

"Not at the gendarmerie tonight," he replies in his sing-song whisper of a voice.

I furrow my brow. "Where is she?"

"At the Tuileries," Gavroche replies as if it's obvious.

"The palace?" I say.

"There is a ball tomorrow night," he says, as if somehow I should have known that.

She is probably there as security.

"Father says to tell the Black Cat of the Thieves Guild that the Ghosts will not be attending the uprising," he says, between mouthfuls of pastry. "He says she would do best to do the same."

My blood runs cold. "What does Orso mean?" I ask with a trembling voice.

"Father has heard that there is a traitor among the sons of rebellion." He takes another little bite, making the pastry last as long as it can. "They march to their doom." He looks at me with his serious eyes. "He bids you tell them on his behalf."

With the pastry finished and the message delivered, he bows formally to me.

"Bonne chasse," he whispers, and fades into the night.

I let him go, my mind a whirl, and steal back into the house, where I walk squarely into St. Juste.

St. Juste looks over my shoulder out the door, but Gavroche has disappeared.

"What were you doing outside?" he asks.

I know I should give him Orso's message, but I hesitate. "Taking the air," I say.

He frowns. He knows I've never "taken the air" in my life.

"You were with someone. Who was it?" he demands.

"My secret paramour," I say, waggling my eyebrows suggestively.

"Don't be ridiculous." St. Juste brushes the idea of a romantic assignation aside.

"Why is it ridiculous for me to have a secret paramour?"

"We have an agreement," he reminds me.

St. Juste has promised to help me in my quest as long as I ensure that the Miracle Court will aid him in his takeover of the city. It is meant to unfold in the course of a single night: arm the students, blow up a few gendarmeries, set the Hyènes to attack any police, while the Ghosts watch and relay where the enemy is. With our combined efforts the city should be ripe for the taking. Yet if I give him Orso's message about a traitor among his ranks, he may call off the rebellion. And if he does, will he still be ready to aid me?

"Have I in any way not delivered?" I retort, offended. "I've brought you everything you asked. I've carried your messages, bought you guns and knives, whatever you required."

"And we're very grateful. But we're so close now, we need every one of us to be focused on the task at hand."

"You think I lack focus?" I ask darkly.

"We realize that you have, er, other priorities. You're a Thief." He stumbles over the word awkwardly. "And we turn a blind eye to what you have to do to survive in this cruel city."

"How generous of you." Sarcasm drips off my every word.

"But should you get caught, or arrested, you could be thrown into the Châtelet right when we need you the most."

"You do remember that time I broke Orso out of the Châtelet?"

His face clouds as he also remembers that I had him arrested as a distraction. Then he smiles calculatingly and closes the distance between us. I ignore my racing pulse.

"You're the most daring girl I've ever met."

"You don't meet a lot of girls, St. Juste," I point out.

His cheeks go red. "We are not playing games here, Nina," he says angrily. "You must take things seriously."

"Why must I?"

"Because this is all for you!" His voice rises. "It's for you and your brethren, all the downtrodden of Paris, that we seek change."

I feign a yawn. I've heard St. Juste's speeches a hundred times.

He's used to being listened to adoringly by his friends, so my lack of reverence infuriates him. He takes my wrists in a painful grip.

"St. Juste." Grantaire, coming out of the salon, frowns, seeing us in the doorway. He's worried St. Juste is being too rough with me. He has no idea the things people have done to me.

"Do you remember how the nobles poisoned the wells?" St. Juste looks manically into my eyes. "Do you remember the bodies?"

"I remember." Many of the Wretched perished of hunger and sickness. Ghosts, Thieves, Bats alike.

"We fight so that such unforgivable evil will never occur again." St. Juste's voice is low now, a caress.

His chiseled face is inches from my own. I think if he put his mind to it, he'd be rather good at seduction.

"And we need you. We need your razor-sharp brain, your skills, your undivided concentration." He sighs then, a hand worrying the end of his cravat as he draws back from me. "Your drive and bravery are unparalleled, Nina. I'm just concerned that you waste all your energy on trying to find that girl."

My stomach drops. I told St. Juste about Ettie only once, and it was in confidence.

"You need to accept that it has been too long. In all probability she is dead." His voice is lower now, gentler. He's trying to choose his words. Something he rarely does. "I think you care about a ghost. And it will destroy you."

I turn my back on him and head for the stairs, refusing to listen. I cannot give him Orso's message now, not when it's clear he thinks my quest is a folly while his will be our salvation.

"You're surrounded by the living here," St. Juste calls after me. "You're useful to us, Nina."

I march into my room, slamming the door as if it could block out his words.

I'd cry, but there's a tall, angular shadow in the corner. It's cloaked in almost-black and playing with a ruby-inlaid dagger.

My heart gives a strange lurch.

Montparnasse.

28

Master of Knives

The stairs creak: someone is coming. There's a knock at my door, and I shoot Montparnasse a look as I open it a crack.

St. Juste is outside, wearing an expression of concern. Grantaire glares at him from behind.

"I'm sorry." St. Juste shifts from foot to foot awkwardly. "That I implied that looking for your friend is a waste of time."

"You don't need to apologize," I say coolly. "You pay me, so you'll still get your guns."

St. Juste looks slightly ashamed.

"Our agreement stands. I help your revolution, and when it's over, you help me destroy a monster," I say a little more gently. Because right now I need these young men as much as they need me.

"You have my word on that," St. Juste says.

"And you have mine that I'll be present and available and focused when Lamarque falls."

Montparnasse glances at me. I've known him long enough that I can read his almost-nonexistent expressions. He wants to talk to St. Juste.

I open the door all the way, and St. Juste and Grantaire step gingerly into the room. Being polite gentlemen, they've never been in my room. Their eyes travel shyly from the old mattress on the floor to the armoire in the corner.

Montparnasse, in typical Assassin fashion, is so still that the other two don't even know he's there. He coughs and Grantaire jumps out of his skin. St. Juste stiffens. He has no idea who Montparnasse is, but the Master of Knives gives off an air that would chill the soul of the purest innocent. The boys give a slight bow of their heads to Montparnasse as I make the introductions; I've taught them well.

It's strange to see St. Juste and Montparnasse in the same room. St. Juste is made entirely of fire and justice, where Montparnasse is darkness and secrecy. From dagger to cheekbone, he's all sharp angles, with cold, expressionless eyes. The past, the Wretched, the Guilds are wrapped in Montparnasse's inky black cloak, while St. Juste . . . he shines like a beacon. A promise of all that the future could be.

Being a man of few words, Montparnasse gets straight to the point. "Madame Corday sends her regrets. We won't be attending your . . . uprising."

Rennart's balls. I had hoped to get a chance to talk to Orso myself, to see if I could change his mind before I broke the news to St. Juste.

St. Juste goes white as a sheet. The disappointment rolls off him in waves. "Why?"

"The payment is not high enough for such a suicide mission."

St. Juste stares at him blankly. "But we're fighting for you too—for *all* of you. Don't your people want things to change? Don't they want their lives to be better?" he asks.

Montparnasse regards him as if he's slightly mad. We've never needed a bunch of well-meaning students to fight for us. The Wretched grow up with a dagger in one hand, trying to fend off Death the Endless with the other.

But the look on St. Juste's face tugs at my heart. He's confused and hurt. He truly believes things can change, which is why he dedicates every waking moment to the cause. It is his dream, his obsession. And he is willing to pay any price for it. He would march to the gates of hell itself if it was asked of him. It's one of the things that I find most admirable—and terrifying—about him.

Montparnasse gives a little shrug. "There has been some question of . . . security."

"What do you mean?" St. Juste demands.

"The Ghosts whisper that there's a spy in your club."

"We're a *société,* not a club!"

Montparnasse nods seriously. "Nonetheless, neither the Dead Lord nor Lady Corday can lend their support to a cause they're unsure of."

St. Juste falls silent, gazing questioningly at me, and I swallow my guilt over the message Gavroche brought, a message I chose not to pass along because it might mean losing St. Juste's support in my own war. But now Montparnasse has suggested there's a traitor in their organization, and Orso, a man who has spoken on freedom and rebellion, has said he is pulling out. The sense of betrayal St. Juste must feel is unimaginable.

St. Juste lifts his chin. "I'll contact the Société. If there is a spy, then they'll advise us how to proceed."

"The courier comes tomorrow," Grantaire adds with a hand on St. Juste's shoulder to comfort him, or possibly to make sure he doesn't fall over. "We can get instructions then."

"Right." St. Juste runs his hands through his hair and looks distracted.

They're standing still, St. Juste because he's thinking about his plans, and Montparnasse, I suspect, because he won't leave St. Juste and Grantaire alone in my bedroom.

I clear my throat. "I need to change now."

St. Juste looks at me and seems suddenly to remember I'm female, something I'm not sure he remembers all that often. He nods and leaves, dragging Grantaire out with him.

I turn to Montparnasse. Our paths have diverged greatly in the last two years. I hardly ever see him, save for a glance across the Miracle Court, or a shadow in the night that makes me wonder if he's lurking somewhere in the darkness, watching.

"Do you think I'm wasting my time?" I ask him. "Do you, too, think she's dead?"

I need to know how well I have done. How much even he believes.

Montparnasse watches me for a while. He doesn't speak.

"I think you care too much," he finally says. "You always have."

He's at the window.

"But you'll never stop looking. You don't know how."

He gives a small bow and is gone without a sound.

The boys' voices float up through the floorboards. They'll talk late into the night, weighing the risks of carrying out their plans without the support of the Guilds. I feel a strange pang, because the events of the next few days will likely bring an end to the life I've come to know with them. Their tall tales and teasing, the talks about sacrifice and the greater good, the discussions of the failed revolution. St. Juste often gets a gleam in his eye during those talks as if he would have liked to live and die in those days when the streets of Paris were bathed in blood, when dreamers like him were fed to Madame Guillotine. They have heated debates about how it ended, how it could have been different, how it will be different. They argue, drink, and laugh.

Sometimes Grantaire notices me in my corner and coaxes me into telling a story. Even St. Juste listens then. I never betray the secrets of the Court, but I can keep them mesmerized for hours recounting the tales of my people. They hang on every word like thirsty men; I can keep them entertained until the sun rises. On those nights, I've gone to bed drunk on the feeling that I've been seen for the very first time.

I've been their little sister for two years now, and I'm fond of them. I like the way Grantaire drinks too much, mostly to annoy St. Juste. I like teasing St. Juste and watching his face go red and his eyes become like flint. I like the way Feuilly is always reading, even in the middle of the most avid debate. He's lent me entire libraries of books in the last year, after being shocked when he learned that I could read. I think it pleases him to see me clutch one of his old tomes and carry it around the house like a well-read alley cat.

I'm their gunrunner, their messenger, their go-between, bringing news and information from the Guilds for a shiny gold coin. But they're not mercenaries, not merchants, not crooks like the Wretched. They don't know how to keep me at a distance. They don't know how to treat me differently, so they treat me like I'm one of them. And for the first time in my life, I began to feel like maybe I could belong to a world that's not the Miracle Court, to a family that's not the Thieves Guild.

I shake my head at these foolish thoughts and begin to peel off my clothes: dress, chemise, skirt hoop, and corset land in a heap on the floor. I wipe my face clean with water from a jug and an old cloth, undo my hair, and braid it, tying the plaits up in a crown that will more easily fit under my cap. I take out my Cat clothes: dark trousers, boots, and a shirt.

I hide all proof of my womanhood under ill-fitting clothes.

First I wind bandages around my soft shape. I erase and re-write myself with a new face and form. The feel of the linen as it slides over the scars on my back reminds me who I am and what my purpose is. I'm no woman, no girl. I've no blood father or home; I've none of the cards this life dealt me at birth. I chose who I am. I'm the Black Cat. A daughter of this city. A child of Tomasis, Lord of the Thieves Guild. No one can take anything from me because the Tiger has already taken it all.

And I'm going to get it back.

Once the revolution is over, I'll get what I've waited, planned, and worked for these last two years. I'll use these boys, as they've used me for their games of war. They'll be my weapon to destroy the Tiger once and for all, because they can do what I, as a child of the Miracle Court, cannot. They can attack, report, and destroy a Guild without bring-ing war to the Court.

They will be my revenge.

I get out my tools—my carved picks, my needles and pins for locks—and slip them into my trouser pockets. I roll up my sleeve and strap my dagger to my lower arm, then pull my cuff back over it. I dip my hands in a small pot of gray dust to keep my palms dry, and I pull out pieces of long gray cloth, wrapping them around my hands as makeshift gloves. I pull on my jacket and tuck the loose hairs into my cap.

I climb out the window to avoid meeting St. Juste again and drop to the ground, creeping into an alley at the back of the house. There I pause, slowing my breathing till I'm completely still. The noises of the night and the darkness of the street swell around me. I listen. The boys' voices are raised inside. St. Juste is sternly telling someone off. I tilt my head, focusing. I can make out their laughter, recognize each voice. Nobody knows I am gone.

I'm the Black Cat of the Thieves Guild, and this is my hunting.

I'm ready.

29

Of Paper and Rats

The meeting place is a warehouse, filled as far as the eye can see with barrels of Japanese sake. I try to stay calm and not dwell on what is about to happen. I sigh and stretch my arms; it will be some time before they come. So I get to work. I uncork the first few barrels, taking care not to breathe in, and I pull the syringe and water pouch from my jacket.

The Bats appear first: Corday, Montparnasse, Col-Blanche, all arriving in silence. One moment they're not there; the next they are. They stand in the shadows watching, saying nothing. I keep quiet too, waiting for the others.

The Dead Lord and Loup appear next, the familiar smell of the Ghosts announcing them minutes before they enter, covered in their layers of gray dust. Orso nods to me and Loup bows.

Then comes Adlen Yelles, Lord of the Guild of Dreamers, which surprises no one, since this is one of his warehouses, where the Smugglers deliver him the drugs that he in turn sells to Those Who Walk by Day. He gives me a small bow, and I see Corday's eyebrow twitch at the sight.

There's chittering and scrabbling overhead. I raise my head and respond in kind to the call of the Rats of the Smugglers Guild. Tamar l'Aure enters first, leading an elderly woman who's bent almost double. Both are swathed in cloaks of matted brown fur, with thick oilskin aprons and boots made to withstand long voyages at sea. Both move with a strange mixture of sleekness and caution. Their hair, where it peeks out from under their furred caps, is a mess of coils and braids, and their skin is burned and leathery with exposure to salt and sun. The old woman is being led; her eyes are wide and milky white, for she is blind. This is Nihuang, the Fisherman, Merveille of the Miracle Court and Lady of the Smugglers Guild.

Tamar is jittery and ill-tempered. Like all the Rats of the Smugglers Guild, she would rather be sailing on the open sea than be here on land. Her gaze meets mine, and she does not smile.

There's a sound like the fluttering of wings, and Femi appears—Aves, the Elanion, the one who summoned them all for me. He slips through a window and smiles weakly at me. Someone coughs behind him, and a small figure emerges from the same window after him.

I bow low to Lady Komayd of the Guild of Letters, who

watches me like an amused auntie watching a small child at play.

"Is that Gayatri?" the Fisherman asks Tamar in a bracing voice.

"It is, Mother," Tamar says.

"Yes, the smell of dusty parchment and ink is unmistakable."

"Better that than salt and fish," Lady Komayd retorts.

"Hmmph," the Fisherman says with a sniff. "And what did such a small Cat do to summon the Lady of Paper?"

"She rescued one of my sons from the Châtelet," Komayd replies. "A . . . *favorite* son. So it is a debt of thanks that the People of the Pen owe you, Black Cat, and that is why I am here." She fixes me in her sight and smiles, lines wrinkling the corners of her large eyes.

I feel the corner of my mouth twitch in response. *Favorite son indeed.*

"Indeed, Cat," Orso says. "And now that you have our full attention, why don't you explain to us why we are here."

I try not to shake as I bow to the group. Fathers and Mothers of the Miracle Court, Guild Lords and Ladies, Masters—they're all watching me. I try to keep a brave face and not think about how I, a mere Cat, summoned five Lords of the Miracle Court. And *they came.*

I clear my throat. "I am going to break in to the Guild of Flesh." I announce. My voice it is not as steady as I would like, but it will have to do.

In the ensuing silence, they all stare at me. Orso looks

dazed. Komayd stares as if I've gone insane. Corday cocks her head to one side, considering me.

Then the Fisherman starts to laugh. Which is not the response I was hoping for.

"She's mad," Tamar says.

"Yes, but this should at least be entertaining," the Fisherman replies, quieting her chuckles. "Do go on, my dear—you were saying?"

"To enter a Guild House uninvited is not only breaking the Law, it is an act of war," Col-Blanche interjects.

"The Law is already broken, and only his ending can mend it," I say.

There is another silence at this. The Lords and Ladies share an unreadable look. Have I gone too far?

"It has been a long time since the Court had a judge among us," says Yelles slowly.

I swallow, unsure whether this is a compliment or a threat. I am not trying to place myself in the position of judge to the Court—how could I? Judges are the keepers of the Law, and distributors of punishment who rose up among the Court in times of threat and war. I am not trying to start a war, no matter what the Lords might think. I only know that there is no other way to save Ettie, and Azelma, and all of the other Sisters.

"He has found her, then?" Orso asks. "Kaplan has found Ettie, and you are going to rescue her?"

The sound of her name makes my heart tighten. I force my feelings down and tell myself that it was worth it.

"Do the stripes on your back not remind you of the foolishness of your plan?" Tamar asks before I can answer.

"They sing to me day and night," I snap. "They sing the hunting song in his name."

Tamar narrows her eyes. "You're not going to rescue anybody, are you?"

"None of us is safe while he lives," I reply.

"You're going to kill him," Yelles says.

Femi shakes his head in disbelief. "No, she's going to get killed trying."

"Child, the Tiger will slit your throat and wear your skin on his back." Corday's voice is as calm as if she's asking me about the weather.

"Probably. But if there's a single chance on this earth that I can destroy him, is it not worth trying?"

"You'll fail," Corday says, emotionless, then turns to Montparnasse with a motion that shows she is leaving. I feel panic lance through me. They can't leave, not yet.

"Nina, you can't even get to the Guild House," Femi says.

He's right. Almost all the Guilds keep the location of their houses secret. Femi knows where they are, but he is bound by the Law never to reveal their location, and I can't ask it of him.

"The Guild of Letters audits every Guild," I say. "They know the location of the Flesh Guild."

Corday pauses at the window.

Everyone's attention turns to Lady Komayd. She smiles, betraying nothing.

"Tell us your plan, then," she says.

Which is better than an outright refusal to help me. *At least they're listening.*

"I know that none of the Guilds can be seen to endorse my quest," I say. "If they're caught, it could mean war. So I ask no Ghosts, Rats, Bats, or Dreamers to join me. I need only information from the People of the Pen, and a gift from the Fisherman and the Lord of Dreamers, to help me.

"If I fail and perish, then what I have done can be left at my door. They will say I was half mad with grief and it drove me to do the unthinkable. You may all wash your hands of me in peace.

"But if I succeed, if Kaplan falls, then I will ask something of you. I will ask that you set free the Sisters of the Guild of Flesh."

"The Sisters are no more—the Tiger destroyed them," Col-Blanche says.

"Many of that Guild live still, under the sway of the poppy," Yelles answers.

"How can we free anyone under the influence of the poppy?" Col-Blanche asks.

The Lords of the Miracle Court are notoriously suspicious; their eyes turn to the bottles I've pulled from the crates and set before me.

"Ysengrim be damned, child, what have you done?" the Fisherman hisses.

"We have awakened those who slumber," Yelles says, his voice a fraction of a whisper.

"We have been diluting the drugs that the Guild of Dreamers sells to the Tiger," I add.

"Have the Fleshers not suspected? Not seen signs?" Tamar asks.

"It took many years to come up with a dilution that is subtle enough for the Fleshers not to notice," Yelles says. "Sons and daughters of my own Guild gave themselves to the experiment—for we had to be sure the addiction could be reversed."

"How many years?" the Fisherman asks curiously as her unseeing eyes glance in Yelles's general direction.

"Since he destroyed my sister, Lady Kamelia, and enslaved her children." Yelles's voice is sharp and raw. "When the Tiger came to me and offered me a fortune if I would make him a brew of the poppy so strong it could force any man to his bidding, I was too young, too greedy, too naïve. I made it and sold it to him, thinking it none of my business what he did with it. And he used it on my own sister, to destroy her and her Guild." His eyes shine with unshed tears. "And when we saw what he had done . . ." He shakes his head mournfully. "We were weak. He had allies, slavers, a hundred ships in our ports. Could we have gone to war with them and prevailed? Our duty was to protect our Guilds, to protect the Court. That is what we told ourselves to justify doing nothing."

He turns his eyes to me.

"Then one day a Cat with a back scarred in stripes came

296

to me saying that she was going to kill the Tiger and set all the Sisters free. She asked for my help. How could I refuse?"

He waves a hand over the barrels of sake. "We have been diluting the poppy the Tiger buys for two years. According to our studies, the Sisters should be coherent enough not to fight you if you reason with them. Some may remember who they are. Most will not, having been too long under the poppy's sway.

"And if the Cat fails—which is likely," he says, giving me a measured look, "then all the blame for the dilution of the drugs will be placed on her. My sons will swear she broke in and tampered with the bottles alone."

"No," says the Fisherman. And there is so much force in that single word that we all look up. "She is asking us to attack a Guild. She stands here among us and admits to planning the murder of a Lord of the Miracle Court. We should drown *her* in shackles of iron in the name of preventing a war and be done with it."

30

What the Lords Said

"There are nine Guilds, nine Lords. Yet the Sisters' seat lies empty and a false lord, a slaver, sits among us!" Yelles shouts, fists clenched and fire raging in his eyes. "The Miracle Court was not created to protect those who trade in the flesh of the Wretched, and yet we have allowed it. It's time we correct our failure."

"Brave words from a man who has been fiddling with bottles in secret," the Fisherman parries, not a whit impressed.

"What I have done in secret I have done to protect the children of my Guild. What I do tonight I will do to avenge my sister and to put right the wrongs that have been committed against all. Even if none else will aid the Cat, I will,"

Yelles says. "Kaplan has no place at the high table. Ridding the Court of him is our duty. It is our duty to the Law."

The Fisherman shakes her head. "I was not yet Lady of Rats when the Tiger was first taken. It is well known that Kamelia and I—" The Fisherman breaks off and looks suddenly very old. "I was at sea when he returned and established his hold on the Court. I arrived too late to save her.

"I have done what I could without putting my own children in jeopardy. I take in more girls than the other Guilds combined, for they are safer on the waters than in the Court, where the Tiger's eye can easily fall upon them."

I glance at the scowling Tamar, wondering if that's how she came to be Master of the Guild of Smugglers.

"We Rats have seen more than this Court has. The slavers control the seas, and though seeing one of them fall would be a boon to us, you must know, Cat, that if the Tiger falls, his brethren will come to avenge him."

I know the Fisherman cannot see me, yet I feel her gaze upon me, piercing my skin.

"They will fall upon the Guilds like a curse."

"Let them come," Yelles answers in a hard voice.

"Yelles, our grief is shared, but do not let it make you foolish. You do not know of what you speak. The Tiger is but one; his allies are legion."

"Are we Those Who Walk by Day, to cower in the face of our enemies? Is that what Kamelia would have done? We have been afraid too long!" Yelles retorts.

The Fisherman laughs in response. "If Kamelia had known what the Tiger would do to her children, she would have torn out his throat. But then, she was Raksha, a she-wolf, and was always much fiercer than we were."

She smiles and turns her head away as if her entire argument with Yelles has been staged to test him, as if it is all a game to her.

She nods in my direction. "What is it you want of us, Cat?"

Beside her, Tamar makes a small sound of discontent, as if she disagrees.

"I want you to give me the voice of Mor," I reply, tensing as I wait for the answer.

"Is that all you will ask of me?"

"Yes, my Lady."

"And for so small a price will we call Death the Endless down upon ourselves and our children." Her milky eyes seem to be looking for something that we cannot see. She sighs. "Very well, then. For Kamelia."

Tamar's face crumples, and she turns to gaze accusingly at me. "You dwell on land, little Cat. What do you know of Kaplan's slaver kin? Why do you think the first Lords let the Tiger be taken as a child? They knew that the Guilds combined could not withstand them. And you would make them our enemies?" she says.

"Enough, Tamar! Your opinion was not asked for," the Fisherman says.

Tamar is silenced. She looks resentfully at me, but I also see something else in her eyes—fear.

"It is a noble ambition," says Col-Blanche, "but we do not know how many dens the Tiger controls, or where they are. Even if we knew, how can we free the Sisters and subdue their captors? We don't know how many sons of Flesh are posted in each, how many weapons are at their command. To go blind into such a fight would be disastrous, and the other Guilds, the ones allied to the Tiger, might take his side. It would be an all-out Guild war," he finishes.

"But one of us does know their numbers," I say.

Everyone waits for me to go on, and I proceed, rolling out a map of the city I painstakingly copied from St. Juste, down to the little red marks he has made for the places where the revolutionaries will erect their barricades.

"Lady Komayd, will you give us the information we need?" I ask in a solemn voice. "The numbers of the Tiger's sons, the locations of his dens, the numbers of his weapons and"—I swallow hard, knowing the enormity of what I am asking—"the location of his Guild House?"

She considers it for a moment, and I hold my breath.

"You ask much, little Cat. Rescuing one of my sons from the Châtelet was indeed a great feat, but the bone debt you seek could mean war." She taps her fingers to the side of her head and quirks her mouth. "And yet the Tiger is a stain upon this Court," she says with resolve, and her small eyes shine behind her spectacles. "The Guild of Flesh is here."

She steps forward to the map and points. "On the right bank of the Serpent la Seine. It stands three stories high, with an underground cellar. The Tiger's quarters take up the entire top floor. There are never guards at the front of the house, so as not to call attention to their location."

"And also because no one in their right mind would ever attack them," Femi says drily. But he uncrosses his arms and steps forward to look better at the map.

"There are walls on the east and south sides of the house," continues Lady Komayd. "There are four guards posted in each corner. Two more guards are stationed at the west side of the house in front of the river. Boats unload their goods there, and the goods are carried through a gate into the garden."

"You will need a distraction there." Femi points to the riverside. "To draw the guards away from the garden."

"I might have something that will bring all the guards to the front of the house," I say innocently.

Everyone stares.

"Angry men wanting to overthrow the government marching up and down every street in the city," I say by way of explanation.

Orso snorts, and I give him a hard look.

"There will be an uprising, and soon," I say firmly. "Those Who Walk by Day are merely waiting for the death of General Lamarque."

Corday's mouth falls open. She recovers quickly but takes long strides to the table and points at me. "You—you are the one who paid us to kill Lamarque?" she exclaims.

Femi sighs loudly again.

"I paid in gold coin, and much more than your usual rate!" I say defensively.

"If I had known your plans, we would have refused the commission."

"Lamarque has been ill for over a year," I say reasonably. "His suffering is dreadful. Death the Endless will be a mercy to him."

"So Lamarque dies—" Corday starts.

"And as he is a man of the people, his death is the sign the revolutionaries will use to begin their campaign," I finish. "We control the hour of Lamarque's death, we control the start of the revolution. People will take to the streets, protesting, fighting, and building barricades. The Flesh Guild will be so distracted, they won't notice me sneaking in."

"Even if you could distract them long enough to get in, you're only a Thief, in a house full of Fleshers," Corday points out. "You won't survive three minutes in their Guild."

"I will go with her," Montparnasse answers from her side.

And I feel a wave of relief flood through me.

Corday stiffens; her gaze sears his face. He has no expression, no reaction. He asks no permission, not even from his Lady.

"And when she fails and you're found in the Guild? It'll be outright war," Corday counters.

"When have I ever been found?" Montparnasse replies.

Corday turns back to fix her gaze on me.

But the atmosphere has changed. If there's one person

capable of entering the Guild, it's Montparnasse. But there's still only two of us, and the whole of the Guild of Flesh between us and the Tiger.

"I might have something else that can help your ascent to the monster's lair," the Fisherman says. "It will slow them down, but it will not stop them."

I shake inwardly. Gifts mean debts, and debts must be repaid. But what choice do I have?

"The sons of Flesh at the Guild House number thirty to forty men at most," Lady Komayd says. "They're all exceptionally strong and violent; the Tiger keeps their numbers low, culling the weakest among them regularly."

"You're not painting us the most hopeful of pictures, Gayatri, dear," the Fisherman says gently.

"They're well armed, with guns, knives, and bludgeoning tools."

"I'll take care of that," I say quietly.

"Nina, there's one of you, and the Tiger's Guild is armed to the teeth," Femi points out.

"I'll do what I can," I say.

Femi frowns. He knows that fighting and disarming hordes of battle-ready bruisers is not one of my talents. He knows there's something I'm not telling him.

"Let us for a minute entertain this wild folly and pretend that you have the luck of Rennart and succeed in removing the Tiger. You then wish us to attack his dens, subdue his men, and free the Sisters?" the Fisherman asks.

I blink. "Yes."

"Komayd?" the Fisherman calls, wanting to know what the Lady of Letters thinks, but Tamar whispers to her that Lady Komayd is already marking spots on the maps to show where the Tiger's dens lie throughout the city.

"How will we know the Tiger has fallen?" Komayd asks, looking up at me.

"The voice of Mor will speak, of course," the Fisherman answers with a laugh, reading my mind.

31

The Dead Lord's Word

When the Lords have gone, I set off after Orso. He knows I am coming and turns to greet me with a grim look.

"Cat," he says.

"I want to know why you are reneging on your word," I say, sounding more accusatory than I should.

"I did not give the students my word. No bone oath was sworn to them."

"You found St. Juste, you put the fire in his eyes and his heart, you set him upon this path. Do not tell me that it isn't so."

"He has his uncle's heart. He would always have—"

"He was standing in the public places and giving revolutionary speeches under the name of St. Juste! It is a miracle that he managed to survive as long as he did. He would have been hanged his first month in the city if you had not taken him under your wing. How can you abandon him now?"

Orso steps away from me, trying to deny it.

"I have been among them, Orso. I know what you did. I know that you showed him how to recruit brethren, how to plan, and what to watch for. There are twenty cells like his across this city. Without our aid they will all be slaughtered."

"And what is the slaughter of Those Who Walk by Day to you?" he asks gruffly, his eyebrows raised.

"I need him," I mumble, flushing for reasons unknown. "I need them to help me overwhelm the Tiger's Guild. I cannot use any children of the Court to enter the Tiger's house, for their mere presence might plunge their Guilds into war." I swallow heavily. "But they will give me their aid only if they survive this uprising—an uprising you and Corday said you would support. That was the bargain we made. You and I both know that without *your* aid they have very little chance."

"It is not the lack of my aid that will damn them," Orso says stubbornly. "There is a traitor in the Société."

"Do you know the identity of the traitor?"

"No. I have merely overheard conversations. Nonetheless, I will not give my children to a cause that is doomed," Orso says.

"St. Juste does not believe it is doomed."

"Then he is a fool, just as his uncle was before him."

Rage rises in me. "St. Juste's uncle was a martyr for this city and a brother to you . . . yet you dare to call him a fool?

You, who were one of them, O tailless one, teller of truths, sixth little mouse of six."

Orso straightens, his hands flexing. I've long suspected that he was the lone rebel who escaped, and his silence tells me I was right.

"You were not there, child," he says in a low, dangerous voice. "You do not know of what you speak. You do not know what it is to see your brethren slaughtered like dogs."

"Then why are you withdrawing your support from them? Don't you know it will happen all over again?"

"You dare question me, child? A *Lord* of the Miracle Court? Have you considered your own ways? You are sworn to serve Tomasis and the Thieves, yet you plan to enter Kaplan's home and attack him. Where is your concern for your own Guild if your plan fails? If you draw us all into war?"

He breaks off, and I feel the sickening truth of his words.

"Your aims are righteous, little Cat. The Court was broken when Kaplan came, and I hate him with all that is within me. But I have weighed the cost. Have you?"

I have not. I have been too busy spinning plans, blindly trying to convince others that this is more than just a suicide mission, that there might be a glimmer of hope. But Orso's words are like my conscience: my own voice now accuses me; my own thoughts now judge me.

"Kaplan broke the Messenger's hands for trying to steal from him once, and not a single Lord objected," Orso continues. "He whipped you like a dog in full view of the entire

Court with their sanction. What might he do to your Guild if your attack fails?"

"Thinking of and fearing what *might* happen is what gives the Tiger his power. He is a cancer among us, and he must be cut out," I insist.

The Dead Lord laughs, and the tension wound so tightly about us eases.

"Ah, little Cat, you are so fierce. You remind me of my fallen brothers. They, too, dreamt of justice, but for all their dreams they still fell to Madame Guillotine, and all who loved them hanged at Montfaucon." He reaches out a ruined hand and touches my cheek gently. "You are small, but you are sharp and bright, and the Court loves you. They see in you a fire and a purity. You could be the Lady of Thieves if you choose your battles wisely."

"You told me once that if I got you out of the Châtelet, you would give me anything I asked."

"That was a long time ago," he says gruffly.

I smile and do my best impression of Thénardier. "Has the word of the Dead Lord changed? There may come a time when you will need angry men with guns and fire in their hearts. It would be a shame if that day comes, only for you to find that they have all died meaninglessly. I'm asking you to help me keep your foot soldiers alive."

I hover there with nervous energy, wondering what the Dead Lord will say, readying myself for a crushing blow of disappointment. Orso eyes me; I can see the gears turning in his great mind.

"If you can convince the Société that their cause is lost, if you can get them to me, then I will help to save them," he says, and I know there is no more arguing with him.

For a Guild Lord to agree to save countless numbers of Those Who Walk by Day is no small matter. It is a bad bargain, for I've no way of convincing St. Juste to give up the fight—but it's the only bargain I'm going to get.

32

⚮

She Who Was Lost

The next evening, I go visiting. The house in the rue Plumet is modest for a genteel neighborhood. It looks perversely cheerful in the fading twilight, with a garden full of greenery and pots brimming with flowers at its every window.

My heart is skittering behind my ribs as I scale the wall. My breath is short, and I find it hard to swallow. But I press on, ignoring the fact that I'm breaking into church property, ignoring the thought of what lies inside. I enter through an attic window and silently glide into an empty corridor.

Or so I thought. A shiver starts at the nape of my neck, and my Cat instincts sing. There is another presence here. I freeze. There's no sound, but it's here. I narrow my eyes, trying to acclimate them to the deep dark. There's a whisper of movement behind me. I try to swing around, when something heavy hits the back of my head. I crumple to my knees, seeing only stars, and the darkness grows thick. There is the ominous click of a pistol being cocked.

A lantern is lit, and I hiss at the brightness. Pain lances my head. A hulking figure of a man stands over me, a giant with a forgettable face. The one I rescued from the Châtelet. Le Maire. For le Maire is the prisoner I freed that day— beloved son of the Guild of Letters, a Merveille of the Miracle Court, lost and found. Orso recognized him that night in the prison and whispered the truth to me sometime later. But a spy of the Guild of Letters is only as good as the mystery that surrounds him, and so his reappearance has been kept quiet from most of the Wretched.

His eyes take me in, and he sighs heavily and lowers his pistol. "Oh, it's only you," he says.

"Ysengrim be damned, did you have to hit me so hard?" I complain as he helps me to my feet.

"I have big hands," he says by way of explanation. He puts his pistol away and stares at me. "You said you weren't going to come here."

Just then a door crashes open behind us with a thwacking crunch. My reflexes kick in and I drop and roll, a dagger in my hand, while le Maire points his pistol at the entrance. There stands Ettie, in a dress that she's since outgrown, wild-eyed, her hair a tangle of curls, a giant ax in her hands. She is taller than when I last saw her that long-ago night when I paid the bread price. But her face is as lovely as ever, and when she sees me, she throws up her arms, waving the ax around, and gives a triumphant cry.

"I knew it! I knew you'd rescue me!" She swings around to le Maire, victory etched across her face. "I told you she'd find me. I told you she'd come for me."

"Where did you get my ax?"

"I know how to pick a lock," she says, rushing toward me, ax still in hand, before stopping abruptly to face le Maire.

"Now you *have* to let me go," she tells him.

Le Maire sighs and sits down heavily on a petite velvet chair, which creaks under his bulk.

"Go with her if you want," he says, his voice dull and tired. "If she no longer needs me to keep you hidden, then my debt is paid and you are no longer my responsibility."

Ettie turns slowly and stares at me.

"Keep me hidden? Nina?"

"Ettie, why don't you put down the ax?"

"I am not putting anything down until someone tells me what is going on," she retorts, eyes shining and crazed. "Why does he say that you needed to keep me hidden?" She's glaring at me suspiciously now, as if she's never seen me before. "You didn't *do* this, did you, Nina? You didn't—"

"I had no choice, Ettie. The Tiger was going to keep coming for you, and eventually he'd have gotten you. I had to send you away, somewhere you would be safe."

Ettie holds the ax before her and points it at me. "Explain," she commands.

313

"He owed me a debt for breaking him out of the Châtelet," I say, pointing to le Maire. "He's a spy, a son of the Guild of Letters. If anyone knows how to disappear from the face of the earth, it's him. So I called in the debt he owed. He went to Thénardier with a price he couldn't refuse. The diamond tiara we took from the Tuileries, do you remember? Valuable enough to tempt Thénardier to cross even the Tiger and secretly sell you to a stranger."

Ettie is staring at me, but she starts to lower the ax, so I press on.

"The only way I could guarantee you'd be safe from the Tiger was if he believed that someone had taken you from both of us, and that I had no idea where you were. I attacked him in the presence of the entire Court. I swore terrible things. There is no one in any of the nine Guilds who, after witnessing my punishment, would believe I had brought it intentionally upon myself."

Blind are the distracted.

The ax clatters to the ground, and Ettie stands before me, shaking.

"I've dreamt of this moment for two years, Nina. I've hoped and prayed and waited and prepared. I thought you'd come and save me from him," she says, looking at le Maire. "I never suspected. I can't believe that it was you who did this to me." Tears fill her eyes, and she buries her face in her hands. My heart twists. Ettie, who has been left by everybody she loved. I was the one she trusted, the one who swore to look after her.

"I'm sorry, Ettie. . . . The less you knew, the safer you would be."

"S-sorry is not close to enough to make up for leaving me with him," she says, raising her head and pointing at le Maire. "Do you know how awful he is? How boring?"

I stare at her. The tears in her eyes are just tears of frustration.

Le Maire sighs loudly.

"He says nothing, he tells me nothing, he confines me to three rooms. I'm not allowed to ask questions, or sing, or breathe, or talk to him."

"It's never stopped you from talking," says le Maire.

"No, but you never answer me, which is pretty much the same thing!" Her eyes are wild. "Nina, I've been talking to myself for two years! Two years! And I know how long it was because I kept track of the days by carving marks into the walls. . . . I'd never have known how much time was passing because *I was never allowed to open the shutters*!

"He keeps telling me his name is Monsieur Madeleine, but it isn't! He has a tattoo, a prison tattoo, and I know the mark of the Guild of Letters when I see it."

"See? She doesn't stop talking," le Maire says with weariness.

"And he doesn't know *any* stories."

"You told yourself enough for the both of us," le Maire offers drily.

I know the signs of two people who have been too long cooped up together.

"And the nuns think he is a saint! The gardener thinks he's the Holy Lord incarnate. He's got them all wrapped around his little finger, and if I ever dare try to get news of the outside world or, Ysengrim forbid, seek out any company aside from his, they all cluck at me that *Monsieur Madeleine wouldn't like it!*"

"At times," le Maire says to me, "at times I have thought that you should have left me to rot in the Châtelet."

Ettie shoots him a reproachful look before she carries on with her tirade. "At first I thought he was one of the Tiger's men, but after a few weeks—"

"During which she tried to escape on twenty-three separate occasions—"

"I realized he couldn't be working for the Tiger. But still he refused to tell me who he was and what he wanted with me." She shivers. "I used to think he had sinister intentions, but after a while I came to understand that he only meant me to die of boredom.

"And all the while, I couldn't know what was happening, to Gavroche, and Orso, and Loup, and Montparnasse . . . and you." She looks up at me, the fury slowly draining out of her. "I could barely sleep each night, wondering what might have happened to you."

My eyes burn at her mournful words. I've missed the sound of her voice, her nonsensical reactions. I've missed her so much it was like a physical ache.

"I tried to be ready because I knew you'd come for me."

The blaze of belief in her eyes puts me to shame. "But he took my weapons, so I couldn't practice with them."

"You tried to stab me with your knife," le Maire reminds her.

"He wouldn't even let me eat with a knife and fork," she says, "which is fine in the Halls of the Dead. But when the nuns are watching you eat with your fingers like you're some kind of animal—"

"You tried to stab me with your *fork,* too."

She ignores him. "I tried to keep up the things you taught me. And I didn't eat too much, so I'd not get slow if we had to escape suddenly. I fed half my food to the birds, and every time I did that I thought about whether you had enough food, whether there was sickness, whether little Gavroche had recovered . . . whether you and St. Juste had declared your feelings for one another."

"Why is everyone convinced I am in love with St. Juste?" I ask, disgruntled.

"I hear he is very handsome," le Maire says gravely. "That he has the face of an angel."

"Oh, Nina!" Ettie says with a sob, and she throws herself into my arms, almost bowling me over. "I've been so miserable without you." Over her head, le Maire gives me look that says she has been far more trouble than she is worth.

He is a grown man, a member of the Guild of Letters, a spy, a hardened criminal, so I try my utmost not to show him how amusing I find the fact that he is being utterly undone by a mere slip of a girl.

"What are you doing here, Black Cat?" he asks.

"I would not have come, le Maire, except—"

Ettie pushes away from me. "Le Maire?" she says, and then she looks at the man who has kept her imprisoned. *"Le Maire?!"*

He looks at me, his eyes heavy with reproach.

"Le Maire?" Ettie is saying again, her voice pitched high in disbelief. "One of the three living Wonders of the Miracle Court? Le Maire, who convinced an entire town that he was their mayor for three years? Le Maire, who infiltrated the Austrian Court and escaped from the Bastille?"

I look between the two of them.

"And you said you had *no stories to tell*?"

I hastily interrupt this one-sided exchange to address le Maire. "I need your expertise, and there is no one else I can ask, no one who can do what I need done."

"The debt was to hide her." He frowns and motions at Ettie as if she is no more than an envelope he has had to secrete away. "There was no talk of further aid."

I smile at him. "If you do this favor for me, le Maire, then you will not need to hide her from the Tiger anymore— your debt will be considered fully repaid."

It takes the space of a heartbeat for him to reply. "What do you need me to do?"

"And what about me?" Ettie says, her voice as sharp as the blade of the ax. "What am I to do while you and le

Maire are off having adventures? You cannot leave me here or hide me somewhere else. I'll not stand for it, Nina!"

I fix her with a cold gaze. "I am going to enter the Flesh Guild and I am going to kill the Tiger," I say.

The gravity of my task should frighten her enough to calm down all her talk of adventures.

But to my surprise, she smiles, a glint in her eyes.

"Good," she says. "It's about time we did that."

33

The Ruined Flesh

Outside in the rue Plumet, night has fallen. The oil lamps are feeble halos of light punctuated by long pockets of darkness, giving ample opportunity for any Wretched looking to carry out a quick mugging. Or to steal someone away.

"You know what to do?" I ask Ettie when le Maire has finally gone.

"Yes," she says grimly.

I give a low whistle, the call of the Ghosts.

Behind me, Gavroche emerges out of the night. He has taken to following me around; I am not sure if it's on Orso's orders or because he is so fond of Ettie and thinks that if he follows me he might find her.

This is his lucky day.

Ettie gives a small cry and takes him in her arms. His smile is so wide it threatens to split his face in two.

"Gray Brother, will you bring Ettie to where she needs to go?"

He looks lovingly at Ettie and nods.

"Are you afraid?" I ask Ettie.

"Everyone is afraid," she says, echoing Azelma's words to me.

"You know we can't survive this, Ettie," I say softly.

"Then we die together," she replies, shaking her curls defiantly. "I'd rather live one glorious night hunting by your side, Nina Thénardier, than a hundred lifetimes without you." She raises her palm and I see the scar where we made our oath in the palace all those nights ago. I raise my own hand and we intertwine our fingers.

"Nous sommes d'un sang," she says. And she and the little Ghost disappear into the night.

My next task awaits me. I slip over an unattended section of the palace walls, which I found years ago on one of my night wanderings, and creep stealthily to an entrance I know to be frequented by servants. In a back closet, I open my satchel and pull out a dress, the first of several items I "acquired" from the Duchesse de Callicèbe one night when she was away. I layer my skin with powder to erase the darkness, pinch my cheeks to add color, and dab scent on my stolen wig. I also helped myself to a weighty pair of diamond drop earrings, which I fasten to my earlobes.

Thus disguised, I slip from the closet and into one of the corridors, where I bump into several large footmen hurrying to and fro with great trays of food. I grab one of the men, seemingly accidentally, and I laugh too loud, pretending to sway.

"Oh my, I don't have the faintest idea where I am!" I giggle.

The footman looks annoyed at being stopped in his tracks, but he pastes a smile onto his face and with great decorum disentangles himself from me. "Let me lead you back upstairs, madame."

He escorts me through the Pavillon de Flore and up the back stairs to the palace. Then he opens a door and everything is light and color.

The ball is a seething tangle of bodies, spread out over two floors off the central Pavillon de l'Horloge. I pause for a minute to appreciate the giant chandelier, which sends sparkling light over everybody. It's said to be the greatest chandelier in all of Paris, even all the world. Perhaps one day I'll steal it and it will hang above Tomasis's head in the Shining Court of the Thieves Guild. But tonight, I have a mission; the last piece of my plan must be set in place.

Everybody who's anybody in society is present tonight: nobility, royalty, foreign dignitaries and ambassadors.

A footman walks past with a tray. I reach out and grab a

glass of pink champagne and take a sip. It's delicious, light, bubbly, and sharp. I survey the ballroom through the bottom of my glass and count the number of servants circulating with trays of champagne, detailing which entrances and exits they use. Twenty guards in blue livery stand, two at each door. I frown. From the corner of my eye I spot a uniform of blue with shining brass buttons. A member of the Sûreté. I count four Sûreté agents in all. They look conspicuous and ill at ease.

I choose the youngest one, a black-haired boy too thin for his uniform but with the right fresh-faced foolishness to tell me what I need to know. I plunge straight into the crowd, letting them bump into me and turn to apologize. My hands are quick, my smile is enchanting, my manners are irreproachable. I make my way to the other side of the hall, pull out the fan that I just acquired, and, fanning myself, approach the young officer.

"*Bonsoir, Officier,*" I say in a coy undertone.

The boy looks alarmed that I'm speaking to him and goes slightly pink.

"I'm looking for the lovely red-haired inspector. She told me to meet with her ten minutes ago, and I can't find her anywhere."

I flutter my eyelashes and gaze at him hopefully.

"Inspector Javert will probably be occupied for some time more, mademoiselle," he answers in a low voice. "She's in a meeting in the Salon de la Reine."

I make a face. "I'll wait. I'm not in a rush," I lie, though it is, in fact, most inconvenient that the inspector is here at the Tuileries when I need her to be ready to play her part in my schemes.

I thank the officer prettily, then turn and almost walk right into . . . *St. Juste?*

For a moment we stare at each other. He's dressed in dark wine velvet with a white-and-gold cravat.

His mouth is slightly open as his eyes travel from my head to my feet. "Well, you look entirely different."

"What on earth are you doing here?" I hiss, tucking my hand into his arm.

St. Juste hates balls, and rich people, and fun, so his being here is deeply out of character and practically shouts that he's up to something. But he's also standing here in a velvet coat looking devastatingly handsome.

St. Juste lowers his lips to my ear in a manner that might seem seductive to anyone around us. "We are planning an act of treason against every person in this room, so I thought, what better opportunity to survey the palace than the occasion of a ball? Why are *you* here?"

"I'm a Thief, St. Juste. Breaking into places where rich people get drunk and leave their jewelry lying around is what I do," I say quickly.

There's a distracted look on his face, and a muscle twitches in his cheek.

"How did you even get in?" I ask him.

"My grandfather on my mother's side was a tutor to

several of the dukes. He's often invited to these sorts of soi-rées and was only too delighted to let me come in his place. He thinks I'm growing disillusioned with my heretical be-liefs."

I lead St. Juste by the arm through the ballroom and toward a magnificent staircase teeming with people going up to the second floor. He clings to me in a way that I tell myself is because of the heaving crowds around us.

"Why did you ask that Sûreté officer where the inspector is?" he murmurs in my ear, his voice as low and intimate as a lover's whisper.

"There is something here that I need to obtain," I say vaguely, giving him a mischievous smile. I don't think St. Juste will like my plans for Inspector Javert.

"Oh? And what might that be?"

I rap him with my fan. "Do you tell me all your secrets, St. Juste?" I ask teasingly.

"Yes," he answers with brutal honesty.

"Well, then you're a fool," I say, leaning into him as if we're two young lovers flirting with impossible desire. Which obviously isn't the case. Because no matter what everyone says, I'm definitely not the slightest bit attracted to St. Juste. Or so I constantly remind myself.

I wait for a chance and drag us both down a corridor in the shadows. I know the layout of this palace intimately, thanks to my previous visit. The northern wing is barely used, so we take the long way around, down deserted corridors and past empty rooms. In the darkness, St. Juste holds my hand, more to keep from bumping into things than out of romantic inclination, but the feeling of his fingers wrapped around mine as I pull him along leaves me slightly breathless.

We go through the servants' stairwell to the corridor of the Salon de la Reine. There are two liveried guards stationed at the door beside a giant clock wrought of ivory and gold. It's a good thing that before I snuck into the ballroom, I set up a few loud traps timed to—

A crash rings out. The guards hurry toward the noise. I dash past them and stop before a tall door outlined in gilt.

I tell St. Juste to stand guard in the shadows behind the clock while I slip through a door onto an open balcony. The fireplace in the room below stands cold and empty, but the room itself is ablaze with other lights, making it hard for me to hide. I slowly lower myself into a corner and take in the room. In the center is a large table with a gigantic map of the city spread out on it that would drive St. Juste wild with envy. There are objects set on the map in perfect rows. My heart pounds as I recognize what they are.

Toy soldiers.

There are four people in the room. Inspector Javert is one of them, recognizable by the long red hair tied into a tight tail at her neck and her uniform of bright blue. Good. I'll just wait for her meeting to be finished; then I'll slip down and waylay her with information that I know will bring her to the right place at the right time. . . .

There's also a dark-haired noble turned away from me.

And a woman in a shimmering dress of silver. I catch my breath. Son Altesse Royale la Reine.

The queen peels off one of her long gloves, and I frown: there's something strange about her hand. The flesh is a mess of shining skin blotched with angry red stains. It no longer looks like a hand.

From this day forth, whoever even thinks of putting death in the waters of this city will cast their own hand into the flames until it is ruined.

I shiver, remembering the words of Corday's curse.

Ysengrim take you.

Oblivious to my silent curses, the queen picks up a toy soldier from the map.

I look again at the map and recognize twenty red marks at strategic locations. And around each mark is a ring of perfectly arranged soldiers.

"Are you sure you're ready?" the queen asks the dark-haired nobleman.

"Do I not look ready?" he answers smoothly. "We know the exact location of each splinter cell. We outman them ten to one. We'll wipe them from the city's memory."

My heart surges—they're talking about St. Juste and the Société!

"Any survivors will be arrested," the queen adds. "They will be publicly tried, and will be found guilty. They, their families, their friends, and anyone who even recognizes their names will be fed to Madame Guillotine."

"You have their names?" asks the nobleman.

The queen smiles and is about to answer, when, on the balcony beside me, the door opens and St. Juste tumbles in, mouthing "Guards."

I lunge desperately for the door he releases behind him, but I'm too late—the weight of it swings shut with a noticeable click.

Every head in the room turns toward us.

"Who's there?" Javert demands.

In a rustle of heavy silk and satin, the queen is at the door of her Salon, commanding her guards to drag us down.

Every lesson Gentleman George taught me whirls through my head as I calculate our options.

If you are ever caught among the nobles, simply pretend you're doing something indiscreet.

There's only one thing for it: I fling myself at St. Juste, throwing my arms around his neck. Shocked, he stumbles backward, and we land in a heap on the floor.

"Listen to me, St. Juste—we are betrayed," I hiss in his ear in the few seconds I have.

His eyes widen at my words; then I kiss him and hope desperately that he doesn't push me away or ask what I'm doing. His arms snake around me, pulling me closer as he kisses me back fiercely. He tastes like coffee and red wine. And I'm pretty sure I hear him growl my name when the balcony doors are flung open and we're torn apart and dragged to our feet. The spectators below can now see us both, so I use all my strength when I send a sharp slap across St. Juste's face.

"How *dare* you, sir!" I say loudly. "Don't think a few kisses meant I was ready for *that*."

St. Juste is dazed. Wincing and confused. The guards drag us out into the corridor while I demand, "Unhand me," and order, "Take this gentleman back to the ball, where he can try his luck with *easier* maidens."

I keep up my flow of dialogue until we're standing before the queen. My skin crawls with fear. What if she recognizes me? When I look up at Her Majesty, I feign shock and drop to my knees. Behind me, St. Juste follows suit quickly.

"What is this?" she asks.

"Forgive me, Your Majesty. I made the mistake of trusting this gentleman." My voice is high with histrionics. "I didn't object to a few friendly kisses, but then he dared to put his hand on my—"

The queen gives me a dismissive wave and I fall silent. Her face is blank, and she barely looks at me. She doesn't recognize me. I'm painted and dressed in finery as I was two years ago, but she didn't look at me then, either. All she saw was Ettie. I might as well have been invisible, except to—

The dauphin steps into the corridor. The past two years have been kind to him; he's still incredibly handsome. Dark hair, artfully disheveled, his muscular frame clothed in a magnificent coat of chocolate velvet and trimmed with bright gold. He looks straight at me, taking in the scene, and turns to his mother.

"You'll be missed from the assembly," he says.

The queen lifts a gloved hand to him. "I trust you can deal with this."

The prince nods. "*Oui,* my queen."

The queen turns on her heel and glides down the corridor, back to the ball.

I swallow hard, unsteady thoughts racing through my mind. I keep my head low. Surely the dauphin won't look closely enough to recognize me. I'm just a random female among the hundreds at the ball.

The prince reaches out his hand.

"Hello, Nina," he says.

34

The Truth

I pale beneath my white powder.

The dauphin looks at St. Juste. "Who's this?"

"No one," I say in a dismissive voice.

I hear a faint splutter from St. Juste.

"Escort him back to the ball," the prince orders the guards.

They take St. Juste firmly by the elbow and lead him away. St. Juste doesn't protest and I don't watch him go. If I want to protect him, I must pretend he's nothing and no one to me. Not that I've much of a choice; the prince has me by the arm and is dragging me into the Salon de la Reine before I can say another word.

"What are you doing here?" he asks.

"I came to find the inspector," I say.

The prince's face falls, but Javert looks at me, frowning darkly.

"Who are you?" she demands.

"My name is Nina Thénardier, Inspector."

"You break into the Tuileries during the biggest ball of the season so you can see the inspector?" the dauphin says incredulously. "I waited and hoped for years to get word of you." He stares at me with an intensity I'm not sure I like. "You and Ettie are the only friends I've ever had. The only people who aren't afraid of me. I think of you every day, every night."

I raise an eyebrow. "Every night?"

He reddens, but only slightly. "Yes, every night," he says boldly. "I've even wished you'd make good on your threat and sneak in one night to slit my throat. Anything so I could see you again."

I don't really have time for these reminiscences, and shift my feet as a familiar feeling of annoyance rises in me. "The night I left you, Ettie was kidnapped, and it's taken me two years to locate her."

The prince stares at me. "Kidnapped?" He steps toward me with arms outstretched. "Nina, I'm so sorry. Do you know who took her?"

I cross my arms. "An ex-convict named Jean Valjean. Rumor has it the inspector has been tracking him for years. And I've found his hideout."

Javert gives a start and stares hard at me.

"I thought the inspector would want to know," I finish innocently.

"Why didn't you come to me for help when this first happened?" the dauphin asks, a slightly hurt note returning to his voice.

"What could you have done? You're no good at finding criminals, and you wouldn't know the first thing about disappeared paupers."

I've responded too quickly, and he blinks at me, wounded.

"I could have been a friend."

I roll my eyes. "I don't need friends. I need someone who knows how to deal with Valjean. I need her." I point at the inspector.

The prince sighs and rubs a hand across his forehead.

"In two days I'll send soldiers to rescue Ettie from this Val—" he begins.

"No!" I interrupt him. "You don't understand. Ettie isn't safe. We must act now."

"Tell me the address and I'll have guards stationed there to ensure she remains safe."

"If Valjean thinks he's been discovered, he'll disappear." I turn in frustration to Javert. "Tell him!"

Javert eyes me coldly. She has no idea who I am or if she can trust me, but from her reaction to le Maire on the Pont Neuf and the conversations I've overheard among the officers at the Sûreté, she *does* know Valjean.

"This girl is correct," she says now. "Valjean is an expert

at evading capture. It's best to leave him be until the moment we plan to arrest him."

"Well, then you'll lead a division of the army to arrest him as soon as we've squashed the rebels."

I can't let them proceed with their plans. They will wipe out all of the revolutionaries. St. Juste, Grantaire, and all the boys will be gone—and with them, all my plans.

"But Ettie's in danger *now*!" I say with real desperation.

"So is France!" the prince barks back at me. "If this city falls to revolutionaries, the whole country falls, and every ruling house in the land will be put to the guillotine. So you'll forgive me if I place the fate of France and the stability of our people before the safety of one girl."

"One friend," I say quietly.

"What?"

"You said we were your only friends."

The prince looks furious.

"Everything is weighing on my shoulders," he growls. "Father is abroad with Général Bonaparte, and he's trusted me with keeping the peace in his absence."

"Peace?" I march over to the table and wave a hand over the soldiers and streets, using precious seconds to familiarize myself with each position so I can report back to St. Juste. "Since when is *this* peace?"

"Since a hundred noble children died of poisoning in one month."

When the children of the nobility fell, their numbers were so great that mass funerals were organized. I watched the processions from the rooftops, hidden in the shadows. I saw the prince seated beside his mother and father. And my heart, which had been sick with fear that somehow he, too, would have been poisoned, felt a pang of relief. All around him the nobles wailed and wept. And when he raised his head and turned, I could see the sharp shine of tears in his eyes. Their grief was his; he was one of them, after all. But had he wept when starvation and poison sent a quarter of the city's poor to *their* graves? There had been no funeral processions then.

After the funerals came the news that doctors had found poison in the stomachs of the dead children. The nobility did not understand how it had been done. But the servants knew; they had seen their masters bid their children to drink from crystal bottles. And so the whispers grew and spread, and although the nobles had no memory of the deed, they somehow came to realize that they had done this unforgivable thing, that they had killed their own children.

The prince's voice is like stone. "Since countless of my peers and family have been struck with the terrible impulse to plunge their hands into fire." His eyes are glittering with rage. His voice breaks. "Since we found ourselves under attack. And no one could say how it came to be. So it was decided that we should root out our enemies by creating the Société."

My blood runs cold. "What did you say?"

"I said we created the Société, a false group aimed at overthrowing the crown, and waited to see who would bite.

335

Who would reveal themselves to be traitors, enemies of the throne." He spreads his arms wide. "The membership has grown into the thousands. And all the while we have been waiting and watching, prepared to wipe them out in one fell swoop."

He falls silent. I make my face into a mask, refusing to betray any emotion.

"You don't remember, do you?" I ask.

He frowns at me in response.

"You don't remember what they did, the ones who are cursed to set their hands on fire."

I look at the prince, at his darkly glittering eyes, at his jaw set in determination. *He is one of them,* I remind myself.

He studies my face and sees it impassive. "I don't believe in curses."

"There was not enough bread, and the poor began to starve," I say. "Out of fear that hunger would lead to a violent uprising, the nobles put poison in the city wells so that all who drank from them would die."

"Don't be ridiculous," he tries to protest, but I ignore him.

"It was in revenge for these acts that the poison was given to the best-loved child of every noble house; it was almost given to you."

The prince blanches. The mesmerist may have hidden the memory of all else from him, but he remembers Ettie and me begging him not to drink from his mother's hand. He looks uncertain.

"You're a liar."

"And you're a fool."

The prince turns to Javert and in a decisive tone says, "She knows too much. Keep her locked up until it's all over. Then you've got permission to take as many men as you need to apprehend this Valjean."

Javert grabs me by the arm more roughly than necessary and starts to haul me out of the room.

"Wait!" The prince hesitates, suddenly awkward, his face flushed. "And—bring her back when it's done."

My eyes flash.

"Ask your mother if what I say is true," I call back over my shoulder. A terrible thought crosses my mind, and I add, "Ask her if she's ever thought of doing it again."

35

Inspector Javert

I know Javert's habits from months of watching her through the gendarmerie windows. I know that she is methodical with her schedules and paperwork, patronizing to the officers, and ruthless with the criminals who come before her. She doesn't say a word as she leads me away, clamping me so closely to her side that it might look to passersby as though we're friends going for a brisk stroll. She marches me down the back stairs and avoids the heavily crowded areas. As we cross a back courtyard of the Tuileries into the breaking dawn and head to where the carriages are waiting, I catch a glimpse of scarlet and gold: St. Juste is tailing us at a distance.

A sudden clamor of bells pierces the dim morning. And yet it's not their hour to ring. I recognize the tongues of Notre-Dame singing a lament. Someone important has died.

Another set of bells starts from the north side of the city. And then another from the east, singing the mourning song.

Javert merely paused at the sound of the first bell. The buzzing noise of the crowd has drawn to a silence.

A voice booms across the grounds. "We ask for one minute of silence in honor of the passing of General Jean Maximilien Lamarque."

I remember seeing the general on the Pont Neuf, shouting at his troops not to open fire on the crowd. He was ever a man of the people. The Death Dealers have done their work well. The general's death is the signal the students—and I—have been waiting for: the start of their new revolution, the start of my hunting.

A long silence is observed. The cold air nips at my cheeks.

"The funeral of General Lamarque will be held this morning."

The announcement rings in my ears, and I look around wildly for St. Juste. I need to tell him what I learned in the Salon de la Reine. If the funeral is today and I can't warn them, they'll go marching into a trap.

At a grubby carriage guarded by two gendarmes, Javert finally addresses me.

"Are you sure it's him?" She is trying to be businesslike, but I can hear the hope in her voice.

"He has a number tattooed onto his right arm: two-four-six-oh-one," I say, recalling it from the posters.

She bows her head as if the news is too much for her.

She is desperate to find Valjean—le Maire—who has

escaped her custody twice. The obsession burns inside her. Perhaps I can use this to get her to postpone their plans, giving me time to warn St. Juste and the others.

Her eyes snap to mine, and I see cold calculation there.

"Who are you?" she asks.

"Just a girl who lost a friend to that criminal Valjean," I say with a sniff. "I swore I would get her back. I made an oath."

Javert frowns. "And what is she like, your friend?"

"She is an innocent—naïve, trusting, and more beautiful than the dawn," I say.

I see it then, a flash of naked pain crossing Javert's face. And jealousy . . . She is jealous of Ettie? But Ettie is just a girl.

The inspector quickly adjusts her expression and eyes me head to toe. "And how are you acquainted with the prince?"

I can feel the judgment in her blue eyes as she takes in the color of my skin.

"We visited the palace, Ettie and I, as children," I say, for the Gentleman taught me that the best lies are the ones nearest the truth.

"I will give you a word of caution, then: no matter what he says, you cannot trust a man like the dauphin. Men easily charm with promises, but when the time comes to choose, they always choose their duty."

I taste her words, knowing deep in my bones that she is speaking about Valjean—le Maire. She has to be.

I look at her with my blankest expression.

"You think it strange that I say this when the dauphin clearly seems to care," she continues.

I think the dauphin is an emotional, lonely boy who would care for a hat if it showed him the least bit of attention, but I'm not about to tell her that.

"But men of his kind do not care for girls like you. You must push him away, protect yourself, or he will take everything from you and leave you with nothing."

Her mouth is a trembling line; her hands are closed into fists, her eyes drowning in pain.

Le Maire broke her heart. And so she hunts him.

"Did someone hurt you?" I ask, my voice gentle and curious.

Her eyes grow flat and cold at my question and she pulls on her gloves. "If they had, then they would come to regret it." She gives me a mirthless smile. "For unlike other women, once ruined, I am not the sort to fade away. I will pursue my enemy to the very ends of the earth."

She pauses, and I decide that her obsession with Valjean is going to serve me well; it is the worm with which I will bait the hook.

"Take her," she orders the gendarmes, who each grab me by an arm and pin me tight.

She orders them to throw me in a cell.

"And keep a watch on her." She eyes me askance. "I shall be most displeased if she escapes."

341

We've barely left the palace gates and my head is spinning.

I look out the carriage window and try to recognize the street we're on. But to my horror, all I see is row upon row of soldiers standing at attention in perfect formation. Waiting.

I must warn St. Juste and the boys. Orso will surely not come to the students' aid, and now that I've seen the prince's plans, I know they'll be marching to certain death. The thought twists itself inside me like a knife.

I must get to them. I must.

Tears spring to my eyes as we roll past the soldiers and into the city proper. I feel as if it is all slipping out of my control. All my plans. All my friends.

If they're all dead, they can't help me take down the Tiger.

The gendarmes are eyeing me. One is leering at my chest. Another is watching me warily, probably wondering what exactly I've done.

I make eye contact with the one who's leering and flutter my eyelashes.

"You couldn't open the window the smallest bit, kind sir?" I ask in my most sugary voice.

He grins at me revoltingly, and leaning over, he opens the window to the carriage.

I take only a second to purse my lips and give a short, sharp whistle, followed by a low one.

The gendarme nearest me backhands me across the face. "None of that!" he says, snarling.

The blow is mild, but I taste blood in my mouth. I think he's split my lip. He glowers at me, authority and dominance pouring off him.

"You'll regret that," I tell him.

They slam the window shut.

He raises his hand to strike me again just as the leering gendarme pokes him in the side.

"What's that?"

"What?" his companion asks, but then he notices it.

I sit there, my mouth closed, in perfect silence. And yet it's the strangest thing: my whistle hangs in the air. It sounds again and again, like an echo. First in faint, short snatches, then growing in volume until there is a chorus ahead of us, behind us. The horses shy, the carriage rocks, I hear the driver curse. And the whistles spin webs around us, drawing near. The horses neigh and shriek, and still the whistles grow louder, wilder.

Then they stop. And the silence they leave is more terrifying than anything else.

One gendarme hits the roof of the carriage with the butt of his gun.

There's a voice—the driver, I assume—cursing. A sound like something heavy being dragged off the roof. Then the frightened tones of a man begging for his life. Praying that God will forgive him.

The gendarmes are staring at each other, pale as death. They cock their pistols.

"We're armed!" they shout at the carriage door.

The door flies opens and they both fire at it, completely unaware that the other door is opening silently under the thunder of their shots. The rush of cold air behind them makes them turn a second too late, and the leering gendarme is ripped out of the carriage backward. His colleague grabs me and puts his gun to my cheek. I can almost taste the metal pressing into my face.

"I'll kill her! I'll shoot her head clean off!" he yells.

I laugh under his hold. "I wouldn't do that if I were you."

There's no response from outside. Only a dead silence. The gendarme, unnerved, forces me to my feet and, keeping the gun firmly planted at my cheek, pushes me out of the carriage.

A hundred Ghosts encircle us in a silent vigil. There's no sign of the driver or of the gendarme's colleague.

At the head of the Ghosts is Gavroche. He takes in the gun pressed to my cheek before his eyes travel to the gendarme's face. He shakes his head in mild warning.

The gendarme blinks suddenly, and I see the whites of his eyes as the tip of a knife is pressed into the back of his neck.

Montparnasse is hanging over the roof of the carriage.

The gendarme drops his gun and raises his hands. One of the Ghosts collects the gun, and it disappears into a gray cloak. They'll sell it to the Smugglers Guild for a week's worth of food for the pot. I grin widely.

Montparnasse slides down from the roof, landing on his feet more gracefully than any Cat, and comes to stand in front of the gendarme. He glances at my face, his eyes resting for the merest second on my split lip before they travel back to the man before him. The gendarme pales.

I told him he'd regret it.

"I found Ettie," I tell Montparnasse. He looks at me. If he suspects it was I who hid her in the first place, I can't tell.

There's a clattering of hooves on cold stone, and like a flustered knight arriving too late to rescue me, St. Juste swoops in on horseback.

"Nina!"

"St. Juste!" I cry, rushing to him. "The army—"

"I know," he says shortly. "I rode through a regiment of them."

He takes in the scene: me, the Ghosts, Montparnasse, and the empty carriage. "You're all right? I was worried," he says as he dismounts.

It is deeply unlike St. Juste to worry. He will brood obsessively, but not worry.

Gavroche reaches for the horse's bridle, and St. Juste lets him take it. Foolish. That horse will feed the Ghosts' pot for a month.

"I need to tell you—"

St. Juste takes in my split lip. "You're hurt."

I push him away, embarrassed—and conscious of Montparnasse's gaze.

St. Juste looks around, frowning in confusion. "Weren't there gendarmes?"

I try to look as blank as I can. St. Juste's gaze wanders back to me and then settles on Montparnasse.

"You didn't kill them, did you?"

I don't have time for this. "St. Juste, I saw the army's plans at the palace," I say in a rush. "You must warn the others. You *must* call off the protests."

His eyes snap to mine.

"It is as Orso warned," I continue. "The revolution is compromised. The nobility know where you'll be, and the army will be waiting to meet you."

"Are you certain?" St. Juste asks, all his concern for me evaporated.

"I saw it in the palace. There's a map of the city, just like yours, with marks for the positions of every cell of the Société."

St. Juste knots his fingers and thinks. "Will you come with me? To explain it all to the others?"

I nod. "We don't have much time."

"But what about the gendarmes?" St. Juste asks.

I wink at Montparnasse. "Forget the gendarmes."

36

A Little Fall of Rain

On the way across the city, Montparnasse leaves us, but Gavroche, my ever-silent shadow, remains. He takes my hand and stretches up to whisper in my ear.

"He has her," is all he says.

My heart contracts.

Focus, Nina. It's all part of the plan. Don't think of Ettie now.

The City knows something is coming and lies silent, waiting. Like a cemetery, the streets are empty, wrapped in thick fog. All around there's a metallic tenseness to the air, the breath drawn by the crowd before the hanging man steps off the platform.

Those Who Walk by Day cower behind their locked doors.

The City has a long memory. The people don't forget.

The last time the children of the City rose, when their numbers were great and their hearts burned for change, there was no mercy for them. Neither woman nor child was spared. The streets ran red with blood.

I shudder.

We take the back way, knowing that the army is probably already on the march. We choose alleys and narrow roads where soldiers would find it hard to walk two abreast. But we can't avoid the smell of saltpeter, and the eerie soundlessness of a city that usually roars with life, even in the latest hours.

St. Juste suddenly comes to a halt. I don't need to look up at the street signs to know where we are. I can tell by taste, by touch. I wear this city on the soles of my feet.

"Rue Villmert," St. Juste says. His eyes narrow. "We're near the first cell. There should be more noise than this. . . ."

He's right. From all the talk, I expected a barricade manned by students drinking and cheering. There should be anything but this unnatural silence. Still, I shake my head.

"Perhaps they heeded Orso's warning and called it off," I suggest, not believing my own words.

St. Juste frowns at me, then makes up his mind and sets off down the street toward the avenue Ficelle, where the cell should be.

At least the flag still flies, red as the blood of angry men—or so Grantaire informed me one particularly drunken night. It protrudes from the top of an impossible structure built of barrels, tables, and chairs, anything that could be spared or ransacked from nearby houses.

"No . . . ," St. Juste says, and I hear the unfiltered rage in his voice.

For this is not the sight of a waiting protest, of young men preparing to fight. A smell hangs in the air—it is a smell of slaughter and death, the air foul with human waste and blood. And when we go closer, we see them: the dead festoon the barricade like garlands, the bodies of men, women, even children tossed up against the structure at awkward, unnatural angles. They lie at our feet, a carpet of ruined flesh. Their shattered remains are not tragic figures made beautiful in paintings, but the bleeding, open corpses of true battle, guts, excrement, and all.

I bend down and force myself to gently touch the corpse of a small girl. She is not yet cold. They have been dead for scarcely an hour.

"Monsters," St. Juste says. "We will show them no mercy."

I glance around, my heart heavy. The barricade stands, not dismantled or burned or broken in any way; there are no soldiers' bodies. The enemy took the cell completely unaware, trapping them against their own wall and killing them where they stood, as they could have done only if they knew where the barricade was going up.

"I told you, St. Juste. Orso told you. You are betrayed! We must get back and call off the uprising. It has no chance of success."

St. Juste's gaze sweeps the dead, the barricade that rises behind them.

"We must recover the flag," he says, an edge of certainty creeping back into his voice.

Gavroche perks up beside me.

"What?" It's such a ridiculously St. Juste thing to want to do. "We don't have time! We must warn the others."

"The flag is the symbol of what these men and women died for," he says, his voice rising in anger, anguish pouring out of him.

"St. Juste, please," I say desperately, fear welling in me, tears in my eyes. "It's a piece of cloth! I'll steal you a hundred flags!"

I don't understand why I'm shaking, or so angry, or so afraid. He is one of Those Who Walk by Day, and a means to an end. . . . Surely it shouldn't matter to me if he wants to pluck flags from barricades and march off to his death.

But I can't turn away from his face, so earnest, even with a long smear of dirt across it and rage burning in his eyes.

Time seems to slow. I see St. Juste's eyes widen in horror. For there, behind us, is Gavroche, high on barricade, reaching for the flag. He's almost got it, just a bit farther to go, but that distance is enough to expose him to any soldiers who have been ordered to remain behind. . . .

I scream for Gavroche and leap at the barrier, but St. Juste is closer. He hurls himself upward. Gavroche has the flag wrapped in his hands now, and he turns and smiles triumphantly at us.

Gunshot pierces the air as St. Juste collides with him, and time speeds up again as they fall and I fall. There is the sharp shock of ground, the rattling of bones, a promise of future pain. And a heap next to me—a small gray boy and a young man in a coat of scarlet.

I wrench myself up and drag myself toward them. Gavroche is facedown, tucked into St. Juste's arms. My heart thuds in my ears; the air is thick with the smell of saltpeter, gunpowder, dust, and sweat. I turn him over. There is blood everywhere.

Gavroche blinks at me. He's still holding on to the damned flag. I grab him, checking him for a wound . . . checking him for any sort of injury. I feel a terrible relief flooding over me. He is not hurt; they must have missed! But where did all this blood come from? Then I notice that Gavroche is looking at St. Juste, his large eyes full of fear.

St. Juste is marble white, the elegantly carved angles of his face in stark relief against the brightness of his blazing eyes.

He has a hole in his side, small and black, and the dark blood blooms around it. I can barely hear my voice shouting at him as I tear a length of his shirt and press it to the wound. I scream at Gavroche to get help. I manage to bind the cloth tight, pulling it all the way around him, and tears start to blur my vision.

"Look at me, you stupid, useless, pointless . . ." My words fail me, but the venom in them snaps him out of his dream and he focuses on my face.

"Nina," he says, lifting a trembling hand to my cheek.

"Don't you 'Nina' me. You've got a bullet in you, and we have to get out of here, because there are soldiers and they are going to kill us."

He smiles then, and it is like the rising sun. Even in the chaos it takes my breath away.

"Here, lean on me . . . ," I say. I try to raise him as I stand, but his body slumps. "St. Juste, for Rennart's sake!"

He blinks up at me.

"It's raining," he says. His voice has lowered to a delirious whisper.

The drops fall gently at first, washing the grime and blood from his face. The City is weeping for her children.

"Rain will make the flowers grow . . . ," he murmurs in a singsong voice.

"Are you singing?" I say in horror.

I slap him hard across the face. And he recoils in shock. He stares at me with wide, focused eyes.

"So help me, St. Juste, if you don't get a grip and stand up, I will shoot you again myself."

He gives a gurgle of weak laughter at that. "You wouldn't," he says with assurance.

"Don't tempt me—it'd be a whole lot easier to get out of here if I weren't dragging a useless Frenchman with me."

"No," he insists. "You wouldn't shoot me because you don't have a gun."

"Of course I do. I stole your pistol ten minutes ago."

37

The Courier

I manage to drag St. Juste down two roads before Gavroche returns with le Maire. The giant takes one look at St. Juste and gently hoists the boy over his shoulder, ignoring his complaints of pain. Le Maire is a machine, and both Gavroche and I jog to keep up with him as he speeds down alleyways to the rue Musain.

Grantaire answers my thundering at the door. There are dark circles under his eyes, and he's got a pistol stuffed untidily into his breeches. He takes one look at St. Juste and yells for Feuilly. Suddenly the students are everywhere, wresting St. Juste from le Maire's grasp and carrying him away.

"Grantaire, you must call it all off!"

The words come tumbling out, though I know that with them I might be losing the boys' aid.

"The palace knows your plans, and the army has been dispatched to all of the cell positions."

I follow him like a shadow, almost tripping over the stacks of rifles piled up in the corridor.

"We just came from the avenue Ficelle. The cell has been wiped out."

Feuilly has set St. Juste up in the kitchen and is shouting orders, getting others to boil water and cut sheets into bandages.

"You can't all be tending to him," Grantaire snaps. "I want the first ten of you ready to go on ahead."

The students break away from St. Juste and rush back into the salon, leaving me alone with Grantaire, St. Juste, and Feuilly. Feuilly has St. Juste sprawled across four chairs. He looks half dead; his eyes are closed.

"Grantaire! Did you not hear what I said? You are not still sending them out? The Société is compromised. You must abort the plans."

Grantaire frowns at me and says firmly, "We shared Orso's suspicions with the Société, and the courier has just this minute brought word back that the plan is to proceed. Barricades are set up around the city. Our time has come."

I gape at him in amazement.

"We've been planning this for years. We know what they're doing," he finishes, slight worry punctuating the veneer of his confident words.

They don't believe me.

They killed one-third of the mice for reason, and one-third for sport. Then the cats hanged the six little mice before all of their brethren to teach the mice fear. The guillotine is for those the City loves; Montfaucon is for the rest of us. These boys will surely hang.

Desperately, I swing around to St. Juste.

"Wake him up!" I tell Feuilly.

Feuilly shakes his head as he ties off the length of cloth around St. Juste's middle. "He's in shock. He needs to rest."

In one movement I grab a bucket of water that Feuilly had the students fill earlier and unceremoniously dump it over St. Juste's head.

He sits up, spluttering, as Grantaire grabs at me.

"St. Juste, tell them the Société is compromised," I demand. "Tell them what we've seen."

St. Juste can barely focus. Feuilly props him up and glares at me.

"Tell them what we saw at the avenue Ficelle," I say again. "Everyone was *dead,* Grantaire. It's a trap. You are betrayed."

"Betrayed? Yes," St. Juste says, color rising in his cheeks. "But the question is, Who has betrayed us?"

I frown.

"You and your allies took our money and provided us with weapons and information, and just when we needed you most, you backed out."

"Wh-*what?*"

I stare at St. Juste, remembering with sudden clarity how he showed up at the palace with the flimsiest of excuses, how he asked me why I was talking to the Sûreté officer.

"The spy in the Société, the reason the Guilds won't back us. The ambush on the street. Did you do it all?" St. Juste asks me.

"Is *that* why you followed me to the ball? You think I am the traitor?"

"You cannot deny that you're known to Sûreté agents and royalty alike. Curious, is it not? We all know you have other priorities. Perhaps we too easily forgot that you and your kind are criminals after all," Grantaire finishes.

You and your kind.

And I thought for a moment that perhaps I could be one of them. Clearly, they never thought so.

"Do you really think I could betray you?" I ask.

"I think you would do anything to find that girl." Grantaire's words are like knives. "She's all that matters to you."

He thinks that I lost her; they all think so. I've played my part so well that nobody believes anything other than what I have shown them.

I snap. With one swipe I pull out the pistol I stole from St. Juste and point it straight at his heart.

"There is no time for these histrionics," I say sharply.

He takes a second to realize what I've done. They all freeze, and I look at them grimly.

"Are you going to shoot me again?" His voice is like ice. *"Again?"*

"I didn't see who shot me at the barricade—were you trying to make sure I wouldn't come back and warn my brothers that we had been betrayed?"

"The day I shoot you, St. Juste, it won't be a flesh wound. *My kind* are unlikely to miss. Being criminals, we tend to have very good aim." I yell for one of the students to come. "Joly!"

Joly enters the kitchen and, seeing me with the gun, stops and stares.

"Where is this courier? Find the courier or I'll shoot St. Juste. You know I'm capable of it. Me being one of those *criminal* elements."

I press the gun deeper into St. Juste's chest. He barely flinches, measures me up with his eyes, and nods at Joly.

Joly goes thundering off, his footsteps echoing as he scarpers to the back of the house.

In seconds the doorway is full of anxious and curious boys. Some have weapons in their hands but hold them in a halfhearted manner, not sure what to do. Then Joly is back, pushing past them and dragging someone with him.

I turn my gaze from St. Juste to the doorway as the boys part to let the courier through.

I stare for a full trembling minute. Then I start to laugh, great belly-shaking, exhaustion-laden laughter that hits me like a wave. I lower my weapon.

Seeing my weakness, St. Juste tackles me, wresting the gun from my loose grasp, and we land in a heap on the floor. The boys are all shouting, but I can't stop laughing.

St. Juste has me pinned to the floor, his body holding mine heavily in place. Mostly because I'm too busy giggling to struggle. With one free hand he passes Grantaire the pistol. Grantaire takes it and trains it on me. Enraged at the tears of laughter pouring down my face, he demands to know what's so funny.

"D-don't you know who that is?" I splutter, trying desperately to calm myself.

They all look at the courier, a woman in a dingy, patched oilcloth coat with a single untidy tendril of red hair spilling from her cap.

"Rennart's balls, St. Juste. You're all fools. That's Inspector Javert of the Sûreté."

"Don't be ridiculous," Grantaire retorts. "This is the courier. She's been bringing us messages from the Société for months."

Of course she has. Her mouth is a grim line, and a vein at her neck throbs angrily.

"She was there at the ball tonight, in the Salon de la Reine with the queen. The dauphin told me that the Société was created to flush out the enemies of the Crown. The Société itself is a lie."

St. Juste looks at the inspector.

"She's lying," Javert spits, but I see her eyes darting around, measuring the distance to the door, counting the people in the room.

"You don't have to believe me. Ask Orso. Ask any of my people. They all know who she is." I grin maliciously at her. "Or you can ask the gentleman I arrived with."

St. Juste orders them to call my companion in.

There are footsteps and a deep voice. Then le Maire

enters, his form filling the doorway. He takes in the scene and stops when he sees Javert.

Her eyes widen. Her face blanches.

"You," she says.

Le Maire looks at her. His face is a strange war of emotions. "Inspector."

She lurches at him, but two of the students catch her between them.

Javert lifts her chin defiantly. St. Juste takes his pistol back from Grantaire and trains it on her.

"You stupid children. You will never succeed." Javert's face wrinkles in a sneer. "We know your names, your associates, each member of your family. There's nowhere you can hide from us. We are coming for you."

St. Juste's face is a mask of rage. His hand trembles, but he cocks the pistol.

For a moment I think he'll shoot her. Then he lowers the gun.

"Take her away," St. Juste says.

An unrepentant Javert is led out, with le Maire following slowly behind.

Grantaire suddenly realizes that I'm still lying on the floor, and he tries to help me up. I push him away.

"You should have shot her," I say to St. Juste as I sit up.

"She's a woman," St. Juste says.

I look at them in despair. Their illogical upper-class breeding so often overrules common sense.

"She was going to lead you to your deaths."

St. Juste's brow is furrowed. He's trying to regroup his thoughts.

"All the information," he says. "All of our orders have been compromised." He looks at me like a lost boy. "She and other couriers from the Société have carried messages to our brothers throughout the city. They've all gone out to fight."

"Then they're all betrayed," I say quietly.

"We can't let them stand alone."

"All probability says they're dead," I say, repeating his words back to him. "If you go out there to join them, you'll die too."

"What else would you have us do?" he asks. His eyes are haunted. "We cannot leave our brothers to lie broken in the streets while we sit here in safety."

I sigh. These boys will no more abandon their cause than I will mine, no matter the odds against them.

"Send some of your men to the remaining cells," I say. "See if you can still sound a warning."

St. Juste turns to the students. Five of them nod at him, wordlessly taking up their weapons and turning to go.

"Be careful," he calls as he watches them go, then turns back to me.

"I owe you an apology . . . ," he says.

"I don't need apologies," I say, looking hard at him. "I need you to help me destroy another monster."

He listens. They all listen. They hang on my every word as if their lives depend on it.

On my way out of the house I find Javert gagged and tied to the banister.

Gavroche is sitting on a step, watching her with satisfaction. Le Maire hovers uneasily nearby.

I give Javert my widest smile.

"Inspector," I say. "Good news."

She growls at me through the gag, which is good. I need her to be angry.

"I found Valjean." I point at le Maire.

She throws him a look of such venom that it makes me pause, and leaning over to him, I whisper, "What exactly happened between the two of you?"

He averts his gaze, a flush rising on his neck.

I shrug and turn my attention back to Javert. Pasting a smirk on my face, I continue. "I'm sure the dauphin will soon be here with his great army, ready to cut down all who stand in their way." I wave my hands dramatically. "But we're moving on. If you want to find us, I leave our change of address here in this note." I pin a piece of paper to her shirt. "We'll all be there, won't we, Valjean?"

I nudge him in the ribs and he looks thunderously at me.

I take one last look at Javert, trussed like a roasting chicken, and blow her a kiss.

"Do send my best regards to His Majesty."

38

The Tiger's Lair

The Tiger's lair is a derelict dockmaster's warehouse. Its windows are mostly broken or boarded up. To unsuspecting passersby, it looks empty.

We watch from across the road, hidden behind a crumbling wall, as a tall, nondescript figure walks straight up to the front door and knocks sharply. There's no answer. He waits patiently. After some time, he knocks again. This time the door groans, opening with an ominous creak of warped wood. From our shelter we see that the tall man at the door is facing down the barrel of a gun.

He doesn't move an inch, doesn't raise his hands. A voice comes rasping from inside the warehouse, demanding to know what he wants.

The tall man's voice is low but clear. It brooks no question and accepts no challenge.

"Guild of Letters," he says. "I'm here to do an audit."

<hr />

The river is a haze of thick fog. A few grubbers still flit about the docks, searching for nails or other bits of metal to sell.

Two boats are tied up on the riverside by the Guild House. In the dimness, I can just see Loup and his Ghosts slip from a sewer grate. Loup begins to cut through one of the heavy ropes that keep the first vessel moored. Gavroche boards the boat and pours something onto the deck, then sets it aflame. He leaps off, and the Ghosts rush back into their hole.

The flames grow as the boat lazily floats away from its mooring. Eventually, the few Fleshers posted by the docks see it and begin yelling and running toward it as it drifts along in all its blazing glory. They're so occupied with catching it that they don't see me slip from the shadows behind them and clamber up the side of the other boat. There I set down a bottle filled with a liquid that the Fisherman has carefully decanted for me.

She warned me sternly not to drop it, so I'm sweating as I let the bottle go, pushing it gently so it rolls down the deck. I take one look behind me. More Fleshers are running from the house now, toward the burning boat. My way clear, I leap from the deck and speed across the moorings and into the catacombs. I follow the dark passage till I come to a grate overhead.

A shadow emerges out of the wall. It has knives.

"You don't have to come with me," I say.

"I thought we were friends," Montparnasse replies. "It would be rude of me not to attend a friend's funeral."

I can't help but smile as we climb up an ancient ladder carved into the tunnel wall. When we reach the grate above, Montparnasse silently lifts it, and I scramble up, practically into his arms, to peer out. The street is empty. Anyone around is down by the river, watching the Fleshers recapture a burning boat.

We emerge just as an explosion thunders through the night and a dark cloud of heavy smoke mushrooms up from the river. It'll be seen and heard from miles around.

Just in case they didn't get my note.

"What did the Fisherman put in that bottle?" Montparnasse asks.

"I don't think I want to know," I reply as we jog down the street toward the Guild of Flesh.

New guards have been posted at the back of the building to cover those who are hunting down the burning ship, or those who got blown half to bits by the explosion. I grin to myself.

Montparnasse eyes the guards. "I can take them."

"Wait."

He raises an eyebrow at me.

"Yes, wait before you murder everything."

I pull out a pocket watch that I stole from Feuilly and look at the time. *St. Juste, where are you? We agreed on a time, and you're late.*

Yells and cheers break out from the front of the building. *"Liberté, égalité, fraternité!"*

We can hear the slogan of the Société being chanted by numerous voices carrying on the wind.

Montparnasse looks slightly taken aback.

"You brought the revolutionaries here?" His tone is half impressed, half horrified.

"The traitor compromised their plans. So I persuaded them to join a fight they stand a chance of winning," I say, winking at him.

The guards standing at the back of the building are pacing, unsure if they should leave their posts to investigate the explosion or the chanting. Someone sticks their head out a door and shouts at them to get to the front immediately. They all go running.

We scale the wall in seconds and drop into the garden. We make our way to the house and crouch in front of a broken window that's been unevenly boarded up. We peer through the gaps into a room with an open door; it's empty. I tie my scarf around my mouth and nose, and Montparnasse does the same with his. I reach into my bag and pull out two skin pouches. Montparnasse holds a match to the leather, and we toss both through the window. They land with a *thunk* and roll to the middle of the floor, small flames eating through them, and then they go out.

The burning pouches let off a thick, dark smoke that I can smell, even at this distance. It's heavy and sweet: the smell of the poppy. Two pouches of pure opium, provided by the Guild of Dreamers, thanks to Lord Yelles. They'll burn for hours and get stronger as they do, dulling the senses of everyone inside.

Montparnasse peers up at the building.

"The whole top floor," he says.

I follow his eyeline.

The Tiger's chambers. That's where we need to go. We could climb, but we would be exposed to anyone outside, and I don't know how long my distractions will last.

"We break into the cellar and enter from within," I say decidedly. "Then you can murder everyone."

We split up and do a quick reconnaissance of two sides of the building. He finds the large wooden delivery hatch on the west side. It has an ancient lock, which I pick in under a minute, and he lifts the heavy door. We drop into the darkness of a cellar, closing the door above us so as not to mark our entry point.

A feeling prickles at the back of my neck when something moves, probably a rat. Montparnasse's knife is out in a second. Then the smell hits us. Sweat, blood, rot, and human excrement. I breathe through my mouth as I advance. It's too quiet.

Montparnasse hesitates in front of me. He lights a match, and its tiny flame hisses to life, illuminating us. And then we see them: rows upon rows of women and children crammed against the walls, leaning on one another.

I look at them. They stare back at me, motionless. One of them blinks.

They're alive.

They're not tied up, but they don't have to be; the Tiger will have already fed them the poppy, so he has complete control over them.

The match goes out, and my mind whirls as I reach for another.

If these women were intended for the city's Flesh Houses, they'd already be there. There's only one reason to pack them like cargo in a warehouse. They're going to be shipped out.

It is known that the Tiger made his fortune as a slaver before taking over the Flesh Guild. And though there have been rumors that he was feeding Sisters from his Guild to brothels abroad, no one has ever known for sure.

Slavery is forbidden by the Law of the Miracle Court, and is illegal by the law of Those Who Walk by Day. That is why I have set bait for Inspector Javert to come. Because whether I live or die tonight, perhaps she will be able to find evidence enough to stop the Tiger's trade.

Montparnasse tiptoes to the door of this dungeon and puts his ear to it.

He holds up ten fingers and my shoulders drop. *Ten guards:* more than we thought we'd find.

We don't have time to stay and help the women, and we both know it. Yet Montparnasse is trying to help them to their feet.

"You've invited the army to this door," Montparnasse whispers. He looks at me, his eyes unreadable. "Do you know what the Fleshers will do to them when the soldiers arrive? They'll throw these women in the river so they don't get caught." His voice is shaking. "They'll drown them, and there'll be no proof they were here."

He's right, of course, and I'll be to blame because I brought the army. Instead of offering them a way out, I've signed their death warrant.

"You get them out," I say. "I must go get Ettie."

He grabs my hand as I turn to leave.

"He's waiting for me, not you," I tell him. "It's not your fight."

Montparnasse's face is shadowed in the flickering match light, uncertainty crossing his features.

"Ettie and I are only two," I insist, motioning to the women. "And they are so many. You must help them."

There are as many as five guards out front, and more will return to the garden soon. I can't get past them all. I'm a fighter, not a killer. Montparnasse is a killer. He knows it.

He knows he's the only one who can get these women out and defend them if it all goes wrong.

His grip on my hand is tight.

"I'm Master of the Assassins Guild," he says. "I've *never* been able to fight your battles. I've not been able to lift my hand to protect you. I cannot risk dragging my Guild into war." His eyes are burning with emotion. "But if he kills you, I'll take his head from his body and I'll set it on a pike in the middle of the Lords' table in the Miracle Court, and none will ever take it down. There it will rot, the worms will eat it to bone, and all who see it will remember you." His voice breaks. "Even if Corday asks my life of me in return, I'll do it. I swear."

In the dirt and the darkness, and with the high probability I will never see him again, I bury myself in Montparnasse's arms, resting my head against his hammering chest. He's muscle, bone, and steel. If he ever had a heart, I know it's mine. I want to tell him things, but I find that I can't put them into words. So I push away from him and, my eyes full of unshed tears, say:

"He won't kill me. I promise."

39

The Black Cat's Father

The sound of horse hooves on cobblestone echoes down the street as I clamber out of the cellar into the garden. The army is arriving, just as planned. Soon they'll have surrounded the building, searching for the revolutionaries. I look up at the façade. The Tiger's rooms are on the top floor. I can't go in through the cellars as we had planned because Montparnasse will be busy getting the women out that way. Although I'll be exposed, I've no choice but to climb. I wrap strips of cloth around my hands, tightening my claw picks in place, and I shinny up the building as fast as I can go.

I pass a window, an empty room, and pause only momentarily to listen; I hear raised voices from inside the house. The Fleshers must have rounded up the students; St. Juste's voice carries. He's trying to convince them to join the glorious revolution. I smile grimly and keep moving.

I'm almost at the top when a voice calls out, clear as a bell.

"Hello!"

I just have time to look up to find a greasy powdered head staring down at me through an open window.

Thénardier.

He cheerfully aims his pistol at me with his good hand and fires.

I throw all my weight onto one arm and let my body swing just as the bullet whistles past my ear.

Thénardier's head disappears and I curse, scrambling down to the lower-level window. I swing myself, sending my legs out and back again, and smash my way through the glass. It shatters around me as I crash into the room.

I lie on the rough wooden floor. My skin is ripped and bleeding; there's glass under my fingertips. But at least the room is empty. The Tiger's men are dealing with the revolutionaries and the soldiers downstairs. Through my scarf I can smell the sweet smoke of the poppy. That's good; it'll make them all slower and less inclined to beat anyone to death. *We can only hope.* I push myself up and wince; I've twisted my ankle.

Ysengrim be damned.

There's a heavy tread of boots on wood.

My dagger is in my hand as I pull myself to the door, trying not to put weight on my ankle.

Is this how it will end? A Cat felled by a sprained ankle in the Tiger's Guild? What kind of fool was I to think I could take him on in his own lair?

The door creaks open. My throat constricts and I prepare myself to attack. If someone is going to kill me, I'd like to get a few blows in first. I'd like to go down fighting.

It takes me a full second to recognize the man looming in the doorway, and when I do, relief floods through me.

"Le Maire!" I sway, and in three steps he has me on my feet, throwing my arm over his shoulder before I can protest.

"That boy of yours is giving them trouble," he says.

"He's not my boy," I protest, smiling as I imagine St. Juste taking on the Tiger's Guild.

Le Maire half carries me down an empty corridor and toward a flight of stairs. The Tiger's rooms are above, and le Maire is by my side.

"The weapons?" I ask.

Le Maire grins widely at me. "I did a full audit—guns, knives, everything. Removed all the ammunition. Emptied all the gunpowder down a privy."

"They just handed them over?"

"No one questions the People of the Pen."

He's right. The Guild of Letters is respected and feared by all.

Perhaps we can do this.

"But we've little time. They'll have discovered the treachery by now."

And if we fail today, his actions will be considered an act

of war between the Guild of Letters and the Tiger's Guild. We both know it.

What have I started?

The sounds of a brawl begin below us: men in a rage.

Then there are thundering footsteps on the stairs from the lower floors. A glance down the stairwell shows three burly Fleshers racing toward us. Le Maire looks at me.

"You can't take them," he says.

He's right. They're huge and murderous, and even without my weak ankle, I'm a Thief, not a Hyène.

But le Maire is a veritable bull of a man, with the strength of four men. He can take them.

"Go," he says forcefully, and pushes me.

I half fall, gripping the banister as the Fleshers reach the landing.

They hesitate when they see le Maire, because he is, after all, a member of the Guild of Letters.

I don't look back.

Not when they swear at him. Not when he answers them. Not when I hear the crunch of club against bone. I climb, dragging my bad leg behind me as I race to the top floor.

There's only one door on this floor, and I know he's waiting for me behind it.

I am the Black Cat; this is my hunting.

I am the Black Cat; this is my hunting.

The handle of the door is a roaring brass tiger. It's cold beneath my touch. I turn it and push.

The door creaks open before me.

Every hair on my head stands on end. The scars that lace my back sing.

They always hurt when *he* is near.

The Tiger's room looks like a bordello, richly decorated with silk pillows, exotic rugs, and low-hanging lamps. I count eight figures in corners of the room: Sisters with painted faces, their eyes blank with the drugs the Tiger has fed them. They lounge in a deep stupor or drunkenness, draped over chairs or curled up on floor cushions. Two appear to be naked; the others are half dressed. One is injecting herself with a wicked-looking needle.

At the far end of the room, the Tiger himself is sitting on a low bed of cushions. Beside him, shrinking stiffly back as far from him as she can, is Ettie.

And standing at his right are Thénardier and Tomasis.

My heart leaps, and I force myself to let out the breath I've been holding. Tomasis is here. I knew he had an understanding with the Tiger, but I didn't expect him to be here in the Flesh Guild's house.

"I told you she'd show up eventually," Thénardier says, waving the stump of his ruined arm at me. "She doesn't know how to leave well enough alone."

"Hello, little kitten." The Tiger's voice is warm as I walk toward them, ever alert.

Ettie's hands are bound. She has the start of a black eye, and a line of blood drips down her face from her nose.

I give a small, disrespectful bow of my head to the Tiger and completely ignore Thénardier.

"There's a shocking lack of familial affection here. Are you not going to greet your father?" the Tiger asks.

"Father." I bow my head at Tomasis. His frowning eyes meet mine.

The Tiger laughs heartily. "A wild little spitfire to the last," he says. "I was talking about Thénardier."

I look over at Thénardier. He's leaning against the wall, watching with amusement.

"He tried to shoot me."

"I always back the winning side," Thénardier says.

"You back the side that'll pay you something."

He laughs without malice. His pursuit of gold is highly impersonal.

I scan the room. There are no visible weapons here save the pistol in Thénardier's hand. There are only tall lamps, candlesticks, and the odd chair.

"You shouldn't have found her," Tomasis says. "I knew where it would lead you."

"Tomasis has had you followed, little Cat," says the Tiger. "He's had your own Guild watching you and reporting back."

I pretend the information doesn't sting.

"I've come here to put an end to this," Tomasis says, pointing at Ettie. "Her existence brings the Guilds to the brink of war." His words are careful and slow, as if it pains him to say them.

"She's a Ghost." I look pleadingly at Tomasis. "You swore an oath when I paid the bread price that you would not harm her."

The Tiger laughs.

Tomasis avoids my eyes. "We've come to an agreement. The girl is the root of all the trouble. If she dies, the struggle between the Ghosts, the Thieves, and the Flesh Guild comes to an end."

"My Lord, the *Law*." I approach Tomasis. "You cannot do this!"

Tomasis strikes me across the face, and I stumble. "I am your Lord. You do not question me," he says. His voice is raised, but he's trembling. "You obey your Lord, trusting that he has the interests of your Guild at heart."

I right myself and he reaches out to steady me. Gripping my arm, he twists my neck to force me to look him in the eye. He speaks in a low voice.

"The first duty of every Lord is to protect his children. You know this. Because you are my daughter, I have done what I can to shelter you from Kaplan's wrath. But I see now that I've indulged you too much, given you too much freedom.

"She is only one Ghost," he continues. "And I will not allow her to endanger you or my other children any longer." His fingers are bruising my skin, but his tone is pleading. "Don't you see, little one? She leads down a path to war, and I cannot allow it."

There are tears in my eyes. I hear his words. He is my Father; I know what he says is true. And yet I cannot accept it.

"Are we not the Wretched?" I say in a broken voice.

"We, the children of the Miracle Court. Are we not bound by the Law?"

He turns away from me as if he can hide from my questions.

"You don't understand. You're too young to remember the last Guild war."

The Tiger watches us, eyes alive with raw delight, and he puts his fingers in Ettie's curls and tightens his fist. She yelps as he drags her toward him.

He tilts her face to his. "Hear that, little Ghost? You're going to die tonight."

I look desperately to Tomasis, but he still won't meet my eyes. He likes none of this, but he won't do anything about it. And it's then that I know I've lost him.

"Leave her alone." I step toward the Tiger, but Tomasis is faster than I am. He grabs me and swings me around, pinning me against him. I struggle, but his grip tightens. I relax my arm, lower the dagger into my hand, and raise the blade in an upward swoop, slicing Tomasis's arm. He swears and, grabbing my arm, slams it hard against his knee. I cry out, sure he's broken it. Yet still I struggle.

"That's enough!" Tomasis orders me.

I don't stop fighting to get free of him, fighting to get to Ettie, who is rigid with fear. I try kicking myself loose. He can pin my hands, but he can't keep my legs still.

Seeing this, Tomasis looks over at Thénardier. "Shoot her in the leg!"

The bullet rips through me. A searing instant of flesh tearing. Then the pain breaks over me in a wave as Tomasis holds me up. I try desperately to focus on breathing and staying conscious, and on watching Thénardier's face as he struggles to reload his pistol with one hand.

"You are my Father. You swore to protect me," I say to Tomasis through gritted teeth. "You took an *oath*."

"I *am* protecting you." Tomasis's voice in my ear is as sure and comforting as it has always been. His words have always been right and true. If I trust him, then I can be safe.

But Ettie will be gone. Azelma will sleep forever. And the Tiger will live.

"Let me kill him, Tomasis. Please."

He freezes. "Are you mad, child? If you listen and stay silent, you might make it out of this alive."

"Do you think I want to live in a world where he exists? Where we all hide and cower in fear of him? He takes what he wants from us. He tears sisters and wives and children from us. He deals in the slavery of flesh. He is a stain upon the Court."

"You don't understand what Guild war is like," repeats Tomasis.

"I've taken an oath to you. I've loved you, my Lord." My words are heavy with tears, because I have loved him, because he is my Father. But whom do I love more? Tomasis or my sisters?

And what of the others, the women huddled in the cellar? The Sisters shut away in filthy beds all over the city?

Something snaps inside me. Perhaps this is what it feels like to have your heart break.

Sometimes we must pay a terrible price to protect the things we love.

I maintain my focus on Thénardier, who's still holding his gun and watching me with mild interest. I make a choice. I meet his eye.

"If you shoot him now," I say, my words tearing out of my throat, "you'll be Lord of the Thieves Guild."

The Tiger laughs. Tomasis turns, eyes wide with horror. He lets go of me and raises his hand, saying Thénardier's name. But Thénardier has already raised his gun, and his good hand is steady.

The smell of gunpowder burns my throat. And as Tomasis falls, someone cries out like a wounded animal, screaming and screaming. It sounds like me.

I drop to my knees beside Tomasis. He's pale, and his fingers frantically clutch his chest. Tears roll down my cheeks, and I hear myself sobbing as I take him in my arms.

"Forgive me, forgive me," I say over and over, as if it will undo what I have done.

He grasps his neck, fingers closing around the Talisman of Charlemagne. He raises it toward me. I take it and he reaches a hand to my face, his fingertips grazing my cheek as the convulsions start. He shivers violently, blood spilling from his mouth as he opens it to choke out his last words.

"Protect them," he murmurs.

I tell Tomasis I'm sorry. I tell him I'll do as he bids. I hold him tight as he spasms and trembles. I keep my eyes fixed on his as he fades, as his limbs slacken, as the glimmer of laughter always in his eye drains away, leaving only an empty shell.

The Tiger rises, forgetting Ettie. He comes to me, his words slicing through my pain.

"Get up." He grabs my shoulder, dragging me to my feet, tearing me from Tomasis. His voice is sharp in my ear. "I know you loved him. I know you trusted him. I know your heart is breaking. But he betrayed you." He shakes me. "Don't cry for him, little Cat," he says, holding my face between his hands. "He was supposed to protect you, and he didn't. Don't waste tears on him. Don't be so weak."

"That's her biggest problem," says Thénardier behind me. "She gets too attached."

Although I am drowning in grief, I can't help but think like a Cat. I scan the room and weigh my chances.

Tomasis is dead.

And now there are only two of them.

40

The Death Song

"I know what you're thinking," the Tiger says, still gripping my shoulders. "I know the pain in every part of you. It's eating its way through you, tearing out your heart."

Thénardier walks over and prods Tomasis with his foot to make sure he's dead.

"You think it's the end," the Tiger says in my ear. "But you're wrong. It's the beginning. I've been thinking about you, little Cat." He frowns. "Don't look so alarmed. It doesn't become you."

He lets go of me and raises his hands to show me he's not about to attack.

"I've been remembering it all from the beginning. I played it over and over in my head," he says. "I said to myself that this one hadn't been with you very long when I offered for her." He looks over his shoulder at Ettie. "Strange that you would be so attached to her. So reluctant to give her up. You even took the stripes for her. But it wasn't her you were trying to save, was it?"

He smiles at me.

"Thénardier told me I took something else from you. A sister . . . What was her name?" He throws the question at Thénardier, who opens his mouth to answer.

"Don't you dare speak her name," I hiss.

Thénardier eyes me and decides it's in his best interest to obey me. "They were close" is all he offers.

"A mother to you, was she? Brought you up? Loved you? Then it all makes perfect sense. I took your sister from you, and there was nothing you could do about it. My taking her made you run to Tomasis. Made you beg him for protection. Everything about you, from your rage to the stripes on your back to the dagger in your hand is because of *me*. I made you, like my father made me the moment he sold me to the slavers' whips."

He reaches out and runs a finger from my forehead down my cheek, drawing a mirror of the stripes on his own face.

"You already bear my scars on your back. I carved my name into your skin. You belong to me."

I flinch. "I belong to the Thieves Guild. You are without honor, without Law—"

He gives a short bark of laughter. "Law? Where was the Law when I was taken, broken by my father so he could live?

He made me what I am. I am the failure of the Law. I am the nightmare it birthed. I am its vengeance."

He takes me by my shoulders and drags me toward him.

"The Miracle Court fears me. They bow, scrape, and hide. They're so afraid that you can smell the fear on them. They're weak."

He cocks his head at me.

"But you . . . you're not like them, are you? You're the little kitten that took the lash. The Cat that attacked a Guild Lord. The only one who dared defy the Tiger," he says.

He leans closer, his lips inches from my ear. I try desperately not to tremble.

"Do you know what you're like?"

His voice is rich and warm.

"You're like me."

He leans back and sees the disbelief on my face. He smiles.

"Who else but you and I would have spent every day of the last two years thinking about Ettie? Who else has spent every waking hour planning how to get her back? We're the same.

"I'm going to break her," he continues. "Not because I want to, not anymore. She's a pretty thing, like other pretty things. But I will break her for you, because I want to see you become a terrible, lawless, honorless thing. I want to see you shatter and twist. I want to see you become like me."

He lifts my chin so that I'm staring into his eyes.

"Today you will be reborn. Born in blood, in pain, in rage." His breath is warm on my cheek as he murmurs,

"After all, you killed your own Guild Father. You're halfway there. You're just a little monster who hasn't grown into her claws yet."

There's the slightest hint of movement behind the Tiger. He's forgotten about Ettie because she is just a weak, pretty thing to him.

Foolish.

I taught her to escape bonds years ago, and now she's on her feet behind him and Thénardier, walking with a sure, silent step. In her hand is the dagger I gave to her. She has kept it sharp all this time.

The Tiger's face is alight with smiles as he continues. "I told you, little kitten, we're the same. You're just like me."

"She is nothing like you." Ettie's voice is heavy with hatred.

The Tiger turns, but it's too late; with every ounce of her strength, Ettie drives the wicked blade right through his smiling cheek.

His screams are horrifying. He falls backward, flailing, blood spattering everywhere. Ettie tries to get to me, but Thénardier, eyes wide with shock, has his gun trained on her now. I jump at Thénardier's back, but my leg is damaged, and he's a man of great instincts. He throws me across the room, and I land facedown.

Deafened by the Tiger's screams, I try to raise myself up on my good arm, but I'm slow and dizzy from the pain.

It's amazing, the strange details you notice when danger is upon you. My eyes take in the wood grain of the floor that shows between the Ottoman rugs. I see the bootlaces of the Sister hiding in the shadows in front of me, the worn blue silk of her dress, how it's faded in patches and stitched unevenly along the hem. I frown, focusing on the lines of that thread.

I know *those stitches,* I think with a shock.

I look at her face and my heart seizes.

Azelma.

My sister.

Of course she's here. Of course the Tiger brought her to mock me.

Her hair is plastered to her face, and she clutches a syringe in her hands. But her eyes . . . She's looking at me. Focusing on my face.

She sees me.

She knows who I am. Her mouth opens as she silently says my name. She sees my arm hanging limp and useless at my side. She sees my ruined leg covered in dark blood. Then she gazes up at the screaming Tiger. And a strange look comes over her.

She drops the syringe and rolls it across the floor toward me. I grab it with my good hand and tuck it under my body as I slowly raise myself. She watches me with a hungry expression. I manage to stand and look down at the syringe. It's full.

The Tiger is yelling unintelligible things to Thénardier. He's clamped his hand across his cheek, but then, it's hard to talk clearly when there's a gaping hole in your face. His blood is everywhere, and his words are incoherent. Thénardier is watching him, gun in hand, cocking his head to one side like a dog considering his options.

"Shoot her!" the Tiger mouths, blood streaming from his lips. That instruction, at least, is clear. Ettie is in a corner, clutching a tall wooden candelabra like a weapon. It looks heavy in her arms, and she's carrying it all wrong.

"I always back the winning side," Thénardier says calmly to the Tiger. "And right now, you might not be winning." And to the Tiger's great horror, Thénardier puts his gun back into his belt and looks to me.

"No hard feelings," he says cheerily. "If you survive the night, I'll make you my Master of Thieves." Then, with a last grin, he leaves the room.

Ettie advances on the Tiger, dragging the lamp with her. The Tiger is crouched low, like a wrestler. His eyes are mad with a rage that burns stronger than his pain. Even injured, he's terrifying.

Ettie's eyes are wide, wary. He lunges at her, and she swings the lamp. But the weight of it makes her slow. He lands on top of her, driving her into the wall with a loud thud, and tries to wrest the lamp from her. She's shrieking and yelling like a hellcat, so he doesn't notice me drag myself across the room behind him. All he feels is the stab of the needle deep in his neck, the drug coursing into his blood, filling him with his own drugs.

He rises and bats me away. One blow and I'm thrown to the floor. He grabs the syringe and yanks it out of his neck. But the drug is strong, and already it is taking effect. He stumbles like a maddened animal, barely able to stand. His movements become slow, stupid, less frightening.

Ettie is on her feet, the lamp in her hand again. She raises it, but he can hardly see her, blinded by pain and dizziness. She swings it at his head, and this time it hits him full force. He crumples to the floor, his limbs trembling, and tries to speak, but all we hear is an animal's growl. Ettie advances on him, and raises the lamp again. She brings it down on his back. He cries out, and tries to crawl away from her. But she follows him like an avenging angel, raising the lamp above her once more; her eyes fill with rage and tears as she brings it down on him a third time.

"Ettie . . ." She can't hear me, so lost is she in her terrible task. I drag myself toward her. "ETTIE!" I grab for her arm.

She wakes as if from a stupor, looks at me. She's shaking and covered in blood.

"It's enough."

Her face says she doesn't agree. She looks down at him.

He lies on the floor, gurgling, twitching, and bleeding everywhere.

From the corner of my eye I see movement. The Sisters. Terrible disjointed shadows, they come from the corners of the room. Expressions hard, hands raised, they creep toward us menacingly.

Ettie grips the lamp firmly, but I put an arm up to stop her.

Azelma is leading them.

"Wait," I say to Ettie, my voice small and piteous. "It's Azelma, my sister."

Ettie holds the lamp out before us to ward the Sisters away. But they pay us no heed.

I close my eyes, and when I open them again, they have passed us by, forming a tight circle around the Tiger. They stand, looking down at him. He is weak from blood loss, from the bludgeoning Ettie gave him, from the poppy coursing through his veins.

He raises a hand to one of them, begging for help.

And I know with sickening clarity what's about to happen.

"Ettie, let's go."

She won't move, hypnotized by the spectacle.

"Ettie, please."

Azelma considers the Tiger's hand, and then she drops to one knee in front of him and gently puts a finger into the wound in his cheek.

He starts to scream.

"Ettie!" I call, but she won't leave; she won't move.

I turn my head away. I don't want to see or hear this.

As long as I live I'll never forget his screams. I wish I could cut off my ears to hide from the sound of them. But I stay for Ettie. Ettie, who stands trembling with eyes wide open. Beautiful Ettie, who was always afraid.

She's not afraid anymore.

Somewhere in the distance, the City whispers. She wraps her clawed fingers around the man who was a monster, and she takes him. It was a good story, a sad one: the boy beneath the lash. But our Mother, the City, demanded a sacrifice, and he was the darkest one I could give to her.

41

The End of the Tale

Ettie helps me go slowly to the stairs; we take them one at a time. She has tied my scarf around my leg to stop the bleeding. Its faded flowers are dark with my blood.

The sight of what awaits us would be humorous if it weren't so serious.

The Guild is overflowing with people, and it's a cacophony of raised voices and pointed challenges. Everyone here is waving a gun at someone.

As we stumble down the stairs, we are greeted by a dozen guns trained on our heads. I raise my good hand and Ettie calls out, "We're unarmed!"

In the center of the room, the women from the basement are huddled together. Making a circle around them are the revolutionaries and le Maire. St. Juste's face is bleeding;

Grantaire has a black eye; Feuilly has lost his glasses. They look furious and are aiming their weapons at the Fleshers, who form yet another ring around them. The brawny Fleshers look murderous and confused at the same time, and I quickly see why: at every window, and spilling in from every door, are soldiers, their muskets trained on everybody they see. I spot Javert among them, her red hair shining like a beacon.

There's a commotion at the door, and the soldiers part to allow a dark-haired man through. He scans the room, clearly shocked at the scene. As he sees Ettie and me on the stairs, he blinks.

"Nina!"

"Votre Altesse," I say to the dauphin, and my slight bow almost topples Ettie.

The prince comes to us and takes in the extent of my injuries.

"You're hurt! Who did this to you?"

"A dead man," I answer, trying to shake off the tiredness that threatens to engulf me. This night is not over yet.

I managed to get the soldiers and Inspector Javert here, so it's time they played their part.

"Altesse, you've ridden across the city and slain every revolutionary cell in your path, have you not?"

The prince's face grows grim, and he gives the slightest of nods.

"There remains only one, and here they are. I believe your mother the queen commanded that any survivors be arrested. Take them. They're outnumbered and won't fight you."

St. Juste's face is completely and utterly furious. "Nina?"

I ignore him.

The prince's soldiers surround St. Juste, who's glaring at me with rage at my betrayal. For a moment I fear that he's going to fight, so fierce is the look on his face. But he hands over his pistol, and his friends follow suit.

And now, dance to the tune that I will whistle.

I gesture to the women. "These women were stolen from the streets of this city and, against every law of this country, were to be traded into prostitution." I point to the Fleshers. "These are the men that have done this."

The prince is horrified, and in a voice of barely contained fury says to his soldiers, "Arrest them all!"

I lean toward him conspiratorially. "I wouldn't arrest that one, however." I point into the shadows where Montparnasse is lurking. "Unless you want a lot of dead soldiers on your hands."

The prince looks around. "Arrest all the others," he says.

The soldiers move forward, and the Fleshers, seeing themselves grossly outnumbered, drop their weapons. The soldiers round everyone up, making them raise their hands above their heads.

"Anything else?" the prince inquires of me with only the slightest edge of sarcasm.

"There are more women upstairs." My voice hitches when I want it to be strong. "All of these women have been prisoners of the Tiger for too long. They need medical attention."

"Take the women to l'Hôpital de la Pitié. Be gentle!" he shouts, his voice like thunder. "They've no need of more pain. And cover them. Are they to be walked half naked through the streets?"

The prince snaps an order at his men to get them moving. They drag everyone outside. The students go first; St. Juste goes quietly. He doesn't even look up at me, doesn't realize that his arrest has saved his life. The army has intervened in time to stop any bloodshed. The Fleshers have not been able to murder the students, and the presence of the rest of us stopped the army from massacring the students in the streets.

"Go with St. Juste," I whisper to Ettie.

She looks at me, confused.

"Trust me."

She lets go of me and steps away.

"If they're going to be arrested, then I'm going with them," she announces loudly to the world, as if she and I have quarreled.

I wobble, unable to stand properly without her holding on to me. I want to cry out for her to stay, to wait. But everything will be much easier if she's with them.

She marches out the door with the prisoners. I hold the banister and inch myself forward, wincing in pain. Montparnasse watches from a distance. He doesn't come to help me. As long as I'm able, he'll let me walk for myself. I lift my chin and meet his eyes. And I could swear, for the first time in his life, he smiles.

The dauphin, however, is by my side in an instant. He stands there in his only slightly dusty uniform while I'm covered with dirt and blood, painfully aware that I reek.

"You need a surgeon for that leg. Here, let me help you."

I shake my head and swat him away. I don't have time; there is much still to do. He follows me out the door, trying to bully me into coming to the palace to recover. He prattles on about providing me with the best doctors. I wonder how it's possible for any one person to be so handsome and so annoying at the same time.

The Fleshers have been rounded up and loaded onto a prison cart. The revolutionaries, St. Juste, Grantaire, le Maire, and Ettie are being piled into another. Javert is making sure they're all together. Ettie watches me from between the bars, exactly where I need her to be. To the right, the Sisters are being loaded onto wagons that will take them to the hospital. I catch a glimpse of Azelma, her worn gown stained with the Tiger's blood. Her eyes are dull and confused; she is skin and bone. My heart contracts. I want to go to her. I want to put my arms around her and take her away. But I know she's safer where she is for now.

She is safe.

She is finally safe.

Content that le Maire is locked in the carriage, Javert climbs up next to the driver and snappily orders him to head for the Châtelet. The driver cracks his whip, and the cart starts to rumble away.

I give a whistle, short and sharp. Ettie turns and looks at me, and I put one hand to the neck of my shirt. She frowns, then lifts her fingers to the blood-soaked collar of her dress, where they close over the two brass hair clips I pinned there earlier. She laughs. It's a glorious sound.

The soldiers are mounting their horses and heading away. A wave of dizziness comes over me. The prince takes advantage of my weakness to seize my arm and steer me to his carriage.

A moment later I'm lying in his arms and we're moving.

"You'll be seen by my own physician," the prince says, gently stroking my hair. "You'll be fine."

His voice is shaking, and I look up at him. He's dusty and dirtier than I thought, and his eyes are red and swollen.

"Are *you* all right?" I ask.

He shakes his head and holds on to me, a hand wound around my arm.

"I—" He breaks off and looks away from me. "I asked Mother about the wells," he says in an oddly detached voice. "She told me it was true. They put poison in the water. She said it was necessary, a merciful thing, or else the poor would grow too numerous and we would not be safe. She said they had risen before and they would rise again if we didn't keep careful control of their numbers."

Ysengrim take them. They are monsters, one and all.

"I asked her if she ever thought of doing it again," he continues mournfully, "and she got up, walked to the fire, and put her hand in the flame." He pauses, horrified at his own admission. "I didn't even stop her." He stares at the empty seat before him like a man haunted. "She wouldn't stop screaming."

He wrings his hands as if they were covered in blood.

"When I told her that I wouldn't lead the attack, she said I had no choice. That if we allowed the rebels to unite, they would march on the palace and turn us over to the guillotine, as they tried to years ago. Every single one of us."

He's right. That's what the six little mice attempted to do in the last revolution.

"How could I let that happen? She said if I didn't go, she would send another captain and charge him with executing every civilian he saw."

He's shaking.

"And so you went," I say quietly.

"The queen said an example must be made. I had to ride at their head and let the soldiers do their job." He shudders. "They ambushed and crushed every cell. They took no prisoners, Nina. None. And when they were done, they lined up the bodies side by side to make it easier for the cart to take them away."

He closes his eyes and I see a tear run down his face.

"We had to cross their names off a list." He swallows. "The plan was thought up by advisors. Father and Mother sanctioned it, but I gave the order. *I* did it, Nina. I killed all those people, as sure as if I were the man firing the gun, the hand wielding the sword."

His eyes are bright with horror. I take his shaking hand in my own and lift my gaze to his.

It is strange, the urge I have to comfort him, when he is telling me of all the people that have died at his hand.

"It's finished," I say gently. Because there is nothing else to say.

He looks at me like a crazed man, like a drowning man. And his lips come down on mine, hard. He kisses me with such force I can barely breathe.

To think, after all these years, he still tastes of chocolate.

When he finally comes up for air and looks down at me, his eyes starry and dazed, I give him a sad smile.

"I'm sorry," I whisper.

He frowns, confused. In a flash I reach up around his head and tie my bloody scarf across his mouth.

His eyes bulge and he tries to struggle, but I tied his hands with a strip of cloth when he was telling me his story.

His expression is raw hurt, longing, and loneliness. The beautiful friendless prince.

I open the carriage door; the street is a blur whirling past us outside.

I wink at him and leap out into the night.

In the early dawn, I stop and pull from inside my coat the Fisherman's last gift: the tongue of Mor the Peacock. I drive one of my lock-picks into it and push it into the ground; then I light the fuse. It shoots into the air with a scream that will be seen and heard across the city. Men and women stop and raise their heads and it screeches across the sky, exploding into fireworks of light and color, a tiger roaring across the heavens.

Now, at this signal, the Wretched all over the city will descend upon the Tiger's remaining strongholds. They will attack each one, killing or driving off the Fleshers and freeing the Sisters.

I manage to limp unsteadily down a dark alley, where I see a prison cart. A little boy materializes out of the darkness and stands before it. The horses stop and refuse to go any farther. Javert rises, shouting at the boy to get out of the way. But the boy advances. Other Ghosts appear behind him, emerging from the fog, forming a wall, blocking the street at both ends, a noseless young man at their head. Javert tries to grab her pistol, but the cart driver pulls out a gun of his own and holds it to her head.

Ettie has the lock open in seconds with the hair clips I gave her, and she quickly tumbles out of the cart. The other prisoners follow her, while Javert roars and rails. Orso takes Ettie into his arms and hugs her fiercely. She buries her face in his cloak and throws her arms around him. Gavroche is there at her skirts, and when Orso releases her, she greets Loup with a kiss on the cheek and takes Gavroche's hand.

Le Maire, meanwhile, goes to address Javert. I can't make out his words, but his manner is apologetic. She screams at him, shouting that he won't escape her, swearing to find him no matter where he goes. Tears are pouring down her face, and le Maire is looking decidedly odd as he turns and leaves her.

I watch from the shadows.

St. Juste is talking in low tones with Orso.

"How many fell?" St. Juste asks.

"All," Orso says. "You are the only ones left."

St. Juste shakes his head, tears brimming in his eyes. "I was ready to die tonight. I should have been with them. Was I wrong? Did I betray them?"

"No," Orso says. "Death the Endless comes for us all. When your time comes, we'll make it count."

Grantaire is asking where they are going.

"We must cross the sewers to get to the catacombs," Loup responds.

Ettie appears at my side, clutching at my sleeve. I know I look bad, because her face is a picture of concern.

"We're alive," I say, sounding chirpier than I feel.

She takes my hand, and the gesture is a powerful declaration of sorrow, of forgiveness, of love, threads of silver and gold wrapping around us: the orphan and the thief. Ettie's arms are around me; her forehead rests against my shoulder. A thousand memories race through my mind as I lean my head against hers.

My sister.

"Go on," I murmur, my voice faint. "We're not out of this yet."

She kisses me. Her lips burn against my cold cheek.

The Ghosts hurry the students down through a grate in the street. Gavroche leads the way, dancing like an excited djinn before them.

Then Orso is before me. "Well, little Cat. What now?" he says.

"Javert won't rest till she finds le Maire," I say. "The boys will be wanted criminals, and St. Juste won't give up fighting."

"No, but he might be better equipped next time." Orso gives me one of his terrifying smiles. "You killed a monster and saved a great many lives. Not bad for a night's work." He frowns at me. "Try not to bleed to death."

I'm so cold and so faint.

I feel the street beneath my feet. Through the soles of my shoes, the echo of a song trembles through me. The City sings me a lullaby. She has drunk enough blood tonight. It's time to sleep.

A wave of exhaustion hits me, and as my good knee buckles, Montparnasse melts out of the shadows, catching me at the waist, and I fall into him.

He holds me up in his thin arms. I feel the beating of his heart as I lay my head against his chest.

Orso's words swirl around my head.

"Let us go," says Montparnasse. "The Dead are calling."

I smile into the rough linen of Montparnasse's cloak, and then the darkness swallows us.

Les milles remerciements—
en ordre chronologique

To my Father, who gave me whatever talent I may possess.

To Mum and Babuji, who gave me words, language, stories, and all the classics.

To Gow, who used to get me to do her history homework, thereby sparking a lifelong passion for tales of French kings and violent revolutions.

To Victor Hugo, who created such spectacularly haunting characters as Valjean, Javert, Éponine, Gavroche, Enjolras . . . threw them into the most tragic of stories . . . and then added Marius Pontmercy, just to drive me crazy. I like to think of this book as vengeance for years of wanting to strangle Marius (how can anyone be so useless?)—and because ÉPONINE DESERVED SO MUCH MORE!

To Messrs. Boublil and Schönberg, for reinforcing my *Les Mis* obsession with their spectacular musical.

To my Husband, who is my rock, without whom nothing could ever get done.

To Jess. I wrote this as if I were telling it to you at bedtime.

Les milles remerciements—
en ordre chronologique

To my Father, who gave me whatever talent I may possess.

To Mum and Babuji, who gave me words, language, stories, and all the classics.

To Gow, who used to get me to do her history homework, thereby sparking a lifelong passion for tales of French kings and violent revolutions.

To Victor Hugo, who created such spectacularly haunting characters as Valjean, Javert, Éponine, Gavroche, Enjolras . . . threw them into the most tragic of stories . . . and then added Marius Pontmercy, just to drive me crazy. I like to think of this book as vengeance for years of wanting to strangle Marius (how can anyone be so useless?)—and because ÉPONINE DESERVED SO MUCH MORE!

To Messrs. Boublil and Schönberg, for reinforcing my *Les Mis* obsession with their spectacular musical.

To my Husband, who is my rock, without whom nothing could ever get done.

To Jess. I wrote this as if I were telling it to you at bedtime.

To my Mao, my first reader, who is the very best of friends and greatest of cheerleaders.

To my Sister, who remains convinced that she is the subconscious inspiration for this book.

To Brendra Drake, who tirelessly created Pitch Wars, which is how I got my agent!

To Rosalyn Eves and Erin Summerill, my mentors therein, for giving Nina and her gang of miscreants the opportunity to invade the world.

To Josh, my agent, who is the very best, for believing in my stories, and all the Adams Lit family for their support.

To those who made me laugh instead of cry along the way. The E.a.F. crew, Rebecca and Tomi.

To Amie Kaufman, for taking the time to share no-nonsense advice and saving me from many anxieties.

To my editors—Melanie, at Knopf, for all her hard work, investment, and wise direction, and Natasha, at Harper, for her passion, as well as all the many dedicated members of the Guild of Letters who serve under them. *In ink is truth.*

Nous sommes d'un sang.